EMPIRE
OF
SHADOWS

MIRIAM FORSTER

HARPER TEEN
An Imprint of HarperCollinsPublishers

HarperTeen is an imprint of HarperCollins Publishers.

Empire of Shadows
Copyright © 2014 by Miriam Forster
www.epicreads.com

Library of Congress Cataloging-in-Publication Data
Forster, Miriam.
Empire of shadows / Miriam Forster. – First edition.
    pages cm
    Summary: "After taking the oath of protector of the Order of Khatar, Mara
travels to the Imperial city with her charge, Revathi; although she knew the
dizzying city would hold its dangers, she never thought her life–as well as her
heart–would be at stake"– Provided by publisher.
    ISBN 978-0-06-212133-2 (hardcover)
    [1. Fantasy.] I. Title.
PZ7.F7765Emp 2014   2013051283
[Fic]–dc23   CIP
                                                                             AC

Typography by Erin Fitzsimmons
14 15 16 17 18 LP/RRDH 10 9 8 7 6 5 4 3 2 1
❖
First Edition

For Dan,
who makes me feel
more human

Dramatis Personae

in the

EMPIRE OF SHADOWS

Mara t'Riala
Emil Arvi

At the Order of Khatar

Vivaksh, head of the Order of Khatar
Gyan, archivist
Samara, weapons master

The Kildi camp

Stefan Arvi, Emil's twin brother
Mihai Arvi, *Kys* of the Arvi clan; Emil and Stefan's father
Nadya Arvi, Emil and Stefan's mother (deceased)
Pali Arvi, Master of Trade
Lel Arvi, Master of Camp
Meri Arvi, Master of Livestock
Rona Arvi, Emil's cousin
Besnik Yanora, *Kys* of the Yanora clan
Kizzy Yanora, Besnik's daughter

In the surrounding forest

Esmer, wild spotted cat
Ashin, wild spotted cat
Rajo the Black, leader of a band of mercenaries
Karoti, Rajo's brother
Biren, a mercenary
Marir, a mercenary
Yatra, a mercenary

IMPERIAL CAPITAL CITY OF KAMAL

At the palace

REVATHI SA'HOI, a young noblewoman
EKISA SA'HOI, Revathi's grandmother
EMPEROR SARO, ruler of the Bhinian Empire
PRINCE PAITHAL, older son of the Emperor
PRINCE SUDEV, younger son of the Emperor
GAREN, head of the Imperial Palace Guard
BHAGI, a bond slave
HANOI, a cook

In the Flower Circle

TAMAS U'GRA, Revathi's betrothed
SATHVIK U'GRA, Tamas's father
AARI, Lord u'Gra's companion
TAPAN U'GRA, Tamas's brother

In the Jade Circle

SUNI, a warrior monk
MANIK, a cook
SANAH, a healer
VIHAN, a member of the Order of Khatar

In the Wind Circle

HEEMA, Lel's sister
GIRI, Heema's companion
ABHRA, tea seller
AVAHAA, a young girl
ASATYA, infantry captain
CAMUS, a Jade scribe

THE CASTES

FLOWER, for the nobility
JADE, for the learned
BAMBOO, for the merchants
HEARTH, for the farmers
WIND, for the wanderers

THE GIRL WITH no name reached the steps of the building a little before Darkfall. Made of weathered stone, the building was almost the same shade as the featureless gray sky. It seemed to fade into the shadows of the thick bamboo forest. There were no windows, just one ancient double door, made of teakwood and inlaid with pale slivers of bone.

Sweat trickled down the side of the girl's face, and the barely healed wound in her side burned. She'd been running since the Elders had named her punishment, fleeing the assembly like the criminal she was. But even before the trial, she'd known that she would come here.

She had nowhere else to go.

Hot air lay like a wool blanket on her exposed arms, making her itch. She pressed one hand against the carved surface of the door, feeling the grain of the wood and the smoothness of bone against her palm.

Shar. The voice spoke softly into her mind. Her shoulders tensed with the feeling of eyes on her back.

Don't say that name, she sent back fiercely. *Shar no longer exists.*

The words in her head were deep and sad. *You know why they ruled against you.*

The girl kept her eyes on the door, fighting the urge to turn around. She wouldn't see the watcher, not with these human eyes. The thick, straight stalks of the bamboo, the dancing shadows of the forest, all of that confused her sight, blurred the sharp outlines she was used to.

I know.

They'd ruled against her because of what she'd done. But they didn't have to live with it afterward. *They* didn't have to figure out a way to go on. She did.

The voice spoke again. *Why are you here? Isn't exile punishment enough?*

The girl closed her eyes, feeling the prick of tears under her lids. Another human sensation. *This isn't about punishment,* she sent. *It's about penance.*

And she seized the iron ring and knocked, three sharp raps.

The door groaned and opened, revealing an older man in a yellow-green tunic, the color of new bamboo shoots. His dark-brown skin was seamed with creases, like the marks on a scratching tree. A tooled leather cuff covered almost the entire bottom half of his left ear.

He fixed her with sharp dark eyes. "Who seeks the Order of Khatar?"

The girl lifted her chin and stood a little straighter. She might not be Tribe anymore, but she would not show fear. "I do. I seek admittance to your Order."

The man stepped out of the building. His eyes moved to her tunic, and she saw that the cut in her side had opened again. Even her quick healing couldn't completely seal a deep wound like that, not in two days. A patch of gleaming blood stained the fabric.

"How old are you?"

She swallowed under his stare. "I'm fifteen."

"And why are you here?"

Again she resisted the urge to look behind her. Instead, she touched the fresh blood on her shirt and held out her red-stained fingers.

"There is blood on my hands," she said. "I would like to wash it off."

The man's hard look turned speculative. "So you do know the purpose of our Order. But do you know the price?"

"I do."

"To redeem oneself, to regain lost honor, it is a heavy task," the man said, and she thought his voice was gentler than before. "There will be sacrifices. Are you ready to give up all you are and any prior loyalties to family or Empire? To pledge yourself to the protection of one person even until death?"

Her throat constricted, blocking her words. She could only nod.

The man didn't seem to notice her silence. "Those who are

ready for the Order must bear the mark before they pass through the doors." He pulled the cuff off his ear and she saw that his earlobe had been cut off. "The mark is the sign of the oath you will take. If you fail in your duty, whether through negligence or fear, you will be stripped of your ear cuff. Your shame will be made visible for the world to see. Are you willing?"

My shame is already visible, the girl thought. It was in her exposed skin, her clawless fingers, her dull human eyes. No one of her Tribe had ever chosen to take a permanent human form. The idea was absurd.

But it was the only part of her that wasn't a monster.

Her face grew tight and hot. "I am ready."

The man slid the cuff back over his mangled ear and pulled out a dagger. The blade of the weapon was double-edged, sharp as the gleam of teeth in shadow. Instead of a traditional solid handle, it had two slender pieces of metal that came down about a hand's width apart. Two closely set handles, like the rungs of a ladder, connected the two sides.

The man slid his veined hand over the handles, so that the long sides of the dagger reached down his wrist and the blade rested on his knuckles.

"This is a *kattari*," he said. "It was invented by Khatar of the Copper Blade during the reign of the Second Lotus Emperor. With it, Khatar became the most feared of fighters." He mimed a swift punching motion that came close to the girl's face, but she didn't flinch. The man looked pleased.

"With this blade, you do not merely hold the weapon, you are the weapon," he said. "Khatar used it for his own glory in the early days. Now we use it for the protection of others. But first it must taste your blood." He stepped closer and took her earlobe in two fingers, his skin and bones pinching into the sensitive flesh.

The girl remained motionless. *This is what I choose,* she reminded herself. *This is my penance.*

She saw the man's hand move, saw the blade flash, and a clap of white-hot pain echoed through her head. Everything went fuzzy and gray.

When her vision cleared, she was still standing. The man was pressing a cloth to her ear, and a stream of something wet and warm was dripping down her arm. She didn't look at it.

The man smiled, showing worn and crooked teeth. His hands on her ear were gentle. "Well done, novice. Welcome to the Order of Khatar. What shall we call you?"

A name. A new one, to fit a new life. Out of the corner of her eye, the girl saw a flicker of striped tail in the forest, the last sight she would ever have of her Tribe. The loss was sharper and more final than the pain in her ear.

Tell them I said good-bye, she sent in the direction of the retreating scout. *Tell them I'm sorry.*

Then she turned her eyes back to the man, who had leaned forward to bandage her wound.

"Mara," she said to him. "Call me Mara."

I tire of killing.

Make me the man I wish to be.

And give me purpose.

The words of Khatar of the Copper Blade
as spoken to Elina the Bow-Singer,
from *The Song of Stone and Blood*

1

Mara

MARA SAT IN her stone sleeping cell, cleaning her dagger. Her hands were busy with the cloth and polishing sand, but her mind was far away.

In a few minutes, she would take the final test to become a full member of the Order. If she passed, her time here would be over. She would walk out the wood-and-bone door for the first time since she'd come to this place. She would leave behind her open cell, with its hard stone shelf-bed. She would leave behind the practice square with its high ceiling and the broad opening in the roof that let in the gray dusty light, the place where for three years she had practiced combat forms until her bones ached and her muscles cramped. She would leave behind her teachers, the other novices, the simple way of life she had held on to in those first dark days of choosing to be human.

For the first time in three years, she would be alone.

The dagger in her hand slipped, slicing the pad of her thumb. Mara hissed through her teeth and put her thumb to her lips. The rich, sweet taste of blood filled her mouth, bringing a rush of memories. Pouncing on the kills her parents brought home, sharing rabbits with her siblings, the swish and rustle of the long grass around her as she stalked her first deer.

And it brought back the last day of her old life. The pain of the sword biting into her side, and the red haze of rage. The feeling of her teeth sinking into unprotected flesh. The sick shame that came when her mind cleared. And the irrevocable verdict of the Elders.

Man killer.

The dagger clattered to the floor and Mara bent over the nearby washbowl and spit red. She spit until her mouth was dry and rubbed the sleeve of her green cotton tunic against her lips until they burned. Then she pressed her forehead against the cool stone of her cell.

I'm afraid, she thought. *Afraid to leave.*

Without thinking, her hand went to her ear, feeling the tooled leather cuff. The smooth, curled design under her fingers calmed her a little. She would not fail this time. She would protect life instead of take it away. She would no longer be a monster.

Footsteps on the dirt floor outside her cell made her straighten. Samara, the weapons master, stopped in the doorway. Light glinted off the smooth brown skin of her bare scalp, and her eyes were as direct and fierce as a hawk's.

"It's time," she said. "Are you ready?"

Mara picked her dagger up and tucked it back into her belt. She ran a hand over her own head, feeling the short, soft strands. "Does it matter?" she asked, trying to smile.

"You could choose to test next year," Samara pointed out.

"No," Mara said. Her hands were damp, and she wiped them on her tunic. "I'm ready."

The low thrum of a gong rolled through the building.

"Then come," Samara said. She left the doorway and Mara followed.

The center of the Order was a wide practice floor, ringed with the open doorways of sleeping cells. At one end of the room were three larger archways that led into the simple kitchen, the small library with its dense piles of scrolls, and the armory. That was it. There were no other rooms, no doors to give privacy. There was no world beyond the stone walls and the square of open sky, with the unchanging gray of the Barrier above them.

Mara wondered what it would be like to live again under that vast space. Unbounded by walls. Free to hunt where she willed.

Travel. Not hunt. Travel.

She would never hunt again.

"Novice Mara." The voice jarred Mara back to the present. Samara had joined the other two trainers on the raised platform. Their yellow-green tunics matched Mara's own simple clothing. The head of the Order, Vivaksh, stood in the center, his arms folded, looking no different from the day Mara had met him on the steps. He did not smile.

"Step forward."

Mara came to the center of the room and bowed, her hands pressed together in front of her chest. The other novices gathered in a loose circle around the open space.

All the novices looked curiously alike, with serious faces and haunted eyes. Some were here to atone for their own crimes; some were here to regain their family's honor. The Order was where you came when you had nothing left to lose.

Gyan, the archivist, stood to Vivaksh's right. He was an old, stooped man, his face lined with both humorous patience and sorrow. He spoke first.

"We will test your knowledge," Gyan said. "For it is knowledge that allows us to make wise choices and enables us to protect our charges. Novice Mara, what is the purpose and goal of the Order?"

Mara closed her eyes, remembering the words she'd memorized by flickering lamplight, the words she'd burned into her mind like a brand so she would not forget why she was here.

"We swear to defend the defenseless," she said. "We take an oath to protect one person and one person only, for even a single life is precious. We are not mere guards; we do not pledge to households, nor do we protect treasure or goods. We accept no payment but the honor of laying down our lives for another. Like Khatar, who gave up his violent ways and pledged to protect Elina the Bow-Singer, we wish only to erase the evil we have done and replace it with good. That is the purpose and the goal of the Order."

"Correct," Gyan said. "And very well spoken." He smiled at her, the lines creasing deeper into his face. Mara smiled back.

More questions came. How to sweep a room for danger, how to stand for hours without losing attention, how to guard against assassins–all the things Mara had learned came spilling forth.

At last Gyan stepped aside, to be replaced by Samara. "Mara, you have passed the test of knowledge," she said. "Now you must show your skills in a fight."

Mara swallowed and pulled her dagger out of her belt, sliding her fingers around the crossbar. Samara stepped down, her dagger appearing in her hand as if by magic.

"You will fight until I say to stop," she said. "If you surrender, or are pinned, you will fail the test."

Mara gripped the crossbars of her dagger, taking refuge in the rush of adrenaline that tightened her muscles. Samara swung the dagger around her head and dropped into the classic starting position. Mara followed.

"Begin."

2

Mara

FROM THE FIRST training session, Mara had loved dagger fighting. The hand-dagger was a part of her, the way her claws
had been, her arms and shoulders as much the weapon as the
dagger itself.

Samara moved first, swinging her dagger in an overhand strike,
followed by a flurry of angled blows. Mara blocked them all, the
clatter of daggers ringing around the open space.

Then Samara struck with her other hand, aiming a close-fisted
blow to Mara's face. Mara ducked. Her feet slid on the sandy
floor as she tried to keep her balance.

Samara pressed her advantage with another overhand blow,
leaving her stomach exposed. Seeing the opening, Mara sprang
forward, arm out, pressing the dagger toward Samara's belly.
But Samara was too quick. She jumped back, swinging her

hand-dagger down to knock Mara's aside.

The two circled again, swaying their daggers back and forth like snakes weaving in battle. Mara fell easily into the rhythm honed by years of training. Strike. Counterstrike. Dodge. Understrike. Overstrike. Block. Turn. Attack.

Mara realized she was smiling, wide and feral. This was fun.

Samara leaped high in the air, her dagger aimed like an arrow. Mara twirled out of the way, digging an elbow into Samara's back as she landed. The woman whirled, slicing her dagger across Mara's sleeve.

There was a brief burning pain and the sharp metallic smell of blood.

Mara faltered. Her eyes blurred, and her mind filled with the shine of another blade. The sword that had cut into her and taken her sanity away. She stumbled back.

Samara slashed at her, and Mara threw herself to the side, narrowly avoiding the strike. She hit the ground in a perfect roll, coming up on her feet.

Focus, Mara. This was her best chance at escaping her past. She couldn't lose it.

Mara raised her dagger again.

Samara sprang forward, her dagger swinging, but this time Mara was ready for her. She grabbed Samara's wrist, seized the woman's shoulder with her other hand and fell backward, using Samara's momentum against her. Mara's feet came up as she fell, dealing a solid blow to the other woman's gut and flipping her onto the ground. Samara's back hit the floor with a crack.

Mara rolled to her knees, her breathing fast and shallow. Sweat rolled down her face like tears, and she fumbled with her weapon. But Samara stood and sheathed her dagger.

"I am satisfied," she said. She held out her hand and Mara took it, allowing herself to be helped up. "You have learned much." Samara placed one hand on her chest and bowed.

"My teachers taught me well," Mara said, returning the bow.

Vivaksh came down the steps of the dais.

"Kneel down, novice."

Mara dropped to her knees on the packed dirt floor, feeling the grainy dust under her fingers. A hand touched her hair.

"As head of the Order of Khatar, I hereby name you Mara t'Riala, the newest member of the Order of Khatar. I name you, and I set you free to seek the one you will swear to."

T'Riala. The name shared by all the members of the Order as if they were a family by blood instead of a group of strangers who had all taken the same vow.

Vivaksh went on. "Seek out those who are worthy, who cannot protect themselves. Once sworn, you must protect the one you choose at all costs, even unto your own life. Under the law of the Empire, if your charge is killed, you may eliminate the one who was directly responsible. Otherwise, you may kill only if you or your charge is in danger. Do you understand this?"

"Yes."

"You may work for your keep until you make your pledge, but once you swear, you are bound for life. You must serve until your charge dies. Are you willing to so swear?"

Mara's voice was steady. "I am."

"You know the penalty for those who do not keep the oath. Do not break faith."

"I won't."

The hand left her hair, leaving cool air behind. Then Vivaksh knelt and pressed something into her palm. It was a bronze earring. "Here is the symbol of your service," he said. "Do not lose it. Now rise, Mara, and go out."

They stood and Mara bowed to Vivaksh. Then she bowed to the crowd of novices and teachers.

"Thank you for my new life," she said, the ritual words coming easy.

"Live well," the others chorused. "And die with honor."

Mara slipped the earring into the special pouch on her belt that had been made for it. It would stay there until she found someone worth giving her life to. Worth giving her life *for*.

The teak-and-bone door groaned like a dying elephant when she pushed it open. The brightness was blinding, but Mara forced herself to walk forward until she stood at the top of the steps.

After the cool shadows of the stone, the air seemed too thick, too hot. The bamboo forest around her was tangled and blurry, buzzing with noise. Mara closed her eyes, trying to convince herself to walk forward. Trying to ignore the thrill of fear along her spine.

"If I may offer a suggestion?" Samara said from just behind her. "The Imperial capital of Kamal lies to the west and south of here, across the biggest of the Five Sacred Rivers. There is a Jade Circle there, a place for healers and scholars and warrior monks to gather. Go to the temple with the *naga* on the gate and ask for a warrior named Suni. Tell him you're my student. He'll give you shelter until you find someone to pledge to."

Mara felt her muscles relax a little. That was what she needed, a direction, an idea of where to start. Get to the capital and worry about everything else later. She opened her eyes.

"Thank you, Samara. And tell the others thank you too."

The weapons master smiled, the first full smile Mara had ever seen on her. Then she put a hand on Mara's head, just as Vivaksh had. Her touch was comforting and Mara leaned into it. Touch was important to all the Tribes. It was how you formed bonds, how you welcomed travelers home.

And how you said good-bye.

"Go in peace, Mara t'Riala. And may the Ancestors see your sacrifice and balance their scales in your favor."

I don't believe in the Ancestors, Mara thought. Her Tribe had worshipped Nishvana the Silent-Pawed. But she was grateful for Samara's blessing all the same. It made her feel a little less alone.

Mara took a deep breath, then turned and walked down the steps. Behind her, she heard the heavy door shut.

She didn't look back.

Water falling from the sky

Where has all the magic gone?

Spots of light in blackest night

Where has all the magic gone?

Earthsleep comes and seasons turn

Flowers grow and flames will burn

Wait for old days to return

Where has all the magic gone?

Kildi children's rhyme

3
Emil

"WE'VE GOT TROUBLE."

Emil Arvi looked up from the toy that he was carving. His twin brother Stefan's broad shoulders filled the doorway to their shared tent.

"Trouble? What kind of trouble?"

"One of the goats is missing."

From where he was sitting, cross-legged on the rug, Emil had to crane his neck to see his brother's face. "Are you sure?"

"I counted twice," Stefan said. His forehead wrinkled into a frown. "We're one goat short on the tie line. It's not being combed out, it's not in the medicine tent, it's not anywhere." He paused. "I think it was taken by a tiger."

Emil set the wooden figure and the carving knife down and rose to his feet. Standing, he was at least a head taller than

Stefan; he had to duck to keep from brushing his head against the striped cotton of the tent.

"There hasn't been a tiger this close to the Imperial capital for decades."

His brother's scowl deepened. "I know the print of a tiger's paw when I see one. Looks like the prints of those cat friends of yours, only the size of my hand." He spread his fingers to illustrate. "Look, I know it doesn't make any sense, but I saw the print and the goat is gone. I can show you if you want."

Outside, one of their younger cousins laughed, a ripple of sound. Fear tightened Emil's shoulders. A rogue tiger could take a child as easily and silently as it took the goat. If Stefan was right . . .

"Here's what we'll do," Emil said. "I'll tell Father while you find the Master of Livestock. We need to do a head count, gather the children in, and make sure everyone is safe."

"There's no time," Stefan said. He pushed past Emil and into the tent, grabbing a long spear. "We need to go after it, get the goat back, and kill the beast."

"Are you crazy?" Emil said. "The goat is probably dead by now." For a moment, he imagined Stefan dead, his chest ripped and bloodied, his eyes blank. The thought made his hands shake, and he put them behind his back. "We need to get everyone together and leave the area."

Stefan stared at him. "We can't leave! The Clothing Fair is tomorrow. As for the goat, it might still be alive. We have to try."

Emil resisted the urge to reach out and shake his brother. Stefan always did this, always charged ahead without thinking of his own safety, or the effect he had on the people around him.

I won't lose another member of my family, Emil thought. *I won't.*

"We can't afford to lose any more goats," Stefan went on, and for a moment, Emil thought he'd spoken his thought aloud. But Stefan just kept talking. "After that sickness that struck them during Earthsleep, we were lucky to get anywhere close to enough from the ones we have. We need this fair and we need that goat and I'll be damned if I'll let some tiger drag it off and put the whole camp's welfare in jeopardy."

Emil and Stefan shared the same black, wavy hair, and the same square jaw, but despite the family resemblance, they were as different as water and stone. Where Emil was lean and sharp, Stefan was blunt and muscled. Emil had the ready smile and dark eyes of their dead mother. Stefan had their father's pale-brown eyes and constant frown. They were different in other, less visible ways, too. Emil was the voice of reason to his brother's rashness, the calm to his brother's temper. But trying to steady Stefan was like balancing on a rock in the middle of a swift-flowing river. One wrong step and you were lost.

Emil took in a deep breath of warm air and let it out. "Stefan," he said, "we are *not* going after that tiger. You and I are going to go tell Father about the missing goat. And we're going to let him decide what to do. All right?"

Stefan's face turned a dull red under his scruff of beard. "You tell Father," he shot back. "You're his favorite anyway. I'll go tell Meri." He dropped the spear with a clatter and stomped out of the tent.

Frustration bubbled up in Emil's chest, and he resisted the urge to bang his head on the tent pole. *Why does every conversation we have end in a fight?* he thought. *Why is it so difficult to talk to my own brother?*

But the silent tent didn't answer him. Emil kicked a stack of blankets just to make himself feel better, then went after Stefan.

Outside, the camp was showing signs of the hectic trading season. The donkeys were tethered to stakes pounded into the ground, not corralled in a pen the way they usually were. The hastily raised tents sagged, and stacks of grain and supplies were piled around them. Many of the Arvi hadn't even bothered with tents, electing to sleep on pads of black goatskin around their cooking fires instead. The *clack clack* of looms mixed with the calls of the donkeys and the bleating of the nearby goats.

Stefan was nowhere in sight.

Fine, Emil thought. *I'll deal with this myself. Like always.* Nearby, his twelve-year-old cousin Rona, a purple scarf wrapped around her dark curls, was brushing a donkey. Emil beckoned her over.

"Rona," he called. "I need you to do something for me."

"What is it?" Rona asked. Flecks of straw clung to her gray cashmere skirt, and her sturdy boots were streaked with dirt. Another scarf, woven in stripes of green and purple, was tied around her waist. Rona tucked a wayward strand of hair behind one ear. "You look worried. Is something wrong?"

Emil smiled at her. "I don't know yet," he said. "But something took a goat last night. Will you gather up the children and make sure everyone's accounted for?"

"Of course," Rona said. "They've been pestering me for another clapping game anyway. Do we know what took the goat?"

"We're not sure," Emil said. It wasn't exactly a lie, and everything would go faster if no one panicked. "But if it can take a goat, it can take a child. Spread the word that no one is to go into the forest, and count the younglings. Let me know if anyone is missing."

Rona darted off. Emil headed for the few caravans parked at the edge of camp. Lovingly carved and painted with colorful birds and flowers, each caravan was a traveling, permanent residence, reserved for the Elders who ruled the Arvi. There was a Master of Trade, a Master of Livestock, and a Master of Camp. And overseeing them all was the *Kys*, the leader of the Arvi and Emil and Stefan's father.

Emil cursed under his breath. Going to talk to your own father should not feel like going into battle. It hadn't been that way when his mother was alive.

Has Father changed that much? Or is it Stefan and I who have changed? Emil stifled a sigh. Maybe it *was* him who was changing. Maybe he was the only one changing, and wasn't that an unsettling thought?

At least a tiger was a problem his family could deal with together. He tried not to think about how grateful that made him feel.

4

Emil

THE *KYS* WAS sitting on the steps of his wagon, his arms resting on his knees. Short hair, lightened by age into a yellow gray, covered his head and face, a striking contrast to his dark, lined skin. A necklace of polished ivory, mahogany, and gold beads hung around his neck, showing his rank.

Emil's uncle Pali, the Master of Trade, stood next to him, wearing a finely woven tunic. There was a roll of rice paper in his hand.

"I hate to put our booth on the edge of the Clothing Fair," Pali was saying. "But these two clans aren't getting along right now, and their booths are next to each other. . . ."

"And a fight at the Clothing Fair hurts everyone," Emil's father said. "Very well, move us down the row and tell the Nuri clan they can have our booth." He glanced up as Emil approached.

"Ah, you're just in time, Emil. This would be a good leadership lesson for you. We've got some problems with the fair tomorrow."

Of course we do, Emil groaned to himself. Once, just once, he'd like to talk to his father without everything being a lesson. "I'm afraid we have more problems than the fair, Father," he said. "One of the goats is missing, and Stefan found a tiger track."

"A tiger?" His father's eyes narrowed. Beside him, Pali tensed. "Are you sure?"

"Stefan is," Emil said. "And I trust his opinion. I've already started pulling in the children, but we should do a head count."

Pali rubbed the gold-and-silver embroidery that lined his hem. "Mihai," he said, addressing Emil's father. "We cannot cancel the Clothing Fair. We're already low on funds for the year, and summer's not even over yet. We need this trade."

"No one is canceling anything," Emil's father said. "But Emil is right, we do need to make sure everyone is accounted for. Then we need to send messages to the other clans and alert them." He looked at Emil. "Have you spoken to Meri yet?"

"Stefan went to find her," Emil said, just as the door of one of the traveling wagons opened. A woman in a dyed black tunic and trousers, her hands stained with medicine and her clothes smelling of goats, walked out. Everyone in camp wore cashmere, but the Master of Livestock was the only one who dyed her everyday clothing.

"I heard my name," Meri said, shaking her shoulder-length hair out of her face and tying it back with a leather thong. "What's going on?"

Something cold and suspicious ran down Emil's spine. "Stefan was looking for you," he said. "Have you seen him?"

Meri looked confused. "No," she said. "I haven't, and I've been right here all morning. What's happening?"

But Emil wasn't listening anymore. Leaving his father and Pali to explain, he turned and ran back to his tent.

The tent looked much as it had when he'd left it. There was the pile of blankets, the bags of dried vegetables, the bedrolls.

But Stefan's spear was gone.

Emil cursed. Flinging open the chest where he kept his belongings, he pulled out a long bundle of waterproof skins.

"What's happened, Son?" His father stood in the doorway, flanked by Pali and Meri. Emil unwrapped the skins, taking out a simple bow and a quiver of arrows.

"Stefan's gone after the tiger."

For the briefest of moments, Emil saw fear on his father's face, harsh lines digging into his dark skin. Then it was gone, and he was once again *Kys* of the Arvi, calm and in charge.

"Pali, send messages to the other camps. Tell them there is a tiger in the area and we need help to track it down. Meri, go find Lel. The head count is his job. The two of you need to make sure that everyone is accounted for and that all the livestock are in. Emil—"

Emil didn't let him finish. "I'm going after Stefan," he said. "I'm going to stop him."

His father studied him. "Be careful," he said finally. "We need you."

"We need Stefan, too," Emil said, making the words intentionally sharp. But his father didn't flinch.

"How are you going to find him?"

"Easy," Emil said, slinging the quiver over his shoulder. "I'm going to get Esmer to help me."

Outside Emil's tent, the cheerful chaos of the morning was gone. The Arvi stood in small groups, whispering anxiously. Rona, along with the other older children, had gathered the younger ones into the center of camp, and they all sat in a circle, clapping and singing.

Earthsleep comes and seasons turn
Flowers grow and flames will burn . . .

Lel, Pali's partner and the Master of Camp, was already busy. He hummed tunelessly as he marked off a scroll of names, making sure no one was forgotten. Emil stopped to check in with him.

"I'm going after Stefan," he said. "Don't let anyone else leave camp."

Lel never looked up from his list. "Be careful," he said, still humming under his breath.

Emil felt a rush of affection for Lel. The man had been a wandering Wind caste scribe, until Pali met him at a trading fair in the south and brought him home. The Arvi—like most of the Kildi—were open to outsiders joining them, as long as they did their fair share of the work and didn't cause trouble in camp. Lel fit into the Arvi family right away. He'd taken over the duties of Master of Camp with quiet efficiency, and he trusted people to do their job properly. If Emil was going after Stefan, then Emil had a good reason.

The goats were still tethered in a line at the edge of camp, and they bleated as he passed, pulling at their ropes. "Someone will come to get you soon," Emil promised, patting one. It studied him, its odd rectangular pupils dilated

"Maaaaaaaaa," it complained. Emil thought it looked like a worried old man.

It took him only a few minutes of searching to spot the track Stefan had seen. His brother had been right—the track was as wide as Emil's hand, the front four toes pressed deep into the earth. There were more, heading into the forest. It could very well be a tiger's print, but Emil needed to be sure.

He took a small wooden whistle out of his pocket and blew a soundless blast.

At first there was nothing. Then Emil heard a faint rustling from the nearby trees, followed by the sound of feet hitting earth. A girl about Emil's age stepped out from the treeline.

The girl was dressed in a simple brown tunic and trousers favored by many of the Sune. Her skin was the color of polished *narra* wood, and a single gray streak ran through her dark hair. Like all the magical shifters in the Empire, she had brown eyes flecked with gold.

"You called?" she asked.

Emil didn't waste time with greetings. "Esmer, why didn't you tell me there was a tiger in the area?" he said, indicating the enormous paw print in the dirt.

"What?" Esmer's voice was sharp. "Let me see." She knelt and put her small hand over the track, tracing the shape of the print. Then she leaned forward, sniffing it. "Well, it's definitely a tiger," she said, sitting back on her heels. "But I swear it didn't come through our territory. I would have warned you."

"So where did it come from, the capital?" Emil snapped. Then he sighed and rubbed the back of his neck.

"I'm sorry, I . . . Stefan's gone after this thing." He heard the break in his voice. "Can you track it?"

Esmer gave a half hiss, half growl that sounded remarkably like swearing. "Stupid boy. Of course I can track it. Tigers aren't nearly as subtle as they like to think."

There was a flicker, a chill of magic rippling over Emil's skin, and Esmer disappeared. In her place was a wild cat, slender and long-legged with gray fur and black spots. The cat looked up at Emil with golden eyes and waved its black-tipped tail.

Follow me, the tail said as clearly as any spoken words. Then the cat turned and trotted off into the undergrowth.

Emil followed.

5

Mara

MARA SWORE UNDER her breath as she tried to keep her balance on the tree branch. One of her hands gripped the branch above her, the rough bark digging into her skin, and the other held her dagger. Her eyes were fixed on the pile of yellow berries that she'd arranged in the crook of the tree. She felt horribly exposed and her shoulder was starting to cramp, but she didn't move.

Come on, she thought, as if by sheer will she could summon her prey. *Come on, you stupid monkey. I know it's the middle of summer, but you have to be hungry. You just have to be.*

Her stomach twitched at the thought. The monkey might not be hungry, but it had been days since Mara had eaten anything but berries. She'd learned to cook in the Order, doing kitchen duty, but she hadn't joined the hunting parties. The idea of leaving the Order walls had been too tempting . . . and too frightening.

Mara had spent time as a human before joining the Order, of course. Even wild Sune had to change sometimes, or they risked going feral. She'd been on trading trips to the nearby villages, watched people point and whisper and shy away from her. She'd learned how to read, been taught the laws of the Empire and the story-songs the humans sang, as well as the songs of her own people. She knew about humans.

But she'd never tried to survive as one outside the Order. This body might be good at fighting, but it was poorly designed in other ways. No claws, no teeth, and even Mara's quick, muscled form couldn't move fast enough to catch a spotted deer. Humans needed *weapons* to hunt, and Mara's dagger wasn't built for throwing.

It didn't help that her senses were so dull. She'd been so full of grief and guilt three years ago that she'd forgotten—or ignored— the difference between her human senses and her animal senses. And it hadn't mattered in the Order, where her surroundings were all stone and dirt and sweat.

But out here, under the blank gray of the Barrier, everything was so *muddled*. And it had only gotten worse as the bamboo forest of her childhood gave way to unfamiliar teak trees. It had taken her days to learn to read her surroundings again, days to stop being startled by a grouse exploding from cover, or the crack of a branch under a deer's foot. Sometimes Mara still felt like she was traveling half blind.

At least she'd figured out how to disguise her scent a bit. By smashing leaves with rocks, she'd made a thin paste that she'd smeared on her face, neck, and hands. She'd also rubbed her tunic and trousers with fresh earth. The camouflage was comforting, especially at night.

Night was the worst. Before her exile, Mara had loved the dark, all soft outlines and cool, clear air. But now, with no night sight at all, the darkness was full of shadows and danger. Sometimes Mara had nightmares that the families of the men she had killed were hunting her. Those nights always ended with her sitting with her back against a tree, her dagger in her lap, and her mind filled with blood and screams.

A rustle brought her attention back to the matter at hand. *There!* A monkey with a black face and silver-gray fur, its small black eyes bright with hunger. The sight made Mara's stomach hurt even more. She remembered hunting monkeys from the ground: the stalking, the brief chase, the sweet-salt taste of raw meat.

Her hand tightened on the dagger.

The monkey crept closer. . . .

There was a screech close to Mara's ear as a flock of birds above her took flight. She jerked, startled, and her boots lost their grip on the bark.

Then she was falling, plummeting, and there was the ground coming at her like a fist. The impact chased the breath from her body and sent a shooting pain through her shoulder. Between the shock and the hurt, Mara felt the carefully built wall inside her crack, and the power in her blood woke with a scream.

Pain. Hurt. Change.

No!

Mara dug her fingernails into her palms, resisting with all her strength. Her vision swam with red. The magic that allowed Sune to change from human to animal was closely tied to instinct, and it was especially strong when there were injuries or danger. Changing to animal form helped you get away, helped you heal. But it could also take over, leave you mindless and furious like a wounded animal.

It could make you kill.

I am human.

I am human.

I am human.

The red started to fade and the overwhelming urge ebbed. Mara went limp with relief. She'd had accidents at the Order, bruises and cuts, once even a twisted ankle. But there she'd been able to shove the urge away, tamp it down. After a while, the instinct to change had faded entirely.

She'd forgotten how strong it was, the sheer *need*. The need to become something else, something stronger, faster, better able to survive. She'd been safe in the Order, but out here her instincts would be harder to resist. She'd have to be more careful.

Her vision was clear again. Mara pushed herself into a sitting position. Her shoulder still burned with pain, and her arm dangled from her side. Dislocated.

Mara grimaced. They'd taught her basic healing at the Order, including how to put in a dislocated shoulder. It was going to hurt. A lot. But she didn't have a choice. As long as she was injured, she was a danger to herself and others.

Just as Mara was bracing herself to put her shoulder back in, she heard a commotion through the trees. Cracking branches, running footsteps . . .

And the high-pitched breathing of a human fleeing for its life.

Mara scooped up her dropped dagger and looked around for somewhere to hide. Gritting her teeth against the pain, she fell to her knees and wriggled into a nearby bush. She tried to make herself small and still, like a baby deer.

The footsteps got closer, and a boy ran into view. He looked about her age, with a dark scruff of beard on his chin, and he was wearing a filthy, buff-colored tunic. The boy's mouth was open, gasping for air, and he cradled his left wrist close to his side. The fingers of his right hand were clenched around a broken spear.

Mara shrank farther into the bush, as the boy staggered closer. He reached the tree she'd fallen out of and leaned against it.

A low growl reverberated through the trees.

The boy's head snapped up. His pupils were wide and dark like a rabbit's, and his chest heaved. A second growl came, and Mara's skin rippled with recognition. It couldn't be . . .

A tiger padded into her line of sight.

6
Emil

EMIL KNELT BY the shredded remains of the goat. Esmer was right; it was easy to track the tiger's path. All they had to do was follow the blood and broken branches. The goat's belly had been torn open, and its intestines were wet and glistening and buzzing with flies. A sour smell filled the air.

Emil thought about the tiger's claws tearing open his brother. He dug his nails into his palms to drive the image away.

"Anything, Esmer?" he called.

"Over here," Esmer called. She was back in human form and examining the base of a nearby tree.

Emil crouched next to her as Esmer touched the grass and old leaves, rubbing them between her fingers. Her forehead was creased with worry.

"Stefan was here," she said. "His scent is all over this area. But he didn't go near the goat."

"Because the tiger was there," Emil said. He took a deep breath, loud and ragged in the still woods. "Which way did he go?"

Esmer scanned the ground. "That way," she said, pointing with her thumb. "They both went that way, not too long ago. If you look, you can see the tracks."

Emil looked down at the line of scuffled marks that led off into the trees. His neck felt tight and stiff, and his feet were sweating inside his boots. "What is a tiger doing this close to humans? We've visited this area every summer for years and never had a problem."

"There are mercenaries camped to the south right now," Esmer said. "The tiger might have been trying to avoid them and ended up closer to your camp."

Emil studied the ground, not really listening to Esmer's words. "I'll follow the tracks. Can you circle the area a little, make sure they didn't double back?"

"Of course," Esmer said. "If you find him, call for me." She flicked back to cat form and vanished into the bushes.

Emil started following the tiger tracks, praying to the Horned God that he would find his brother alive. *I won't lose another member of my family.*

"Stefan!" he called as he went. "Stefan, are you there?"

7

Mara

THE TIGER WAS beautiful, with inky black stripes over fur the color of molten bronze. It held its broad head low, muscled shoulders rippling under its silky fur as it stalked forward. The boy made a whimpering noise. Mara bit her lip.

There was no way she could fight an adult tiger and win, not in her human form. But if she let this boy die right in front of her, it would be one more death on her conscience. One more thing to atone for.

Her deliberations were interrupted by the last thing she expected, a mocking female voice inside her head.

Wait right there, my brave, foolish boy. I'm coming to you.

Shock froze Mara in place. Her eyes snapped to the tiger, which was pacing closer. A Sune? She hadn't seen another Sune since she'd walked through the doors of the Order.

You interrupted my dinner, the tiger drawled, her attention still on the human. *That was rude, you know.*

Mara couldn't breathe. It had been years since she'd heard another voice in her head, years of living with her own lonely thoughts. And now, another Sune. Just within reach . . .

But what was she doing here? She wasn't Mara's Tribe–the coloring was wrong–so she couldn't have followed her. And there were no tigers in this area.

More important, why in the name of Nishvana was she hunting *humans*? None of the Sune Tribes Mara knew would allow such a thing. And the tiger didn't look wounded or angry or any of those things that could make a Sune act on instinct. If anything, she seemed . . . bored.

Mara saw the boy's hand tighten on the broken spear, and he drew himself up.

The tiger-Sune chuckled silently. *Yes, yes. Fight me, human child. It's so much more fun when the prey has some spirit.*

Anger burned through Mara's shock. Only the oldest and most powerful Sune could reach through the layered confusion of the human mind and make themselves heard. The boy clearly could not hear the tiger, yet still she taunted him.

The tiger-Sune was *enjoying* this.

As carefully as she dared, Mara got to her feet. Her arm throbbed, but she ignored it. She stepped forward, making herself as tall as possible.

"Hey!" she yelled, waving her good arm at the tiger-Sune. "Hey, you!"

The tiger blinked. *Another one?* she drawled. *How delightful.*

Mara put all her will behind her answer. *Think again*, she sent, hoping her mind-to-mind speech wasn't too rusty. *I'm no unarmed human to be played with and tormented.*

The tiger sat back a little. Her ears went back, and she hissed. *A loner? I thought I was the only one in the area. Where did you come from?*

That is none of your concern, Mara sent firmly, making sure not to break eye contact. *What is your concern is that this boy is now under my protection. I've claimed him.*

On what grounds? The tiger sounded interested, rather than angry, but Mara didn't relax her stance. *This is my territory, young one, not yours. By rights all prey belongs to me.*

Humans aren't prey! Mara sent back. *And hunting them is forbidden. You shame yourself and our kind with your actions.*

That's one of the benefits of being a loner. The tiger opened her mouth, revealing teeth the size of Mara's fingers. Blood stained her muzzle. *There are no Tribe Elders here to stop me.*

Beside her, the boy shifted. "Don't move," Mara whispered, and he stilled. At least he was smart enough for that.

I'm here, she sent to the tiger. *I'll stop you.*

Really? The tiger crouched low, tail snapping. *Let's see if you can.* The muscles under the tiger's skin twitched, tensing for a leap.

Mara stepped in front of the boy.

"Stefan!" The shout carried through the air, followed by the sound of someone crashing through the brush. "Stefan!"

The tiger recoiled. *More vermin*, she sent, disgust making the word slick, like spoiled meat.

Mara pressed her advantage. *Yes, more humans*, she sent. *Coming* with their spears and their bows and their anger. *How many can you fight?*

The tiger's eyes met Mara's again. *Have it your way. But I'll remember you, young one.* Then she was gone, slipping through the woods.

Another boy burst through the trees. He was tall and lean with the same simple clothing and dark-brown skin as the boy Mara was protecting. His eyes scanned the clearing, and when he saw the injured boy, his shoulders sagged with relief.

"Stefan!" he called out. "Esmer, I found him!"

"Emil." The first boy exhaled, slipping down the tree to a sitting position.

Mara's shoulder chose that moment to throb, and she hissed a breath through her teeth, stepping back from the humans. Maybe she could slip away while they were distracted.

The new boy wasn't looking at her at all. He knelt down by Stefan, his whole body tight with anxiety. "Stefan, are you all right? What happened?"

"I was tracking the tiger," Stefan said, his voice short with pain. "I wasn't going to try to kill it, I just wanted to find it, and follow it so it couldn't get away. But it must have smelled me, because it started chasing me." The other boy started examining Stefan's wrist.

"What happened here?"

"I fell down at one point," Stefan said, then winced. "Did something to my wrist. Sprained it, I think."

"More like broke it." The other boy sat back on his heels. "Honestly, Stefan . . ."

"No lectures, Emil," Stefan said, shifting positions. His face was gray under his brown skin. "I'm going to get enough of that from Father."

Mara was about to step behind a clump of trees when there was a flash of fur and a spotted wildcat came bounding thorough the brush. Its gray-and-black fur stood up on end, and it was clearly agitated.

Then, between one leap and the next, the cat flickered into a girl. A girl with a gray streak in her hair and gold-flecked brown eyes.

Not another one, Mara groaned to herself. *That's not fair.*

The girl walked up to Stefan and slapped him. It wasn't a hard slap, just enough to redden the skin, but the boy rubbed his cheek and glared at her.

"What was that for?"

"For being stupid," the girl said. Her voice was soft, at odds with her no-nonsense tone. "Because your brother won't say it and you won't listen to your father. So that leaves me." She put her hands on her hips and glared at him. "Do you have any idea how dangerous that was? How are you still alive?"

Preoccupied with watching the other Sune, Mara forgot to look where she was stepping. A branch snapped under her foot.

Stefan looked up. "Because of her," he said, waving his uninjured hand at Mara. "She jumped in front of the tiger, waving and shouting. I think it might have attacked us anyway, but then we all heard Emil and it ran away."

Mara fought the urge to run away too, as three pairs of eyes landed on her.

The cat-Sune tilted her head. "Confuse the tiger, make it think the prey isn't worth the fight. Not a bad plan."

The other boy stood. He was even taller up close, with the slight stoop of someone used to having to duck through doorways. His black hair was thick and wavy, and his eyes were the dark brown of freshly turned earth. He smiled at her, his eyes crinkling, and Mara found herself wanting to smile back.

"Thank you," he said, and his voice was as warm as his eyes. "That was very brave of you. I'm Emil Arvi, and this reckless one here is my brother, Stefan."

Mara swallowed. "I'm Mara," she said. "I'm pleased I was able to assist." She turned to Esmer, unable to resist the urge to speak mind-to-mind, just one more time. Just this once.

Well met, cousin, she sent, reaching out tentatively to brush against the girl's mind.

Oh. The girl's eyes widened in a visible expression of surprise, and Mara could almost see her ears go back. *You're Sune.*

Please don't tell the humans, Mara hastened to send. *I'm just traveling through, and I don't want trouble.*

I see. Esmer's mind-voice was as sharp and bright as a polished sword. *Well, with a rogue tiger in the area, I can see why not. You are tiger-Sune, aren't you?* She paused. *I mean, I haven't met many, and you smell more human than anything, but you* sound *like a tiger.*

I was, Mara sent. She kept her thoughts bland and harmless, not showing how Esmer's question had surprised her. Sune mind-voices could carry impressions as easily as they carried words, and if you were listening, you could usually tell what kind of Sune you were dealing with. It was a necessary skill, especially for smaller Sune like Esmer. But Mara hadn't realized hers was still so distinctive.

I've given up my tiger form, she sent at last. *And as I said, I'm only passing through.*

Before the other girl could reach further, Mara broke the connection, pulling back into the cold, solitary reaches of her own mind. The loss of contact felt like being gutted, and Mara wondered if it was possible to suffocate from loneliness.

That was when Emil reached out and touched her good hand. "Mara? Are you all right?"

The feel of his skin on hers sent a jolt through Mara. It had been so long since she'd touched anyone outside her fellow novices. And even in the Order, it had been only a hand on her head, a pat on her shoulder. Small gestures, comforting but mostly fleeting. Not like this. Emil's hand was almost curled around hers, his light touch holding her in place.

Mara was suddenly conscious of her dirty tunic and dirt-streaked skin. But Emil didn't seem to notice or care.

"Do you need help?" he asked. "You're holding your shoulder as if you're hurt."

The brush of his fingers against her skin was suddenly more intimate than Mara could bear. She pulled away.

"I can't—I'm not—"

Desperate, her mind reached out for Esmer's. *Please,* she thought. *I can't be around them. Not while I'm injured.*

Esmer narrowed her eyes, then nodded. *Go,* the cat girl sent back. *I'll keep them here.*

Mara backed up and started to babble. "I have to go," she said.

"I'm glad your brother is safe."

Emil moved as if to follow her, but Esmer put a hand on his arm. Her voice slipped into Mara's mind again.

I forgot to give you my name. It's Esmer, of the Marjara-Sune.

Thank you, Mara sent back. *I . . . thank you.*

And she turned and ran into the woods.

8

Emil

"I DON'T UNDERSTAND," Emil said, staring after the girl who had saved Stefan's life. Despite her obviously injured shoulder, the girl moved with grace, slipping deeper into the trees until she was gone entirely.

"That girl is hurt, Esmer, and that tiger's still out there. She shouldn't be alone."

Esmer's hand was firm on his sleeve. "Trust me, Emil. She doesn't want or need our help. And we have your brother to worry about."

Emil dug his feet in. "Esmer, we can't just let her go. Even if the tiger is gone, there are the mercenaries. And my father is gathering hunting parties for the tiger. She could get hurt by accident."

The cat girl paused, her forehead creasing with thought. "I

hadn't thought about hunting parties." Her fingers drummed on Emil's arm.

"How about this?" she said finally. "I'll help you get Stefan to his feet, and then you take him back to the camp while I go make sure Mara is safe. Will *that* satisfy you?"

"It satisfies *me*," Stefan said. His face was sallow, and sweat dampened his hairline. "That tiger might come back, and I don't want to be here when it does."

Guilt curled in Emil's chest. Of course his brother had to be his first priority. He moved to one side of Stefan, Esmer going to the other, and they lifted him to his feet.

"Can you walk?" Emil asked.

"I broke my wrist, not my ankle," Stefan snapped. "Of course I can walk."

Esmer and Emil exchanged a glance. Stefan was touchy at the best of times, but when he was hurt he was like a wounded bear, all growls and swipes.

"I'm going to check on your rescuer," Esmer said. She patted Stefan's shoulder. "Try to get home in one piece, all right?"

"I'll do my best," Stefan said gruffly. "And thanks, Esmer."

"Anytime," the girl said.

"Be careful, Esmer," Emil cautioned. "There's still a rogue tiger out there."

"No tiger is going to catch me," Esmer said. "I'd like to see them try." She flicked into cat form, then leaped gracefully to Emil's shoulder. Emil staggered with the sudden weight.

"All right, all right," he said. "I know. You're quicker and

sneakier than I will ever be, and you can take care of yourself."
Claws dug into his shoulder, and he winced. "Now could you get
off? You're heavy."

Esmer purred, and her black-tipped tail curled across the back
of Emil's neck. Her claws gripped him as she jumped. In midair,
she blinked back to human form and landed like a tumbler, rolling and coming up on her feet.

Emil rolled his eyes. "Show-off," he teased.

Esmer brushed the leaves off her tunic and grinned.

"I'll make sure she's all right before I come back," she said.
Then she ran into the trees and disappeared.

Emil turned back to his brother. His twin was still cradling his
broken wrist, but at least Stefan was standing and his eyes were
clear. Relief made Emil almost giddy. He wanted to say something like *I'm glad you're safe* or *You frightened me*. But habit took
over and what came out wasn't like that at all.

"Father is going to kill you."

"I know," Stefan said. His laugh was bitter. "And he'll probably
throw you some sort of party for finding me."

"Stefan . . ."

"Don't," Stefan said, cutting him off. "Just . . . don't, all right?
I got myself into this, I'll take the consequences. Let's just go
home."

Emil rubbed his forehead. Once again he'd failed to reach
across the ever-widening gap that separated him and his twin. He
gazed around the clearing, trying to think of what to say next.
Something near the base of the tree caught his eye.

"What's this?"

This turned out to be a small leather pouch with something hard and round inside. Emil reached in and pulled out an earring, a squat bronze hoop with an odd dagger symbol pressed into the metal.

Stefan leaned forward. "That's strange," he said. "I've never seen an earring like that. It's still shiny, so it hasn't been here long. You think it belongs to the girl who saved me?"

Emil examined it. "Maybe." He'd been too concerned about his brother to really study the girl before, but now he closed his eyes and cast his mind back.

She'd been short, he remembered. About Esmer's height. But where Esmer was quick and slim, this girl moved with muscled power. It was her face that stuck in his memory: wide, high cheekbones, full lips, and eyes the color of darkest honey. Her hair was a little longer than a bond servant's, and there had been a leather decoration hiding one of her earlobes.

Emil opened his eyes. "She's from the Order of Khatar. She was wearing the ear cuff they always have. But I don't think her other ear was pierced."

"Then maybe it's not hers." Stefan winced. "Can we go home now?"

Emil sighed and slipped the earring back into the pouch. "You're right," he said. "I'm sorry. Let's get you home."

9

Mara

MARA MOVED THROUGH the trees as quickly as her injured shoulder would allow. When she was sure she was out of range of the humans, she stopped, sagging against a tree. Already she could feel her instincts rising, pleading with her to change. Her shoulder hurt more with every step she took. Magic coiled in her belly, waiting to be used. It felt sour and angry and made her stomach hurt.

A place to sleep, Mara thought. *I need a safe place to sleep first. I'll be too tired afterward to find one. And then I can put my shoulder in and ride out the pain.*

But first she had to get herself under control. She focused on the meditation techniques that her teachers at the Order had taught her, breathing and clearing her mind. Gradually the pain in her shoulder dimmed to a sharp ache, and the urge to change receded.

A cautious voice brushed against her mind. *Mara? It's Esmer. Are you all right?*

You shouldn't be here, Mara sent. She straightened up and scanned the trees. *The humans aren't with you, are they?*

The boys went back to their camp. Esmer's mind-voice was soothing. *But you need to know that this forest is about to be full of hunters. The Kildi clans are gathered for the Clothing Fair tomorrow, and the boys' father is putting together hunting parties to search for the tiger.*

Hunters. The word sent a twist of panic through Mara's chest. Hunters with blades and spears, looking at her with flat, empty eyes, as if she were an animal ready for the slaughter. . . .

Mara! Esmer's voice cut sharply though the flashes of memory. And Mara realized she was gasping, fast shallow breaths. Her whole body was thrumming with magic and power and fear.

Hunters were coming.

Mara, breathe, Esmer commanded. *You're in no danger right now. I promise. It's just you and me here.*

Mara forced one ragged deep breath, then another. She clenched and unclenched her fists, feeling the bones and muscles move, feeling the press of her feet into the earth, forcing the overwhelming terror away.

It ebbed slowly, leaving her trembling. Mara's shoulder ached, and she felt an unaccountable urge to sit down and cry.

I'm so tired, she thought, not caring if Esmer heard her.

There's a large banyan tree a little to the south, Esmer sent back. *I know a human can squeeze between the roots, and it's covered in leafy vines in the summer. No one would find you there.* Her mind-voice was deep with sympathy. Mara knew she didn't deserve the kindness, but she was grateful all the same.

Thank you. You didn't have to come back.

Emil was worried about you, Esmer sent. She sounded amused. *He wouldn't leave until I promised to make sure you were safe.*

A flash of warmth ran through Mara, and despite her exhaustion, she smiled. *I'll be all right. I just need to put my shoulder back in and get some sleep.*

You haven't changed in a long time, Esmer sent.

No. Mara tensed, waiting for the questions.

There was a moment of quiet, then Esmer spoke. *I think you must be very strong. Good fortune go with you, Mara, whatever path you choose.*

Mara's eyes stung. *And to you,* she replied. *Tell Emil I said thank you.*

He's going to be at the Clothing Fair tomorrow, if you want to tell him yourself, Esmer sent back. *It'll be on the main road to Kamal. You won't be able to miss it.*

Then she was gone.

Mara pushed herself up and staggered in the direction Esmer had indicated. It wasn't until she reached the banyan, with its tangled roots and branches, that she thought to check her weapons belt.

Her dagger was there, but earring pouch was missing. One of the ties was broken, the other cut, as if something sharp had caught it. It must have happened when Mara was falling out of the tree.

Mara's fingers clenched. Without the earring, she could not pledge. She had to go back, she had to find it–

But she couldn't. Not now. If she went back now, wounded and weak as she was, and ran into hunters . . . well, no telling what would happen. It wasn't worth the risk.

Mara reached out her good hand to steady herself on the rough bark of the banyan tree. She would go back tomorrow, she promised herself. And the earring would be there.

It had to be.

EMIL SAT IN the grass outside his father's wagon, his fingers tapping on the yellow-painted wood of the wagon wheel. There was a healer from one of the other Kildi camps in there, setting Stefan's broken wrist. Emil couldn't help but feel sorry for the woman. His brother was yelling so loudly that he could hear every word.

"I was trying to protect the camp!"

A rumble of anger, his father's voice.

"Well maybe if you gave me any responsibility, I'd actually do that!" Stefan shouted. "Just because I'm not Emil . . ."

Emil winced. He hated when Stefan and Father dragged him into their fights. And they both did it, his father holding Emil up as a standard that Stefan could never, would never meet. And Stefan resenting, pushing back.

Of course, no one had ever *asked* Emil if he wanted to be the standard. Or the next in line to lead the camp.

No one really asked him anything.

Emil shifted at the thought, feeling the Wind caste scars on his shoulder pull. The truth was, Emil didn't want to be a leader. He liked trading, liked reading faces and body language, guessing what would make a customer buy. He liked chatting with people and matching wits, the subtle contest of offer and counteroffer. He wanted to be Master of Trade someday, like his uncle Pali, traveling with the camp, going outside it to small villages to sell goods. He wanted to be responsible for wool and paper and numbers and profits. Not people.

Around him, the camp was returning to normal. The weavers had gone back to their looms, and the children were playing in small groups, each under the watchful eye of an older child. Most of the goats were sleeping off the afternoon heat between the caravans, curled up like the rolls of wool they produced. From where he was sitting, Emil could smell the three male goats, their distinctive scent mixing with the smells of curry and other spices from a nearby cooking pot. It was a combination as familiar to him as the feel of his own skin. Home wasn't a place for the Arvi. It was people. These people.

Then why don't I want to stay here?

Sometimes Emil wondered if his caution and care–the traits his father praised so much–were simply cowardice. Emil felt like he was afraid all the time. Stefan didn't seem to know what fear was.

Father has it wrong, Emil thought, not for the first time. *I'm not the strong one.*

The door to the caravan slammed open. Emil scrambled to his feet as Stefan stormed down the steps. His brother's wrist was splinted with bamboo and wrapped with thick linen, and his face was pale with pain and fury.

The *Kys* emerged, followed by the healer, a young woman a little older than Emil. She was wearing an undyed cotton tunic and skirt and had a green scarf tied around her waist.

"It wasn't a serious break," she said to Emil. "I gave him some herbs for the pain; if he doesn't overstrain the wrist, it should heal just fine."

"Thank you," Emil said. He elbowed Stefan, who was scowling at the ground.

"Thank you," his twin muttered.

The woman bowed to Emil's father and left. Emil thought she looked relieved.

"Thank you for bringing your brother back, Emil," the *Kys* said. "It was very brave of you."

Emil stifled a groan. Their father didn't have to make it sound like he was such a hero. Stefan had been just as brave, if more foolish. And, there was the girl who'd stood between Stefan and the tiger. Emil opened his mouth to say as much, but his father wasn't finished.

"Stefan," he said, and his voice was heavy with disappointment. "You are too old to punish like a child. But you put yourself and your brother in danger, and I cannot have that. Therefore, none of the Arvi will speak to you until Darkfall tomorrow."

Stefan sucked in a breath. Emil flinched.

Silent treatments were rare. A Kildi's entire life revolved around his clan. To be deliberately excluded, even for a day or two, was like cutting a branch from a tree.

Stefan's face hardened. "Fine," he said, biting off the word. "It's not like anyone ever listens to what I say anyway." Then he stomped off.

The *Kys* put his hand to his eyes, pinching the bridge of his nose. "Emil, will you find Pali and tell him that you're going to be working at our booth in the Clothing Fair tomorrow instead of Stefan?"

Emil hesitated, the words sitting like broken glass in his mouth. *Father, I'd really like to start doing more trading. Maybe train under Uncle Pali to be the next Master of Trade.*

I don't want to be leader.

"Father . . . ," he started.

"We'll talk later," his father said, waving his hand in dismissal.

Emil pressed his lips together. To hide his disappointment, he glanced up at the Barrier, the blank gray sky that had separated the Bhinian Empire from the rest of the world for five hundred years. It grew darker and lighter according to the time of day, but it never changed, not really. Nothing changed in the Empire. Not the caste system, not the Kildi traditions. And not his father's mind.

"Yes, Father," Emil said. "Of course. Esmer can help too."

His father frowned. "You've been spending a lot of time with that Sune girl. Is there something going on that I should know about?"

The unexpectedness of the question jerked Emil around. "With

Esmer?" he said. "No. We're friends, that's all."

His father raised his eyebrows. "You spend more time with her than with practically anyone else in camp, even your own brother."

Because Stefan resents me, Emil thought, swallowing the words. "Esmer and I have been friends since we were small," he said. "And there aren't that many people in camp my age to talk to."

"The Arvi are free to choose who they love," his father said. "It has always been so. But as leader, you should be considering more than just yourself. It would be best for you to choose a mate who strengthens your position, not weakens it. There are plenty of Kildi girls you could make profitable clan-alliance marriages with. . . ."

"I'm not looking for a mate," Emil said. "Esmer and I are just friends."

Without waiting for his father to answer, he turned and walked away, a slow anger burning in his stomach. His father never had time to hear Emil's concerns, but he always had time to tell Emil what he should be doing to become a better leader. Sometimes Emil thought he could replace himself with a wooden statue and his father would never even notice.

He might be hard on Stefan, but at least Father sees him, Emil thought. *The only thing he sees when he looks at me is a copy of himself.*

Still, he was going to work in the Arvi booth tomorrow. That was something. And maybe, at least for a little while, he could pretend to be someone else.

Listen to how it was in the beginning.

Before the Barrier rose, the Empire worshipped the Horned God, overlord of the world. The Horned God was both just and merciful, male and female, sky and earth. Now this god had two children, the son, the Sacrificed Bull, and the daughter, the Eternal Flame. And the people worshipped these three gods and respected the magic that flowed through the land and through the people of the land.

But in their prosperity, the people grew arrogant. They thought themselves as powerful as the gods. And one day they cast a spell they could not control, a spell that ripped the magic out of the land and flung it outward, forming a Barrier that no one has crossed in five hundred years. All that had magic died, including every man, woman, and child with a shred of power.

The loss was more than the people could bear. Grieving and angry, they threw down their leaders and abandoned their old gods. And the world as we knew it ended forever.

The words of Aishe Yanora, Rememberer of the Kildi

11

Mara

THE NEXT MORNING Mara wriggled out of the cramped space between the banyan roots. The air was thick with noise: the snap and hoot of monkeys in the branches, the high-pitched buzz of cicadas. A yellow-crested woodpecker added its *rat-tat-tat* to the chorus. Thin tendrils of mist drifted over the ground, rare for summer.

Mara got to her feet and stretched her stiff shoulder. Putting it back in yesterday had hurt just as much as she'd feared, but she'd managed to stay in control. Now, after a night of sleep, the pain was only a dulled memory.

Even in human form, Mara healed quickly. The thought made her feel bitter and grateful at the same time.

She rubbed her neck, thinking. If she really had dropped the earring pouch when she fell, it should still be near the tree somewhere. Mara broke into a jog, retracing her steps from yesterday.

The spot where she'd met the other tiger-Sune looked curiously empty now. Mara saw signs of people, tracks and broken branches, but whoever they were, they were long gone. She located the tree she'd fallen out of and searched the ground around it. Then she searched it again. And again.

But the pouch–and the earring–weren't there.

Mara forced herself not to panic. If the pouch wasn't here, then someone must have picked it up. One of the Kildi hunting parties. Maybe even Emil, the boy with the warm smile, the one who'd touched her hand.

And the best place to find the Kildi–any of them–was probably the Clothing Fair that Esmer had mentioned.

Mara dusted off her clothes, rubbed some of the dirt and leaf stain off her face, and headed for the road.

Mara paused on the outskirts of the fair. The Clothing Fair turned out to be a sprawling collection of booths and entertainment tents spread out on either side of the main road. The road itself was a river of hard-packed dirt, and Mara knew from her studies that it ran from the nearby capital into the wide, flat farmlands of the west. Kamal, the capital city, wasn't in the exact center of the Empire, but it was close. It housed the Imperial Palace and the royal family, most of the important noble families, and many of the wealthier merchants.

But all that seemed very far away right now. Mara took a deep sniff, savoring the smell of pastries fried in butter and dipped in sugar. Her stomach rumbled.

A few horses stood tied to nearby trees, watched over by gray-clad servants. The sound of their snorts and neighs mingled with the music of flute and drum and the buzz of conversation. As Mara watched, two nobles rode up, a broad-shouldered man in a peacock-blue tunic and a girl Mara's age dressed in brown. They appeared to be arguing.

Mara drifted closer. She'd never seen a member of the noble Flower caste up close before.

". . . don't like these Kildi markets, Revathi," the nobleman was saying as he dismounted. Gold embroidery glistened from his collar. It matched the gleaming *kanak* flower tattooed on the inside of his arm. "Why can't you buy your pretty things from respectable people? I don't mind normal Wind caste—they know their place—but these Kildi . . . you know what my father says about them. They're dangerous."

The girl slid off her horse. She had copper skin and a mass of glossy black hair pinned in a low knot at the base of her neck. Her asar was wrapped loosely around her slender legs, allowing them to move freely.

"I like buying from these people better, Tamas," the girl said, tugging down the sleeves of her undertunic. "I like buying goods from the people who make them, instead of purchasing them from some merchant in the Bamboo Circle. Besides," she said, as the nobleman opened his mouth. "It's cheaper this way."

The man stopped mid-answer and grimaced. "True."

"Come on, Tamas," the girl said, her eyes crinkling. "This will be fun."

"It better be," the man mumbled. "I don't like soiling my clothes in Kildi dirt without there being some benefit."

The girl checked her horse. "That's why you don't wear court clothes to a fair," she answered, still smiling.

This time, Tamas smiled back. "Lesson learned then," he said, offering her his arm. "Shall we descend into the masses?"

"Gladly, good sir." Revathi took his arm and they walked into the swirling crowd.

Mara watched them go, then shook herself. She wasn't here to eavesdrop. She was here to find Emil and Esmer.

But it was hard to stay focused, especially once she dived into the thick press of people. There was just so much to see. Men and women from every caste of the Empire were here. Heavily jeweled merchant families mingled with nobles and with farmers wearing the beaded collars of Hearth caste. There were even a few mercenaries loitering about, trying to look harmless. They weren't doing a bad job of it, but Mara had been trained to see weapons under clothes and inside boots. She made sure to avoid them.

Mara spotted a few Jade healers, their hands painted with dark-green patterns, and was tempted to strike up a conversation. Healers were a favorite choice for members of the Order because they often needed protection as they traveled. And what better way to regain honor than protecting someone who healed others?

But she couldn't pledge to anyone until she got her earring back. Mara scanned the booths around her. Most of them seemed to be manned by Kildi. There was a booth that sold fine thread, where the sellers wore richly embroidered tunics. An older woman sat nearby, stitching sample designs onto swatches of fabric. At a dye booth, a girl dressed in deep purple held up bowls of brightly colored powder and bottles of shimmering liquid.

Kildi clans rarely traveled through the bamboo forests of Mara's childhood home, and she studied them curiously. They were certainly better dressed than most of the Wind caste Mara had seen, and their clothes looked sturdy and well made. No cobbled-together rags here.

There were other differences, too. Many of the Kildi had dusky brown skin, a shade or two darker than the more common amber and copper hues. And while they spoke respectfully to those of higher castes, they also held themselves with a dignity that drew the eye. The stories Mara's Tribe told said the Kildi were the descendants of the original rulers of the Empire, cast down after the Barrier was raised, and looking at them, Mara could believe it.

The main part of the fair was clumped around the road, but there were a few booths and tents scattered around the outside as well, and Mara moved in that direction. She passed an unoccupied booth full of undyed cashmere and stopped to run her hand over one of the rolls of fabric. It felt glorious, soft as a flower petal.

This was one thing she did like about her human form, the sense of touch. She liked the tickle of grass on her arms and the roughness of tree bark under her fingers, all wrinkles and lines like a handprint. Touch was such a decadent thing. It didn't help you hunt or sense enemies or call a mate. Aside from telling you if something was too hot or too cold, Mara couldn't see that it helped you survive at all.

Maybe that was why human were such emotional creatures. Maybe it was something that just happened when you lived without fur or feathers or armor of any kind. In a world so based around how things *felt*, maybe your heart became as sensitive as your skin.

As Mara stroked the cashmere, something caught her eye. Sitting off to one side, almost hidden by the rolls of fabric, was a perfectly carved miniature tiger. It was made out of polished rosewood, and the dark pattern of the rings formed the stripes on the tiger's side. Flecks of ebony stone made the eyes, and the tail was curled around the feet so perfectly that Mara had to touch it.

The wood was smooth against her skin, and the small tiger fit into her palm perfectly. She closed her fingers around it.

"Just a moment," came a muffled voice from somewhere inside the booth. "I'll be right there."

Mara jumped back as a tall young man stood with a roll of cashmere in his arms. It was Emil. Their eyes locked, and a smile lit his face.

"Mara?"

12
Mara

EMIL LOOKED SO genuinely happy to see her that Mara's wits deserted her. She fumbled with the wooden toy in her hands and put it down quickly.

"Emil, right? We met yesterday in the forest?" Mara cursed the breathless sound of her human voice.

"Yes." The boy set the roll of cashmere down and gave her another of his disorienting smiles. "You saved my brother's life."

Heat rose to Mara's face. "I just did what anyone would have done."

"I'm not sure just anyone would have jumped in front of a hunting tiger," Emil said. "But I'll stop mentioning it if it makes you uncomfortable." His eyes met hers and Mara looked away, her flush deepening.

"I'm glad you're here," Emil continued in a more casual tone.

He reached under the counter, pulled something from a hidden shelf. "I found this and I thought it might be yours."

It was her earring pouch.

Mara gasped, her hand reaching for it, even as she tried to be calm. "Yes, that's mine," she said, her words coming too fast, too eager. "Can I have it back, please?"

Emil handed the soft skin pouch to her. When Mara felt the round edge of the earring still inside, something tight and painful inside her loosened.

"Thank you," she said, clutching the pouch close to her chest. "Thank you for finding it. I . . . this is important to me."

Emil's eyes didn't leave her face. "I can see that."

Mara suddenly felt like he did see, as if she'd turned as transparent as a mountain river. She didn't like the feeling at all.

"Thank you," she said again, stepping away. "I have to go. I'm glad your brother was all right."

"Please." The quiet word stopped her midstep. "Wait."

Mara turned around. "What do you *want*?" she said sharply. What was it about the man that made her feel so off balance?

Emil studied her, as if she were a puzzle box he was trying to open. "To talk to you," he said. "You saved my brother, and I know nothing about you." His smile wrinkled his eyes, and Mara found herself wanting to smile back.

"Besides, I've been here all day by myself," he continued. "The friend I was counting on to help me had to do something else this morning, and I've done nothing but talk about cashmere with customers and read people's palms. You're the most interesting person I've seen all day. Don't go yet. Please?"

Mara knew she should say no. But it was so nice to just talk to someone, someone who wasn't afraid of her. Someone who touched her. Emil was open and genuine in a way that Mara hadn't known humans could be, and somehow when she was with him, she didn't feel lonely.

So she turned and walked back to the booth.

"You can really see the future in someone's hand?"

"Or the past, depending on which hand you give me. Tradition says the future is shown in the right hand and the past in the left."

Mara put her left hand firmly behind her back, and Emil chuckled. "All right. The future it is." He held out his hand, his eyes daring her.

Slowly Mara put her hand into his. He cradled it as if it were a bird's egg.

Emil stared down at her palm. "Hmmm. I see you belong to the Order of Khatar."

"Very funny," Mara said "You don't need to look at my hand to see that."

Again he smiled, as if she had delighted him. "Ah, but it helps." He flipped her hand over.

"See these calluses, here and here?" Emil rubbed his thumb across her knuckles, then brushed against the sensitive skin between her thumb and first finger. "Only a hand-dagger leaves marks like that."

He ran one finger up to her wrist bone. "And the edges of the handle leave an imprint on your arm, see?"

"Does . . . does my hand tell you anything else?" Mara asked, clearing her throat.

Emil flipped her hand back over, studying the palm. "You will meet a tall, dark man in the near future."

"That's likely," Mara said drily. "Considering how many tall, dark men there are in the Empire."

Emil grinned at her. "You're spoiling my trick."

Mara raised her eyebrows at him and Emil laughed, and for a moment, it almost felt like being home. Like curling up with her family on cold nights, the heat of their bodies against her back. Everything at the Order had been routine and training and study, and like Mara, most of the other novices were so wrapped up in their own hurt that they had little time for anyone else's. They'd been fellow warriors, but not really family.

Her real family was gone forever.

"Mara, are you all right?" Emil said. Mara looked up to see him studying not her palm, but her face. "You looked really sad just now."

Mara suddenly felt exposed and transparent all over again. "I thought you were supposed to be reading my palm, not my expression," she said, yanking her hand back.

Emil looked as surprised as if she had slapped him. "I'm sorry," he said. "I didn't mean . . ." He rubbed his hand over his neck. "I'm making a mess of this, aren't I?"

Mara drew a breath. "No, I just . . . I can't . . . talk about it."

"Of course," Emil said. "Look, I owe you for yesterday." He

took the wooden tiger from the counter and held it out to her. "I had carved this for my cousin, but if you like it, it's yours."

Mara's fingers itched to take the tiger from him, hold it tightly. "Are you sure?" she said, not caring that her voice was harsh with want.

Emil tucked the tiger in her palm and wrapped her fingers around it. "I can make another one easily. Consider it a gift. And an apology for making you sad."

Mara felt a strange urge to cry. Instead she pulled the tiger close and turned her face away. When she had herself under control again, she looked back and allowed her mouth to curl at the corners.

"Thank you."

The silence stretched between them as they smiled at each other. To break the moment, Mara asked the first thing that came into her head. "Was I really that obvious? Just now?"

"Not really," Emil said. "But I'm good with faces, people's expressions. My uncle is the Master of Trade for our camp, and he knows all the merchant tricks. You're actually pretty difficult to read most of the time."

"Good," Mara said, feeling a bit better. The idea of everyone being able to read her that way was frightening. Mara could read body language and someone's tone of voice, but faces? Human faces were so changeable. Emotions flickered faster than she could follow. She wanted to ask Emil how he managed it. She wanted to put her hand back into his and listen to his laugh and watch his eyes crinkle when he smiled.

He wouldn't be so kind if he knew what she'd done.

The thought chilled her, and Mara stumbled back a step. "I'm sorry," she said. "I really do have to go. Thank you again for the tiger."

And without giving him a chance to stop her, she turned and ran into the crowd.

13
Emil

WHAT DID I say?

Emil watched, perplexed, as Mara hurried away. He wanted to go after her, ask her what was wrong, and apologize if he needed to, but he couldn't leave the booth.

Emil replayed their conversation in his mind. Up close, Mara's eyes had reminded him even more of dark honey, thick and sweet with secrets. He'd wanted to ask her all kinds of questions about where she'd come from and why she'd joined the Order of Khatar. But asking felt too personal, too invasive.

So he'd settled for trying to make her smile. She didn't look like someone who smiled very much. During their conversation, she'd held herself perfectly still and watched him with steady patience. Then suddenly . . . sadness. It was an expression Emil had felt often on his own face, the sudden spasm of missing someone so much you could barely breath. Mara had lost some-one, just like he had. He'd reached for that connection without thinking.

He'd hurt her, and it shamed him. And in his shame, he'd offered the only thing in the booth that was his to give, the wooden tiger.

And she had seemed to like it. More than liked it, she'd clung to it, and had finally given him the smile he'd been angling for.

But then she'd run away. Why?

Two women, one older and one younger, both wearing Bamboo caste jewelry walked up to the booth, their eyes bright with inter-est. Emil reluctantly put the question of Mara's strange behavior aside. He was here to sell Arvi goods, not to think about girls, no matter how intriguing they were.

Maybe if he did well today, it would give him the opening he needed to talk to his father.

Emil put on his best smile. "How can I serve you ladies this day? Would you like to see the finest cashmere in all the Bhinian Empire?"

Both women smiled back at him. Like most Bamboo women, they were dressed in flowing tunics and loose pants in finely woven cotton. They wore matching pairs of gold hoop earrings, and thin golden bangles jangled on their wrists.

A wealthy artisan family, Emil judged. Probably high-end tai-lors or clothiers looking for materials. The younger girl wore a small gold hoop in her nose, signaling that she was unmarried. Emil directed his next smile at her.

"I have thick wools, fine wools, medium-weight. Soft as mist and sturdy as the goats we take them from. Of course, none of them are as lovely as you ladies."

The girl blushed and cast her eyes down. The woman gave her an indulgent smile. "I am teaching my daughter how to trade for goods. I see I'll have to teach her to beware of flattering tongues as well." She unrolled some of the cashmere and studied it with a practiced eye.

Emil grinned. "I can see you are a woman who knows what she wants, and a fine judge of fabric, and that, ma'am, is not flattery."

"This *is* very fine work," the woman said. "But perhaps a little steep in price?"

"Our yield was low this year," Emil said. "Less supply sadly makes for higher prices."

The woman frowned. Emil pretended not to notice. "Of course, lower yield also means that this fabric will be rare this year. Perhaps rare enough to fetch a higher price from some of your more exclusive clients?" The curve of the woman's mouth relaxed, and Emil went on.

"Rare Kildi-made cashmere, cut from goats that have grazed on the green mountains, with no equal in luxury. Just think how well that sounds." He lowered his voice to a conspiratorial whisper. "You and I both know that nobles are always looking for ways to outdo one another. It's part of the Great Game that they play. No price is too much if an item is rare enough."

"Hmmm," the woman said. "I see your point." She made an

offer, and Emil countered it.

This was the part he loved. It was like a dance: the haggling and dramatic gestures, the offers made and accepted and the weighing of coin. The two women walked off, each holding two rolls of cashmere, and Emil turned to put his handful of silver into the strongbox.

"That was impressive." Esmer walked around the corner of the booth. Her hair was in a loose braid, hiding the gray streak, and she was dressed in her usual browns. "I feel like I should applaud."

Emil gave her a theatrical bow. "Always a pleasure to entertain you, milady."

The young cat-Sune shook her head at him, a dimple creasing her cheek. "I swear, Emil, one of these days that tongue of yours is going to get you into trouble. You'll start out to sell something and find yourself engaged."

"My father would hate that," Emil said. The words sounded unexpectedly bitter, and he smiled to soften them. "Actually, he seems to be under the impression that you and I might be . . . attached."

Esmer burst out laughing. "With you? I'd rather stick my tail under a cart wheel."

"Hey!" Emil protested, a little offended in spite of himself. "What's wrong with me?"

"Not a thing," Esmer said. "You're very sweet, for a human. But if you think I'd give up my cat form for anyone, you're sick in the head." She held up a finger. "And don't tell me I wouldn't have to, at least most of the time. I have friends mated to humans. Love is hard enough for people who are always in the same form. Besides, I don't want to mate with you."

"Well, thank you very much."

Esmer raised her eyebrows. "Would you prefer that I was perishing of love?"

Emil's neck was hot, and he tugged at his scarf. "Of course not."

"Then stop complaining." Esmer sat down on the ground, pulling her legs up. "You don't want to mate with every girl you see, do you? So why should every girl want to mate with you?" She gave him a sharp look. "You're unusually grim today. What's wrong?"

"What *isn't* wrong?" Emil started tidying up the booth, arranging the soft rolls of cashmere in gradients of shade, white and cream to darkest browns and grays. "Stefan's under silence for the entire day, not that he'd be speaking to me anyway. Father's too busy to let me get a word in edgewise, but not too busy to concern himself with my eventual choice of wife. And I ran into that girl who saved Stefan yesterday, and I think I made her angry."

"Mara?" Esmer sat up straighter. "She's here?"

"She came by the booth. We were talking and she just . . . ran off. I don't even know what I said."

"Huh." Esmer rested her chin on her knees. "Mara's situation is complicated, Emil. I wouldn't take it personally."

"You're probably right," Emil said. He could tell that Esmer knew more than she was saying, but he didn't press. Esmer held on to her secrets like greedy men held on to gold. If she didn't want to tell you something, she wouldn't.

It was probably for the best, Emil thought. He really should be thinking about other things right now. Like the fact that he couldn't even talk to his own brother.

As if the thought had summoned him, Emil spotted Stefan down the row of booths. His twin was wearing his festival clothes: a clean red shirt and dyed brown trousers. He was balancing two bowls of *roti* bread and rice in his good arm, and his broken wrist was tucked into a sling.

Emil watched as Stefan made his way toward a booth that sold bottles and bowls of dye. That was the Yanora clan. They traveled the Empire searching for roots and plants, their path often crossing the Arvi's. The two clans were on friendly terms.

Stefan handed one of the bowls to a tall young woman Emil recognized as Kizzy Yanora. She was wearing a skirt that had been dyed a vivid purple, and there was a bright yellow shawl around her shoulders and neck. She said something to Stefan, poking him in the shoulder. Stefan made a face at her, then laughed.

Emil frowned. How long had it been since Stefan had laughed like that at home? His brother shouldn't be more comfortable with strangers than he was with his own family. Maybe if they could actually talk, maybe if Emil could show his brother how much he mattered, and how much he cared about him, they could be allies instead of rivals.

It was worth a try. Even if it made his father angry.

Emil looked over at Esmer. "I'm going to go talk to Stefan," he said, pulling his embroidered red scarf off his neck. "Can you watch the booth?"

"Of course." Esmer stood up and stretched her limber spine. Emil offered her the scarf, and she wrinkled her nose. "Do I have to?"

"Only if any Hearth caste come to trade," Emil said. Hearth caste people wore beaded collars that symbolized their tie to the land. They paid better prices if the Kildi sellers kept their necks covered too. "Please, Esmer."

"Fine." Esmer rolled her eyes. "The things I do for you." But her smile was warm as Emil left the booth.

ONCE OUT OF the booth, Emil let himself relax into the flow of the fair. Not even the mingled smells of perfume and unwashed bodies bothered him. It was just another familiar piece of the landscape, like the musicians and dancers, like the noise of haggling and laughter, like the smell of spiced meat and fried bread in the air. People snacked on pickled gooseberries and drank generously sized cups of *sulai*, a sweet alcohol made from molasses.

Everything exactly as it always was.

Then Emil's eye caught something that wasn't usual—the shine of a blade. He turned.

Standing near one of the entertainers' tents was a man as tall as Emil. He wore a black vest over his bare muscled chest, and the dark scars of his Wind caste mark showed plainly on the brown skin of his shoulder. He held an unsheathed short sword with an ebony handle, examining the edge as he talked. Brass throwing circles hung at his waist. Probably a mercenary of some sort.

The man was spinning a story about fighting a beast in the Eastern Forests.

"Lost two of my best men taking that monster down," he said, as the rapt group of people around him listened. "But what else were we going to do? Elephant that size could level a village. He almost did. And it's not like Emperor Saro's men are going to do anything about it."

His audience nodded in agreement. Emil turned back to look for Stefan.

His brother had left the Yanora booth and was weaving his way through the clumps of people. He was balancing his own clay bowl in one hand, and it looked like he was trying not to bump his injured wrist in the crowd.

Which was probably why he didn't see the nobleman coming out of the entertainer's tent until it was too late.

It happened so fast, Emil barely saw it. The man's head was turned to the girl next to him, and he stepped right into Stefan's path. The bowl went flying, spattering the rice and sauce all over the nobleman's gold-embroidered tunic.

The crowd fell silent.

"You idiot!" the man cried. He was about Emil and Stefan's age, maybe a bit older. "Look at what you've done to me. Do you know how much this tunic is *worth*?"

The young woman with him put a calming hand on his sleeve,

but he shrugged her off. "Apologize at once," he ordered.

Stefan swallowed his temper with a visible effort. He bowed low. "Forgive me for bumping you."

"Forgive me, *sir*," the nobleman said. "Don't any of you Kildi know how to speak to a Flower caste?"

Emil saw Stefan's hands tremble and knew his brother was close to exploding. He tried to push through the crowd to reach him first, but there were too many people between them.

"Forgive me, sir," Stefan said in a barely audible voice.

"Tamas, it was an accident." The girl spoke for the first time. "You promised to help me pick out fabric for a new asar." She opened her large dark eyes wider and put her lip out in a pretty pout. "I'm bored, Tamas. Let's go."

Tamas ignored her gentle attempt to redirect his attention. "In a minute, Revathi," he said. A cruel smile crossed his face. He held out one sandaled foot. "You got food on my feet, dog. Lick it off."

Stefan hesitated and for a moment, Emil thought his brother might actually do it. Then he saw the telltale curl of Stefan's fists. *Oh no.*

Emile gave up all pretense of politeness and shoved his way through the crowd. But before he'd gone two steps, Stefan punched the noble in the nose. It was an off-balance hit with his unhurt hand, but it still managed to connect with a solid *crack*.

Tamas staggered back, blood pouring from his nose. "You *dare!*" he howled, drawing his sword. "I'll kill you for that!"

Emil threw himself forward. But it was going to be too late.

There was a flicker of movement behind Tamas, and the noble-man stumbled forward, as if someone had shoved him. The sword cut through empty air, missing Stefan completely. Tamas fell into an elderly farmer, knocking the man down.

A woman screamed. The relaxed, tipsy mood of the crowd shifted. Someone tried to help Tamas up. Someone else reached for the farmer, and the farmer's wife, misinterpreting the gesture, hit the helpful stranger with her walking stick. He staggered back into the crowd. A drink spilled. Another punch was thrown, and suddenly everyone was fighting.

Emil ducked a stave as it whistled over his head, and stepped out of the way of a musician wielding an instrument case like a club. A merchant smelling of *sulai* grabbed the front of Emil's tunic and swung a fist at him. Emil blocked it, then head-butted the man, making him release his grip. There was a crash as one of the booths fell over.

Emil saw a flash of blade next to him and whirled to face the attack.

It was Mara. Her short hair was mussed, and there was a scratch on her cheek. "Come on!" she yelled to him, her cheeks flushed. "I didn't keep a tiger from eating him yesterday just so he could get himself killed today."

She plunged into the crowd, using her fist and the flat of her dagger to beat them a path. Emil followed her, watching her back and praying to the Horned God with every step. *Please let Stefan be all right.*

When he got a glimpse of his brother again, the rush of relief was overwhelming. Stefan's eye was rapidly purpling, and a cut on his cheek streamed blood, but he was standing. He had picked up his thick clay bowl, and was swinging it in his good hand as if it were a cudgel. There was an expression of fierce glee on his face.

By this time, the fighting had degenerated into a full-out brawl, weapons abandoned for fists and feet. Many people were simply punching anyone within reach. The Kildi had abandoned their booths and were running for the woods, coin boxes and merchandise clutched to their chests.

Emil looked for Tamas, the nobleman who had provoked Stefan. Tamas was fighing one handed, and had his other arm around the young noblewoman who sagged limply against him. Her brown asar was rumpled and her eyes were closed.

Despite the fighting around him, Emil grinned. The girl must have fainted in the madness, giving Tamas something else to worry about besides going after Stefan.

A hand touched his, and he looked down into Mara's dark eyes.

"I have to help that girl. The idiot with her is going to let her get trampled."

Emil impulsively reached out and brushed the sweat-damp hair back from Mara's forehead. His fingers lingered at her hairline, and he thought he saw her flush deepen. "Thank you," he said. "Again."

"You're welcome," Mara said, smiling up at him. She squeezed his hand, sending a jolt of warmth up his arm. "Go to your brother," she said. "He needs you."

Emil stepped away reluctantly. But Mara was right. Soldiers

would be here soon, and they would be looking for someone to blame. He had to get Stefan away.

His brother barely glanced at him when he ran up. Emil had to grab his shoulder to get his attention. "Come on," he yelled, pointing to an open space between booths, with a clear trail to the forest. "Let's get out of here."

Stefan hesitated, then nodded, throwing the bowl away. Mara was fighting at the nobleman's side now, her movements as smooth as a bird in flight.

Be safe, Emil thought in her direction, as if she could somehow hear him. Then he and Stefan ran for the trees.

15

Mara

MARA KNELT IN the dirt, cleaning her dagger. The fair
was a far cry from the cheerful mix of colors and sounds it had
been a short time ago. Abandoned weapons littered the ground.
The air smelled of sweat and metal and blood. Most of the brawling had stopped when a squad of Imperial foot soldiers showed
up. They'd arrested a handful of people, questioned others, and
sent everyone else home. Mara had noted with relief that none of
the prisoners seemed to be Kildi.

The sergeant in charge was an older woman with a worn face
and deep-set eyes. She wore a long tunic of heavy silk, and a
square plate of iron trimmed with copper that fastened over
her chest. A short spear and a curved sword hung at her side.
There was a tired, patient quality to her, as she listened to
Tamas rant.

"I don't care if they move around!" Tamas's voice rose. His rich tunic was muddy, and he was sporting the beginnings of a respectable black eye. "I want that Kildi."

The sergeant folded her hands. Her leather wrist guards were studded with bronze, a sign of her rank, and she spoke to Tamas as if he were a very small child.

"Yes, I understand, sir. We will do our best, but there are quite a few Kildi clans in the area. Do you know which family the assailant belonged to?"

"How should I know that?" Tamas said. "They all look the same. Can't you just . . . I don't know, start arresting people?"

"No, sir, I cannot." The woman sounded even more tired than before. "If you want mass arrests, you'll have to appeal to the Emperor."

"If you can find him," Tamas muttered. The soldier gave him a sharp look, and he flushed. "Never mind. Forget I said anything."

"Of course, sir," the sergeant said. She started walking toward the end of the fair, and Tamas followed. "I just keep the peace on this road. Now can you think of anything else about the person who hit you?" Their voices dropped to a low murmur, their feet treading on scattered gooseberries and crumbs of bread as they walked.

Mara's feet itched with the need to start moving again, start looking for her charge. She didn't like it here, and the soldiers made her nervous. But Tamas's companion hadn't come out of her faint yet, and it wouldn't be honorable or kind to leave her unconscious on the ground.

Mara frowned at the thought, then leaned over to examine the girl more closely. She had a thin, fine-boned face, and her lips were slightly parted. Her loosened hair spilled over the dirt like dark, frozen water. Mara could see the glitter of a golden flower tattoo on the inside of her narrow wrist.

Mara went back to cleaning her dagger.

"You know," she said, keeping her voice low, "most true fainting spells don't last very long. If I were you, I'd start recovering before that friend of yours gets worried and calls for a healer."

Out of the corner of her eye, Mara saw the girl blink. Then she started to move and make the soft murmurs of someone coming back to consciousness.

Mara hid a smile and set down her blade. "Oh, good," she said in a voice that was slightly louder than normal. "You're awake. No, don't move too quickly; let me help you."

She lifted the girl to a sitting position, leaning her against a nearby booth. She beckoned to a nearby guard.

"Can we get some water for the lady, please?"

The guard brought water in a clay cup and the girl sipped it, her black-brown eyes never leaving Mara's face. When she was finished, she handed the cup back to the guard with murmured thanks, then waited until he had walked away.

"How did you know?" she asked.

Mara picked up the dagger she'd been cleaning. "Educated guess. There was a little too much tension in your muscles for it to be a true faint."

"It's hard to go limp when you're in danger of getting skewered or stepped on," the girl said, her mouth twisting in a smile. "I probably would have had to wake up and move sooner if you hadn't been there."

"You did very well," Mara said. It was a strange and awkward conversation, but the girl was smiling at her and she was smiling back and it felt . . . nice. A little more uncertain than speaking mind-to-mind, but nice all the same.

"I'm Mara t'Riala," she said.

The girl put her hands together and bowed from her sitting position. "Revathi sa'Hoi. You haven't asked me why I pretended to faint."

"I assume it was to keep your companion from killing Ste–that Kildi."

Revathi's eyes narrowed, and Mara held her breath.

"Save a Kildi boy I've never met?" Revathi said, but the smile was back. "Why would I do that?"

"Because you didn't want him to get killed?" Mara said, relieved the girl hadn't commented on her slip. "I assumed you were being nice."

"Nobles aren't nice," Revathi said, tugging at the edges of her sleeve and brushing at her crumpled clothing. "But thank you anyway."

Mara scratched the back of her head. "Well," she said after a moment. "I wouldn't be so quick to deny it if I were you. Pretending to faint in the middle of a riot was a really stupid thing to do otherwise."

The girl tilted her head back and laughed. "I suppose it was."

She looked like she was about to say more, but Tamas's voice interrupted her.

"Revathi, you're awake!"

Tamas knelt down and put one hand under her chin, examining her smudged face. "Are you all right? No one stepped on you?"

"I'm fine, Tamas," Revathi said. "I just fainted. Everything happened so fast, and all that fighting . . ." She gave a delicate shudder. "It was such a shock."

"Of course," Tamas said, running his hand over her hair. "This is why I didn't want you to come here alone."

Revathi folded her hands into her lap. "You know, after we're married, you won't be able to come with me all the time. You'll have important duties in the court. Maybe you could teach me to use a dagger so I could defend myself?"

"Darling, what would you do with a dagger?" Tamas said. "You're too small to fight anyone. No, what you need is a minder, someone to watch you while I'm not there."

Some of the spark disappeared from Revathi's face, smothered like campfire embers under mounds of dirt. "I'm not a child, Tamas. I'm perfectly capable of managing my own affairs."

"Oh, I know *that*," Tamas said, and there was a bite to his voice. Revathi's mouth tightened.

Tamas took a deep breath. "Please be reasonable, Revathi," he said in a softer tone. "I don't want to be worrying about you all the time. And if that girl over there hadn't helped us, you might have been seriously hurt." He nodded at Mara. "Thank you for that, by the way. Let me give you something for your efforts."

Tamas reached into his tunic and pulled out a handful of silver and copper coins. Mara backed up a step, shaking her head.

"I'm not allowed to accept money."

"There must be something I can do for you," Tamas said. "If you won't take money . . ." He trailed off, looking from Mara to Revathi. "Would you like a job?"

Revathi's head jerked up as though she'd been bitten. "Tamas, don't!"

"Me?" Mara said. "You want to hire me?"

"Why not?" Tamas said. "You're Order of Khatar, aren't you? Isn't guard work what you people do?"

"I am," Mara said. "And it is. But–"

"Are you pledged already?" Tamas looked around the fair. "I didn't see any–"

"No." Mara said. She planted her feet against the urge to run, and tilted her chin up. "I'm not."

"You're a good fighter," Tamas went on, relentlessly persuasive. "A very good fighter. I saw the way you protected my betrothed. You could pledge to her, couldn't you?"

"Tamas!" Revathi sounded horrified. "You can't just tell a member of the Order of Khatar who to pledge to!" Her voice softened. "I appreciate your care for me, but it's very insulting to her." She gave Mara a swift smile. "I knew a man who had an Order of Khatar guard. They always spoke of it as an incredibly personal decision."

"It is," Mara said, relieved that someone understood. "We join the Order of Khatar to regain honor. It's a lifelong pledge. So we're careful to choose someone who can balance us, someone honorable, who needs our help. It's not a choice we make lightly."

Tamas huffed out a breath. "I suppose I understand that." He frowned. "But what do you do until you find your person? How do you live?"

"Take odd jobs, mostly," Mara said. "We're only allowed to work for our keep, though. Food and lodgings, the occasional set of clothes. No wages. And when we pledge . . ."

"You'll leave, yes, yes." Tamas waved a hand. "So I *can* hire you."

"Tamas," Revathi protested. "I don't need a bodyguard."

"Don't be silly, love," Tamas said. "This is a perfect solution, at least until I can find a trustworthy guard." He held up a hand, forestalling Revathi's answer. "It's about time you start letting me make this kind of decision for you. I'll be doing it anyway, once we're married."

He looked at Mara.

"What do you say? You can watch over my girl here, and in return you'll have whatever you need."

Mara hesitated. She hadn't thought to hire out so soon. But if she followed her original plan, she'd be living in the city anyway. And as the bodyguard to a noble, she wouldn't be dependent on the kindness of Samara's friends. She could earn her own way. The idea was appealing.

"I suppose . . . ," she said. "As long as it's only for a little while." She glanced at Revathi. "And if it's all right with her."

"Of course it's all right," Tamas said. Revathi closed her eyes and let out a breath.

"Yes," she said. "It's fine."

"See?" Tamas said. "Now that everything's settled, we should head back. I'm hungry."

"Why don't you ride on ahead, Tamas?" Revathi said. "I'm still feeling a little woozy. I don't want to get on a horse quite yet."

"I suppose that's all right," Tamas said. "The soldiers are still around, so no one should cause any trouble." He offered Revathi a hand and pulled her to her feet. "I have Imperial Guard rotation tomorrow, but I'll try to come see you."

"That will be nice," Revathi said.

Tamas nodded to Mara. "You'll stay with Revathi for now, of course. She'll show you where to go." Then he walked off toward the line of tethered horses.

Neither girl spoke. Revathi dusted off her asar and shook out her hair, tying it back with a green ribbon she pulled from some hidden pocket. Her eyes were almost black with an emotion that Mara couldn't identify.

"I wish you hadn't done that," she said. The tentative feeling of connection Mara had felt was gone, and Revathi's voice was distant, frustrated. "I know I said it was fine, but really, I don't need a bodyguard."

Mara folded her arms. She was tired and hungry and starting to wish she'd just gone on to the capital. "I need work until I find the person I'm going to pledge to. If you don't want me, I'll go."

Revathi gave a very unladylike snort. "It's a little late for that.

No, you'll have to stay, at least long enough for me to convince Tamas that I don't need you." She pressed her lips together. "What a mess. At least you didn't tell him I faked the faint."

"Why would I do that?" Mara said. "I'm a bodyguard. Not a spy."

Revathi raised her eyebrows. "We'll see." She dusted off her hands and looked around the deserted fair. "I don't have a mount for you. If I walk the horse, will you be all right traveling by foot?"

"Of course," Mara said. She was torn between walking away from the whole job and an odd desire to prove herself. "I can keep up with you."

A swift, wry smile crossed Revathi's face. "Like I said, we'll see." She walked off toward the line of tethered horses. After a moment's hesitation, Mara followed.

One of the more curious things to happen since the Barrier rose is the use of the caste marks. It started with the branding of the old rulers, those who would become the Kildi. The marks were intended to shame them, to serve as reminders of how they had failed the people. Then others were marked as well, criminals and debtors, the first true Wind caste. And before more than two generations had gone by, the caste marks had spread to every level of our Empire. Perhaps people adopted it as a way of solidifying their own identity. Or as a way to connect with others of their caste. We can't be sure.

What we do know is that only two castes have permanent caste marks: the Flower caste, whose children bear a golden flower tattoo–or white, if they belong to the Imperial family–and the Wind caste, who are marked as they have always been, with raised dark scars on the sholder. These scars are made by packing shallow cuts with ash and can be easily felt through a tunic.

The beaded collars that the farmers and fishermen of the Hearth caste wear can be cast aside for the night. The earrings and nose jewelry of Bamboo caste merchants and artists can be removed, even if the holes remain. Even the green dye that Jade caste healers and scholars use to paint their hands and faces will fade. It is only in the highest and lowest castes that identity is permanent, only at the extremes of society that people can least afford to forget who they are.

From the writings of Vaydhish, Jade scholar

16

Emil

"HOW COULD YOU *do* this?"

Emil had never seen his father so furious. He was pacing back and forth in front of them as he shouted, his frame vibrating with rage. Emil could feel the curious glances of the rest of the Arvi as they pretended to go about their tasks. At least he and Stefan were half hidden behind the *Kys*'s caravan instead of in the middle of camp. It wasn't much more than an illusion of privacy, but it was better than having everyone stare openly.

Nearby stood Besnik Yanora, his muscled arms folded over his chest. The *Kys* of the Yanora clan, Besnik had deep-set eyes and a gray-streaked beard. His nails were splotched with color from dye testing. He watched the unfolding drama calmly.

Emil's father, however, was far from calm. And he wasn't making any effort to keep his voice low.

"I never thought a son of mine could be so *stupid*. Do you ever stop to think of anyone but yourself?"

Stefan shrank into himself, and Emil's heart twisted.

"That's not fair . . . ," Emil started. His father whirled on him.

"And you," he snapped. "You're supposed to be an example. You should be conducting yourself like the future leader of the Arvi, not brawling like a common thug!"

The weight of his father's disapproval was like a physical thing, pushing at Emil, making him stiff and defensive. He wondered if this was how Stefan felt all the time. He hunched his shoulders, waiting for it to be over.

"Emil was trying to help me," Stefan spoke up, to Emil's surprise. "He wasn't close enough to stop me, and once the fighting started, all he did was find me and get me out of there. He wasn't brawling."

"I don't need your opinion," their father said. "You're in enough trouble as it is. What in the name of the Horned God were you *thinking*? You know how precarious the Kildi position is in the Empire. We're only allowed to sell what we make with our own hands. We're forbidden to trade inside the cities, and we can't even camp too close to them. Many people already think we're thieves. You've just given the Emperor even more reason to label us as troublemakers. He could send the army after us, he could put more restrictions on what and when we can trade, and there would be nothing we could do to stop him."

Stefan flinched, shame flashing across his face. Then his mouth set in its familiar sullen scowl. "I didn't start this, that nobleman did! He tried to humiliate me for his own amusement."

"It doesn't matter!" their father shouted. "Listen to me, Stefan. *It. Does. Not. Matter.* The world isn't fair. The Empire isn't fair. The nobles have hated and feared us since the day they overthrew the First Lotus Emperor and condemned him and all his family to wander. They have the power. And you'd better learn to accept that or you're going to end up skewered on the end of some high-born sword!"

Stefan's fists were clenched. "You're saying I should have just licked his feet? Is that what you wanted me to do?"

The *Kys* hesitated, and Emil knew why. If Stefan had licked the noble's feet, it would have been a serious humiliation for him, and by extention the entire Arvi clan. It could have damaged their reputation and made it harder for them to get fair prices for their goods.

But their father wasn't about to back down.

"You could have turned around and walked away," he said.

"That wouldn't have helped," Stefan pointed out.

"Maybe not. But you didn't even try. You just went in swinging. You put your family and the entire fair at risk. Do you have any idea of the damage that was done?" Their father gestured at Besnik. "His daughter's booth was knocked over, and they lost some very expensive dyes."

Oddly, this seemed to affect Stefan more than is father's scolding. "Is Kizzy all right?"

"She's uninjured," Besnik said. "A little shaken up and embarrassed, but otherwise well."

"Embarrassed?" Stefan said.

There was no mistaking the proud smile as the man answered. "Kizzy hit a mercenary in the back of the head with a bottle of *kunkuma* powder and it broke. A lovely shade of red, but not really meant for face paint. She's a bit . . . streaky. The mercenary got the worst of it, though."

Stefan relaxed and smiled back at Besnik. "Good for her."

"The point is," their father said, "your actions endangered Kizzy, and everyone else at the fair, and cost everyone a lot of money."

Stefan squared his shoulders. "It was my choice to fight. I can work for the other clans to help ease the loss."

"I'll help too," Emil put in, and both his father and Stefan glared at him.

"I don't need your help," Stefan said at the same time as his father spoke.

"You're needed here."

"Clearly, *I'm* not needed," Stefan said, under his breath. "But you've got *leader* things to do."

"I was involved as much as Stefan was," Emil said, trying again. "I should bear some of the consequences."

"I appreciate your desire to own your mistakes," his father said. "But this is Stefan's mess to clean up."

"It's *always* my mess," Stefan said. "Because I can't do anything right in your eyes."

"Maybe if you had a little self-control . . ."

Emil blew air through his lips and rubbed his forehead with two fingers. Trying to calm himself, he turned away from the squabbling and touched the clusters of white jasmine that his mother, Nadya, had painted on the caravan's back wall.

Emil pressed his hand against the wooden surface, feeling the echo of his mother's touch in the brushstrokes. He missed her, with a sudden intensity that sucked the air from his lungs. Her ready laugh, the way she could always talk his father down with a hand on his arm and a few words. She'd been so bright and warm, the comforting hearth fire at the center of their family. His father hadn't been so hard on Stefan and him when his mother was alive, and Stefan hadn't been so angry. Now the only person standing between the two of them was Emil, and neither one of them wanted to listen to him.

He caught Besnik Yanora's eye, and the older man smiled at him sympathetically.

"Mihai," Besnik said, interrupting the growing shouting match, "I should probably return to my own camp. The riot has drawn Imperial soldiers, and I want to take my family far away from here."

Their father calmed himself with a visible effort. "A wise move, Besnik," he said. "We can discuss our other business later. My deepest apologies for the rash behavior of my son."

Besnik shrugged. "We were all young once," he said. "And if Kizzy's account is accurate, he was sorely provoked."

"That's no excuse," their father started, but he was interrupted by a deep voice behind Emil.

"I think it is."

Emil whirled to see the mercenary from the fair standing behind them.

17

Emil

UP CLOSE, THE dark-eyed man was an imposing sight, broad-shouldered and muscled like one of the elephants on the mountain. He bore several fresh cuts and bruises under his open vest. And there were others with him, three men and two women with such a variety of weapons that Emil couldn't help but be impressed. He saw daggers and short swords, throwing circles and cudgels. One of the women sported a *lati* fighting staff tipped with iron, and the other had a quiver and bow slung on her back. She had an wickedly barbed arrow in her hands, fingers playing idly with the tip.

"Who are you?" Emil's father put a hand to his tunic, reaching for the dagger he kept hidden there. "Why have you come into my camp with drawn blades? The Arvi are a peaceful people."

The large man threw back his head and laughed. "A peaceful

people? When your sons start a riot at the Clothing Fair and you are ready to pull a blade at the sight of me?"

"Who are you?" the Kys repeated.

"I know," Besnik said. He put his head to one side, an expression of mild interest on his face, as if the mercenary were a particularly odd plant. "You're Rajo the Black."

Emil tensed. Rajo the Black and his mercenary band had earned their reputations in the wild places of the Empire, battling animals and bandits for paying villagers. They were said to be the best. They were also said to be very expensive.

"So I am," Rajo said. He sheathed his sword and bowed, hands pressed together against his chest. It was a strange gesture from him, like a tunic that didn't quite fit. "And I have come to honor fellow fighters. Your son stood against that noble's cruelty, and your other one protected him well. You should be honoring these boys, not scolding them like an old farmwife."

A small smile crossed Stefan's face.

"There is no honor in endangering others for the sake of hurt pride," their father said. "A true Kildi"–here he glared at Stefan, whose smile disappeared–"a true Kildi cares about what is good for his clan, and fighting is rarely good for anyone."

"That depends on who wins," Rajo countered. "Doesn't it?"

"Spoken like a mercenary," Emil's father said dismissively. "Battle for the sake of battle, thinking only of your purses and your bellies."

Emil saw the other mercenaries stiffen at the insult. He stepped forward to stop his father's words before another fight broke out, but Rajo spoke first.

"That's where you're wrong," Rajo said. "We fight to live, just like you. I have battled men worse than any monsters from your tales. And animals from the Eastern Forests that can kill a man with one swipe. The Emperor sends his soldiers to control the cities and patrol the roads, but what about the rest of us? Who do you think holds the predators off the villages, protects those no one else cares about?"

"For money," Emil's father repeated. His face was still flushed with anger. "You don't protect those villagers for free."

One of the other mercenaries stepped forward. He was a slim man with an open face only partly hidden by his neat beard. And he was the least armed of the group, carrying a knife at his hip and a soft skin bag over one shoulder.

"We never take more than a village can afford," he said in a quiet, crisp voice, startlingly different from Rajo's bellow. "We have even worked for free when the need was great. But every man must eat, and unlike you, we have no talent for goat herding."

Rajo gestured at the other man. "This is Karoti, my second in command."

"Second in command?" Emil's father said. "Never heard of you."

"Father!" Stefan said.

Karoti seemed amused rather than offended. "A mercenary band runs on its accounts, but accountants make bad figureheads. I prefer to stay in the background. But I can assure you that we charge a fair price and do not resort to violence or coercion to collect what is owed us. Not all mercenary bands can say the same."

"And who are you working for now?" The words escaped Emil's lips before he thought. Every head in the group swiveled to him.

"What makes you think we're working for someone now?" Karoti asked. His voice was casual, but his bright brown eyes were sharp.

Emil swallowed, but plowed forward. "Like you said, you work in the wild places, the mountains and the great forests of the East. You'd have no reason to come this close to civilization unless there was work for you here."

"Clever reasoning." Again the accountant-mercenary seemed amused. "Very clever. But we're on a restocking trip. New weapons, replacing worn-out gear. Harmless." He winked at Emil, who frowned.

"You could at least *pretend* not to be lying," he said.

Rajo burst into another round of laughter. "Truly you should be proud of your boys," he said to Emil's father. "Strong, loyal, and smart."

"I'm glad someone thinks so," Stefan muttered.

"Don't get too cocky, youngster," Karoti said. "If I hadn't shoved that noble in the back when he went to draw his sword, you would have been gutted like a fish. You should learn to court death a bit more carefully."

Stefan looked down. Emil noted with interest that his brother actually looked chastised for once.

"Never mind, boy," Rajo said. "It was foolhardy, but we all

make mistakes." He turned and bowed to Besnik Yanora. "I would like to salute you as well. I was told a daughter of your clan was responsible for one of my men's rather . . . unusual color."

Besnik bowed back. "We are proud of all the Yanora children," he said. "And if your men wish to avoid unusual colors, perhaps they should not brawl near our dye booths."

Rajo raised his eyebrows. "Karoti, make a note of that," he said. "The Yanora dye booths and all other dye makers are to be left alone if at all possible. I won't be able to frighten people if my men are colored like court peacocks."

"So noted," Karoti said. "I will add it to the bylaws."

Besnik nodded graciously. "I thank you."

"Enough of this," Emil's father said. He folded his arms. "My son's behavior is for me to deal with, mercenary. If you have stated your business, then be gone."

"Father!" Stefan said.

"I do have one more thing to say," Rajo said. He turned to face Emil and Stefan. "Change is coming to the Empire. I need strong men at my side, and I'd be honored to have the two of you join us."

"Absolutely not," Emil's father said. He pushed himself between Rajo and Stefan. His voice was low and savage, a tone that Emil had never heard from his father before. "Try to take my sons and I will carve your heart from your chest myself."

Raj held his hands up. "I meant no harm. It was simply an invitation." He bowed to Besnik Yanora and then to Emil's father. "Forgive me for disturbing your peace. Should you change your mind"–he jerked his thumb in the direction of the forest–"we'll be in a clearing to the south of here until dawn tomorrow. Then we have business in Kamal." He smiled, wide and hungry, like a wolf. "For restocking, of course."

"Get out of my camp," Emil's father said. "And stay away from my children."

"As you choose," Rajo said. He nodded to Emil and Stefan. "It was an honor to watch you fight."

Karoti bowed to the group. "Good travels to you and your clans." Then he turned and followed Rajo, the other mercenaries falling behind them like silent shadows.

No one spoke for a moment, and then Besnik broke the silence. "Well, it sounds like things will become very interesting around here, very shortly." He sighed heavily. "How inconvenient."

"You don't like interesting things?" Emil said, trying to dispel the tension in the air.

Besnik smiled. "I prefer my life and the lives of my people to be as boring as possible," he said. "Interesting times upset my routine. And it's bad for the dyes." He bowed to Emil, Stefan, and their father. "I think we'll head to the edge of the Eastern Forests. It's a little late for cinnamon alder cuttings, but the bark and shoots should still be harvestable."

"Perhaps we'll follow you," Emil's father said. "Anything that gets us away from those cursed mercenaries. And we do have business to discuss."

"We do," Besnik said. "Until next time then, Mihai. Emil, Stefan."

When Besnik had walked away, Stefan turned to his father. "What business?"

"Nothing that concerns you," the *Kys* said. "And since we're moving out, I'm lifting your punishment. For now. Go pack and tell Lel and Meri that we're leaving. I want to be gone by first light tomorrow."

Stefan hesitated. "Father . . ."

"Be silent!"

Stefan took a step back, and even Emil recoiled a little at the anger in his father's voice. Then the *Kys* dropped his head and Emil saw the telltale signs, the eyebrows high and drawn together, the strain around the mouth.

His father was afraid.

"You've done enough damage for one day," their father said, and his words were tired. "And we *will* be discussing your punishment. But right now, I don't wish to see you. Go pack up your tent."

"Very well, Father," Stefan said, and his voice was soft. "As you wish."

Emil moved to go as well, but their father held out his hand.

"Emil, I would speak to you in my wagon."

"Me?" Emil said. "Why?"

"Just . . ." His father pinched the bridge of his nose. "Just come with me. I need to talk to you about something."

Emil watched the back of Stefan's head disappear around the corner of the caravan. "Of course, Father," he said. "Whatever you need."

18

Mara

MARA'S FIRST GLIMPSE of the capital city of Kamal left her breathless. One moment she was jogging down the packed dirt road behind the swishing black tail of Revathi's horse, teak trees towering on either side, then the road took a sharp right, the trees stopped, and there it was. Situated on a wide, jutting piece of land where two of the Five Sacred Rivers met, the city was surrounded on two sides by swiftly flowing dark water. It was built on a low hill, each section set a little higher than the last, the flat roofs of noble houses and the decorated roof of the palace visible above the rest. A thick wall of worn brown stone looped the city's base.

"Is this the first time you've seen Kamal?" Revathi asked, looking over at Mara.

The back of Mara's neck turned warm as she realized she was staring. "It's . . . large."

"It was rebuilt after the Barrier went up," Revathi said. "It was the biggest city in the Empire then, and it still is, though Deshe is a close second. That's where most of the noble families go during the hot season, in fact, to Deshe, and the farms in the west. It's a little cooler near the mountains, and those nobles who own land there can check on the growing crops."

"So most of the nobles are gone?" Mara asked, disappointed. If the court was mostly empty, it would make it harder for her to find someone to pledge to.

"I'm afraid so," Revathi said. "I prefer the quiet, but it will probably be very boring for you." When Mara didn't answer, she turned the head of her mare toward the gate. "I'll get you some new clothes with my house colors on them and show you around." She paused. "I suppose you'll want to sleep in my room."

"In your room or close by," Mara said. "At least that's how it would work if you were my charge."

"Sounds horribly suffocating," Revathi said. "Like a built-in chaperone . . ." A sly, considering smile crossed her face, then she laughed. "Oh, that's perfect," she said. "I'll just keep you with me as much as possible. Tamas won't be able to get me alone, and if I'm lucky, he'll get so frustrated that he'll give up this bodyguard idea entirely."

Mara kept her face blank, masking the small stab of hurt she felt at Revathi's crisp words. She supposed she was going to have to get used to difficult clients, at least as long as she was working for her keep. When she pledged, it would be different. Her charge would want her help, need it even. They would be a team.

The main gates of the city were huge, heavy and dark with age, and even though they were open, Mara felt as if they wanted to shut her out. The sight of those gates, and the thickness of the walls, made Mara's neck tight and her stomach hurt. She had a sudden wild longing for the tangled shadows of the forest. But she squared her shoulders and followed Revathi forward.

To one side of the gate was a long table. Two soldiers in the silk and copper of infantrymen stood on either side of it, spears held at attention. The table held piles of paper and parchment and scattered writing implements. A small, fat man was engaged in sorting them out. He wore a dark-green tunic embroidered with silver, and there was a spot of green dye the size of a thumb pressed into his forehead.

A Jade scribe, Mara thought, remembering the variety of caste marks she'd learned in the Order. A keeper of records.

Revathi pulled up her mare. "Good day, Camus."

"Lady Revathi," he said, pressing his hands together and bowing from his seat. "Good day to you. And who is this?"

Revathi waved a delicate hand back at Mara. "This is Mara, my new guard. She needs a work permit."

"A guard?" one of the soldiers spoke up. His leather wristbands were studded with gold, the mark of a captain's rank. "Are you in some sort of danger, Lady Revathi?"

"Of course not," Revathi said. "Tamas is overly concerned for my safety, is all." Her voice dropped. "Honestly, I think he was just tired of carrying my parcels."

The other soldier snickered, but the captain frowned. He stared at Mara, as if trying to see under her skin. Mara raised her chin a little and stared back.

"She's a bold one," the man said, disapproval showing in his folded arms. "And she's very wild looking." Mara flushed, torn between anger and embarrassment. "That won't do at court, Lady Revathi, you know it won't. Her manners . . ."

"Are my concern," Revathi finished for him. Her voice had taken on a decided chill. "I'll deal with it. Can you enter her on the rolls, Camus?"

"Certainly." The scribe looked at Mara, his gaze sharp and analytical. "Pledged?" he asked.

Mara shook her head. "Work for hire," she muttered, feeling awkward. The man nodded briskly.

"Still t'Riala then." He made a note on one of the parchments, then handed it to Mara. "Here is your work permit," he said. "Keep it with you at all times. It allows you to stay in the Inner City and the outer portion of the palace. You'll have to see someone in the Imperial Palace Guard about going behind the Lotus Wall. I'm not cleared to authorize that."

Mara wasn't sure what he meant by Lotus Wall, but she took the thin piece of parchment anyway, tucking it into her tunic. The soldiers waved them through the gate. And as soon as she saw the inside of the city, Mara couldn't register anything else.

It was chaos. Every piece of space was thick with human bodies, clogging the air with their voices, overwhelming her with their smells. For the first time in three years, Mara was grateful for her human-dulled senses.

She was standing on a strip of land bounded on one side by the wall and on the other by a canal full of sluggish gray water. The far side of the canal rose steeply, placing the next level of the city on a higher plane, and a wide, wooden bridge connected the two levels. The area at the foot of the bridge was packed full of sleeping pallets and rumpled travelers. Some of them sat up at the sight of Revathi's horse. They stretched out their arms, their voices desperate.

"Work, miss?"

"Do you have any work?"

Revathi shook her head at them and guided her horse into a clearer area just near the main gate. "Sorry," she said to Mara. "I should have warned you. This is the transients' area. Once they enter the city, Wind caste people have three days and two nights to get a work permit. If they succeed, they're allowed to move into the Wind Circle."

Revathi nodded to where the sleeping pallets gave way to rows of tiny cobbled-together houses with beaten paths of hard dirt running between them. "They can move into an empty house if one is available, or build one. The builders and masons sell their broken or inferior materials to the Wind Circle, and there's a small market where Bamboo merchants and artisans sell the cast-off clothing and tools they can't sell elsewhere. If these people don't find jobs by the time the three days are up, they have to leave Kamal."

A fight broke out between two men in the crowd, a brief,

violent tussle. The loser picked up his bedroll and moved away to the edge of the crowd.

"They do that all the time." Mara turned to see that the captain had followed them inside the gate. The man folded his arms. "Fight over the best spots, that is. The farther away they are from the gate and the Hearth Bridge, the less likely they are to catch the eye of an employer." He paused. "Watch for yourself. Here comes one now."

A man in embroidered gray silk was walking over the bridge, his steps brisk. Mara assessed him, trying to remember her training. Gray meant he was a house servant, but the rich material meant he was of a higher level, probably the manager of a household.

The eyes of everyone in the area swiveled toward him, heads turning as if pulled on strings. The man stopped at the foot of the bridge and crossed his arms. "No moving, and no speaking," he shouted, in a deep voice that carried over the suddenly silent crowd. "Raised hands only. Who among you can sew a straight seam?"

About twenty hands went up. The man made a palms-down gesture. "Come forward, just you lot."

Murmurs of disappointment followed the owners of the hands as they picked their way to the foot of the bridge. They were a ragged-looking bunch, men and women, young and old. The man in gray walked among them.

"What's he looking for?" Mara asked.

"He's looking at their clothing, examining the mended parts," Revathi said. "Someone with good sewing skills will repair his own clothing whenever possible. Buying thread is cheaper than buying new clothes."

Finally the man in gray stopped and put his hand on the shoulder of a stooped older man. "You. Come with me." He turned and headed back across the bridge, the old man following. The ones who hadn't been chosen made their way back to their pallets, their shoulders slumped and their steps heavy.

"So that's how it's done?" Mara said.

"For the most part," the captain said. "That man is lucky. He'll be part of a noble household, well fed and well clothed. If he'd been hired by a Bamboo merchant, he'd draw a wage, but probably still have to live in the Wind Circle."

"Are you ready, Mara?" Revathi was looking up at the gray sky. "It's starting to get dark."

The captain bowed to both girls. "Yes, you don't want to be late, Lady Revathi. I know your father gets . . . concerned when you are late."

Revathi stiffened. "As my father is in Deshe right now with my mother and brother, he won't be worrying much at all, will he?" She urged her horse forward through the crowd, and Mara followed, ignoring the outstretched hands all around her, the pleading for work.

"Interfering busybody," Revathi muttered as soon as they were on the bridge. "Ever since my parents left for Deshe, every merchant, soldier, and lesser noble has been prying into my family's affairs." Her voice took on a sarcastic, mimicking tone. "'Are you sure your father would approve of this purchase?' 'Does your mother know you're in this part of town?' 'Whatever would your parents think, dear?'" She scowled. "Bunch of river sharks, that's what they are."

She looked down at Mara. "And now I have you to deal with. Another person watching my every move. That's really the last thing I need." She slapped her mare's shoulder lightly with the leather reins, urging the horse forward, so that Mara had to jog to keep up. "The sooner we get home, the happier I'll be."

19
Mara

MARA FOLLOWED REVATHI over the bridge and into a part of the city that was as different from the Wind Circle as anything could possibly be. Here the streets were full of fruit trees, vegetable gardens, and animals. Mara trotted past a few pigs in a pen and some bored-looking cows. Every intersection was peppered with booths selling produce and other foodstuffs. The scents of baking bread and roasting spiced meat filled the air.

Revathi slowed her mare to a walk again.

"Are you sure this is a city?" Mara asked her, trying to lighten the mood. "I thought there'd be taller houses and fewer chickens."

Revathi smiled for the first time since they'd entered the city. "This is the Hearth Circle," she said. "If it has anything to do with growing things, animals, cooking, or hospitality, this is where you find it. The village farmers and fishermen keep booths here all year, and this is where most of the food supplies in the city are sold." She gestured back at the bridge they'd crossed. "The bridges are named after the circle they lead to. That was the Hearth Bridge. The Hearth Circle and the Wind Circle together are called the Outer City."

They crossed another sturdy wooden bridge. This one was polished and gleaming, its pillars carved into the shapes of different Ancestors and monsters of legend. Groups of women in beaded collars and brightly colored asars knelt on the wide steps at the edge of the canal. They laughed and chatted as they washed their clothes.

There were soldiers at the end of this bridge. Revathi nodded to them, and they let her through. She pulled up her horse to let Mara catch up. "Does this look more like a city to you?"

Tall row houses jumbled together, keeping the wide streets in perpetual shadow. Shops on the ground floor displayed everything from brilliantly embroidered fabric to wooden kitchen utensils. On one corner, a girl in a peach-colored tunic and trousers danced to the beat of another girl's drum. At another intersection, a man was blowing glass using a clay blowpipe and a small oven. Everyone was wearing some kind of jewelry. All the men sported at least one earring, many had two or three, and the women bore jewels in both their nose and ears. The air smelled of dust, sweat, and perfume.

"This must be the Bamboo Circle," Mara called up, pleased that she didn't sound out of breath. Her training at the Order seemed to be paying off; she kept up with Revathi's horse easily. "Merchants, craftsmen, and entertainers, right?"

"Very good," Revathi said. "At least you're not walking in here entirely ignorant."

"We're very well educated at the Order," Mara told her, straight-faced. "A good bodyguard has to know more than just which end of the weapon is the pointy one."

Revathi didn't smile this time, but Mara thought she heard a touch of amusement in the girl's voice. "Oh, Garen is going to love you."

"Who's Garen?" Mara kept an eye on the shifting crowd as they walked. She knew from her lessons that the Bamboo Circle was the largest part of the city, and it certainly seemed to be the busiest. People got out of the way of Revathi's horse—many giving respectful bows as they did so—but there still wasn't much room.

"He's the head of the Imperial Palace Guard and Emperor Saro's primary bodyguard," Revathi answered. "He's also the person you need to ask for permission to access the inner part of the palace."

"So the palace is in two parts?" Mara said, trying to get a sense of where they were going. "The man at the gate said something about a wall. . . ."

"The Imperial Palace isn't all one building," Revathi explained. "It's actually more like a giant park with a lot of different build-ings, and it's divided into two parts by a wall. The larger half is the public part of the palace; it holds the Shrine of the First Emperor, the Palace of Rippling Leaves—where the throne room is—and a few other buildings. The smaller part is the private quarters and gardens that belong to the Imperial family alone."

Mara squinted. "Sounds confusing," she confessed.

"Oh, it is," Revathi said. "But you'll learn. The sa'Hoi are distant cousins of the Emperor, and we supervise most of the administrative tasks of the palace, so you'll be spending a lot of time on the palace grounds." She said it carelessly, as if she wasn't confessing to being one of the most powerful nobles in the city. As if it didn't matter.

Mara kept her face blank. Revathi might be trying to intimidate her, or she might not. Either way, Mara wasn't going to let her know she'd succeeded.

They walked in silence after that, soon reaching yet another bridge. This one was of heavy dark wood and led into what Mara knew was the Jade Circle. Here there were no shops or booths, no music or shouting or animal noise. Just street after street of white courtyard walls, wide metal gates, and carefully trimmed bushes and trees. There was almost no scent in the air. A few people walked the streets, most of them wearing dark-green tunics, with green dye on their hands or marking their foreheads.

Mara slowed her steps as she passed a bronze gate stamped with the half-human, half-snake body of a *naga*. This was where Samara, the weapons master, had told her to go, where Samara's friend the warrior monk lived. Mara had a sudden urge to knock on that gate and find the welcome she knew would be waiting. Revathi didn't want her, and Mara knew nothing of human courts or nobles. Everything sounded so complicated in Revathi's world, and it would be so easy to stop here. . . .

"Is something wrong?" Revathi looked back, and Mara realized she'd stopped walking.

"No," Mara said, with one more glance at the bronze gate. She was more likely to find someone to pledge to if she wasn't hiding behind walls. She'd follow this path and see where it led. After all, she could always come back. "Nothing's wrong."

Revathi gave her a sharp look. "We're almost there. Do you need to rest?"

Mara shook her head.

Revathi lifted her thin shoulders in a shrug. "Suit yourself."

True to her word, it didn't take long to reach the next bridge. Unlike all the rest, this one was made of thick gray stone. Vines hung from the bridge in green sheets, and red and yellow glory lilies peered through the narrow leaves. And as soon as she stepped foot off the bridge, Mara understood why the nobles' part of the city was called the Flower Circle.

Blossoms were everywhere. Orchid trees grew at each street corner, and a colorful riot of flowering bushes lined the stone-paved roads. Noble houses all seemed to be built around large, open courtyards, and Mara caught glimpses of gardens and sparkling fountains through their half-open doors. Men in embroidered tunics and women in patterned asars could be seen walking on the flat roofs, and many of those roofs were also full of green and growing things.

It was lush and decadent . . . and overwhelming. The scent of the flowers alone was enough to make Mara light-headed, especially after the clearer air of the Jade district. Everywhere she looked, there was someone dressed in silk or chiffon or brocade. Even Revathi's brown asar looked dim here. As for Mara, she felt grimy and dirty and horribly out of place.

Then she saw the palace.

20

Emil

THE *KYS*'S WAGON was small but comfortable, with carved furniture and flower-painted walls. Emil's father sat on the wooden bunk that stretched across the back. Behind his father's legs, under the bed, Emil could see the copper gleam of a handle: the handle of the trundle bed that he and Stefan had slept in until they had been old enough to have a tent to themselves.

Emil leaned against the dresser that had been fastened to one wall and waited.

"Emil . . ." His father shifted on the bunk. "Emil, what do you think of Kizzy Yanora?"

"Besnik's daughter?" Emil straightened up. "She's very nice. And I guess she's good with a dye bottle in a fight."

His father didn't smile at the joke.

"Well, Besnik and I were talking," his father said. "And it's been several generations since the last clan alliance between the Arvi and the Yanora. I told him that I thought your affections might be elsewhere, but if you and that Sune girl are truly just friends . . ." He spread his hands.

Emil blinked, the words taking a moment to sink in. "You want me to marry Kizzy Yanora?" he said, and his voice was loud, too loud in the small space of the caravan.

"Why not?" his father said. "She's been eligible for marriage for several years, she's around your age, and she's one of the most talented dye makers in their camp. She would be a valuable addition to the Arvi."

"She's not a goat, Father!" Emil pushed his hand through his hair, torn between laughter and anger. Even in the middle of a crisis, his father couldn't stop trying to arrange his life.

"It's just a suggestion," his father said. "The Arvi have had a hard year. A clan-alliance marriage would be good for us right now, if you were both willing."

"Is she?" Emil asked, curiosity winning over his frustration for a moment. "Willing, I mean?"

"I don't know," his father admitted. "Besnik was going to speak to her, just like I'm speaking to you. But you should consider it. She's attractive and intelligent, and I'm sure she finds you agreeable."

"Or at least amusing," Emil muttered. He didn't want to marry Kizzy Yanora, whose calm smile hid a wicked sense of humor and who always seemed to be gently laughing at people from behind her bright brown eyes.

"Was I wrong?" his father asked. "Has someone else caught your eye?"

Emil thought about Mara, the way she'd fought for him and his brother, the way every smile she gave him felt like a gift. But Emil had as much chance of wooing a member of the Order of Khatar as he did of touching the gray roof of the Barrier.

"No," he said. "There's no one else. I just don't want to marry right now."

"A leader should—" his father started, and the banked embers of Emil's anger flared to life.

"Maybe I don't care about what a leader would do!" The words spilled out of his mouth, jagged and harsh. "Maybe I don't want to be a leader at all."

The silence that fell was so stiff and heavy that Emil felt flattened. He curled his fingers into fists, resisting the urge to reach out and snatch back what he'd said.

"You don't want to be a leader," his father repeated. "Since when?"

"Since . . . I don't know when." Emil waved his hands in a helpless gesture. He groped for a way to describe the growing restlessness, the unease that had grown since his mother's death, strangling him like a creeper vine. "For a while. I wanted to tell you, but there never seemed to be a good time."

"And what, if I may ask, would you like to do instead?" Emil's father said. His voice was flat, and his face could have been carved from stone for all Emil could read it.

Emil gathered his courage. "I want to apprentice to Uncle

Pali and go with him when he travels. I want to see more of the Empire than the parts where we've always camped. I'm good at trading, and I think I could be better with some training. And then maybe someday I could be the Master of Trade myself."

"I see," his father said. His voice sharpened. "And what happens to your family while you're off chasing mist? What happens to your brother?"

"Stefan's eighteen, the same as I am," Emil said. "He doesn't need me to take care of him."

"But you're the only one he'll listen to," his father said. Emil opened his mouth to protest, but his father wasn't finished. "And what about the rest of the Arvi? What happens to them, if something happens to me? Who will lead then?"

"Stefan could—"

"Stefan could *not*. Your brother has heart, but he is not mature enough to be the leader this family needs."

Frustration crawled up Emil's throat, choking him. "Stefan would walk through fire for this family," he said. "He might not be the most levelheaded person, but he cares about what's good for the camp and for us. He just needs time."

"We don't have time," his father countered. "There are no other boys your age in our family, and who knows what could happen in the future? I need a successor now. We can't wait for your brother to decide to grow up."

"What about me?" Emil said. He felt like a snare was closing around him, binding him tighter than any rope ever could. "Don't I get a choice?"

"There is always a choice," his father said. "You can walk away from the people who need you anytime you like."

Emil flinched, and his father's voice softened. "But I don't think you'll do that. And it's not a bad life, being the leader."

"Is that what you told yourself when Mother died?" Emil said. "When you couldn't be there with her? Did you tell yourself it wasn't a bad life?" The words felt wrong on his tongue, flat and emotionless. Words like that shouldn't be said; they should be screamed in anger, thrown like weapons.

But Emil was too tired to fight anymore.

Without looking at his father, he turned and left the caravan, shutting the thin wooden door of the wagon behind him.

Once outside, he took a deep breath and closed his eyes, taking comfort in familiar sounds: the giggles of children, the clatter of tools. The hot air wrapped around him, and he felt the muscles in his neck relax.

Maybe there is something wrong with me, he thought. His father wasn't asking anything of Emil that he hadn't done himself. In lean times, the *Kys's* food share was always the smallest. When the bitter cold of Earthsleep came, he let the younger children sleep in his caravan, where the thick, wet mist couldn't touch them. On those nights, he bunked with Emil and Stefan, all of them huddling under goatskins and woven blankets, shoving for space.

He smiled at the memory. His father would give anything for the camp, and Stefan was the same way. But Emil . . .

He put a hand over his chest, fingers digging into his skin.

If only he could reach inside with his bare hands, pull out his dreams, and throw them away. He imagined leading the camp, living in this very caravan, marrying someone his father approved of. Sacrificing everything for the Arvi, even, if necessary, the people he loved.

The image left a dry, burned taste in his mouth, like ash. Or maybe it was the aftertaste of the words he'd just said to his father. He wanted to turn around and apologize. But if he went back now, he'd agree to anything his father said. Even to marrying Kizzy Yanora.

I'll speak to him tomorrow. Emil pushed his hands through his hair. All he wanted to do now was pack up his tent, get some of the peppery mutton stew he could smell cooking, and get some sleep.

Stefan was in their shared tent, packing. He was shoving things into bags and boxes with unnecessary force, a dark scowl on his face. He didn't look up when Emil entered.

"What a mess, right?" Emil said, trying out a small smile. Stefan turned his back, bracing his foot against a sack of dried onions and tying the mouth of the bag shut with quick, hard jerks.

"Here, let me help you with that," Emil said, moving forward. "You shouldn't be trying to use that hand right now–"

"Don't touch me!" Stefan turned on Emil, his face filled with such fury that Emil took a step back.

Emil didn't think Stefan could hurt him, not with his arm in a sling. But he also wasn't in the mood for a fistfight.

"Don't take this out on me!" he snapped. "I'm not the reason Father's furious with you."

"Of course not," Stefan snarled. He picked up a small carved statue of the Horned God and put it in his chest, slamming the lid shut. "Nothing is ever your fault. Innocent Emil, just doing what Father wants; no one could blame you. You could leave me something, you know, instead of taking it all for yourself."

"What are you talking about?" Emil said. "I'm not taking anything away from you." He drew a breath. "Look, I know you're upset, but Father won't be angry forever. I could talk to him again–"

"Oh yes, come and save me." Stefan started pacing back and forth, his angry footsteps muffled by the rugs. "Then maybe I'll think you're wonderful, just like everyone else. Isn't it enough that the whole camp practically fawns over you? Everything is always offered to you, everything you do is praised. Why can't you be happy with that?"

Happy. Laughter burned like bile in the back of Emil's throat. "Why do you care if I'm happy or not?" he said. "No one else does."

"Yes, your life is so hard," Stefan mocked. "I feel so sorry for you. It must be terrible being Father's favorite."

Emil's frustration boiled over. He was sick of always being in the middle, sick of trying to keep everyone happy, sick of feeling restless and empty.

Sick of his family.

"Stefan, shut up!" The words came out quick and hard, like a slap. "I'm tired of hearing you whine and moan all the time. And I'm tired of cleaning up your messes, too. I don't want to be the leader, but I'm going to have to because there's no one else but you, and you would tear this camp apart! In fact, you're already doing it. Father's right: everything you touch turns to chaos. You're not a leader, Stefan, you're a disaster!"

The two stared at each other across the tent, Emil's ragged breathing filling the space between them. He braced himself for Stefan's blow.

But instead of throwing himself forward with a roar of rage, Stefan just . . . stood there. He didn't yell, he didn't scowl, he just stared at Emil, his face wiped clean of expression.

"If that's what you think, then I guess there's nothing to say," Stefan said finally. He grabbed his bedroll and a sack of clothes. "I think I'll sleep outside tonight." Then he pushed past Emil and out of the tent.

Emil stared at the empty space where Stefan had stood, still littered with blankets and sacks of grain. Then, with a deep sigh, he started packing up the rest of the tent. Maybe having someone call him on his attitude was just what his brother needed. Maybe he'd take what Emil said seriously and actually try to do something about his situation.

The thought didn't soothe the sour feeling of guilt in his gut. First his father, now Stefan. He'd never spoken to his twin that way before. He'd never spoken to *anyone* that way before.

He must be more tired than he thought.

He'd apologize to both of them tomorrow. After they both got some sleep and Emil could trust himself again. He'd apologize and they'd start over again.

Tomorrow.

Never trust a human who wants something from you.

Sune proverb

21

Mara

MARA COULD NOT stop staring.

Situated in the exact center of the Flower Circle, the walls surrounding the Imperial Palace rose above the houses, drawing the eye. The bottom half of the walls were smooth gray stone, polished until there could be no foothold for intruders to climb over. The top half was a series of graceful pavilions on strong stilts, their roof edges trimmed with fantastic swirls and carved monsters. The palace complex was encircled by a canal of its own, a pure expanse of sparkling water dotted with lily pads and lotus blossoms. A delicately carved bridge ran up to the front gate.

Unlike the infantry in the rest of the city, the guards of the palace were dressed in dark-blue quilted silk. There was one at each end of the bridge, both holding long spears, and Mara saw several archers patrolling the top of the walls. The guards on the Imperial Bridge saluted Revathi as she passed by.

Once inside the walls Mara saw that Revathi was right. The palace resembled nothing so much as a large, perfectly kept park, scattered with pavilions and graceful buildings. Revathi took a sharp right and followed the wall until they came to a stable complex the size of a small village. "Finally," she said, jumping off her horse and handing the reins to a stable servant. She pulled her heavy, dark hair loose from its tie and shook it a few times. "I get *so* tired of being Lady Revathi sa'Hoi. All anyone out there sees is a title and a pretty face. Sometimes I wonder why I ever leave the palace."

"So you live here?" Mara looked around. "Not in the general Flower Circle?"

"We do indeed," a crisp voice answered, and an old woman stepped out of the shadows of the stable. She wore an asar of rich white-and-silver brocade and a long braid of heavy gray hair. Her eyes were sharp and quick, like a sparrow's.

"I've been looking for you, Granddaughter."

Revathi knelt and touched the woman's feet. "Hello, Grandmother," she said. "Are you feeling well today?"

"Worse than I would like and better than I deserve. Why is your hair down?"

Revathi put her hands to her head. "I was just about to rebraid it."

"Well then, do so," the woman said. "Sathvik u'Gra has been prowling the palace all day, waiting for you to get back. The

Ancestors only know what he'd say if he saw you in this state."

"Tamas's father?" Revathi ran her fingers through her hair and started to braid it back up. "What does he want?"

"To invite us both to supper, apparently," the old woman said. "At least that's what he told the servants. I managed to avoid him, but I wouldn't put it past him to find an excuse to come back." Her eyes flicked to Mara. "You haven't introduced me to your friend."

"Forgive me," Revathi said. "Grandmother, this is Mara. She's my new guard."

The woman gave Mara a startled look. "She is, is she? And why do you suddenly need a guard?"

"There was a riot at the Clothing Fair," Revathi said. "Nothing serious. No one was killed that I know of. But Tamas was . . . concerned. So he hired me a guard."

"And of course, she'll be well paid to report on you," Revathi's grandmother said, frowning at Mara.

"I'm not a spy!" Mara blurted out, too annoyed to worry about politeness. "For Nishvana's sake, what kind of world do you people live in that you think everyone's paid to spy on you?"

Revathi made a choked noise, but the old woman burst out laughing. She bent her head in Mara's direction, long years of practiced grace in every movement. "A dangerous one, child. A very dangerous and very subtle one, not for the timid or the dull. Please forgive my rudeness. I am the Lady Ekisa sa'Hoi. I've overseen this family and the administration of the Imperial Palace since my husband died."

Mara knelt as Revathi had, touching the woman's sandaled feet in respect.

"It is an honor to serve one of your house, lady," she said. "I apologize for my outburst."

Lady Ekisa looked at her carefully. "Order of Khatar?"

Mara nodded.

"Pledged?"

"Not yet, Lady sa'Hoi," Mara replied, deciding that honesty was the best tactic. "I hoped to find a suitable charge here."

A smile twisted Lady Ekisa's face. "Lord and Lady sa'Hoi are my son and his wife," she said. "Since I am widowed, you may call me Lady Ekisa. As for finding you a charge, I'm afraid there is a sad lack of worthy candidates among the nobility. You would be better served offering your skills in the Bamboo Circle, or to the Jade scholars and healers."

"It might come to that," Revathi said. She finished braiding her hair and pulled it over one shoulder. "It probably will. But I need to keep her around at least long enough to convince Tamas I tried. It would be best if letting her go was his idea and not mine."

"True," Lady Ekisa said. She looked at Mara again. "And it might be nice for you to have a girl your own age about. You spend too much time alone."

"Grandmother," Revathi said, her voice warning.

"Don't 'Grandmother' me, young woman," Lady Ekisa said. "One of the few pleasures left to an old person like me is the ability to speak my mind whenever I choose. Especially when it's the truth."

Her voice softened. "When I was your age, I had formed friend-ships with other women, friendships I can still call on to this day. The world is not an easy place, Revathi. You'll need those connections to support you."

"Yes, they've been very helpful so far," Revathi snapped; then she sighed. "I have my duties to the princes, and I have my fam-ily. That's enough for me."

"And when you marry?"

Revathi tugged at the edges of her sleeves. "I'd rather not dis-cuss that now," she said abruptly. "Servants gossip, and you said Lord u'Gra was lurking around. You may not have to play the Great Game anymore, but I do."

Lady Ekisa pressed her lips together. "You missed the evening meal. You must be hungry." She reached out and caught the sleeve of a stable servant who was hurrying by with Revathi's saddle. It was a boy with a shaved head and the bronze cuffs of a bond slave on his wrists.

"Bhagi," she said. "As soon as you've finished with Lady Revathi's tack, go to the kitchens in the Palace of Flowing Water. Have them send two trays to Revathi's room at once."

The boy bowed deeply. "As you wish, Honored Lady." A faint gleam of humor creased his eyes as he straightened up. "For you, I will brave the cook's prickly temper."

Lady Ekisa smiled. "Tell Hanoi I'll buy him a nice tender lamb as a present. He's been complaining that all he gets to work with these days is mutton and fish. And tell him I said to give you a sweet roll as well."

The boy bowed again. "Thank you, Lady." Then he hurried off.

"Bribing the servants again, Grandmother?" Revathi said.

"People want to be seen," Lady Ekisa said. "If they feel appreciated, they work harder and are more loyal. The Ancestors know your grandfather never learned that lesson. He was heavy with his anger, and the servants lived in fear. Things run much smoother this way. Remember that, my dear, for your own home."

"I *said* I didn't wish to discuss that," Revathi said.

"Tamas's two years of service are almost over, dear. You're not going to be able to avoid it forever."

Revathi folded her arms.

"Very well," Lady Ekisa said. "We'll discuss this later. Go and get your dinner, and I will see you tomorrow." She looked at Mara. "You and your new addition."

"Good night, Grandmother," Revathi said. She bowed, and Mara copied her.

Mara watched the gray-haired woman walk away, the line of her back straight and proud. "Your grandmother seems . . . nice," she said, carefully.

"No, she doesn't," Revathi said. She smiled fondly as she watched Lady Ekisa leave the stable. "My grandmother is many, many things, but nice has never been one of them. All that talk about being too old for the Great Game was a ruse. She's a master at it, and one of the most dangerous people I know. But she seems to like you."

The idea didn't comfort Mara much.

"You should see the rest of my family," Revathi continued, bending down to retie her sandals. "Well, you can't, because they're in Deshe. But I'm probably the least dangerous person in the palace."

"I'm not sure I believe that," Mara said.

"Good." Revathi straightened up. "Rule number one in the Lotus Court? Everybody lies."

22
Mara

IT WAS FULLY dark by the time Mara and Revathi left the stables. The stable yard was lit by square wooden lamps, light flickering from their carved sides. Farther out, spots of light glistened from the windows of scattered buildings. On the far side of the garden was a wall, lined with torches and guarded by more soldiers in dark-blue uniforms. Revathi headed toward it, and Mara followed, hoping they would get some food soon. Her legs ached from all the running, and her stomach felt hollow.

Revathi didn't speak as they walked across the smooth expanse of lawn toward the wall. She nodded to the guards as she passed inside, and the guards bowed back.

"Was that the Lotus Wall? The one dividing the palace?" Mara asked once they were through. "I thought you said this inner area was only for the Emperor's family."

"Family and attendants," Revathi corrected. "Including those of us who were assigned to look after the princes when the Empress died." She paused and frowned. "I'll have to get you a pass tomorrow. If you're found without a pass on the Emperor's side of the wall, you'll be thrown in prison." She said it casually, as if her mind was somewhere else.

Mara swallowed.

They walked in silence until they reached another building. Mara couldn't see much in the shadows, but it looked larger than the stables. Stone steps flanked by thick pillars led up to where torches flickered on either side of an elaborately decorated bronze door.

Revathi pushed it open and gestured Mara inside. "Welcome to the Palace of Flowing Water."

The interior of the palace took Mara's breath away. It was lit by steady lamps affixed to the walls, and the warm glow illuminated carved arches and pillars made of rich dark wood. The walls were inlaid with precious stones. Thick woven carpets cushioned their feet as they walked.

"It's beautiful," she whispered.

Revathi paused and looked around. "It is, isn't it? I suppose I don't really notice anymore." She started walking again, down a seemingly endless corridor. "Here we are." She pushed through a thickly curtained doorway. "Home."

Mara paused, instinctively checking the room for enemies. It was a lovely open space, separated into two areas by graceful ivory pillars. The walls and arches were also inlaid with ivory, as intricate as a spiderweb. Around the edges of the rich blue carpets, Mara could see tiles of a lighter blue.

A thick mattress with a dark-blue silken cover occupied one side of the room and a fire in a wide beaten copper bowl sat at the other, with a low desk in front of it. The light flickered off arched windows, several plush seating cushions, and a long shelf full of scrolls and copper figurines.

A pot of tea sat in a small warmer on the desk, a tray of savory fried pastries next to it. Mara's stomach rumbled, and she was suddenly ravenous. Following Revathi's example, she dipped her hands in the nearby washbasin and dried them. Then she pulled a fat cushion close to the desk and sat. Revathi picked up the teapot, paused, and set it down again.

"You're not going to insist on trying all my food for poisons, are you?" she asked. "Because that would be tiresome."

"Only if we think someone is trying to poison you," Mara said. "Is someone trying to poison you?"

"Probably not," Revathi said. "But in the Lotus Court, one never knows."

She slid a thin packet of paper out of her desk and poured a little of the pale amber tea into a saucer. As Mara watched, fascinated, Revathi sprinkled some powder from her packet into the saucer of tea and stirred. She examined the liquid with a critical eye, then lifted it to her lips and sipped it. "No poison tonight," she said, sounding cheerful. "Not that I was expecting any, but it's good to check now and again."

She set the testing saucer aside and gestured at the food. "Go ahead. You look hungry."

Mara didn't hesitate. The pastries were filled with slices of mutton and served with a spicy red chili paste on the side. She gulped them down, trying to show good manners while Revathi poured fresh tea into two gold-leaved cups. She handed one to Mara, then took one of her own.

"What was that?" Mara asked, as soon as her mouth was free of food. "The thing you did with the tea and the saucer."

"A trick my grandmother learned from a friend of hers," Revathi said. "The powder is a special mix. Mostly tasteless unless it meets certain kinds of poison—then it becomes very bitter. Emperor Saro uses it too, I think." She finished her tea and yawned. "Well, it's been a rather trying day and I'm tired." She indicated the roll of blankets next to the bed. "It looks like Grandmother had the servants bring a bedroll. Will that do?"

Mara sipped her drink. The tea was hot and sweet, and the fire was making her drowsy. It had been a long day for both of them. "That will be fine," she said, standing. She made a proper sweep of the room, the way she'd been taught. She also scanned the garden outside, checking below the windows before drawing the thick drapes.

Revathi watched her. "My, you *are* thorough."

"I'm practicing," Mara told her. "You're the first person I've ever actually guarded, you know." She grabbed the bedroll and rolled it out in front of the door. "In case of assassins," she said, joking, but Revathi didn't laugh.

"Not a bad idea," she said as she turned her back and quickly slipped into a loose sleeping tunic. "Though I've been told assassins usually prefer windows."

Mara narrowed her eyes, but Revathi had already climbed into bed.

Mara moved her bedroll to the window, then thought better of it, placing it near the foot of Revathi's bed instead. Revathi blew out the last lamp so that the room was lit by only the dying fire at the other end of the room.

Mara lay down on the bedroll without bothering to change. For a while she stared into the dancing shadows of the bedroom; then her hand slipped into her hidden pocket and pulled out the wooden tiger that Emil had given her.

For a long time she held it, running her thumb over its smooth back. She remembered what it felt like to wear that form, to have fur and ears and a tail. And she remembered how it felt to take the tiger from Emil's hand, skin on skin. Both sensations were things she could not have again. But maybe it was all right–here, alone in the dark–to pretend.

Just for a little while.

23
Emil

EMIL WOKE TO the braying of donkeys and the cries of goats. He sat up, rubbing his eyes, and tried to shake the sleep-fuzz from his sight. His dreams had been restless, full of anxious searching, a sense of something lost. The smell of boiling *kafei* and cooking flatbread wafted into the tent, waking him further. His stomach growled.

Pushing himself to his feet, Emil yawned and tried to rub some of the early-morning soreness out of his neck. His personal belongings had been crammed into a rough brown sack that waited by the tent entrance,. Stefan had put his own possessions in the cart last night, before bedding down outside. All that was left was to tie up the bedrolls and take down the tent and they'd be ready to leave.

"Emil!" Lel poked his head into the tent. The Master of Camp looked far too awake for this time of morning, his smile bright. "There you are, my boy. Glad to see you're up and ready. Is Stefan with you?"

"He slept outside," Emil said, trying not to sound as guilty as he still felt. "Near the back of our tent. He should be there, if he's still asleep." A particularly shrill donkey call made him wince. "Which I doubt."

"Excellent," Lel said. "I'll go find him." His head vanished, then reappeared through the tent flaps. "Rona has breakfast for you."

"Thanks," Emil said as his stomach gave another demanding rumble.

Preparations to leave camp seemed to be going smoothly. Most of the tents were down and the donkeys stood in a line, hitched to wide, flat carts. Meri was overseeing the goats, which were— wonder of wonders—all gathered together without protest. The younger children stood around them with long sticks, ready to nudge stragglers back into the group. Other Arvi packed up looms, wrapped up rolls of cashmere, and moved sacks of grain.

Emil made his way to the cooking fire and said good morning to Rona, who gave him a piece of flatbread wrapped around some pickled vegetables, and a clay cup of dark, fragrant *kafei*. Emil sipped it, letting the earthy, bitter taste clear the last of the sleep-cobwebs from his mind, and started on the flatbread roll. He was almost finished eating when Lel came back.

"Emil, I can't find your brother. There's no sign of him near your tent, and no one has seen him this morning."

The taste of the pickled vegetables turned sour in Emil's mouth. He swallowed. "What? What do you mean, you can't find him?"

The Master of Camp twisted his fingers together. "I've asked everyone, and checked every tent. No one knows where Stefan is. He's . . . missing."

"Missing?" Emil's voice rose. Fear as hard and rough as ice formed in the pit of his stomach. "No, he's got to be around somewhere. Look, his things are still in the cart. . . ." He waved at the cart that he and Stefan had packed their belongings onto last night.

But there was a gap. One of Stefan's bags was missing.

Emil stared at the cart, his own angry words echoing through his mind.

. . . tear this camp apart . . .

. . . you're already doing it . . .

"No," Emil breathed. He was barely aware of Lel asking him a question, of Rona's wide, worried eyes.

Everything you touch turns to chaos.

Emil ran for his father's caravan.

Pali and his father were bent over a map when Emil burst in. "Stefan's gone," Emil blurted. "I think . . . I think he's run away."

I think I drove him away.

The *Kys* looked up, his pale-brown eyes sharp. "Are you sure?"

Emil nodded. "Some of his things are gone, and no one has seen him this morning." He forced himself to breathe, to think. Stefan might have left in a fit of rage, but he wouldn't still be missing unless he'd found somewhere else to go.

"Could he have gone to one of the other Kildi camps?" Pali asked, echoing Emil's thoughts.

"If he has, then it's soon mended," his father said. "We can send messages to each camp to look for him."

"And bring him back?" Pali asked. The *Kys* shook his head.

"It might do him good to travel with another family for a while."

"Father . . ." A horrible idea was growing in Emil's mind. "What if he didn't go to another camp? What if he joined the mercenaries?"

The thought seemed to strike them all silent. Emil was almost ashamed for suggesting it. Kildi were Kildi. They joined other clans, they manned trading posts for the family, but they didn't outright *leave*. They didn't abandon their way of life entirely.

"We can't rule it out," the *Kys* said. "Pali, send those messages to the other camps and then you and I will go to the mercenaries."

"I want to go with you," Emil said.

"Pali and I are perfectly capable of bringing your brother back if he's there," the *Kys* said. "And there might be violence. We can't risk you. You're our future leader, and a leader must learn how to delegate."

Emil felt as if the carved walls of the wagon were closing around him. Nothing had changed from yesterday. His father always chose the good of the Arvi over everything else, and now he was pushing Emil into the same kind of life.

He left the wagon before his father could see him shaking.

Once outside, he leaned against the side of the caravan and tried to calm himself.

My father left my mother behind when she was sick, and I lost her. What if he leaves Stefan behind, too?

The thought stayed with him while he packed. He thought of his mother as he tied his bedroll and knapsack together, as he helped gather up the dogs and tie down the last of the carts. His mother, getting sicker and sicker, slipping away from him, even as he begged her to stay. Both of them waiting for his father to return.

But it had been too late. And it had been thirteen-year-old Emil, and not his father, who'd been there to watch Nadya Arvi draw her last breath.

Take care of Stefan, she'd whispered to Emil. *And be a good boy.*

And Emil had promised. So he ignored the heavy certainty in his limbs, the fear that grabbed him every time he looked in the direction his father and Pali had gone. He ignored it all, playing the good son, obeying his father as well as he could, and praying to the Horned God that Stefan would be found.

Then the messengers from the other camps came back, with no word of Stefan. And when he saw his father and Pali emerge from the woods alone, Emil knew his prayers hadn't been answered.

He ran up to them. Pali shook his head in response to Emil's unspoken question.

"The camp was deserted. They must have moved out very early this morning. Signs say they're going in the direction of the capital."

"Then we should follow them," Emil said. "Follow them and get Stefan back."

Pali glanced at the *Kys*. "I'm going to check the trade goods," he said, then he retreated.

There was a moment of silence. Emil's father had his arms folded, and his eyes were unreadable.

"Father . . . ," Emil said.

"It's too risky, Emil," he said, not ungently. "If Rajo does have a job in the capital, then that means there will be violence. Soldiers are already patrolling the roads because of the riot yesterday. The farther away we get, the safer we are. I have to protect the Arvi."

"Then what are we going to do?" Emil said. Because surely his father had a plan. They weren't just going to abandon Stefan. He was family.

Sorrow and anger pinched his father's face. "Your brother is a grown man, and he has chosen his path. I'm sorry, Emil."

Emil stared at him. "You know Stefan has a broken wrist," he said. "There's no way he can fight. Those mercenaries are going to get him killed. We don't have to take the whole camp to Kamal. You can just send me. I'll find him."

"Emil, we've been over this." His father ran a hand through his gray hair. "The Arvi need you."

"Stefan needs me more," Emil said. "And I won't throw him away. I'm going."

"I know it's hard, Emil," his father said. "But a good leader puts the good of the many over the needs of one person."

Emil felt a cold calm wash over him. Everything seemed to recede, the noise of the camp, the faces in front of him. He felt numb and light and . . . curiously free.

"Well," he said quietly, "I suppose this proves I'm not a leader. Doesn't it?"

His father flinched, as if Emil had struck him. Then his face closed off. "Go then. I will not stop you." Without looking back, he walked toward the waiting wagons.

Emil swallowed, then walked to where his bedroll and knapsack were waiting. He slung them on his back, tightening the fastenings. Out of the corner of his eye, he saw Pali and Lel whispering together, sneaking glances in his direction. Other voices murmured and hissed around him, but he couldn't tell if they were approving or disappointed. It didn't matter anyway.

The only thing that mattered was finding his brother and keeping him alive.

24
Emil

"EMIL!"

Emil didn't look around as he slung his pack over his shoulder. "You can't talk me out of this, Lel," he said.

"I know." Lel moved into Emil's line of sight. He was fidgeting with a scrap of paper. "Here," he said, in a low voice. "The city . . . it's a bad place for people to be alone. Take this." He shoved the paper into Emil's hands, then turned and walked quickly away.

Emil opened the folded piece of rice paper. It bore a single name. *Heema.* He looked over at Lel, but the man was once more deep in conversation with Pali. Emil caught Pali's eye. He was too far away to be sure, but he thought his uncle nodded to him.

Emil tucked the paper into his tunic and started walking. Lel's words rang in his ears. The man was right. Finding Stefan in a city that size would be hard, and going there alone would only make it worse. Emil needed help.

He needed Esmer.

Emil waited until he was out of sight of the camp before setting down his pack and putting the wooden call-whistle to his lips. After a few minutes of silence, he blew again. Still there was no response. Emil picked up his things. Esmer's Tribe scattered in the summer heat, roaming for food, sometimes miles apart from one another. But Esmer preferred to stay in the area, sleeping in trees or underneath the small wood huts that served the cats as shelter during Earthsleep.

If Esmer wouldn't come to him, he'd go to her.

After checking several of her favorite spots, Emil found Esmer dozing in a tree. The gray spotted cat was stretched out on a branch, one paw dangling down. There was another cat-Sune with her, a tawny gold male with ink-dark spots. His sleek head rested on her hindquarters, and he was batting lazily at Esmer's twitching tail.

"Esmer," Emil said.

Esmer's eyes opened into thin slits. Then she closed them again and turned her head, a gesture Emil knew meant *Go away. Not today.*

"Please, Esmer. I need to talk to you."

The male cat chirped at Esmer. She purred back and pushed herself up, arching her back in a luxurious stretch. Then she leaped down, changing to human before her feet hit the ground.

"What's going on?" she said, covering her mouth as she yawned.

"I need your help," Emil said. "It's about Stefan."

"Again?" Esmer looked up at the male cat. "Sorry, Ashin. Looks like our afternoon's been canceled."

There was a flicker, and a man with dark-gold hair and an annoyed expression sat on the branch, swinging his feet. "Pity," he said. He looked down at Emil. "Hello, human."

"Hello, cat," Emil responded. Ashin was one of the wilder members of Esmer's Tribe. Over the years, he and Emil had settled into a kind of thorny respect.

"Come to drag Esmer off to deal with more human problems?" Ashin continued.

Emil bit back his retort. Because that was exactly what he'd come to do.

"I just wanted to tell her I'm leaving," he said instead. He shifted his gaze to Esmer. "Stefan's run away to Kamal, and I'm going after him."

"What?" Esmer's head whipped around. "Ashin, I'll see you later."

The man groaned. "Really, Esmer? You're really going to follow him into who knows what?"

"Am I wearing a collar?" Esmer snapped. Her voice was a low growl. "Is there anyone's name around my neck? No. I do what I want, Ashin."

"I know, *striikaaraka*, I know." Ashin jumped down and ran a hand over Esmer's cheek. "Please be careful."

Esmer leaned into his touch. "I will."

Ashin touched his forehead to hers, then shifted back into cat form. He leaped back into the tree and away.

"He doesn't like me much," Emil said.

"He doesn't like being disturbed after a hunt," Esmer said. "And he worries." She hummed softly, a lazy smile crossing her face. "But he does have his good qualities. Now tell me what happened with Stefan."

Emil told her the whole story, including the fight with Stefan.

"I told him he was a disaster, Esmer, that he was tearing the camp apart." Saying the words again made them sound even worse. Guilt twisted inside Emil like sharp wire. "I told him Father was right about him. And now he's gone. If he gets killed . . ."

Esmer put a hand on his arm. "Stefan's too stubborn to get killed. Besides, we'll find him first."

"We?" Emil said.

"Of course," Esmer said. "Like I'd let you go alone." Her words were brisk, but her gold-flecked eyes were wide, the pupils dilated.

Esmer, Emil realized with a start, was frightened.

He set down his things and took her by the shoulders. She was so small, and her head barely reached Emil's collarbone. Her black hair was coming out of its loose braid, the gray streak plainly visible.

"Esmer, I'm going to the capital," he said. "That means walls and chaos and people everywhere. I admit, I was going to ask you to come with me. But Ashin's right: this isn't your problem. It's mine."

Esmer looked up at him. "Emil, when we met, I asked you for a promise. Do you remember?"

Emil remembered. Esmer in human form, crouching on a tree branch, her thin legs pulled up and her eyes round and frightened like they were now, Emil looking up at her.

Come down and play with me.

How do I know you aren't dangerous?

I'm not. I won't hurt you.

Humans lie.

I don't.

Swear you won't lie to me, ever. I'll smell it if you do.

It was the first pact he and Esmer had ever made, back when their friendship was an awkward thing, full of sharp edges and fears.

The Sune possessed the ability to speak mind-to-mind among each other, and Esmer had been nervous about playing with a human, someone whose thoughts were murky and dark to her. So Emil had promised.

I'll never lie to you. I swear.

"Look me in the eye and tell me you can do this alone," Esmer said. Her hands came up, grabbing his wrists with surprising strength. "Look at me and tell me you don't need help finding Stefan."

Emil let go of her. "What about Ashin?"

"He'll keep," Esmer said. "Stefan may not, though. Now do you want my help or not?"

Emil opened his mouth, then shut it again. "Damn it, Esmer," he said after a moment.

Esmer picked up his bedroll, slinging it over her shoulder. She flashed him a feral, triumphant smile.

"That's what I thought," she said.

25

Mara

MARA WOKE TO a soft scratching noise. For a moment, she couldn't remember where she was; then it came back: the fair, Emil, Revathi, Kamal, the palace. She was still holding the wooden tiger, cradled in her palm. Mara tucked it under her pillow and sat up, squinting in the light that came through the broad, arched windows. She must have been more tired than she thought.

Revathi was sitting at the low desk, her legs folded under her as she wrote. She still wore her long-sleeved sleeping robe, and her hair fell loose around her shoulders.

"You're up," Revathi said. "Good." She set down her reed pen and sprinkled sand on the ink to dry it. "I keep asking Grandmother if we can move to charcoal writing sticks instead of ink, but she doesn't like them. Says a lady should never have smudged hands." She lifted the document to her lips and blew. "I'd rather have charcoal smudges than all this grit."

Mara padded over to the desk, enjoying the coolness of the carpet on her bare feet. "What are you writing?"

"Nothing special." The noble girl waved the rice paper gently to finish drying it and then rolled it up and tied it with a small piece of twine. She placed it onto a small pyramid of similar messages nearby. "Orders for the kitchens, a few notes for the head servants, approvals of hiring requests, and suggestions for some new ideas for the gardens. Grandmother and I are splitting my parents' duties for the summer. She's handling the delicate political problems, which leaves me with the day-to-day management."

Scattered clumps of inky sand covered the surface of the desk. Mara rubbed one between her fingers.

"Sounds like a lot," she said.

"It is," Revathi said. "At least when I marry Tamas, I'll have a smaller household to run." She smiled as she said it, but her voice was wistful, and her hand touched the scrolls lightly as she rose. "There's some fresh chai in that pot if you want any. I'm not with the princes today, so I thought I'd give you a tour of the palace. You can watch me do all my most boring noble duties. Also, we still need to talk to Garen and get you permission to stay here."

"If you think it's necessary," Mara said. Despite what Revathi had said earlier, she was wary of drawing too much attention to herself.

"It is." Revathi knelt by the clothes chest at the foot of the mattress and pulled out a dusky purple asar with silver embroidery.

"Like I said, access behind the Lotus Wall is forbidden to anyone not directly serving the Imperial family. According to the rules, I shouldn't even have let you stay here last night, so the quicker we fix things, the better." Revathi turned her back on Mara, stepped out of her sleeping robe, and pulled a long-sleeved undershirt over her head. Mara could see the movement of her ribs under the skin.

Mara poured herself some tea. It was hot and creamy and spicy, and even breathing in the steam made her feel more alert. The warmth of the cup was comforting, too, and Mara held it close. She'd have to ask Revathi about free time, at some point. She wouldn't be able to find a charge if she was spending every minute in the palace.

"Should be easy to find Garen," Revathi continued. "Lately he's been spending most of his time with the princes."

"I thought you said he was the Emperor's bodyguard?"

The noble girl wrapped the asar around herself with a quick, practiced ease. "Usually, yes. But the Empress died this spring, and Saro is still in mourning. He mostly stays in his private quarters. If you do meet him by chance, don't take it personally if he doesn't notice you. Just bow and then wait until he passes by."

Revathi pulled the curtains open, then took some seeds from a small glazed jar. She scattered them on the windowsill, whistling as she did so. A crowd of songbirds fluttered to the sill, their feathers flashing red and black and green.

Mara held out her hand and imitated one of the birdcalls, a liquid fall of notes that brought a scarlet-and-brown bird to her hand. Revathi let out a delighted squeal.

"Oh, that's wonderful!" she said, clasping her hands together. For a moment, all her reserve was gone and her face glowed. "How did you do that?"

"I grew up in the woods," Mara said. "I heard more birdcalls than I did human speech." The bird decided her empty hand wasn't going to yield any food and flew back to the others.

"Could you teach me?" Revathi asked, eagerness in every line of her body. "Please? I taught them to come to my whistle, but I'd love to know the calls."

"They're pretty easy once you get the trick," Mara said. She and her siblings had learned the birdcalls as youngsters. Originally, it had been just something to help them hunt, but it turned into a game, a way to spend the sleepy summer afternoons. The memory sent a spasm of pain through her chest, and she turned away. "So the Emperor's in mourning?" she asked, changing the subject. "And half the court is in the west for the summer. Not to be rude, Revathi, but who's running the Empire?"

"I am," said a smooth voice.

Standing in the doorway was a heavyset man in the most elaborate court outfit Mara had ever seen, even in the scrolls in the Order's library. A silk, indigo-colored robe brushed his feet, and over it he wore a heavy vest of deep saffron yellow. Both the vest and the robe were so thickly crusted with silver embroidery that it looked like the man's clothing was covered with frost. He had peculiar gray-brown eyes, set in a lined face, and there was gray in his beard. He didn't appear to have any weapons.

"Lord u'Gra," Revathi said, and her voice was so completely neutral, so unemotional, that Mara had to push down the urge to shove this stranger out of the room. But when Revathi put her hands together and bowed, Mara did the same.

"Lady Revathi," the man said, inclining his head. "I hoped to find you yesterday."

"I was with your son yesterday," Revathi said. "He was kind enough to escort me on a shopping expedition."

"Ah, young love," the man said, stroking his beard. "The boy I raised would rather face a herd of angry elephants than a market. You are a remarkably softening influence on him."

"Tamas is very concerned with my safety," Revathi said. "He came as my protection." She ran her fingers through her loose mass of hair. "May I ask what prompted you to call on me in my private quarters before I'm fully dressed? Surely not a desire to discuss my shopping habits."

The man smiled, a hollow smile like a painted mask's. "I wished to invite you and the Lady Ekisa to dinner with Tamas and me. A . . . family affair, shall we say?" His eyes slid to Mara. "Though if you wish to bring a friend, you may."

"Mara is my new guard," Revathi said. "Tamas thought I might need one."

The man studied Mara as if he was assessing her for market. "I would not have thought Tamas to have such initiative," he said. "She looks competent enough, I suppose." He looked back at Revathi. "I assume tonight will be acceptable."

"You assume incorrectly," Revathi said. "As flattered as I am by your generous invitation, tonight is far too short a notice. We haven't a free night for at least a week."

The man's fingers curled almost into fists, then relaxed. "Forgive me for my presumption," he said. "I thought that with your parents away and the court quiet, you would be searching for ways to occupy your time."

Revathi's back tensed, but the pleasant expression on her face didn't change. "Sadly, the house of sa'Hoi carries too much responsibility for that," she said evenly. "And my parents' absence only increases the burden on my grandmother and me. Our days are more than full."

Mara thought she saw a frown cross Lord u'Gra's face, but she blinked and it was gone. "Of course," he said, bowing. "Perhaps you could consult with your grandmother and settle on a date that would work for both of you?"

"Of course," Revathi said, her voice sweet. "We'll let you know as soon as possible. I do have things to attend to this morning, so unless you have anything else to discuss . . ."

"Don't let me keep you from your duties. I look forward to having you in my house very soon." Lord u'Gra bowed again. Then he turned and strode away.

Mara waited a few moments, then poked her head out of the room to make sure he was gone. "Well," she said, trying to sound casual. Best to hide her intense dislike of the man until she knew more about him. "He was certainly insistent."

"Sathvik u'Gra is a self-important, vicious warthog," Revathi said, twisting her hair a little tighter with every word. She pinned it into a low knot and scowled. "But when he says he runs the Empire, he's not far off the mark. He's very close to Emperor Saro right now."

"How did *that* happen?" Mara asked, startled out of her caution. She wouldn't have put a man who smiled that way in charge of *anything*.

Revathi went to her shelf and pulled off a carved wooden box inlaid with ebony. She pulled something out of it, a long, thin metal object topped by a butterfly made of amethysts.

"Sathvik u'Gra lost his wife last year," she said, sliding the object into her thick hair so that just the butterfly was visible, sparkling against her dark waves. "It gives him a card to play, a way to connect with the Emperor in his grief. People in pain are easily swayed. Not to mention that Sathvik is the current head of the Council of Lesser Princes, which is where all the powerful nobles sit. He's good at what he does, and like his son, he's very charming when it suits him."

She put both hands on her hips and looked Mara up and down. "Enough about court politics. We need to get you cleaned up and properly attired."

"Oh, right." Mara looked down at her dirty tunic and trousers and put a hand up to her short, messy hair. "I'm not used to thinking about how I look."

"I've noticed," Revathi said, a smile playing around her mouth. "It's refreshing." She gestured Mara out of the room and followed her. "But rule two in the Lotus Court is this: never forget that appearance can be a weapon."

Revathi led Mara to a bathing room as large as the bedchamber they'd just left. It was tiled with pale stone painted with swirls of blue and white. On one wall, someone had painted a large portrait of one of the Ancestors, a woman with loose, wavy hair and an owl on her shoulder. Her hand was held up, palm facing out, and her face was calm and kind. Several bronze sculptures of owls had been placed about the room as well.

There were several women already in the sunken tubs. Water gleamed on their brown shoulders and shone on their wet, dark hair. Flower petals filled the water around them, drifting swirls of red, yellow, and purple. The air smelled of roses.

Servants moved between the baths, refreshing the water, adding more flowers, or offering trays of sliced fruit. Revathi gestured to them, and before Mara knew it, she was stripped and pushed gently into one of the unoccupied baths. The next half hour was a blur of sensation, the feel of warm water on her skin, soft petals between her fingers, and firm fingers washing her hair.

When she was allowed to dry off, one of the servants gave her new clothing, a supple leather tunic and matching trousers. The clothes were dyed a soft gray and trimmed with red and brown embroidery. Mara slid them on and buckled her dagger belt around her waist. The familiar weight on her hips was reassuring.

There was a mirror on the wall and Mara walked over to it, unable to resist the urge to look at her human form. There were no mirrors in the Order, only the distorted reflections on metal and rippled glimpses in water. It had been years since Mara had truly seen herself at all.

The girl in the mirror had a straight, unsmiling mouth. Her wet hair had been combed back, making her face look severe. The gold flecks in her eyes had faded to invisibility, and she moved like a trained warrior, not a wild thing.

She looked . . . human. As if she'd never been anything else.

Suddenly Mara couldn't bear to look into her own eyes. She turned and left the room.

26

Emil

WHEN EMIL AND Esmer reached the high walls surrounding Kamal, Emil stopped to stare. "It's bigger than I
remembered."

Esmer didn't comment. She'd changed to cat form a couple of
times on the way to the city, running circles around Emil and
darting off into the woods. Now she looked up at the huge main
gate, her lips thin and tight.

"Esmer . . ."

"Emil, if you ask me one more time if I'm sure, I will scratch
you."

Emil swallowed the words he'd been about to say and walked
forward to the registration table.

"Emil Arvi," he told the scribe at the table. "Here to look for
work."

The scribe nodded to a nearby soldier, who stepped forward and grabbed Emil's scarred shoulder. His grip was hard and painful, his fingers grinding into the raised pattern of Emil's scars. "He's Wind caste," the soldier said.

"Of course he is," the scribe muttered. "All right, boy, listen up. You'll have three days and two nights to obtain a work permit." The scribe spoke in the rapid monotone of someone who says the same thing many times a day. His reed pen scratched across the papers in front of him. "If at the end of that time, you have not obtained a permit, you must leave the city. It will be another three days and two nights before you're allowed back in to try again. If you fail to leave the city when your trial time is up and we catch you, you'll be marked with white-flower dye and thrown out. You won't be able to come back until the dye fades."

"How long does that take?" Emil asked.

"Anywhere from thirty to fifty days," the scribe said. "Long enough to starve. I wouldn't recommend it."

Emil swallowed. "Understood."

"Good." The scribe finished writing, blotted the paper, and handed it to Emil. It had the mark of the day and season on it and was imprinted with a seal. "Present this to the person who hires you, and they will give you a full work permit. Next!"

Esmer strode forward to the registration table, her neck straight and her chin up. The scribe raised his eyebrows.

"Name?"

"Esmer, of the Marjara-Sune."

"Huh." The scribe looked her up and down. "Asatya, how's the Sune quota?"

A man wearing captain's cuffs unrolled one of the rice scrolls on the table and scanned it. "Five working in the Wind Circle and three in the Bamboo pleasure quarters. There's that pet of Lord u'Gra's, and of course, Garen. . . ."

"Garen doesn't count," the scribe said, his voice sour. "The Emperor has made that very clear."

"Well, he's the Emperor." The captain shrugged. "If he wants to make exceptions to the law, who are we to object?"

"I still don't like it," the scribe muttered. He'd started writing again, not even looking in Esmer's direction. "It's not orderly. The whole reason to have a quota is so we can keep an eye on them, and keep out the really dangerous ones. We wouldn't have this problem if they were in a caste of their own."

"Good luck with trying to convince the Council of Lesser Princes of that," the captain said. He rolled the scroll back up. "Anyway, looks like we have nine Sune right now. The quota's fifteen, and her Tribe is listed as spotted cats. Harmless. She'll pass." He turned to the soldier who had checked Emil's scars. "Mark her and let her go through."

Throughout the conversation, Esmer hadn't moved, just stared straight ahead with no expression. But now Emil saw her fingers bend a little, as if she were flexing nonexistent claws.

The other soldier grinned. He grabbed one of Esmer's hands, drawing an X in black dye across it.

"Going to work in a pleasure house too, sweet one?" he asked, rubbing a thumb across her skin. He lowered his voice. "I hear there's quite a demand for exotic pets there."

Emil took a step forward, but Esmer jerked her free hand at him, a clear signal to stop. She put her chin down and stared at the man holding on to her. The gold flecks in her brown eyes were very bright, her pupils dilated wide. The look of a hunter about to pounce.

She stared at him until the soldier's grin faded, and he dropped her hand. "Get out of here," he said, taking a step back. "You're holding up the line."

Esmer walked through the gate. Emil following.

The transients' area seemed more chaotic than he remembered, a barrage of noise and smells and shifting people. Esmer had one hand up, as if to shield herself from the noise. Emil put a hand on her shoulder and steered her through the collections of sleeping mats, looking for a quieter place to stop.

Soon the transients' area gave way to narrow streets and small, jumbled dwellings. Most of the houses were made out of scrap wood, or tent material, or some combination of the two, and they were piled together like rolls of fabric in a sack. The noise of the gate quieted, replaced by the soft buzz of conversations and the shouts of children. But the smells were as chaotic as ever: sweaty skin and muddy feet, boiled rice and spiced tea, and the pervasive scent of dirty water from the canal.

Emil pulled Esmer into a small corner between two houses. "Back there, with the soldiers . . . is it always like that?"

The gold in Esmer's eyes was dull, like tarnished bronze, and her shoulders slumped. "No," she said, then fell silent as a man pushing a wooden tea cart walked by their alcove. The cups stacked on the cart clanked and rattled in protest as he passed, and Esmer watched him for a moment before speaking again. Her voice was soft.

"Sometimes it's worse."

Emil frowned. He'd just assumed Esmer never went to Kamal because she hated the crowds and the noise and the smell of the city. He'd never actually asked her why she didn't like it.

"I'm sorry," he said. "I didn't know."

"No reason for you to," Esmer said, lifting her shoulders in a brief shrug. "Haven't you ever wondered why the Sune and the Kildi get along so well? It's because your people are the only ones who see us as human. Mostly, anyway."

Emil thought of his father, the disapproval on his face when he spoke of Emil and Esmer possibly being in a relationship. Had that been because Esmer was a Sune? "I don't understand," he said. "What are they all afraid of?"

"Everything," Esmer said. "Sune live outside the system; we don't fit into the social order. We're not slotted into neat, controllable boxes; we live wild and as we please. And we remind them of something they would like to forget, that once there was powerful magic in this land. Our transformations are fueled by magic; it runs in our blood and strengthens our bones. It's one thing to tell stories and legends about magic, but actually having it in your city, walking your streets?" A faint smile crossed her face. "It makes people uncomfortable. The fact that some of us can turn into huge, dangerous animals probably doesn't help."

"I didn't realize . . . ," Emil said, the words hanging awkwardly between them. *I didn't realize your people were as hated as mine are. I didn't realize you were hurting too.*

"Well, now you do," Esmer said. Her voice was back to its calm, practical tone, but her fingers rubbed against the black mark on her hand. "So now what? Are we going to camp out by the gate like everyone else?"

Emil reached into his tunic and pulled out the paper Lel had given him. "Not yet," he said. "I have someone I need to find first."

He started walking again, and Esmer fell into step beside him. They walked until the street opened up into a wide square of rough stone with a gurgling fountain in the center. Cramped booths lined the edges, selling everything from sticks of skewered meat to rough-made daggers and glass bead necklaces. A few sellers had splurged on jasmine vines that crawled over the wood of their booths. The scent of the tiny flowers made the air seem a little fresher.

All the sellers—and they were all men—bore either the small gold hoops in both ears that marked Bamboo merchant families or the single earring of a craftsman. They were dressed in rougher clothes than Emil had seen on most Bamboo caste, and most of them had swords or daggers hanging in plain sight on their belts.

"Doesn't look like the safest place to conduct business," Esmer remarked, and Emil had to agree.

"They're selling the castoffs of their trade," he said. "But there's still enough value in their goods to make robbery a problem."

"You've been here before?" Esmer asked.

"Not for several years," Emil said. "I came on a trip with my uncle Pali. Kildi aren't allowed to sell inside the walls, but he comes here a few times a year to make connections with the clothiers and tailors and arrange for future sales." He scanned the square. It was thronged with Wind caste workers, most buying mugs of hot tea and slices of sour bread. "One of his biggest customers sells scrap here, and the family should have a booth right over . . . there."

The booth in question was held by a lanky man in a blue tunic. A life of bending over counters had hunched his back and rounded his shoulders, but his smile beamed like a candle flame as Emil approached.

"Need scraps for mending and sewing?" he called. "I have good quality ones, all double-washed and durable. Cotton, silk, thick wool, even cashmere."

Emil examined the baskets of scraps on the counter. They were organized by color, and he spotted a basket of undyed material that looked familiar. "Is that Kildi cashmere?"

"It is indeed," the man said. "My family has a contact in one of the Kildi clans who sells us the castoffs for a good price."

"Pali Arvi?" Emil asked.

"Why, yes," the man said. "How did you know?"

Emil put his hands together and bowed. "I'm his nephew."

The man's smile widened, and he bowed back. "How wonderful! Always nice to meet a member of the Arvi. Are you here to talk to the merchants? Pali usually speaks to my brother, and he isn't here today."

"Actually," Emil said, "I'm looking for someone." He held up Lel's scrap of paper. "Do you know anyone by this name?"

The man's face closed, his smiling mouth flattening into a thin line. "That way," he said at last, pointing with two fingers to the other side of the market. "The red doors." Then he looked past Emil to a pair of Wind caste girls. "Sturdy scraps for mending, ladies? I've got all kinds."

Emil stood there for another moment, waiting to see if he could get any more information, but the man ignored him.

"That was strange," Esmer said as they moved away from the booth. "Who is this Heema person anyway?"

Emil looked down at the scrawled name on the paper. "I think we're about to find out."

27
Mara

REVATHI WAS WAITING outside the bathing room, her dark hair still damp from her own bath, giving instructions to yet another servant. She looked up as Mara came out.

Mara spread her hands and gave a little spin. Her short, damp hair flopped over her forehead. "Well?"

"You'll do," Revathi said. She turned back to the waiting woman and rattled off a complicated set of orders, most of which seemed to be about schedules and laundering. She dismissed the servant and turned back to Mara. "Come on. I'll introduce you to Garen and we'll get some breakfast."

Mara's stomach rumbled at the mention of food. Revathi led her down another long hall, ducking through a sheer silver curtain. "That was the women's area of the palace," she explained, gesturing back to where they had come from. "When the Empress was alive, it was strictly women only—no men allowed—but since she's gone and there are no princesses to guard, people are getting lax." She paused. "Mara, there's something you need to know about Garen. . . ."

"Who needs to know something about me?" said a deep voice.

Mara's head snapped up, and she stepped in front of Revathi without thinking.

But there was no danger—it was only a man and a boy in the hallway. The man was tall and broad-shouldered, with graying brown hair and muscular arms. He wore a sword the length of Mara's leg buckled over his dark-blue tunic. Mara let her gaze flicker up, meeting his eyes.

His surprised, *gold-flecked* eyes.

Mara sucked in a sharp breath. The man's eyes narrowed and he sniffed the air. Then he stepped in front of the boy, shoulders up. A muffled growl rose from his throat.

Who are you? he roared into her head. And the force of his will, the sheer power of it, struck Mara like a body blow. Her spine hit something hard and she realized she'd backed into the wall.

This is my territory. The man stepped forward. *And I don't know you.* His mind-voice was deep and strong, with a rumbly under-tone that Mara recognized.

One of the Great Bears, she thought. *Nishvana help me.*

The bears that lived in the forests of the East were the stuff of legend. Huge and fierce and massively strong. Even Mara's Tribe avoided them.

The magic uncoiled inside her, hot and insistent. *Danger. Change now.*

No, Mara thought fiercely, digging her fingers into the inlaid wall behind her. *No. I won't.*

As if from far away, she felt Revathi tug her arm and heard voices, sharp and questioning. But Mara couldn't look away from the man in front of her. He was still watching her, not attacking. Not yet. But his eyes never left hers, and his hand was on his sword.

Identify yourself, he commanded. *You don't smell Sune, not entirely. But I know what you are. Identify yourself before I lose my patience.*

Mara raised her chin and exposed her throat. *I am* nikrysta, she sent, using the ancient word for outcast. *My name is Mara. I have confined myself to human form of my own free will and sworn the oath of Khatar. Your Emperor and his court have nothing to fear from me.*

The man took a step back and broke eye contact.

Mara pulled herself away from the wall. Her legs were shaking, and her breathing was ragged and loud in the silent hallway.

Mara turned to see Revathi staring at her, eyes wide. The boy who'd been standing with the bear-man was staring at her too. He was about ten years old, wearing a midnight-blue tunic that went down to his knees, with silver embroidery around the neck and sleeves. There was a lotus tattooed at the base of his neck. Unlike Revathi's flower tattoo, this one wasn't gold, but white. The mark of the Imperial family.

"Garen," the boy said, and his voice was calm and unafraid. "I would like an explanation, please."

The big man bowed very low. "I have caused you anxiety and confusion, Prince Paithal, and for this I am deeply sorry. I was taken by surprise."

"By her." The prince gestured at Mara. "Why?"

"She is . . ." The man hesitated, glancing at Revathi. "She is also Sune, my lord."

And so the Third Lotus Emperor made his peace with the Sune

With those strange creatures

Neither animal nor human

Creatures of magic

In a world that had left magic far behind.

And this was his decree:

That they would take no human life

That they would consent to bear an identifying mark while inside
a city

And that they would allow humans in their territory to hunt and
live as they wished.

And the Sune elders agreed

For they were tired

Of being hunted

Of being hated

Of being feared

And there was no war anymore.

From *Battles of Spear and Claw*, a story-song of the Sune war

28

Mara

MARA HEARD REVATHI'S swift intake of breath. The prince put his head to one side.

"You didn't know?" the prince said, eyeing Revathi.

Revathi shook her head. Her eyes flicked to Mara. "You–you–"

"I'm sorry," Mara said, hunching her shoulders. "I should have told you, but . . ." But that would have meant explaining her past and her shame, would have uncovered her own private wounds still raw and bleeding.

It took her a minute to realize Revathi wasn't angry. Instead she was . . .

"Are you *laughing* at me?" Mara asked.

"No," Revathi said, her voice gasping and strangled. Her hands came up to hide her face, and her body shook.

The prince was smiling, his head tilted to one side. Even Garen looked amused.

Mara couldn't share their laughter. Her hands were still trembling. She'd forgotten what it was like to wander into another powerful Sune's territory. All Sune were territorial to some degree; it was an instinct as strong as the magic itself. Most of the time, the confrontation involved force of will instead of actual fighting, but not always.

Standing between the tiger and Stefan hadn't felt like this, probably because the other tiger hadn't felt truly threatened. And Esmer was a spotted cat, not a top predator like Mara was. Had been.

Mara would have to be more cautious. Confrontations like this were dangerous, to her and her control.

Revathi finally managed to stop laughing. Her cheeks were flushed and her huge, dark eyes shone.

"I'm sorry," she said. "I'm not laughing at you. Well, not just at you. I'm also laughing at *me*." She straightened her asar. "I thought I had you all figured out. It's been a really long time since someone's surprised me like that."

Mara frowned. Surprises were not a good thing in her experience, certainly nothing to giggle about.

I do not understand humans, she thought.

It's all right, tiger child. Garen sent in response. *I don't understand them all the time either. And I've been protecting Saro and his family since he was only the heir.*

Mara looked up, startled. She'd forgotten to shield her thoughts. It had been so long since she'd had to worry about being overheard.

Garen was smiling with understanding. It made Mara feel a little less lost.

Revathi turned to the prince and knelt down. "Forgive us if we frightened you, Your Highness," she said, bowing her head. "It was unintentional."

After a second's hesitation, Mara copied her. "Forgive me," she mumbled, ducking her head. "I wasn't prepared."

Prince Paithal put out a hand. "Both of you may rise. You are forgiven." He looked up at his guard. "Lots of people aren't prepared for Garen, are they, Garen?"

"It's not my place to say, Highness," Garen said gravely, but Mara thought he sounded amused.

The prince moved his eyes back to Mara. "Are you a bear too?"

"No," Mara said. "I'm not."

A gap-toothed smile flashed against Paithal's brown skin. "That's too bad," he said. "I like bears."

Revathi put a hand to her mouth, hiding a snicker. Mara felt a flush creep up her neck.

Do I need to tell him I was a tiger? she sent to Garen. *I don't want to scare him.*

Paithal doesn't frighten easily, Garen said. *But if you don't wish to discuss it here, I can tell him later. But Revathi has a right to know who she's dealing with.*

Garen turned to Paithal. "You will have time tomorrow to speak further with Revathi and her new friend, my lord," he said. "Now we must get you to your lessons."

"Of course," Paithal said, looking startled. "I forgot." He

dipped his head. "I look forward to our next meeting. You are dismissed."

Mara and Revathi bowed again and waited as the two walked away. Mara thought that they made an incongruous pair, the young prince and the huge guard walking together. There was an ease in the way they stood together that spoke of more than master and servant, something that reminded Mara of her own family. Paithal looked up at Garen and said something, and the man laughed.

Maybe someday Mara would have that kind of relationship, that kind of trust with someone. In the meantime, Garen was right. Mara owed Revathi an explanation.

There was a tray of hot rice cakes, as well as a bowl full of apples, papayas, and pomegranates, in Revathi's room.

"How do they do that?" Mara asked. "Make sure the food is still hot?"

"I've honestly never thought about it," Revathi said. She sat down at her desk and reached for a rice cake. She tore a piece and dipped it in one of the small bowls next to the tray.

Mara stood and watched her, feeling awkward.

"Oh, for goodness' sake," Revathi said. "Go on and eat." She gestured to the food. "The dips are mint, lime, and tamarind chutneys. I don't care for spicy food in the morning."

Mara sat. Anxiety swirled inside her. She ate in silence, steeling herself to answer Revathi's questions.

"So," Revathi said, licking the remains of the mint chutney off

her fingertips and reaching for another rice cake. "You're Sune."
She waited for Mara's nod, then continued. "And you don't want
to talk about why you left your Tribe."

Mara almost choked on a piece of rice cake. "How did you
know?"

"Mara, I'm not stupid," Revathi said. She started ticking off
things on her fingers. "I know loner Sune are very rare, so this is
something you chose for a reason. And I know that the Order of
Khatar has a reputation as place where someone can regain lost
honor. I'd be a fool to assume that those two things aren't connected, and as I said, I'm not a fool." She dipped her next piece of
rice cake into the lime.

"I'd like to know what kind of Sune you are," she said. "But
that's just because I'm a curious person. As far as I'm concerned,
your past is your own."

"Thank you," Mara said, meaning it. A faint smile drifted
across Revathi's face.

"Tamas won't be pleased," she said. "He doesn't care for the
Sune."

"Why not?"

"Oh, he thinks they're dangerous," Revathi said. "And they live
outside the caste system and worship their own gods and aren't
under enough control. Plus, his father employs one, and I don't
think Tamas likes her." She made a face. "I don't care for her
either, actually."

"Tamas's father employs a Sune?" Mara asked. "What kind?"

Revathi put her head to one side. "You know, I'm not sure. I don't think he's ever said." She shrugged. "Anyway, Tamas doesn't like Sune, for much the same reasons that he hates the Kildi."

"Are there a lot of people who feel that way?" Mara asked, making a note to ask about the other Sune later.

"About the Kildi or the Sune?"

"Both."

Revathi spoke as if she were choosing her words carefully. "Most nobles don't really interact with Kildi or Sune much," she said. "We barely interact with regular Wind caste, except to hire them on occasion. We're not familiar with you, and unfamiliar things are frightening. Some people let that fear tip into hate."

Mara shifted uneasily. "Do we have to tell people? About me?"

Revathi paused. "I don't see why," she said finally. "I mean, you should be registered on the Sune rolls, but if Garen doesn't insist, I'm not going to worry about it." She shrugged. "It's not the worst secret I've ever had to keep. Besides, no offense, but I really don't want the kind of attention that having a Sune bodyguard will bring."

"None taken," Mara said. She took a moment to center herself.

"I am . . . I *was* Kishna-Sune." The words felt strange and distant on her tongue. "My Tribe lives in the north, at the base of the mountains." She swallowed. "The humans call us the dark tigers. Shadow beasts."

Revathi's eyes widened, but she didn't flinch. "I've heard of those. Mostly in stories around fire pits, though. I've never known anyone who's actually seen them."

"We . . . they are very hard to see," Mara said. "That's one of the reasons for the name." Her smile felt shaky and small. "Humans don't like things that come out of the darkness."

"I suppose we don't," Revathi said. She studied Mara for a moment. "Would you be angry if I said I'm relieved?"

"Relieved?"

Revathi's eyes crinkled at the corners. "Because I know Tamas wouldn't have hired you if he knew you were Sune, and that means you're probably not a spy."

"I *told* you I wasn't," Mara said. "I said it repeatedly."

"Repeating a lie doesn't make it true," Revathi responded, unruffled. "You would have said the same if you had been a spy."

"I suppose that's true," Mara admitted. An idea teased the edges of her brain, an idea for how to thank Revathi for keeping her secret. "Revathi," she said, "would you like me to teach you to fight?"

Revathi's hand—which had been going for the fruit bowl—stopped midreach. "You mean teach me to use a blade?" she asked. "So I can defend myself?"

"If that's what you want," Mara said. "Some of my fellow novices in the Order knew how to knife fight." She touched the blade at her waist. "It's a bit different from using a *kattari*, but I can teach you the basics, show you how to stand and roll and use what's around you to your advantage. I can show you the stances tonight, and we wouldn't have to tell Tamas."

A slow smile bloomed on Revathi's face. "No," she said softly, her eyes sparking. "We wouldn't have to tell Tamas, would we? All right, I accept. And . . . thank you."

"It will be my pleasure," Mara said, smiling back. For the first time since she'd left the Order, she felt . . . hopeful. Confident. She didn't have to hide from Revathi that she was a Sune. She had a whole city full of people who could be her charge, and she had someone to help while she was looking.

Maybe she would land on her feet after all.

29

Emil

EMIL AND ESMER walked in the direction the scrap man had pointed, leaving the open square of the Wind Market behind.

"So assuming this Heema person can help us, what's our plan?" Esmer asked. "How are we going to find Stefan?"

Emil ducked under a line of laundry that had been strung across the road. "I have to find someone to give me a work permit. There's no way we can find Stefan in three days."

"While you're looking for work, I can start searching," Esmer said. "That will help."

"Good idea," Emil said, dodging another drying line. The tunics hanging were still wet and smelled faintly like canal water. "We can start in the Wind Circle and work our way inward. The Inner City is going to be a problem, though. No one from Wind caste is allowed in, not unless they work for someone who lives there."

"Let's worry about one thing at a time," Esmer said. She gestured to a nearby cluster of dwellings. "Look, red doors."

It was hard to miss them. Three crooked little entrances, each covered with a curtain of thick red fabric, a splash of color on the chaotic street. There was a symbol embroidered on the doors in gold thread, a symbol Emil didn't recognize.

Emil tapped on the frame of the first door with his fingers.

The curtain was pushed aside and a little girl peered out. Her black hair was matted, and smudges of dirt darkened her copper skin. Her shoulder blades were thin and sharp under her shirt, and the hand holding the curtain open was missing a finger.

"Hello," Emil said, squatting down a little to avoid looming over the child. "We're looking for Heema. Is she here?"

The girl stared at him with wide, dark eyes. Then she disappeared, the curtain swishing shut behind her. There were footsteps and the sound of murmuring voices.

Emil straightened, stepping backward as a man appeared in the doorway. He was short and thick, with a full beard. A broad scar ran from the top of his eyebrow, straight down over his cheekbone, almost to his jaw. The eye in the path of the scar was white and unseeing. The man held up a thick club.

"Who looks for Heema?" he said.

"Emil Arvi," Emil said, loudly enough that whoever was inside could hear him. "I was sent here by a man named Lel."

"Let them in, Giri," a female voice called. "I will speak to them."

The man scowled but stood aside, holding the curtain open. Emil ducked inside and Esmer followed.

The house was a single dirt-floored room, with several bed-rolls stacked in one corner and a small fire pit in the center. The ceiling was made from beams of wood with pieces of goatskin stretched across them. Emil saw that one of the pieces had been tacked back, creating a hole in the ceiling, where light and air could come in.

A veiled woman sat cross-legged on the floor, slicing onions and eggplant with a battered knife. The little girl squatted beside her. The woman looked up as they came in.

"You are of the Arvi?" she asked, and her voice was rich and deep, the tones of a trained singer. "Then show me your clan mark."

Emil hesitated, then pulled up his sleeve, revealing the stylized tiger inked just below the inside of his elbow.

The woman leaned forward, the thin pink fabric of her veil moving with her breath. After a moment, her grip on the knife relaxed. "It's all right, dearest," she said to the man with the cudgel. "He is who he says he is." Her head swiveled back to Emil. "Lelkhan sent you?"

"Yes," Emil said, exchanging a glance with Esmer. "But . . . I'm afraid I don't know why."

He held out the piece of paper, and Heema took it.

"That is his writing," she said. "Avahaa, go next door and join the other children. I'll call you when the food is ready."

The little girl nodded. Then, with another anxious glance at Emil and Esmer, she moved toward the door. The man with the cudgel put a hand on her head as she went by.

"It's all right, little bird," he said. "I'll keep her safe."

The girl smiled up at him and then darted out of the room.

Heema rose in a fluid movement, placed the knife in a small utensil pot, and bowed. "Welcome. May the road be easy on your feet, and may you find a place to call home."

Emil smiled at the traditional Wind caste blessing. "Same to you, lady," he said, bowing in return. "Forgive us for intruding."

"Welcome guests are never an intrusion," the woman said. She gathered up the slices of onions and eggplant from the woven mat and sprinkled them into a large iron pan that was suspended over the fire. The food sizzled as it hit the hot surface. "And if my brother sent you here, he had a reason."

"Your brother?" Emil couldn't stop his surprised reaction. "Lel is your brother?"

Heema laughed, and her laugh was as glorious as her voice. "He is indeed. And protective as only an older brother can be. I am not a secret he shares lightly, and I'm curious as to why he told you to find me." Her voice was still pleasant, but her shoulders were tense. Emil knew he was being tested.

"We're looking for *my* brother," Emil said. In a few brief sentences, he sketched out the situation: the riot, his and Stefan's fight, and Stefan running away. He included the confrontation with his father but didn't mention the mercenaries. Whatever Rajo and his men were up to, there was a good chance it wasn't legal. Stefan could be arrested, or worse.

"I have reason to believe he's somewhere in the city," he said instead. "And the people he's with . . . they're trouble."

"People often are," Heema commented. "So Lelkhan saw you

headed into the city alone and gave you my name. He must like you a great deal."

"He's family," Emil said. It must have been the right thing to say, because a bit of the stiffness left Heema's shoulders.

"How did you find us?"

Emil hesitated, and it was Esmer who answered. "We asked someone in the Wind Market," she said. "They were not . . . eager to help."

"If you asked one of the Bamboo merchants, I imagine not," Heema said, sounding both amused and sad. "The next time you're looking for something in the city, try and find a tea seller. They know everything." She made a sweeping gesture with her arm, indicating the tiny room. "We don't have much to offer, but you're welcome to stay as long as you need to."

The man in the doorway made a protesting noise. "Heema, we don't know who these people are!"

"They are Lelkhan's family, Giri," the woman said. "He sent them here, and we must help them. We can put them in the far room; there's no one there right now."

Giri blew out a breath. "Woman, your kind heart will be the death of me." He set down his club and crossed to Heema's side of the fire. Gently he kissed her forehead through the veil. "Why don't I take them outside so you can finish cooking? I promise not to rough them up."

Heema leaned into his touch. "There's clean water in the jar," she said. "I ran it through a cloth and boiled it this morning. They're probably thirsty after their trip."

"You're a jewel," Giri said. He grabbed three thick clay mugs from a stack of dishes and tossed one to Emil and Esmer each. "Water jug's the big one by the door," he said, gesturing. "You'll live longer in the Wind Circle if you don't drink the canal water."

Emil caught the cup with relief. In the Arvi camp, waste was done outside and discreetly covered up. But here the people used chamber pots, emptying them every night into the canal, where the steady flow of water would sweep it away by morning. But the river still smelled, of people, of waste, of muddy water. The idea of drinking from that foul-smelling water made his stomach turn.

The three dipped lukewarm water from the jar. Giri slid the lid back on and led them out of the warm room and across the beaten dirt path to the edge of the canal. Here the steady stream of people was more of a trickle, and the noise was less.

"Smells like an old stable, but at least there's a breeze," Giri said, as he sat down. He sipped his water. "Heema's decided to trust you, and I trust her. But if you bring any danger down on us . . ."

"Believe me," Emil said. "That's the last thing I want. I just want to find my brother."

"Kamal's a big place," Giri said, gesturing with his mug for emphasis. "It's going to be hard to find him if he doesn't want to be found. And you have to find a job, too. I won't hide you if you don't. Not even for Heema. She and those kids are the only family I have, and I won't risk them."

"I understand," Emil said. He ran a finger around the rough

edge of the clay mug. "Any ideas for how I can get a work permit?"

"Got any special skills?" Giri asked. "Sewing or cooking or a decent fighting style?"

"I can break down a tent," Emil said, a little bitterly. "I can clip a goat and shovel dung and I'm a fair hand at bargaining."

"What about your girl there?" Giri said, nodding at Esmer.

"I'm not his girl," Esmer snapped. "And I don't need a work permit to stay in Kamal."

Giri held his hand out in a gesture of peace. "No offense. I was just thinking the two of you might be able to hire out together. You move like people who trust each other, and that's a rare thing."

Esmer's face relaxed, and she gave the man a smile. "Sorry. It's been a difficult day."

Giri's one good eye rested on her face, then on the black X on her hand. "I can imagine," he said, reaching up to rub his shoulder. Emil saw the dark shadow of Giri's Wind caste scars under the thin shirt. "Sometimes it feels like the mark goes clear through to your soul, doesn't it?"

Esmer stared down into her mug. "Yeah," she said softly. "Sometimes." Emil put a hand on her arm, and she leaned against his shoulder for a brief moment.

Giri raised a mug. "To the outcasts. The tossed-aside, unwanted, and ignored. Long may we survive."

"To the outcasts," the other two echoed.

As Emil sipped his water, his thoughts drifted back to Mara. He found himself scanning the people passing in the street, looking for someone with messy cropped hair, someone who slipped through crowds like a shadow.

It was all nonsense, of course. Mara was gone. She'd moved on after the riot, on her way to find whatever it was that she was looking for. But Emil couldn't shake the feeling that she was close by. It was a ridiculous thought, but it made him feel a little better.

30

Emil

HEEMA CAME OUT of the ramshackle house, a bowl of eggplant rice in each hand. She handed them to Emil and Esmer.

"Better get your food now," she said. "Before the horde descends."

"Horde?" Emil asked, taking the bowl.

Giri grinned. "Watch."

Heema put her hand under her veil and whistled, a sharp, carrying sound. A small wave of children boiled out of the house next door. They were every age and size, all of them painfully thin. One of the children was still holding a wet cloth and rubbing his face with it.

"Everyone wipe their hands?" Heema asked. The children nodded. Heema gestured to the interior of the house. "Rice is in the big pot, vegetables on the fire. Watch the little ones and make sure they don't touch the hot metal."

"Yes, Heema," the kids chorused. Then they started to file inside.

Esmer made a questioning noise. "They're not all hers, are they?"

"If you ask her, they are," Giri said. "But no, not hers by blood. Life in the Wind Circle isn't easy. Sometimes parents vanish. They get thrown out of the city and can't get back in, or they simply don't come home one day and no one knows why. Sometimes the kids run away. Heema started taking them in. One became two became five and six, and so on. She found a patron to help her feed them. It's not much, but it's better than what they had."

There was a crash from the house, and Heema ran inside. Emil could hear her scolding the children in her melodic voice.

Giri chuckled and drained his water. "Ancestors, I love that woman," he said. "One of the kindest and smartest people I've ever met."

"Does her patron provide her with a work permit, too?" Emil asked. Giri shook his head.

"Heema doesn't need one," he said. "She's Bamboo caste."

Emil almost dropped his rice. "She's *what?*"

Giri gave a grim smile. "She's Bamboo caste. They don't acknowledge her anymore, but she's still one of them. So she doesn't need a work permit to live in the city."

"But–but–" Emil's mind was churning. "But she said Lel was her brother, and I *know* he's Wind caste. I've seen his mark."

"It's a long story." Giri's bearded face darkened with anger. "Heema and Lelkhan grew up in a family of famous singers, rumored to be descended from the great Elina herself. Unfortunately, Lel didn't inherit the talent."

Emil tried to remember if he'd ever seen the marks of earrings on Lel's ears. If he was Bamboo caste, from a performing family, he would have had several. But Lel always wore his hair a little long, and Emil had never really looked. . . .

He wondered if his uncle Pali knew.

"Anyway," Giri said. "Lel was sent off to apprentice to some accountant in Deshe, and Heema stayed here. One day she was performing at a wealthy merchant's house, and the son of the house fell in love with her. Nothing would do but that they be married at once."

"Sounds like a story-song," Esmer said.

"You'd think so." Giri looked down at the gray water of the canal. "After a year, when her dowry was spent and there were still no children, he changed his mind. Threw a pot of boiling water on her during a fight. A neighboring glassworker family heard her scream and rescued her. But her husband no longer wanted her, and her family was embarrassed by her. They shut her away from everyone."

"That's horrible!" Emil said. Beside him Esmer growled.

"What happened to her husband?" she asked. "Something awful, I hope."

Giri's face tightened. "Nothing happened to him. He was given a reprimand and a fine to pay to Heema's parents. *His* family shipped him down to Deshe to wait out the scandal. But he's dead now."

He took another sip of his water. "Lel was tried for his murder."

Emil's mouth fell open.

"I don't know what really happened," Giri said. "And Heema won't say. But they didn't have enough proof to execute him, so he was exiled to Wind caste instead. Heema was furious. She ran away from home and ended up here."

Emil swallowed, still speechless. He couldn't imagine calm, soft-spoken Lel killing anyone. But if someone had hurt Rona or another of Emil's family like that . . . well, you never knew what someone could do if they were pushed.

Giri stood. "I wouldn't ask her about it if I were you. She's incredibly protective of her brother and won't hesitate to kick you out if she thinks you're being nosy. But I thought you should know, Lel being family and all."

"I appreciate that," Emil said.

Giri smiled sadly. "Let me show you where you'll sleep tonight, and then I have to go to work. And you'd better start looking too. You don't have a lot of time to waste."

Emil stood and extended a hand to Esmer. Giri led them to the third red-curtained door. "Heema and I have the first house, and the kids sleep in the second one, and sometimes in this one. But right now it'll be just you and Esmer."

Emil poked his head through the curtain. It was a bare room with a few thin sleeping mats and a pile of ragged blankets. He pulled his head out.

"Should we just take a mat?" he asked. Giri nodded.

"We can't provide you with much food," he said. "Because of the children. But you can have one rice bowl a day and a place to bed down at night where you won't get knifed for your shirt. It's better than a lot of people around here have."

"Thank you," Emil said, meaning it. "Do you think . . ."

What he was about to say next was interrupted by a rattling clatter. He looked up to see another tea seller coming down the street. This man wore a thin cotton tunic and a blue head wrap. A collar of dark blue and bronze beads encircled his neck.

The man stopped in front of Heema's doors. "New tenants, Giri?" he said.

"Afternoon, Abhra," Giri said casually. But Emil noticed he put his hands together and bowed. "Yes, some relatives of Heema's come to look for work. This is Emil and this is Esmer."

They bowed.

"Respectful," the man said. "I like that." His smile gleamed against his oak-dark skin as he poured two cups of spiced tea. He handed one to Emil and one to Esmer.

"Welcome to the Outer City, youngsters. May the land be kind to you."

Emil sipped the tea. It was hot, just on the edge of burning, and made his mouth tingle pleasantly. "Thank you, sir," he said, and repeated the Hearth caste greeting, "May the land be kind to you as well."

"I'm alive and my tea is well brewed," the man said. He had a lined, well-used face and very deep-set eyes, and he leaned against the cart as he poured his own tea. "What more could I want?" He gave them a considering look.

"You're Sune, I see," he said to Esmer. "What Tribe?"

"Spotted cat," Esmer said cautiously. But the man's expression was bland and friendly as he drank his tea.

"I haven't seen a spotted cat in the capital since I was smaller than this cart," he said. "Some advice, young woman? If I were you, I'd stick close to Heema's home, or try to stay in animal form. Enough stray beasts around here that no one should notice you, and that mark on your hand might as well be a target, as far as a lot of these Wind caste folks are concerned."

Esmer looked down at her cup and didn't answer.

"Why?" Emil asked after a moment.

"Jobs," the tea seller said. "Some people around here don't like competing with Sune for employment. Makes them resentful."

"Thank you for the warning," Esmer said. She lifted her head and gave the man a brief smile. "And the tea."

The man smiled back at her. "Good luck to you both," he said, as they returned the cups to the cart. "Giri, I would speak to you a moment."

"Of course, Abhra," Giri said. "I'll walk with you." He nodded to Emil. "You'd better get started on finding some work."

"Right," Emil said. "Work."

They said good-bye to Giri and Abhra, and he and Esmer plunged into the stream of people.

"Where to first?" Esmer asked.

"Well," Emil said. "Might as well start with what I know. Let's see if any of those Bamboo merchants are hiring."

31
Mara

MARA DUCKED AS Revathi swung at her with her practice knife. Avoiding the blow easily, she stuck out her foot as Revathi's momentum carried her past. Revathi tripped, hitting the soft carpet with a thud. Mara grinned down at her, twirling her dagger in its protective padding.

"You're still telegraphing too much," she said. "A blind man would know you're coming."

Revathi shook her head. "I really thought I had you that time," she said, jumping to her feet. This morning she was barefoot, dressed in a knee-length tunic and loose trousers, eyes sparkling with exercise and laughter. She pushed her sleeves up over her elbows and waved her knife at Mara.

"Again," she said. "I'm going to take you down at least once if it kills me."

"Slow down, it's only the second lesson," Mara protested.

Revathi swung her loose braid back over her shoulder. "Don't care," she said, holding the knife close to her body the way Mara had shown her. "I want to learn as much as I can before you leave."

The words seemed to echo in the sunlit room. Revathi's face was bright and a little desperate, and Mara suddenly felt the odd urge to apologize, for what she didn't know.

"Revathi . . . ," she started, then stopped as something caught her eye. There was a dark, ugly bruise on the underside of Revathi's wrist, just underneath the golden flower of her noble's tattoo.

"What's that?" Mara asked. She reached for Revathi's arm, but the girl snatched it back.

"Nothing," Revathi said. "I hit it on something in the dark."

"Do you need to see a healer?" Mara asked. "It's a nasty bruise."

"No." Revathi said. She pulled her sleeves down, covering the mark. "It's fine. I'm sure I'll get worse doing this." She held up the blade in her hand for emphasis.

"Possibly," Mara admitted. She readied her dagger. "All right, so this time we're going to work on–"

Someone knocked on the door frame.

"Revathi!" Tamas called. "Revathi, are you awake?"

Mara sheathed her dagger and Revathi dropped the knife, kicking it under one of the floor cushions. Then she moved with quick strides to the curtained doorway.

Tamas had his mouth open to shout again, when Revathi

pulled him inside. "Tamas, what are you doing here?" she hissed. "It's not appropriate for you to visit me in my quarters. People will talk."

"People always talk," Tamas said. He was wearing the dark-blue padded silk of the Imperial Guard, and his sword was strapped to his side. He slid a hand up Revathi's arm. "It's only for a few minutes. And I didn't see you at all yesterday. Where were you?"

"Tamas." Revathi stepped to one side, gracefully avoiding both the touch and the question. "Not in front of my bodyguard."

Tamas pulled back, frowning. "Of course. I forgot. How is she working out?"

"Wonderfully!" Revathi said, her tone sticky-sweet. "It's such a comfort to have someone with me everywhere I go."

"Glad to hear it," Tamas said, but there was still a faint frown on his face. He looked Revathi up and down. "What are you wearing?"

"Sleepwear," Revathi said. "I haven't managed to get dressed yet." She gave him a flirtatious smile. "You shouldn't call on me so early. It hurts my vanity that you're seeing me in such a state."

Tamas's frown mellowed into an indulgent smile. "It's not that early," he said. "The men have been awake for hours. I even saw the Emperor wandering around." His voice dropped to a conspiratorial whisper. "He really looks like a ghost these days. Does he even go to see the princes anymore?"

Revathi frowned. "Tamas, you know I don't gossip about the Imperial family. And you should be kinder. Emperor Saro is really grieving."

"He needs to get married again, that's what he needs to do," Tamas said. "A pretty young noblewoman would cheer him right up. As it is, he doesn't even go to the Council of Lesser Princes half the time–"

"Tamas!" Revathi's voice cracked out like a whip. "Stop it!" She took a deep breath, controlling herself with an obvious effort. "It's dangerous to speak that way. It could be read as treason." She stepped closer. "I wouldn't want anything to happen to you."

"Nothing's going to happen to me," Tamas said, smiling down at her. He brushed a strand of loose hair out of her face. "I promise." He leaned in to kiss her, but Revathi turned her head so that he only caught the corner of her mouth.

Tamas pulled back and cleared his throat. "I spoke to my father. He's very anxious to have you and your grandmother over."

"So he said yesterday," Revathi answered with a neutral smile. "I told him we'll let him know a suitable time."

"What about tonight?"

"Tonight?" Revathi said. "No, Tamas, I'm with the princes today, and Grandmother has meetings and things to do and we have dinner plans already. . ."

"These plans aren't more important than *me*, are they?" Tamas's hands came up to rest on Revathi's shoulders. His fingers brushed her collarbone, and Revathi stiffened. "I mean, I've hardly seen you at all lately."

Revathi didn't answer.

"I want you to come tonight," Tamas said, his voice coaxing. "I went to the Clothing Fair with you, didn't I?"

Servants' voices floated in from the hall, muffled and low. Revathi swallowed.

"Mara, could you please guard the door?" she asked. "I don't want anyone to walk in."

"Of course," Mara said, glad to be able to do something. She slipped out of the room and stood in front of the curtain, her arms folded. She stared at the inlaid wall of the hall, trying not to eavesdrop on the murmuring voices behind her. At one point, Tamas's voice sharpened, angry.

"Why won't you *listen*?"

Revathi's answer was too low to make out, and Mara shifted, wondering if she should go back in. But Revathi had asked her to stand here. . . .

Finally Tamas came through the curtain. He was smiling.

"It's all settled," he said. "Will I have the pleasure of seeing you at dinner as well?"

"If Revathi brings me," Mara said. She watched Tamas walk down the hall, then turned and went back into the room.

Revathi stood in front of the long square mirror on the wall. She'd wrapped a robe around her practice clothes and was busy combing out her black hair. It hung long and thick between them, obscuring Mara's view of her face. Her voice was bright.

"So it looks like we're going to dinner," Revathi said. "I would have preferred to put it off longer, but I suppose it can't be helped."

"Why did you want to put it off in the first place?" Mara asked. She felt oddly uneasy, as if some danger had brushed by her, but she couldn't pin down the feeling at all.

"Oh, just to keep us on an equal footing," Revathi said, running the ivory comb through the ends of her hair. "Sathvik u'Gra wants to use my family's influence to strengthen his position in the Lotus Court. And he's been pushing to move the wedding date up. I'm sure that's what this dinner is about. Putting him off is a way of reminding him that we're just as powerful as he is, even if we aren't as rich. Plus, it'll be a lot of really civil arguing, and that's never my idea of fun."

She shook her hair back from her face. "Sorry about the interruption," she said to Mara. "I really wanted to finish that lesson."

Mara bent down and reached under the cushion to retrieve the knife Revathi had kicked there "We can do it again tomorrow," she said. "And you're learning quickly. I think you'll do well."

Color rose in Revathi's face, the first time Mara had ever seen her blush. "Thanks," she said. "You're a good teacher." Her fingers tugged at her sleeve, and she wrapped the robe closer around her. "We'd better get ready. I wasn't lying when I said I had to attend the princes today. Do you want to come?"

Mara shrugged. She really needed to start looking for her charge, but one more morning wouldn't hurt. And she was curious about the Imperial family. "Sounds like fun," she said.

Revathi laughed. "That's one way of putting it."

Mara glared down at the boy in front of her, resisting the urge to cuff him like a naughty kitten.

"Highness," she explained for what must have been the tenth time, "I'm not going to change to animal form for you."

Prince Sudev, Paithal's younger brother, stuck his lip out and scowled at her. He was a plump boy of about six, with large, dark eyes and a habit of hiding behind his older brother. Unlike Prince Paithal, who was quick to smile and always full of questions, Sudev was shy and serious. And he had a very firm idea of his own importance.

"Garen does it," Prince Sudev said. "He lets us ride on his back."

"Really?" Mara asked, giving the small boy a level stare. He shifted from one foot to the other. "Garen changes for you?"

"Well, sometimes. If we're really good."

Mara stifled a sigh. "Well, that's nice of him. But I'm not going to change for you, I'm sorry. Is there another game you'd like to play instead?"

Sudev's scowl deepened; then he abruptly gave in. "All right," he said. "Let's play the hiding game!"

Mara eyed him, suspicious. That had been too easy. "I don't know the hiding game," she said.

"I hide and then you look for me. If you don't find me, then you lose."

Mara looked over at where Revathi and Paithal were playing a complicated-looking game with a checked board and ivory statues of animals and people.

"What happens if I lose?" she asked. Sudev was intelligent, and very stubborn, and she didn't trust him.

"You're not supposed to ask me direct questions, you know," Sudev said. "Asking direct questions to royalty is very rude. It implies that I have to answer it, and I don't. I'm a prince. Also, you shouldn't look me in the eye. I'm above you."

Mara controlled her expression with an effort and moved her eyes to Sudev's chin. "All right, I would like to know what happens if I lose. And you have to tell me, or I won't play."

"You have to," Sudev said, stomping his foot. "I command you."

Mara looked him in the eye again. If he was going to be obnoxious, so was she. "No."

A dark flush stained the prince's face. "If you spoke like that to my father, he'd cut off your head," he said, raising his voice.

"What's going on?" Paithal called from his seat at the gaming table. "Sudev, you can't cut off heads. I've told you that already."

"Paithal," Sudev said, a distinct whine entering his voice. "This new companion is very rude. She won't play with me or stop asking me questions, and she keeps looking me in the eye when she's not supposed to." He flopped down onto a huge nearby cushion, rubbing at the white lotus mark on his neck. "I don't want her anymore. Send her away."

Paithal exchanged a glance with Revathi, then left his board to kneel down beside his little brother. "Sudev," he said, and his voice fell to a gentle murmur.

Mara sat down next to Revathi. She felt an unaccountable urge to stomp her foot and pout, just like the younger prince.

Revathi shook her head. "Sorry about Sudev," she said. "Ever since the Empress died, it seems like Paithal is the only one he'll listen to. Don't worry, though. Sudev knows asking a Sune to change is very rude, and he shouldn't be asking you to follow court manners, either. Those rules are only for formal audiences and things like that."

Mara tilted her head up, studying the mosaic ceiling. The princes' room was huge, with two wide, soft beds and a door leading to their private bath. The carpets were thick woven cashmere, and the golden pillars and arches were inlaid with red and green jewels in an intricate flower design. It made Revathi's room look like a fisherman's hut.

Everything was so *complicated* here. It made Mara homesick for the life she'd given up, the simple round of eating and sleeping and play. Not this tangle of human relationships and manners and politics.

For a moment she pictured Emil in her mind, remembering their last conversation. Thinking about him was becoming almost habit, a way to center herself when things got overwhelming. Human life was all she had left.

Revathi patted her arm in silent understanding. "Paithal," she called. "Come and make your move, or I'll hide one of your pieces."

The older prince stood up. "Coming, Lady Revathi," he said. Then he poked Sudev in the arm. "Go on," he said.

Sudev frowned, but he got up and came to stand before Mara.

"Paithal says I'm being rude to demand formal manners, and to ask you to change," he said. "He says if I keep being rude, no one will want to play with me. I apologize."

Mara bowed to him. "I accept. How about we make a bargain?

I'll play whatever game you like, so long as I don't have to change."

"Do you know how to play goat and tiger?" A wistful look passed over Sudev's face. "My father and I used to play goat and tiger all the time."

"I don't know that game," Mara said, smiling at him. "But I'd love it if you taught me."

32

Emil

"ANY LUCK?"

Emil didn't look up from where he was drawing aimlessly on the ground with a stick. "No," he said, hearing the sulk in his own voice. He gestured to the pallets and people surrounding him. "Esmer, we spent all yesterday looking. I've been sitting here most of the morning. Most people just walk by without even looking at us. It's like we don't exist. And the ones who *are* looking are usually trying to find someone with a specific skill. The merchants in the Wind Market aren't hiring, and to everyone else, I'm just an uneducated goatherd."

He stood, ignoring the protests and curses as he stepped over bodies. Esmer followed, gracefully slipping through the crowd. Her hands were curled into her tunic, hiding the mark on her hand, but people still looked at her suspiciously. Emil quickened his step.

"I don't know how anyone finds a job this way," Emil continued, when they were a safe distance away from the transients' area. He threw his stick into the canal and watched it swirl away. "It's hopeless."

"I think it's supposed to be," Esmer said. As usual, she looked neat and clean, hair pulled back, face washed. There was a fresh purpling bruise on her jaw.

"What happened to you?" Emil said, forgetting his own problems for a moment.

Esmer shrugged. "Some Wind caste boys and I had a little . . . disagreement."

"What?"

"It's all right," Esmer said. "I won." She smiled, showing all her teeth. "They'll think twice before going after a Sune in the future."

Emil stared at her, torn between pride and horror. He wanted to take Esmer in his arms and tell her he was sorry. He wanted to go looking for those people and punch them himself.

But there was a fierce gleam in Esmer's face that warned him pity would not be welcome. So Emil merely nodded.

"Good."

Esmer gave him a warm smile. "It doesn't really hurt," she said, answering his unstated worry. "Sune heal fast. I'm just sorry it was for nothing. There's not a sign of Stefan in the Wind Circle or the Hearth Circle so far. And I haven't so much as smelled a mercenary either. I might be able to widen my search, but I need time."

"Which I don't have," Emil said, frustration making his voice sharp. "I've only got tonight and tomorrow to find a work permit."

"You know," Esmer said, and her words were gentle. "I always figured that someday Stefan would get into trouble not even you could get him out of. Maybe it's finally happened."

Emil felt his shoulders sag at the thought. He slumped to the ground, putting his feet over the edge of the canal. "I have to keep trying, Esmer," he said, staring out over the gray, swiftly flowing water. "I have to. I just know if I leave now and something happens to him, I'll never forgive myself. But you don't have to stay."

He felt Esmer's hand slide into his hair, stroking the unruly strands into place. She touched him lightly, scratching his scalp with her nails, as if he were a kitten she were cleaning.

"Idiot," she said, and her voice was fond. "Then who will get *you* out of trouble? If you stay, I stay."

Emil leaned into her touch. "I suppose I could go farther into the city," he said. "Try to find a job in the Hearth Circle. I'm not getting anywhere here, that's for sure."

"I'll start searching the Inner City," Esmer said. "I don't need a work permit to do that. I'll start in Bamboo and work my way farther in to Jade and Flower. If I stay in cat form, I can catch my own food and find small corners to sleep in."

"Just be careful when you're sneaking around, all right?" Emil said, still staring into the canal. "I don't want to lose you, too."

"I'm always careful," Esmer said. She poked him in the arm with a sharp finger. "But if I get caught, you had better come get me. I'm not going to be some noble's pet with a jeweled collar and a golden cage."

"I don't know," Emil said, looking up at her. His despair was rapidly leaking away now that he had a plan for the rest of the day. "You'd look pretty fancy with a jeweled collar."

Esmer hissed at him. Emil grinned.

"Of course I'll come. I'd be lost without you." He said the words jokingly, but he knew they were true.

"I'm counting on it," Esmer said. Then she took a graceful leap, changing in midair to cat form. The black tip of her tail vanished behind a nearby building.

Emil stood up, stretching his stiff muscles, and pulled his red scarf out of his tunic, where he'd tucked it that morning. If he was going to look for work in the Hearth Circle, he'd need to look the part. He tied it around his neck and headed over the Hearth Bridge.

The Hearth Circle felt more like home to Emil than the Wind Circle. Fruit trees grew in small yards, white cattle lowed from pens, and there were even a few goats. Like Wind caste, Hearth caste sold only what they–or their home villages–grew, raised, or made themselves. Some booths sold milk and cheese, vegetables, and fresh-baked bread. Other booths displayed lengths of sturdy cloth, raw precious metals mined by Hearth workers, and reed mats woven in the village style. There were fresh water fountains and the road was wider, with channels to wash away human and animal waste and grates to send it deep underground.

Emil had managed to keep his Arvi clothing pretty clean, so

he didn't stand out much in the crowd of chattering Hearth folk. The men wore simple shirts and head wraps, the women dressed in bright, solid-colored asars. Everyone wore the bead-and-wire collar that marked the Hearth caste. Many of them had worn, tired faces, and there were dark circles underneath their eyes.

Emil quickly figured out why when he started to ask around for a job. They would love to hire another person, he heard over and over again, but they simply couldn't afford it. Most of the Hearth booths seemed to be family-run affairs, open from Firstlight to Darkfall. Families with older children fared better, but he saw a few booths run by a single couple where the owners looked like they were about to drop. It was hard not to compare them to the Hearth caste folk he knew in the villages. Those people worked hard, but also had times of rest, like Earthsleep. In the city, it seemed, there was no rest.

But none of that helped him find a job, and Emil was starting to get discouraged again. He stopped at a fruit cart and examined the mangoes on display. Maybe he could dip into his small amount of coins and buy one for lunch. . . .

His thoughts were interrupted by a familiar bellowing laugh. Behind him, bargaining with a nearby bread seller, stood Rajo the Black.

The mercenary was wearing a rough brown tunic, and his sword was conspicuously absent. He looked like an ordinary Wind caste worker, but Emil could see the gleam of his throwing circles on his hip. He seemed to be alone.

Rajo finished bargaining for the bread and moved away,

munching on the loaf. Emil bolted after him.

He wasn't hard to follow. Rajo walked like he owned the street and made a wide trail through the colorful crowd. Emil followed him along the canal, being careful to keep a safe distance. If he could follow Rajo without being seen, Rajo would lead him to Stefan.

Just before he reached the bridge that led to the Bamboo Circle, Rajo seemed to sense someone watching him. He swung around, examining the crowd with suspicious eyes.

Emil ducked behind a nearby spice cart, his heart thudding. The scents of garlic, cardamom, and *ajamoda* seeds almost made him sneeze. He rubbed his nose until the urge passed, then peered around the cart edge, just in time to see Rajo crossing the Bamboo Bridge.

Emil scrambled to follow. He was so intent on not losing Rajo that he didn't hear the guard call him until a rough hand snagged his arm.

"Didn't you hear me?" the guard said, frowning at him. He wore copper-studded cuffs and held a curved sword at his side. "I said, you can't come in here. Wind caste aren't allowed in the Inner City without a permit."

"But . . ." Emil pointed his thumb at Rajo, who was now almost out of sight. "That man there, you let *him* through."

The guard laughed, showing crooked and stained teeth. "And when you get yourself a work permit signed by a noble house, you can come through too. Until then, be off with you."

"Noble house?" Emil's head snapped up. "What noble house?"

"What business is it of yours?" the guard said. "Now go away before you ruin my good mood and I throw you into the canal."

Emil retreated until he was off the bridge. His head was spinning. If Rajo had a permit signed by a noble, did that mean he was living in the Flower Circle? And was Stefan with him?

And without a work permit of his own, how could Emil ever find out?

His thoughts were interrupted in their frantic circle by a clinking, clattering sound. He looked up just in time to see a tea seller walked by.

"Hot spiced tea," the tea seller called, pushing the heavy cart. His head scarf sagged over his forehead, and he looked no older than Emil. "Hot spiced tea for sale."

An idea bloomed, fully formed, in Emil's mind. A way for him to stay in the city *and* get access to the Flower Circle.

But he was going to need some help.

33
Mara

MARA AND SUDEV had played three games of goat and tiger and two rounds of the hiding game before Garen arrived to take the princes to their combat lessons.

Where do they train? Mara sent as she watched Paithal pack up the game he and Revathi had been playing. Sudev was watching too, she noticed, his eyes fixed on his older brother adoringly.

The princes take lessons with the warrior monks in the Jade Circle. It's a privilege accorded only to the royal family, Garen sent.

The Jade Circle? Mara felt a small fissure of excitement run through her. Surely in the Jade Circle she could find a worthy charge. *Where?*

Time had not made Garen appear less massive, but his smile was friendly. *Would you like to come and see?*

Mara hesitated, but the idea of possibly starting her

long-awaited search was too alluring.

Yes, please, she sent. *Let me check with Revathi first, though.*

"Revathi," Mara spoke out loud, and the girl turned. "May I have a free afternoon to visit the Jade Circle? I'd like to start looking for my charge."

Revathi blinked. "Oh," she said. "Of course. Take all the time you like."

"Will you be all right?" Mara asked.

"Don't worry about me." Revathi waved a hand. "I have a lot to do getting ready for the dinner tonight. Go on. Have fun."

Mara darted after Garen, her steps light.

How many warrior monks are there? she sent as they walked. She liked being able to talk to Garen this way, knowing no one else could overhear her. Only another Sune would be able to hear their conversation. Mara couldn't say why that comforted her, only that it did.

Not many, Garen sent back. He smiled down at her. *A few groups of them here, some in Deshe, and some in Aranya, the fortress city to the north. Once they pass their final test, Jade warriors are forbidden to leave their enclaves unless directly ordered by the Emperor. They spend their whole lives behind those walls.*

Mara wrinkled her nose. Those three years in the Order had been confining enough; she couldn't imagine shutting herself away for the rest of her life. Her thoughts were interrupted by Sudev's squeal.

"Father!" He darted forward, throwing his arms around the leg of a worn-faced man in silver and blue who had just turned the corner with Lady Ekisa. The man put a hand on Sudev's shoulder, and the boy buried his face in the man's tunic.

Paithal looked very much as though he wanted to hug his father too, but instead, he came forward and gave a respectful bow. "Good morning, Father, Lady Ekisa." He reached forward and gently disentangled his younger brother, who was still clinging to the Emperor. "Sudev," he said reprovingly. "We're in public."

Sudev flushed and scrambled backward. "Good morning, Father," he said, mimicking his brother's bow.

The Emperor's smile was deep and genuine. Mara thought it made him look even sadder. "Good morning, my sons," he said, nodding in acknowledgment. "And what are you two monkeys up to this morning?"

"Staff practice!" Sudev blurted. "And Mara played goat and tiger with me!"

The Emperor's gaze moved to Mara. "Did she?" His gaze sharpened, and suddenly Mara was reminded that she was in the presence of royalty. "I don't believe I've had the pleasure of meeting you. Are you new to the palace?" He glanced at Garen as he said it, and it was Garen who answered him.

"Mara is companion to Revathi sa'Hoi," Garen said calmly. "She expressed an interest in meeting the Jade warriors, so I invited her to accompany us." A swift look passed between him and the Emperor, a question and an answer. The Emperor's shoulders relaxed slightly.

"Excellent." He nodded to Mara again. "Welcome to the palace, Mara."

Mara put her hands together and bowed as low as she could. "It's an honor to serve, Your Majesty."

"I'm sure it is," the Emperor said. He glanced at Lady Ekisa next to him. "The sa'Hoi family is close to my heart. You choose your friends well."

"As always, Your Imperial Majesty is too kind," Lady Ekisa said. Her voice grew regretful. "I hate to pull you away from your sons, but I do need to discuss some things with you."

"Yes, of course," the Emperor said. He reached out to ruffle first Paithal's hair, then Sudev's. "Be good, boys. I'll see you for dinner."

"Yes, Father," the boys chorused. The Emperor smiled at them one more time, and then walked away with Lady Ekisa. Mara watched them go.

That was a little terrifying, she sent to Garen.

You should have met him before the Empress became ill, Garen sent back. *Saro could cow a roomful of nobles with one look.*

Mara noticed that Sudev kept glancing over his shoulder as they walked. *The princes miss him, don't they?*

They do, Garen sent *He's got little time these days to visit them, and as you saw, they're expected to keep a certain level of formality in public. It's hard on a child.*

Poor boys, Mara sent, thinking of her own childhood. Pouncing on her father's tail, being washed and nuzzled when she got muddy. Her mother's exasperated breaths against the back of Mara's neck as she carried Mara away from whatever mischief she'd gotten into.

At least Mara had *had* her parents while they were alive. Not only had the princes lost their mother, they seemed to be losing their father as well.

The Jade Circle was as clean and sparse as before. The princes seemed restless after seeing their father; Sudev was alternately sulking and fussing, and Paithal was quiet and sharp. Mara was so busy trying to keep the peace that she was surprised when Garen stopped in front of an iron gate. It was the same one that Samara had told her to look for. The gate with the *naga* on it.

"We're here," Garen said out loud. The princes stopped poking each other and straightened up, folding their hands behind them. Garen winked at Mara. "Suni insists on discipline inside these walls."

Mara glanced at Paithal and Sudev, who were looking straight ahead. "Impressive," she commented.

"Suni's the best warrior in the city," Garen said. He reached for a silken rope hanging by the gate and pulled it. Mara could hear the soft peal of bells from inside. "And he's as good at teaching as he is at fighting. Not that you'd know it to look at him."

As soon as they were welcomed inside, Mara understood what Garen meant. The gate opened onto a wide courtyard, surrounded by low buildings. There was a training exercise going on, a bent, old man in a dark-green robe facing off against a young girl. The girl was small and dark with a braid of black hair down her back and a cleft lip, a common sight in some of the poorer villages of the Empire. She was dressed in dusty traveling clothes and she held her *lati* fighting staff with confidence.

The old man twirled his staff in a complicated pattern. Despite his frail appearance, his voice carried over the gathered crowd in the courtyard. "Your teachers said you have skill in the combat arts," he said. "Well, we will see. Defend yourself!"

The girl swung her staff, but the man moved faster than anyone Mara had ever seen. He knocked her to the ground and disarmed her.

"Again," he commanded.

The girl rose, picked up her stick, and faced him again. There was nothing but determination in her face. And when she went down for a second time, she stood up before she was told to. A smile drifted across the old man's face.

"Again then," he said. Over and over, he knocked her down, and over and over she got right back up. Dirt and sweat streaked her face, but her eyes were alert. She was watching her opponent, Mara realized, trying to match his fighting style. A few times, she even managed to get in a block and strike of her own before he knocked her down.

"How long will you keep fighting?" the old man asked. He didn't even seem to be out of breath. "How long will you keep getting up?"

The girl lifted her chin. "As long as it takes," she said, speaking for the first time. Her voice was low and deliberate, each word carefully pronounced. "As long as I can."

The older man nodded. "Excellent," he said. He gestured to one of the green-clad warriors on the edge of the crowd.

"Take her to the novice quarters and get her new clothing and a proper weapon." He bowed to her, hand on chest. "Welcome, my dear."

The girl copied his bow. "Thank you, Master Suni." Then she allowed herself to be led off, and the crowd started to disperse.

Mara realized she was smiling. She could see why Samara had suggested this place to her. It seemed very like the Order.

"New student, Suni?" Garen said. The older man turned and bowed again, this time pressing both hands together.

"Highnesses," he said to the princes. "It's a pleasure to see you again."

The princes bowed back, almost as low as they had for their father, then stood straight, hands at their sides. Suni clapped his hands.

"What are you waiting for?" he said. "Go start on your warm-up exercises."

The boys hurried to obey, and Suni turned to Garen. "Yes, the girl is new. She's from that estate that the Emperor runs, the one that trains orphaned girls. She was originally studying to be a healer, but . . ."

"But she kept sneaking out to take lessons from the Combat Mistress," came a female voice, and a woman and a man emerged from the crowd. The woman's green robe was too loose for fighting, and her hands were marked with the swirls and patterns of a Jade healer. "She still wanted to be in Jade caste though, so we decided to bring her here. A warrior spirit like that should not go to waste."

"A wise decision," Garen said. "Though not all warriors fight with staffs and spears."

The dimple in the woman's cheek deepened. "As my guard constantly reminds me," she said.

"I do," the man agreed, speaking for the first time. Mara's eyes flicked over him, and she bit back an exclamation of surprise. The man was wearing a leather ear cuff over one ear and a bronze earring in the other. A pledged member of the Order.

The man's eyes rested on her, and Mara resisted the urge to duck behind Garen. She hadn't thought to meet another one of her Order so soon. But the man's face held nothing but friendliness.

"Well, well, well!" he said. "This is a pleasant surprise!" He put a hand on his chest and bowed. "Well met, sister! I am Vihan, pledged to Sanah the healer."

Mara flushed as everyone turned to look at her. "Well met, brother," she said, returning the bow. "I am Mara, unpledged. I . . . I haven't been out of the Order long," she added, feeling shy and awkward.

"Have you come to stay with us?" Suni asked. "Their weapons master sometimes sends the new ones here if they have nowhere else to go," he explained in an aside to the healer. "We are old friends."

Mara glanced at Garen, who was listening with interest. "No, I'm working in the palace for now. Just until I find my charge."

"Excellent," Vihan said. "That will be great practice. Have you any idea where to look?"

"I thought here, maybe?" Mara said, stumbling over the words. "I mean, a healer . . . or someone like that . . ."

Vihan's face creased into an understanding smile. "Ah yes, the dream of every new member." His voice dropped to a conspiratorial whisper. "Take it from me, Mara. Guarding healers isn't as good as the stories say. They run headlong into all kinds of danger, and they serve you horrible-smelling medicines just because they can."

The healer—Sanah—laughed. "I wouldn't give you those medicines if you didn't become so snappish. One would think you had marsh flu instead of a simple cold."

Vihan grinned. "I don't know what you're talking about," he said. "I was clearly dying."

Sanah shook her head. "Of course you were. But we should be getting back. I have some delicate herbs soaking, and I don't trust my novices not to strain them wrong." She bowed to Suni. "Always a pleasure, Master Suni."

"For me, too," Suni said. "Travel safe. I'll look after your girl."

"I know you will." The healer looked at Vihan. "Coming?"

"Yes, Sanah," the man said. He put a hand on Mara's shoulder. There was kindness and sympathy in his face. "Remember, little sister," he said. "The goal of the Order is not just about regaining our own honor. It's to defend those who need us. To look after those who have no one else."

Those who have no one else.

The words echoed in Mara's head even after she and Garen took the princes back to the palace.

Let them take the name of those they guard. Let them treat the bond as stronger than marriage, stronger than family. And let them care for their charges, not only as one cares for a treasure, to protect and guard it, but with sincere affection and honesty of heart. For there is no greater honor–and no greater love–than to lay down your life for someone you call friend.

Excerpt from the founding documents of the Order of Khatar

34
Emil

"HEEMA, I NEED to know how to get a job with the tea sellers."

The veiled woman looked up from her mending. The little boy beside her ducked his head, hiding behind her shoulder. She ruffled his hair.

"The tea sellers are a pretty closed-in group," she told Emil in her expressive voice. She was wearing blue today, a fine, pale color at odds with the shabby surroundings. "They don't hire outsiders."

"That's why I need your help," Emil said. "I don't need them to hire me on permanently, I just need a work permit that will allow me to get into the Flower Circle. That's where Stefan is."

Heema was silent for a moment, stroking the toddler's hair. "Come back in an hour's time," she said. "I'll see what I can do."

Emil nodded and ducked out of the curtained doorway. He might as well use some of his coins to buy a little meat for dinner.

He returned an hour later with a rabbit dangling from one hand. Heema was standing outside her home talking to Abhra, the tea seller who Emil had met once before. Emil presented the rabbit to her, and even through the veil, he could sense her smile.

"Thank you, Emil," she said, her voice low and delighted. "The children will love it." She nodded to Abhra. "I'll leave you two alone."

With a graceful bow, she ducked back into the house.

Abhra poured a cup of tea for himself. He didn't offer one to Emil, and he didn't speak.

Emil waited. His eyes wandered over to the canal. A group of boys was having a water fight, shirts off and skinny arms splashing. One of them tipped his head back and laughed. Emil looked away.

The tea seller sipped his tea. "You know," he said finally, "all kinds of people come to Kamal, and they're usually looking for something."

"Is that so?" Emil said, following the man's lead.

"Oh yes," the tea seller said. "Usually it's a work permit, but sometimes it's something entirely different."

"And do they find it?"

"Every now and then," Abhra said. "Sometimes we find it for them."

"We?"

"The tea sellers," Abhra said. He adjusted the heavy cart. "Few notice us, but we're allowed everywhere, Inner or Outer City. And we hear everything. There's nothing like a good cup of tea for loosening tongues and greasing gossip."

"And what do you do with it?" Emil asked, still being careful. "The gossip?"

"We use it," Abhra said. "To protect ourselves and others who need protecting. We are not informants." He smiled, quick and sharp. "Though the Emperor's men wish it were otherwise. And would pay well for what we know."

"But you don't sell your secrets," Emil said, beginning to understand. "You keep them close."

"Do you judge us for that?" Abhra asked.

Emil shook his head. "No." He took a deep breath. "I'm looking for my brother," he blurted. "He's about my age, broad-shouldered, and he stands this high." He made a gesture. "Hair as long as mine and a broken wrist. The people he came here with . . . they're up to no good. And I think they're in the Flower Circle."

Abhra took another sip of his tea. "What's his name?" he asked finally.

"Stefan," Emil said, hope climbing, sharp and frantic in his chest. "Stefan Arvi."

The tea seller pressed his hands together and bowed. "I like you, Emil. You have a cautious tongue and an honest heart. I'm willing to help you. For a price."

"What price?"

Abhra stepped forward so that his face and Emil's were inches apart. His dark eyes were very sharp. "Information. Something is going on in this city and I don't like it. Strangers appear, stir up trouble, and then disappear. People are restless, angry. Now you tell me there are people up to no good in the Flower Circle. When you find your brother, I want to know who he's with and what they are doing. That is my price for helping you."

Emil's throat was dry. "All right," he finally said. "I agree."

Abhra stepped back. "Excellent," he said, pulling a charcoal stick and a sheet of rice paper from one of the lower shelves of his tea cart. "We'll see about getting you into the Flower Circle this evening," he said. "But first I'll show you around, so you know how to act." He signed the paper and handed it to Emil.

It was a work permit.

"Congratulations," Abhra said. "You're a tea seller."

A little while later, Emil stood at the foot of the Bamboo Bridge, trying to control his nervousness.

"Stop fidgeting," Abhra said. "You look like you don't belong here." He straightened the scarf around Emil's neck. "To move freely in the Inner City, you must appear harmless. Look at everyone and smile, wide and stupid, like this." He gave Emil a wide, vacant grin, the gaps in his teeth plainly visible. "They will think you only want to sell them tea and will ignore you. It'll be all right."

Emil stiffened his shoulders and pushed the heavy tea cart onto the bridge. The clay cups rattled as the wheels jarred over the seams in the wood. The guards paid the two of them no attention at all, as Emil pushed the cart through into the streets of the Bamboo Circle. Abhra followed.

It was a different world entirely from the Outer City. The richly painted houses clustered together like gossiping crowds, and the air rang with voices: voices haggling, voices hawking wares, voices laughing and singing and shouting. Everyone seemed to be wearing perfume or scented oil, and the constant flash of gold and jewels made Emil dizzy.

Emil was so busy staring that he didn't see the pile of horse dung in the road. He tripped, tried to regain his feet, and lurched into a dancer who was performing on the corner. The dancer, a slim, muscled man, stepped easily out of the way, and Emil went sprawling.

Abhra cackled. "Gotta watch your step in the Inner City, boy," he said.

Emil gathered himself up and dusted off his clothing, trying to keep his dignity about him. Abhra was still laughing.

I'm going to find Stefan, Emil vowed to himself, as he started pushing the cart. *I'm going to find my brother and if he's alive, I'm going to kill him.*

After a full circuit in the Bamboo Circle, Abhra led him to the Jade Bridge. It was made of a darker wood than the Bamboo Bridge and smelled of fresh pitch. Abhra joked with the guards as they bought his tea, then led Emil farther into the city.

Emil liked the Jade Circle. He liked the wide, bare streets and the clean-smelling air. They sold their tea to ancient men leaning on staffs and to serious young women holding piles of scrolls. At last they stopped at a small side door, set deep in one of the white courtyard walls. Abhra knocked on the door, and it opened, revealing a heavyset man wearing an apron tied around his waist. He had a wooden spoon in his hand, and flour dusted the front of his gray servant's tunic.

"Oh, thank the Ancestors," the servant said, a wide smile splitting his face. "I'm simply perishing for a good strong cup of tea. You have no idea the kind of day I'm having. New assistant, and the boy's simply hopeless. Can't even boil rice properly!"

Abhra chuckled. "Emil, this is Manik, my favorite customer."

"Oh, go on with your flattery," Manik said, waving the spoon about as he talked. "You only like me because I give you all the best gossip."

"It's possible," Abhra said, pouring Manik his tea. "Though now that you mention it, I am looking for someone. A young Wind caste worker with a broken wrist."

"Oh?" Manik's eyes were sharp and dark in his round face. "Why so?"

"He owes me money and he's disappeared." Abhra said. His voice had gone quiet and steely, and suddenly he didn't look so harmless anymore. Emil felt his eyes widen at the sudden change. "It's very . . . inconvenient."

"Someone's trying to duck out on a debt to the Lord of the Outer City?" Manik said with a low whistle. He sipped his tea. "Boy's either brave or suicidal."

Abhra smiled, showing all his teeth. "Now, Manik," he said, still in that softly dangerous tone. "You know you're not supposed to use that title here. I'm just simple Abhra, humble tea seller."

Manik paled, then cleared his throat. "Of course you are," he said. "My apologies."

Emil realized he was staring, but neither of the men seemed to notice. Manik continued,

"I haven't seen anyone like that around here. Just the men working on the Jade Bridge. They're recoating it before Earthsleep." He swallowed the rest of the tea and gave Abhra the cup back. "Have you already given this boy a warning?"

Abhra smiled again, this time closed and tight. "How do you think he hurt his arm in the first place?"

Manik's chuckle followed them down the street.

Once out of earshot, Emil stopped and grabbed Abhra's arm. "Lord of the Outer City?" he whispered.

Abhra didn't stop pushing the cart. "Don't worry about it," he said, once more the mild older man. "It's a silly title anyway. I've tried to squash it, but you know how it is." His shoulders lifted in a shrug. "People have to name everything. It's how they feel safe."

"But you're not . . . you're not just a tea seller," Emil said. It wasn't a question.

"Hush," Abhra said. They turned several corners before Abhra stopped, pulling the tea cart into a narrow, deserted alley. Then he turned and looked at Emil.

"I *am* a tea seller," he said. "But you're right; that's not all I am." He smiled slightly. "The soldiers don't care what happens in the Outer City as long as it doesn't inconvenience the merchants and nobles. Someone has to keep order."

"And that's what you do."

"That's what I do," Abhra said. His smiled widened. "I keep order, and I help people like Heema, and this evening I will sneak you into the Flower Circle, and tomorrow, I must wash all my teapots and leave them to soak. I'm a very, very busy man."

Emil had to laugh.

35
Mara

THE OUTFIT REVATHI wanted Mara to wear to the dinner was pink.

"I can't wear that!" Mara said, staring at the length of fabric that Revathi was holding out. "And how will I put it on? There aren't any sleeve holes or anything!"

"Mara, you're acting like you've never seen an asar before," Revathi said. "I know you saw me put one on this morning. I wear them all the time."

Mara gave the dove-embroidered fabric a suspicious stare. "I didn't realize it was just a tablecloth."

Revathi started laughing. "I'm sorry," she said, when she'd gotten her breath back. "It's just . . . you're looking at that asar as if you're expecting it to attack you."

"I don't understand why I have to have an asar at all," Mara said. "Can't I just wear my normal uniform?"

Revathi shook her head. "Lord u'Gra invited us to a family dinner. I can't bring you as my bodyguard without insulting him. You have to come as my . . ." She coughed. "As my friend."

There was a moment of awkward silence, then Mara rubbed the back of her neck. "Better hope I don't have to fight anyone," she muttered.

"As far as I know, you won't," Revathi said. "If Lord Sathvik is planning an assassination, he's supposed to inform us ahead of time."

Mara squinted at her. "Are you joking? Sometimes I can't tell."

Revathi just smiled.

"That color is going to show every dirt mark and stain," Mara pointed out.

"So don't do anything that gets you dirty," Revathi countered. "Look, colors have special meaning in the Lotus Court. It's one of the most successful ways to play the Great Game. If you choose the right color and pattern, you can communicate everything from anger to lust, and still make sure everything that comes out of your mouth is polite and civil. Basically this asar tells everyone you're not a threat."

"I'm *supposed* to be a threat!"

"Not tonight, you're not," Revathi said. "It's rude." She rubbed her shoulder, wincing a little. "Please Mara, just trust me."

Mara huffed a breath through her teeth. "All right," she said. "What's wrong with your shoulder?"

Revathi dropped her hand. "Nothing," she said. "It's fine."

Mara stepped closer. Revathi was wearing the loose tunic that she'd put on after her bath, and she smelled of jasmine and sandalwood. Mara reached out and carefully pulled the neck of Revathi's tunic aside. There was a new bruise just under Revathi's collarbone, a dull red, darkening at the edges.

"Did that happen during our lesson?"

Revathi pulled away from her hand. "Yes," she said. "But don't worry about it. I have an undershirt that will cover it."

Mara frowned at her. Revathi hadn't taken any bad falls that morning. If the noble girl bruised so easily, Mara would have to be more careful about where she struck her. They should probably talk about that before they had another lesson. . . .

"Stop stalling," Revathi said, advancing on Mara with the asar. "You're going to put this on and you're going to look amazing."

Well, amazing is one word for it, Mara thought, staring at her reflection in the mirror later.

She'd been wrapped and pinned into the asar until Revathi had pronounced her perfect. The pink silk glowed against her brown skin, and the loose end dangled over her shoulder, leaving her arms bare. Mara had flatly refused to wear any jewelry, so Revathi had pinned a tiny cluster of jasmine into her hair. She'd also put dark lines around Mara's eyes that made them look impossibly huge, like a baby animal's.

Revathi adjusted the loose end of Mara's asar, pinning it so it wouldn't slip. "You look beautiful," she said, stepping back. "What do you think?"

"It's uncomfortable," Mara said honestly. The cream-colored, short-sleeved undershirt was tighter than she was used to, and the delicate sandals left her feet exposed and cold.

"It's only for one evening," Revathi said. She went to her shelf and pulled out a carved box. "You can change as soon as we get back to the palace, I promise."

Mara scowled at her reflection. She didn't *want* to look harmless. She liked her short hair messy, her clothes loose. She liked being able to move easily and fight without fabric getting in the way. But it couldn't be helped. Mara turned to watch Revathi finish getting ready.

Revathi's asar was a dark, shimmering silver, woven in a pattern of green and brown vines. Tiny mirrors were sewn into the fabric, scattering light as she moved. She had put up her heavy black hair and rubbed a deep red stain on her lips. A ruby hair ornament in the shape of a hibiscus flower glistened against the dark waves like a single drop of blood.

"*You* don't look harmless," Mara said.

Revathi adjusted a wayward strand of hair. She pulled a thick silver chain from the jewelry box and fastened it round the high neck of her dress. "I don't need to look harmless, because I'm not dangerous. At least not physically. The Great Game is all about subtlety, about strategy, about communicating on many different levels and trying to outmaneuver each other."

Revathi gestured to her asar. "Silver is a color of power," she explained. "It's used often to mark those who speak for the Emperor and will serve as a reminder to Lord u'Gra of my family's position. The design is of *malati* vines. They sometimes stand for love offered, but these aren't blooming. I'm trying to remind Lord u'Gra that I don't belong to him *or* his son. Yet." She slid a silver cuff on her wrist, covering her noble's tattoo. Her fingers tugged at the long sleeves of her undershirt and straightened the high collar.

"It's unusual, going in such dark colors to a social dinner. If I'm lucky, Lord u'Gra will read it as me being unhappy, and that will make him tread carefully. He cares very much about this alliance."

Revathi picked up a silver-painted fan. "Come on," she said, tapping Mara with it. "We're going to be late."

Mara sat down and pulled up the hem of her asar. "Just a minute," she said, tying her dagger and sheath to her calf with two leather thongs. She didn't care what Revathi said, she wasn't going anywhere without her blade. Revathi shook her head but didn't comment.

Mara stood up, readjusting her asar. "What's the fan for?"

"Communicating with Grandmother," Revathi said, with a grim little smile. "I hate fans, but they can be very useful."

"Wait, I read about this," Mara said. "In the Order. You send messages with them, right?"

"Exactly. Fans were originally just a court fad," Revathi explained, as they walked through the palace grounds. "Until the women of the court figured out that they could use them to signal to one another without the men noticing. We change the code every now and then, just to keep it fresh. It adds another level to the Game, and it's really useful, especially for women whose husbands or fathers prefer them silent."

"Clever," Mara said. "I like it."

They paused just inside the palace gate. There were a few workers on the Imperial Bridge, painting it with what smelled like pitch. Mara's nose twitched at the strong smell.

"Fans turned out much better than some of the other fads," Revathi continued. "Like the one about wearing fresh fruit. That got messy *really* fast. The newest thing is this kind of communicating through poems. I think it's boring, but the younger nobles love it."

"I don't understand poetry," Mara confessed. "If you have something to say, why not just say it?"

Revathi shook the fan at her. "That's why you're not allowed to play the Great Game. You're far too direct." She looked in the direction of the palace. "Here's Grandmother."

Lady Ekisa came up, leaning on the arm of a very handsome and muscular guard. "Thank you so much," she was saying, as she gazed up at the young man with obvious admiration. "It's such a comfort to have strong men around to help me."

"My pleasure, Lady Ekisa," the guard said. He disentangled himself from her hands and bowed to Revathi. "Lady Revathi."

"Thank you for helping my grandmother," Revathi said. Her voice was overly sweet. "She is getting a little frail lately."

The guard bowed again and retreated. As soon as he was out of earshot, Lady Ekisa put her hands on her hips and glared at Revathi.

"Frail? Really, Granddaughter . . ."

"Really, Grandmother," Revathi said. "What else was I supposed to say, since you clearly needed the help?" She raised one eyebrow. "What were you doing, anyway?"

Lady Ekisa smiled. She was wearing her usual white-and-silver asar, but she'd added a silver necklace similar to Revathi's and draped an almost transparent white silk scarf over her hair.

"If I choose to portray myself as a slightly dotty old person with an eye for young men, it's my choice. I do what I want. Besides, men always underestimate silly women." She opened her hand, revealing a set of metal guard keys. "I really just wanted the key to the armory, but it seems I've taken all of them. What a shame." She tucked the keys into her asar and winked at Mara.

"You picked his pocket?" Mara asked.

"Whose pocket? I don't know what you're talking about." Lady Ekisa straightened her asar, the bent old woman of moments before disappearing. "We should go. We're going to be late."

Mara shook her head. "Revathi wasn't kidding when she said you were dangerous."

Lady Ekisa's only reply was a serene smile.

Tamas's family's house was a large, two-story building made of reddish stone. A gray-clothed servant answered the door. He bowed low.

"Honored ladies. You are expected."

He ushered them through a narrow hall and into the center courtyard. The house smelled of amber and of rose incense. The walls were painted pale yellow, and the floor was mosaic tile patterned in swirling blues and greens. The courtyard itself was open to the sky and ringed by slender pillars. A balcony with a carved mahogany banister ran around the inside of the second level. Mara could see what looked like bedrooms through the partially curtained doorways. A fountain sat in the middle of the space, burbling to itself.

"Welcome!" Lord u'Gra came forward, dressed in a midnight-blue tunic with a cream-colored vest. Unlike the last time Mara had seen him, the noble wore no silver, and only a bit of gold embroidery on his collar. His beard was freshly trimmed, and his smile was as wide and irritating as ever. Tamas stood a few steps behind him in an almost identical outfit.

Mara saw Revathi's fan flutter in a complicated gesture. Lady Ekisa tapped her fan on her wrist.

Lord u'Gra didn't seem to notice. "It is an honor to have the most beautiful flowers of the house of sa'Hoi in my home." He pressed his hands together and bowed. "Ekisa, you look as young and fresh as ever."

"Sathvik." Lady Ekisa bowed in return. "Your manners, as always, are exquisite, though I can't say the same for your eyesight."

Lord u'Gra laughed. "Even a blind man would appreciate such company." He snapped his fingers, and a servant appeared with a tray of cheese dumplings. "Please," he said. "Accept my hospitality."

Lady Ekisa took one of the dumplings, as did Revathi. Mara hesitated.

"It's all right, Mara," Revathi said. "It's tradition."

Copying Revathi, Mara slid the dumpling into her mouth. It was sweet and milky on her tongue and she swallowed it down, wishing she dared to eat another.

"Hospitality is sweet," Lady Ekisa said. "We accept it with pleasure."

Lord u'Gra clapped his hands. "Excellent! Then we shall feast!" He turned, reaching out a hand. "One more thing, though. I need to make an introduction."

A woman about Mara's height came to his side. She was wearing an amber-colored knee-length tunic and loose trousers and carried herself with such calm assurance that Mara instantly felt overdressed and silly. Her brown hair held hints of gleaming copper, her skin was the color of honey, and her eyes were pale gold-brown. Mara caught a glimpse of golden flecks in her eyes and remembered that Revathi had mentioned a Sune in Lord u'Gra's household.

"This is Aari," Lord u'Gra said. "My companion."

Mara copied Revathi's bow. "Pleased to meet you," she murmured.

The corner of Aari's mouth curved up in a half smile. *But don't you remember, young one?* she sent, her mind-voice a languid drawl. *We've already met.*

36
Emil

EMIL LANDED HARD, rolling across yet another roof. His knee struck a rock, and sharp pain radiated through his leg. He rolled to a stop and lay still, catching his breath.

Why would there even be a rock there? Emil rolled onto his side, pressing his face into the dirty sandstone roof. He took several deep breaths, waiting for the throbbing pain in his knee to lessen. There was no sound from the house beneath him.

Abhra had been as good as his word, helping him sneak into the Flower Circle and even guiding him to an empty alley between two houses. Emil had used an iron hook and rope he'd purchased to scale the wall, and now he was searching all the unoccupied Flower Circle houses he could reach.

He pushed himself up, favoring his sore knee, and looked around. The roof was spotted with pale bird droppings and dry plant clippings. An abandoned wooden tub and several coiled clothing lines lay nearby, along with the flat stone he'd bashed his knee into. Emil scowled at it.

Probably used for washing. Stupid rock. Feeling grumpy and stiff, Emil limped for the stairs that led down to the inner courtyard of the house.

This home was even more deserted than most of the ones he'd looked at. The inner walls were covered in mosaics of white and green, and delicate iron balconies ringed the second floor, but the glossy stone of the inner courtyard was covered in dust, and the only tracks were the skittering marks of rats. The stone had been removed in places, leaving room for dark earth and a few spiky green bushes, but they were overgrown with weeds. This wasn't the careless decay of a house uninhabited for the summer. This was a house that no one had lived in for a very long time.

Emil sat down on the stairs to think.

He was searching empty houses because Abhra had pointed out that no noble family would share space with a group of Wind caste workers. Rajo hadn't been dressed as a servant, so he and his crew might have been hired to refurnish an empty house or one that had been abandoned for the summer. It made sense to Emil, so he'd been going house to house, looking for signs of the mercenaries.

He'd creep across a roof, peer around to make sure no one was looking, and then leap across the gap. Once inside, Emil would search the house. He'd found secret notes about trysts and packets of what he was pretty sure were dream root and poppy leaves.

He'd found stolen jewelry hidden away in servants' rooms and spoiled food in the pantries. He now knew more about the lives of the Flower caste nobles and their excesses than he ever wanted to.

But he hadn't found any sign of the mercenaries, or his brother.

Emil's legs ached and his hands were streaked with scrapes and dried blood. He couldn't keep this up much longer. Besides, it was getting dark.

One more, Emil told himself, rubbing his knee. *One more and I'll stop for the night.*

He pulled himself up and climbed the stairs again.

Now that it was getting darker, Emil could see that he was reaching the end of this stretch of empty houses. Light flickered from occupied homes around him, the courtyards turning into glowing squares in the gloom. There was one house nearby without lights, though. The roof was the same level as the one he was on, and the gap didn't seem to be too wide to jump across.

Emil stepped up onto the narrow stone wall, feeling it crunch under his feet. Then, taking a deep breath, he launched himself into the air.

As soon as his feet left the wall, Emil knew he had miscalculated. It might have been his weakened knee, or maybe the house was farther away than it looked. Instead of sailing over the next wall, he hit it with his leg. He felt the stone scrape and tear, and then he was spinning like a cart wheel, without a way to control the fall.

His head hit the roof with a crack that jarred his teeth together. The taste of blood filled his mouth.

Emil lay still, letting the shock pass. Everything hurt, especially his leg and his head. He'd just lie here a little while, then go downstairs and find a bed. He didn't care if it was dusty, or if there were bugs. He just wanted a soft mattress and some sleep. Then he could restart his search in the morning. . . .

Suddenly, from the darkened courtyard beneath him, he heard the last thing he was expecting. Footsteps.

"Who's up there?" a rough voice demanded. There was a spark, then a light flamed somewhere below. "Hello? Who's there?"

Emil shoved himself up, ignoring the pain that shot through his leg. A wave of dizziness made him stagger, but he lurched forward anyway. If he got caught . . . He didn't even want to think about that.

The footsteps were coming up the stairs.

Emil's head ached as he hobbled toward the edge of the roof. The house next door was a little shorter than this one and close enough that he wouldn't have to leap to it. Emil put his hands on the rough wall and braced himself.

Drop softly. Don't cry out. Don't get caught.

The light was almost to the top of the stairs. "Identify yourself!" the voice said. "Who's there?"

Emil flung himself over the edge, landing on the lower roof with only a quiet thud. Ignoring the scream of pain through his leg, he rolled toward the darker shadows of the roof, moving away from his landing point as fast as he could. He stopped when he felt the cool of a sandstone wall on his back.

A hand holding a flickering candle appeared over the wall of the house he'd come from. Emil held his breath.

He heard another set of footsteps, and a second dark shadow loomed behind the candlelight. A voice spoke into the dark. A voice that Emil knew.

Rajo the Black's voice.

"What's going on, Marir?" The mercenary spoke quietly, his words barely audible to Emil.

"I thought I heard a crash and someone moving around up here," the man with the candle replied. "But I don't see anyone."

Emil imagined Rajo peering into the gloom with narrowed eyes. The image made him want to jump up. He forced himself not to move.

"Set another guard at the top of the stairs," Rajo said, his voice still low. "But keep him out of sight. And put out that candle."

"Yes, sir," the man said. The light disappeared. The footsteps retreated.

Emil let his head fall back against the wall. Despite the pain in his leg, a fierce triumph filled him, and he could feel the smile growing on his stiff and aching face.

He'd found the mercenaries. Stefan couldn't be far away.

Now he just had to figure out a way to slip out of the Flower Circle and back to the Jade Circle without getting caught. Maybe he could swim the canal. . . .

Emil's jubilant thoughts trailed off, replaced by a growing sense of something wrong. It wasn't as dark up here as it should be, for one. Now that the sparks from the candlelight had faded from his eyes, he could see that. And under his cheek, he could hear the sound of low voices and the clinks of cups and dishes.

He'd landed on an occupied house.

Emil cursed himself. He'd been too dizzy from his fall and too worried about escaping to even check this house for people. But there *were* people here, and from the sound of it, they were having some sort of party.

He rose to a crouch and scanned the roof. Like all noble houses, this one was square, and built around an open courtyard. It was surprisingly bare for an occupied house, no roof gardens or wash lines. But that was good; it meant he didn't have to worry about tripping over anything. In the faint light from the courtyard below, he could see that his trousers were torn. A dark, sticky stain spread across the fabric, and his knee felt like it wouldn't hold his weight much longer. He couldn't afford another fall.

Emil reached into his tunic. The rope and hook were still there, though the hook had scored a mark across his chest when he had fallen. Only the red scarf wrapped around the tip had saved Emil from stabbing himself with it.

Stupid. What were you thinking?

Moving as quietly as he could, Emil started to make his way around the roof, looking for an alley or a quiet street. If he managed to climb down the wall without being seen, he could sneak away. He was still searching for a good spot, when a burst of polite laughter from inside the house made him pause.

There was something familiar about those voices.

Leaving the rope and hook next to the outer wall, Emil crept back to the low wall that ringed the opening above the courtyard.

Raising his head, he peered down into the lighted courtyard.

It was a dinner party. Rich fabrics glittered in the candlelight, and the smell of spiced meat and curry wafted up, making Emil's stomach growl. Two noblemen were talking to an older woman in silver-embroidered white, while a girl dressed in gray and green spoke softly to her companion, a girl with a soft dark cap of hair and a pink asar. Then the girl in pink smiled, and Emil's breath caught.

It was Mara.

37
Mara

MARA SAT AT the low table in the middle of Lord u'Gra's courtyard, feeling uncomfortable. The cushion she was sitting on was plump and silky, and she'd been provided with a small basin and towel to wash her hands. The table was loaded with food: lamb and chicken curry, savory vegetables, piles of soft, steaming flatbread, and bowls of fine-grained rice. A bouquet of bloodred hibiscus flowers sat by each plate. There were tiny decorative lamps scattered between the guests, and they cast a warm, bright light over the faces at the table.

But Mara couldn't enjoy the meal. Not with Aari's pale brown-gold eyes fixed on her.

Stop that, Mara sent finally. *I don't like being stared at.*

I can't help it, Aari sent back. *I've never seen a Sune look so . . . human. How long has it been since you've changed?*

Mara ignored the question and turned to Revathi next to her. "Your cup is getting low," she said, picking up the delicate ceramic pitcher. "Let me fill it."

"Thank you, Mara," Revathi said.

Lord u'Gra had provided a cold drink that tasted of lemon, honey, and dates, and Mara studied the faces around her as she poured it. Lady Ekisa was to the right of Lord u'Gra and Aari was on his left. Tamas was seated across from Revathi, both of them talking quietly.

Still not looking at Aari, Mara set the pitcher down and started in on the food on her plate.

I know who you are! Aari's mind-voice rang with triumph, as if she'd just figured out a particularly difficult puzzle. *You're Shar!*

Mara jerked, sending a piece of bitter melon spinning into her lap. The sauce made an ugly stain on her asar, and she kept her head down, trying to wipe it off.

How do you know that name?

Oh please, Aari sent. *You were the first tiger in years to be cast out of her Tribe.* Everyone's *heard of you.*

Mara dabbed at her asar with a towel, but the stain wouldn't come off. Her face felt hot.

Shar is gone. She died with her family.

That's a pity. Aari took a piece of lamb and popped it into her mouth. *You're famous, you know. I mean, the dark tigers of the north are legendary anyway, but you . . .* She licked her fingers. *How many hunters did you kill? Five? Ten?*

Mara closed her eyes, remembering the red wash of fury, the

mindless need to rend, and under it all, pain. So much pain. *Too many*, she sent. Her head was starting to ache.

They deserved it, Aari sent. *Trying to hunt Sune like that.*

Mara took a helping of one of the spicier chicken dishes. It tasted of garlic, tomatoes, and saffron and gave her tongue a pleasant burn. She added some green chili curry, pretending that it was the peppers that were making her eyes water.

At the end of the table, Lady Ekisa and Lord u'Gra were baiting each other.

"But surely," Lord u'Gra was saying, "you would agree that the sa'Hoi family is vastly overworked. Especially with your son and his wife away, as well as your grandson."

"They will return in time," Lady Ekisa said, her serene face showing nothing. "All three will be home by the end of the summer."

"It will be a happy day," Lord u'Gra said. "But still, I worry–"

"What a coincidence," Lady Ekisa interrupted, reaching for the yogurt. "I worry about you as well. With no wife to help you and your oldest son commanding the cavalry in Aranya–which is quite an honor, by the way, you're to be congratulated–plus all your court duties *and* spending so much time with the Emperor. I simply don't know how you manage."

"Visiting the Emperor is no hardship," Lord u'Gra said, his teeth bared in a smile. "We have a shared sorrow. And my service to the court is really very little. But I do look forward to having Revathi in my household. Is there no way the wedding date could be moved up? The start of Earthsleep is so far away."

Mara stole a glance at Revathi. The girl seemed totally focused on wrapping rice and lamb in a piece of flatbread. But when she lifted it to her mouth, Mara saw that her fingers were trembling.

Lady Ekisa laughed. It was a surprisingly young sound, bright and pealing like a copper bell. "Oh, Sathvik, would you take my right hand from me before my left returns? Besides, Tamas is still serving his two years of service with the Imperial Guard. You know the law. No nobleman can wed until he finishes his duty to the Empire."

"But surely your family is so close to Emperor Saro that you could get a special . . . dispensation."

"Be patient, Sathvik dear." Lady Ekisa wiped her mouth. "To want things before their proper time is nothing but greed. And as the wise ones say, greed is the root cause of sorrow."

"I was thinking of Revathi, of course," Lord u'Gra said smoothly. "You know the longer she waits to marry, the worse it looks. People talk, you know."

Revathi's lips tightened and her fan fluttered in her hands.

Lord u'Gra continued, "If you had accepted my original offer for her to marry my oldest son, Revathi could be wed by now and the happy mother of children."

Tamas shoved aside his cup with a clatter, splashing his drink on the table. "You there," he said, motioning to one of the gray-clad servants. "Bring me strong palm wine."

"People will always talk," Lady Ekisa said, fiddling with her own fan. "And Revathi is a sa'Hoi. Our family stays near the Emperor and the palace. Always. You knew that when the betrothal was agreed to."

"Betrothals can be broken." Sathvik u'Gra took a bite of his salad, bits of onion and cucumber falling from his fingers. His tone was perfectly pleasant, but Mara knew a threat when she heard it.

"Oh, I'm fully aware that betrothals can be broken," Lady Ekisa said, taking another sip of her drink. "I find the idea quite comforting."

Lord u'Gra choked on his salad, and Lady Ekisa smiled at him. "But then, I'm a selfish old lady who just wants to keep her granddaughter around a little longer. And wealth does not appeal to me the way it appeals to Revathi's parents. If you truly find our conditions so onerous, perhaps I should speak to her father."

"I was speaking hypothetically, of course," Lord u'Gra said, swallowing. "I wouldn't dream of letting such a wonderful alliance go. And Revathi's certainly improved my feckless younger son. He's quite taken with her."

Tamas drank his wine down and gestured for more.

Lady Ekisa picked up the bouquet of hibiscus flowers and took a deep whiff. "I'm glad we understand each other, Sathvik," she said, face half-hidden by the blossoms. "Now please, no more talk of moving up the wedding. It's getting tiresome."

Lord u'Gra's hands clenched, and his uneven smile faltered. "Of course, Ekisa. My apologies."

His eyes landed on Tamas, who was draining his second cup of wine and beckoning the servant for another refill. "Tamas! Don't be rude. This is not a drinking party, this is a family meal." He turned to one of the silent servants. "Take my son's wine away from him and give him only water from now on."

Tamas's scowl deepened.

Inside Mara's head, Aari snickered.

Look at them all, with their petty human maneuvering. Even the best of them can't see beyond their long noses. But they can be useful. She smiled at Lord u'Gra and put a hand over his clenched fist. The man relaxed a little, his face smoothing out.

Take Sathvik here. He treats me with the respect I deserve and allows me to do what I like without interference. It's more than I got in my own Tribe.

Mara felt her stomach turn, the food sour in her gut. *And what do you do here?*

I do the work of Kapih. The voice in her head was a self-satisfied purr.

The Trickster. Mara's mouth was dry, and she took another drink of water. *The human lord of chaos. You've chosen to serve him over Nishvana?*

What has the Silent-Pawed ever done for us? Aari sent. *Nothing. I prefer Kapih. He at least took action against his enemies.*

You mean humans, Mara sent. *You think humans are our enemies. That's why you hunt them.*

Why not? Aari sent back. *They hunt us, don't they? Take our forests for their farmland and drive us away.* She lifted her cup to her lips, and Mara could see the black *X* on the back of her hand. *They mark us as if they own us, as if they could. But we are stronger then they are. And one day . . .*

What? Mara tamped down her rising anger. *Another war? Is that what you want? More Sune to die?*

Who says it has to be Sune who die? Aari sent. She gave Mara a wide, slow grin, then leaned over to speak to Revathi. "Have you quite recovered from your shock at the Clothing Fair, my dear?" she said out loud. "It must have been horrid being in the middle of that riot. What could the Kildi have been thinking?"

Mara's spine tightened at the mention of the Kildi. Lord u'Gra's face became ugly, twisted.

"Kildi," he spit out. He seemed to welcome something to vent his still-simmering anger on. "Vermin. We should send them all to the copper mines."

"Come now, Sathvik," Lady Ekisa said, accepting a bowl of sweet rice pudding from a servant. "Surely that's a bit extreme."

"They're dangerous, Ekisa. They don't behave like proper Wind caste, they don't show respect like proper Wind caste, they don't even revere the Ancestors properly. Who knows what they're capable of? If the magic comes back . . ."

Revathi choked and hid her face behind her fan. Tamas slumped on his cushion, his arms folded over his chest.

"The magic is gone, Sathvik," Lady Ekisa said, digging into her dessert with a wooden spoon. "The Jade scholars say it's all up there in the Barrier."

"Well," Aari drawled. "Not *all* of it."

Lady Ekisa inclined her head in Aari's direction. "Forgive me. But surely you would agree that Sune magic is as out of our reach as the magic in the Barrier. Mere humans cannot use it, in any case."

"How fortunate for us," Aari said sweetly, then went back to her food.

"But what if it does come back?" Sathvik said, waving his

hands. "The Kildi are all that's left of the old rule. If the magic returns, it will likely come back through them. They should be eradicated."

Mara thought of the way Tamas had taunted Stefan, of the fear in Emil's eyes. Her hand curled around her cup, and she resisted the urge to throw it at Sathvik's face.

You see? Aari yawned, showing teeth that Mara thought looked a little too sharp for a human. *The humans can't get along with one another. All it would take is a spark. One flame bright and true enough to start a fire, and there will be a war. But this time instead of killing us, the humans will kill one another. Then when they are scattered and disorganized, we will drive them from the forests of our homes and make them afraid to ever, ever come back.*

Mara set down the cup and reached for the hibiscus bouquet by her plate instead, burying her nose in it. The feel of the soft petals soothed her. Aari's mind-voice grew a little gentler.

Don't you ever get tired of pretending to be something you're not? Of trying to make yourself small so the people around you don't get too frightened?

No.

You lie.

Mara didn't realize she was crushing the flowers until she looked down and saw her hand was full of red petals. They looked like fresh blood against her skin.

I am nothing like you, she sent.

Aren't you? Aari sat back, a glint in her eye. *We'll see about that.*

38
Emil

EMIL WATCHED, FASCINATED, from his hiding place above the dinner party. He couldn't hear everything that was said, but the faces and motions below him told a story all on their own. The older woman and the nobleman especially interested him. They were clearly rivals, battling each other for status. The lord was good, but the woman was better, and Emil wanted to cheer every time she manipulated the conversation and backed her opponent into a corner.

The younger noblewoman didn't speak as much, but when she did, she was just as deft with words as her older companion. And she had a way of playing with her fan that almost looked like she was sending messages with it.

Things grew considerably less amusing when the nobleman started ranting about the Kildi. The word *eradicated* was clear and hard, even from up here, and it hit Emil like a physical blow. He knew people felt that way, of course, but hearing it was somehow a hundred times worse. He dug his fingers into the stone and forced himself to stay quiet. He was grateful when the conversation turned back to court matters.

The younger nobleman said something Emil didn't catch. The girl waved her fan again.

"Revathi, dear, are you too warm?" the man at the head of the table asked, his voice oozing concern. "I can assign someone to fan you while you eat, if that would make you more comfortable."

The girl smiled innocently. "What a gracious offer," she said. "But I'm perfectly comfortable." She settled the fan back in her lap and glanced at the older woman, who set her spoon down.

"I'm afraid, Sathvik, that I'm not as young as I used to be, and your generous table has made me feel quite sleepy." She bowed from her seat, pressing her hands together. "May I make a toast to end the meal?"

"Of course. Allow me to fill your drink," the man said. The others hastened to fill one another's cups as well. Then everyone held them up.

"To your health, Sathvik," the older woman said. "And to the health of those dining under your roof tonight. May our family alliance be profitable and pleasant for us all."

"May it be," everyone echoed.

Emil shifted his eyes back to Mara. The asar certainly made her look beautiful, but there was something about the way she looked that he didn't quite like. Maybe it was how uncomfortable she seemed. He preferred Mara as he'd seen her last, with messy hair and flushed cheeks. Vivid and fighting and *alive*. This Mara looked tense and unhappy, and when she drank the toast, Emil saw her hands were shaking.

He turned his attention back to the party just in time to hear Lord Sathvik offer to escort the older woman home.

"We can leave the younger ones to themselves," he said with a wink. "With Aari and Mara here, it's perfectly proper."

The older woman hesitated, but the man she'd called Sathvik wasn't taking no for an answer. He handed her a bouquet of hibiscus flowers and firmly took her arm.

"Now don't argue, Ekisa," he said. "I would speak to you of some . . . delicate matters. Surely you do not find my company so disagreeable that you would deny me the benefit of your advice."

"Of course not," the other woman said, but her voice was a little too sweet and her fan fluttered near her face. "Don't stay too long, Revathi. I don't want you walking about late at night."

"Yes, Grandmother," the girl said.

As soon as the two older nobles were gone, the younger man grabbed Revathi's arm and pulled her aside, ending up almost directly under Emil. There was a furious whispered conversation, and Emil could see their faces more clearly.

Emil frowned. That was Tamas, the noble who'd almost killed Stefan. And that was the girl who'd been with him. But what was Mara still doing with them?

He glanced at Mara, but she was on the other side of the courtyard, staring at the other person present, a woman dressed in amber. Mara's face was distant and Emil thought a little despairing. The woman gave her a superior smile, and Emil was suddenly furious. He wanted to march down there and take Mara away from those people, find whatever was hurting her and make it stop.

Tamas's voice rose.

"You *know* what you should have said. Say you're happy to be marrying me, say you're content, say *anything*. Don't just sit there like a lump. My father will think you really did want to marry Tapan."

"I don't want to marry your brother, Tamas," the girl said. Emil thought she sounded tired. She put a hand on his arm. "I want to marry you."

"I don't believe you."

The girl sighed. "Tamas, please. It's late and you've been drinking. Why don't you walk me home?"

"No." Tamas reached out and grabbed her arm hard enough to make her flinch. His voice dropped to a growl. "Not until you tell me you're glad to be marrying me. Say it." His hand tightened, and Emil winced in sympathy. "Say it."

"I'm glad to be marrying you," the girl said. She lowered her voice. "Please, don't do this here, Tamas. You're embarrassing yourself."

She pulled away, and Tamas yanked her back. Then he struck her across the face with the back of his hand.

Mara whirled at the sound. The girl staggered backward, lost her footing on the stone of the courtyard, and fell. Her head struck a heavy iron statue with an audible crack . . .

And she crumpled.

Choice is a most gracious and most deadly gift.

Gracious for its infinite possiblilties.

Deadly for its infinite consequences.

It is like a rock thrown into the sky.

You cannot see where it will land.

You only know that it will.

Jade caste teaching

39

Mara

"REVATHI!"

Mara was moving before Revathi hit the floor. Tamas was frozen, his hand still upraised, and Mara resisted the urge to strike him, to hit him as hard as he'd hit Revathi. Her vision swam with red.

Later. Check Revathi first.

Anger thrummed through Mara's bones: anger and worry and guilt. Because she should have *known*. Revathi's bruises, the way she brushed Mara off, the way she stiffened sometimes when Tamas touched her. It had been right in front of Mara the whole time, and she hadn't seen it. She'd been so focused on finding her charge that she hadn't even suspected anything was wrong.

Mara knelt down, her fingers searching Revathi's scalp. There was a long, shallow gash near her hairline. It bled freely, staining Mara's fingers. Revathi's eyes were closed, but at least she was breathing.

"Revathi," Mara said, trying not to shake the girl too much. "Revathi, can you hear me?" The girl's head lolled slightly, her body limp.

Mara looked up at Tamas. "Call for a healer," she snapped.

"It was an accident," Tamas said. "I didn't mean to hurt her."

"I don't care," Mara said. "Call a healer."

Tamas shook his head. "I can't," he said. "If my father finds out, he'll be furious."

"Revathi could be seriously hurt!" Mara said. "She needs help." She stood, heading for the door. "If you won't call a healer, I will."

Tamas grabbed her by the shoulders and shoved her back. "You're not going anywhere," he said. His voice rose. "No one is going anywhere."

Mara had her dagger out before she even knew she was going for it.

"Step aside," she ordered.

"You can't threaten me," Tamas said. "Who do you think you are? I *hired* you."

Mara shifted her stance. "Then I quit. Now get out of my way or—"

There was almost no warning, only a small rustle and a prickle along the back of Mara's neck. She barely had time to react before pain exploded through her back and shoulder.

Mara's spine snapped back. As if in slow motion, she turned

her head to see Aari holding a slender knife of her own, its blade red and glistening.

"Aari, what are you *doing*?" Tamas said.

"She was threatening you with a dagger," Aari said. "What do you think I'm doing?"

Mara forced herself to take a step. Pain seared through her. *Why?* she sent.

You're not the only one with a job here. Aari smiled, slow and satisfied. *Besides, you said we're nothing alike. Now's your chance to prove it.*

The ground lurched, and suddenly Mara's dagger was gone from her numb fingers and she was falling and someone was shouting and there was so much pain. She hadn't felt anything like this since . . .

Since the day her family died.

As if summoned by the thought, her memories surged up with a scream, all red vision and coppery blood in her mouth. Her fingers were already flexing, wanting to tear and scratch. Magic pooled hot and sour in her stomach.

Hurt. Pain. Enemies.

Kill them all.

No!

But the memories and the flashbacks were like an undertow, sucking her down into the past. Mara could taste blood in her mouth now–her blood–and didn't know if it was from a bitten lip, or something worse.

Stop resisting, little one. Aari's voice was as smooth and sharp as the knife she'd plunged into Mara's flesh. *Give in to it. Embrace your heritage.*

Tears blinded Mara's eyes. She curled in on herself, as if she could hold the magic and the anger in the hollow of her body. As if she could keep it from spilling out, hurting anyone ever again.

I am human, she thought desperately. *I am human.*

Is that what you're telling yourself now? Aari laughed inside her head. *No wonder you're so weak.*

Mara shoved Aari out of her head and tried to breathe. She needed something to focus on, something to keep her from changing.

Touch. She could remember touch, what the air felt like without the protective covering of fur. She could remember the feel of a warm bath and flower petals under her fingers. The softness of cashmere and the smoothness of carved wood. Things that were real, human. She tried to think of Revathi, but that only made her angrier. Because someone had hurt Revathi, like they'd hurt Mara's family.

Hurt them back. Kill them.

No.

She needed something else. Something with only good memories attached.

Emil.

Her frantic mind latched onto the name. She could hold on to Emil. She could hang on to his earth-brown eyes and his slow, kind smile. The concern in his face when he ran into the clearing, the way he'd fought to get to his brother at the Clothing Fair. The first time he'd touched her hand, the unexpected shock of his fingers on hers. His gentleness when he read her palm. The way he'd brushed the hair off her forehead before saying good-bye. She'd felt his touch on her skin long afterward, like the echo of a dream.

That was good, that memory of lingering warmth. It was another human sensation. She could use it as an anchor stone, keeping her in this body. But it was hard, so hard. The pain was a monster of its own, it had claws and teeth; it was ripping her apart along with the magic and she just wanted it to stop. . . .

"Mara!"

Arms slid around her. Arms that smelled like earth and wool, arms that held her up, held her *in* in a way she couldn't explain. And someone was calling her name, a voice straight out of her red-washed imagination.

Mara's eyes flew open.

"Emil?"

40

Emil

"NO!" THE STRANGLED sound of his own voice echoed in Emil's ears. The image of the woman in the amber-colored tunic coldly stabbing Mara while her back was turned was burned into his mind, as he ran for the stairs. Mara was in danger, and he had to get to her.

Tamas and the woman were arguing.

"Your father specifically told me to take care of you. You were about to get yourself killed."

"I don't need a babysitter, Aari! And how is this going to look to everyone else? She accepted our hospitality and you attacked her!"

"She attacked you first!"

Emil stumbled down the last few steps, falling to his knees next to Mara's body.

Not a body. Not dead. No.

She was still breathing, little whimpers coming from the back of her throat. Her fists were clenched as if she were battling against an invisible foe. Emil gathered her into his arms, paying no attention to the blood that streaked his hands.

At his touch, her eyes flew open.

"Emil?" The hope in her voice when she said his name hit Emil harder than his fall on the roof had.

"Yeah," he said, trying to smile, though he felt like crying. "It's me. Shhh. Lie still."

Her hand came up, gripping his shoulder with painful strength.

"Don't let me . . . ," she whispered. Tears leaked from the corners of her eyes. "Talk to me. Please. Don't let me slide away. I can't do it again, I can't. Don't let me do it."

"Of course not." Emil smoothed her hair with his fingers. "I won't let anything bad happen to you. I swear. I'm here. It's going to be all right."

He lowered his head to hers, so their foreheads touched. "Just hang on," he whispered. There was a deep stab wound along the inside edge of Mara's shoulder blade. Carefully, Emil put a hand on her back, gathering as much of the asar material as he could and pushing it against the injury. Mara cried out at the pressure. "It's all right," Emil soothed. "I'm just trying to slow the bleeding. You're going to be fine."

"Who the hell are you?"

Emil looked up to see Tamas and the woman who had stabbed Mara staring down at him, with very different expressions on their faces. The woman looked disappointed, as if Emil had taken something away from her, and she wasn't sure what to make of him. Tamas just looked angry.

"Who are you and what are you doing in my house?"

"Trying to save the girl who was stabbed under your roof!" Emil snapped back. He scooped up the nearby knife and waved it at the nobleman, keeping him away. The handle was sticky with blood.

Tamas flinched. "See, Aari! Even a low-caste thief knows how this looks. If this gets out, both Father and I will lose a lot of face, and I don't think he'll be very happy with you if that happens."

There was a murmur and a groan from nearby. A slow smile spread across Aari's face. "I think I can get us out of this," she said. "But you'd best go see to Revathi first."

A guilty flush crept up Tamas's neck, but he went to Revathi, who was starting to stir.

Mara started whimpering again, and Emil whispered soft, comforting words to her as he watched Tamas help Revathi sit up.

The noble girl held a hand to her head. "I don't need your help, Tamas," she said, her words cold. "I think you've done quite enough." She got unsteadily to her feet. "I think it's best if I take Mara and go home. . . ." Revathi trailed off, her eyes finding Emil and the bleeding girl in his arms.

"Mara!" Revathi ran to them and knelt down. Her fingers found the the knife wound, and her expression went from concerned to furious.

"What happened?" she asked, looking up. Her face was bright and fierce. "Who did this?"

Emil opened his mouth, but Aari spoke first.

"He did," she said, pointing two fingers at Emil. "He came running downstairs right after you passed out. Mara tried to stop him, and he stabbed her."

"No!" Emil said, his arm tightening around Mara. "That's a lie!"

"Oh, really?" Aari asked, her eyes sparking with malicious enjoyment. "Then why are you still holding the knife?"

Emil looked down at the blade in his hand. "I picked it up to protect her!" He stared at Revathi, willing her to believe him. "I didn't stab Mara. I wouldn't do that."

"Don't say her name," Revathi said, and there was such fury in her face that Emil had to resist the urge to scuttle backward. "Don't you *dare*. Get away from her."

In his arms, Mara gave a little gasping cry. "Shh, it's all right," Emil said, rocking her. "Shhhh." He looked up again, meeting Revathi's eyes. "I'm holding pressure on her wound," he said. "If I move, she could bleed to death."

Revathi glared at him. "Tamas," she snapped. "Call the guards. And send someone to the palace for Garen. We're going to need help getting Mara out of here."

Tamas frowned. "I don't know if we should . . ."

Aari threw up her hands. "Save us from stupid men," she said. "We have the man who stabbed her, right? So of course we'll call the guards. I'll do it. You watch the dangerous criminal and make sure he doesn't escape."

Tamas straightened his shoulders. "Of course." He grabbed a sword that was lying nearby and prodded Emil with it. "Don't move."

"I'm not going anywhere," Emil muttered. Then he turned his attention back to Mara. He wasn't afraid of Tamas or Revathi. It would take more than a few guards to tear Mara out of his arms.

In the end, it took four. They pried Mara away from him, giving her to Revathi. Mara cried out in pain at the movement.

"Mara!" Emil pulled against the hands restraining him. "No! I'm not leaving."

He struggled and kicked until he received a swift blow to his head that made his ears ring. By the time his vision cleared, his hands were tied behind his back.

"Take him away," Revathi said. She looked up from where she was holding pressure on Mara's shoulder. Her hair fell around her narrow face, and there was a streak of blood on her cheek. Her voice was cold. "I'm going to deal with him personally."

The soldier holding Emil laughed. "I wouldn't want to be in your shoes, thief."

Emil didn't care. His eyes were fixed on Mara, bloody and limp in Revathi's arms.

"If you let her die . . . ," he started.

Revathi's eyes glittered. "If she dies," she said, very softly and precisely, "so will you."

Her words rang in Emil's ears as the soldiers dragged him away.

41
Mara

EMIL. EMIL!

Mara whimpered, the sound broken and harsh against her lips. Emil was gone and without his presence to ground her, she felt herself slipping back into the red flood. Everything inside her screamed to change.

And it was tempting, so tempting. But what lay under the pain was more than magic, it was rage and fury and the instincts of a wounded animal. The past was here now, the flashes of memory as real to her as the present. If she changed and lost control . . .

She could kill everyone in this courtyard.

There was someone else holding her now, someone who smelled of jasmine and sandalwood, and there were more voices and more hands. So many people around her. So many lives at stake.

Help. I need help.

Mara started breathing, focusing inward, like her instructors at the Order had taught her. Then she took that little bit of strength and reached out with her mind.

It was less like calling and more like screaming, less like reaching out and more like groping blindly, but Mara was desperate enough to make it carry.

Help me, anyone. Please.

Mara? It was Garen's voice, solid and soft and powerful. *Mara, what's happened?*

It hurts, Mara whimpered. *Garen, I can't fight it. You have to get here, you have to protect the humans. Please.*

I'm right outside the house, Garen rumbled. *I won't let you hurt anyone.*

Mara! A new voice cut in, welcome and familiar.

Esmer! Mara was breathing ragged and hard, each inhale sending new waves of pain through her. *Esmer, help me.*

I'm coming as fast as I can, Esmer answered, and even her mind-voice felt slightly out of breath. *Hang on.*

Hands touched her, large and gentle on her skin. *I'm here, Mara,* Garen sent. *I've got you.* Strength flowed down the mental link, pouring over Mara like water from a pitcher. Her memories of being human sharpened, became solid things for her to hang on to.

I'm going to lift you, Garen's mind-voice was soothing. *Hold on.*

And she was being picked up, and Nishvana, it hurt. Another flashback rocked her, another memory, her family dead and dying around her. Mara could feel her tenuous hold on her sanity slipping, feel the urge to change rising, and with it the rage. *I can't do this.*

You can, Esmer sent firmly. *I'm almost there, Mara. Don't give in.*

She was being carried, they were walking somewhere, and every step made Mara feel like she was being stabbed again.

I am human. I am human.

But the refrain wasn't working anymore. Awash in Sune strength and Sune magic, Mara couldn't pretend she'd never been anything else. Her grip on her human memories was fading, and without them, she couldn't find the human parts of her again.

Voices jostled around her.

"Garen, is she going to be all right? What are you doing to her?"

"Not now, Revathi. Go find us a room to put her in."

Then there was another hand on hers, and new strength was added to the mental link, as firm and comforting as a sword in her hand. *I'm here, Mara.* Esmer's voice was sharp and anxious. *Tell us what you need. Tell us how to help you.*

Mara wanted to answer, but the blackness had her now, sucking her down. The voices faded away until all that was left was pain and anger and the memory of earth-brown eyes. Her last lifeline. Her last hope.

Emil.

42

Emil

EMIL SAT IN the small stone cell of the guardhouse. His muscles were cold and stiff and his leg throbbed, but he didn't notice. His mind was filled with Mara. Had they gotten her help in time? Was she still alive?

Would he stay alive long enough to find out?

He stood and ran his fingers over the walls again, looking for a weak spot, a hole, anything. He reached up to the small slit that served for a window, measuring it again with his hands. Too small for him, just like it had been the other five or six times he'd checked.

Emil stood on his toes, trying to get his mouth up to the window. "Esmer!" he called. "Esmer, are you out there?"

There was no answer, not that he expected one. Esmer was probably still searching for Stefan somewhere. If he'd had a

Sune's mind-speaking powers, he might have been able to reach her, but now . . .

Emil looked down at his hands, still covered with Mara's blood. His desperation hardened, turning into a thick, scalding rage that burned through his marrow.

He hated Stefan for leaving and he hated the mercenaries for taking him. He hated his father for letting it happen and he hated the city that had swallowed his brother and refused to give him back. He hated this cell and the soldiers outside and the fact that his word was worth less than that of the woman who had stabbed Mara. He hated Revathi for not believing him and he hated Esmer for not being here to help him and he hated Mara for letting herself get hurt.

But most of all, Emil hated himself. Because no matter how hard he tried, he couldn't save anyone. Not even himself.

The rage blurred his vision, turning everything red, and Emil threw himself at the unyielding walls. He tore at the stone until his fingernails bled and he shouted until his voice was hoarse, and he rattled the door until the guard threatened to come in and give him another blow to the head.

And when the anger was gone, Emil collapsed onto the filthy stone floor, put his head on his knees, and let out a single, broken sob.

It was over. Someone would come at Firstlight to pass judgment on him. If they thought he had stolen anything, they would cut off his hand. At best, they would give him a fine, and if Emil couldn't pay it, they would wrap bronze cuffs around his wrists and put him to work.

He would never see his family again.

It was the pain in his leg that finally pulled Emil out of the fog of despair. Fresh blood glistened on his already bloody trousers. His wound must have broken open again.

Gritting his teeth, Emil pulled the fabric away from the skin. The cut was full of small rocks and dirt and surrounded by scrapes that were tender to the touch.

Emil pulled his scarf out of his tunic, where it had stayed when they took away his climbing hook. He tried to use it to clean the wound, but the thin material just smeared the blood around. Finally he gave up and just started tearing strips from his tunic.

At least the rest of him seemed to be intact. His knee was a little swollen and sore, but it held his weight. The tips of his fingers were bloody from scraping on the cell wall, and his throat hurt from shouting, but those were minor problems. . . .

The iron-banded door to his cell creaked open.

"They said you'd be here," a familiar voice said.

Emil's head jerked up so fast that he actually struck it on the cell wall. Sparks filled his vision, and he blinked them away in time to see Esmer slip into his cell.

"Easy, Emil. Don't hurt yourself," she said. She knelt swiftly and put her hand under his chin, looking into his face. "You're in worse shape than I thought. What in the name of the Long-Tailed Cat were you doing?"

"What was I doing . . . ?" Emil stared at her. "How did you find me?"

Esmer looked up, and Emil realized she hadn't come alone. A huge man in the dark blue of the palace guard stood in the doorway, holding a torch. Emil had an impression of a large-jowled face and a pair of sharp, dark eyes.

"This is Emil?" he said. The man's voice was deep and tinged with worry.

"Yes, help me get him up." Esmer slid an arm under Emil's right side while the man moved to his left.

"Wait," Emil said, struggling to his feet between them. "What's going on?"

Esmer didn't answer. Her smooth hair hung in wisps around her face, and her mouth was tight with an emotion Emil couldn't read. And her hands, too, were streaked with blood.

Fear, like a chasm, yawned under Emil's feet. "Esmer, has something happened to Stefan?"

Esmer shook her head. "It's not Stefan." She looked like she might say more, but the man with her spoke firmly.

"Young man, you're needed at the palace. That is all you need to know."

The palace. Where they'd taken Mara.

"Mara," Emil breathed the name. "Are you taking me to her?" He put a hand on Esmer's arm. "Please . . ."

Esmer put her hand over his and squeezed. "We can't talk here," she said. "Trust me."

Emil forced himself to smile. "Always."

They followed the large Imperial Guard out of the guardhouse and through the night-softened city without stopping until they reached the palace. Torches glowed from the high pavilion, and two enormous fires in scooped stone basins lit the gated entrance. The guards at the gate only nodded at the man in blue as he hurried by. They paid no attention to Emil or Esmer.

Their guide led them through the dark gardens and to a long, low building. Torchlight gleamed on copper-and-silver trimming. Emil thought they would go in the door, but the man veered off at the last minute, walking swiftly around the building. He stopped at the curtained arch of a window and knocked softly on the pillar.

A girl's face peered through the rich, heavy fabric, and Emil recognized it as Revathi's.

"Oh good, you brought him," she said. "I'm trying to keep her still, but I don't think she can hold out much longer."

"Who?" Emil demanded. "Mara? Where is she?"

"Keep your voice down!" Revathi said. "Do you want the whole palace to know what's happened? It's bad enough I had to bring her to my grandmother's room. . . ."

Emil was about to argue, but Esmer put her hand on his arm, her fingers digging into his skin. "Get inside, Emil," she said. "Please."

"Through the window?" Emil said.

Revathi rolled her eyes. "I would think after climbing on the roof earlier, a window wouldn't be any problem. Do you want to help Mara, or not?" She pulled away, leaving the opening clear.

Emil climbed in the window as gracefully as his stiff and sore body would allow, which turned out not to be very graceful at all.

He got tangled in the heavy curtains and half stepped, half fell into the room.

Revathi scowled at him, and he scowled right back as he untangled himself. Esmer, in cat form, easily leaped to the windowsill and inside. The big soldier followed, his light movements at odds with his large frame.

It was a noble's room, richly decorated in red and silver and as large as half a campsite. But it didn't smell like a noble's room. It smelled like blood and medicine and pain. And on the bed was Mara.

Emil ran to her. Mara lay still and tense. Her brown skin had an unhealthy pallor, and her fists were clenched so tightly that her arms shook. Blood soaked the folded fabric under her shoulder.

"Why hasn't this been properly bandaged yet?" Emil demanded.

The big man knelt on the other side of the bed, smoothing Mara's hair. Emil resisted the urge to slap his hand away.

"She's barely holding on to herself as it is," the man said softly. "We can't stitch the wound until she stabilizes emotionally, or she might lose control."

"Lose control?"

Mara groaned and whispered something that Emil couldn't hear. He leaned closer. It was one word, repeated over and over, like a prayer.

She was calling his name.

Emil felt like he couldn't breathe. He dropped to his knees, his fingers finding hers. "Mara," he said softly. "Mara, it's me. I'm here."

The girl's eyes flew open. "Emil," she said. A whimper spilled from her lips. "Please don't leave me again, please, you can't let me change. I can't go through it again, I can't."

"Shhh," Emil said. Without thinking, he laced his fingers through hers and put the other hand on her forehead, stroking her sweat-damp hair. "Shhh, I'm here." Mara seemed to relax a little under his touch, and her eyes closed again. He looked up at the others.

"What is she talking about? Why hasn't anyone helped her?"

The man exchanged glances with Esmer, who bit her lip.

"Emil," she said, "Mara is a Sune. Like us."

"What?" Emil looked down at the girl. She seemed so small, so fragile, so . . . human. "A Sune? Are you sure?"

"Of course I'm sure!" Esmer snapped. "That's the whole problem."

"What do you mean?" Amazement and bewilderment twisted and swirled inside Emil, but he pushed them both aside. "Why would being Sune be a problem?"

The guard gave him a sharp look, but answered easily enough. "A Sune's driving instinct when injured is to change to animal form. It makes it easier to fight or escape, and the magic helps us heal. But sometimes a Sune in great physical or emotional pain doesn't always have control over herself." He paused. "Have you ever tried to get a thorn out of a cat's paw? Mara is like that wounded cat right now, only bigger and stronger. She could kill someone and she knows it."

"But that's not the real problem." Revathi knelt down on the other side of Mara's bed. "Even if she doesn't hurt anyone, there's a good chance that if she changes, she'll run. And a tiger loose in the palace? The Imperial Guard would put a spear in her heart before you or I could blink."

"No," Emil said, his hand tightening around Mara's. "That's not happening."

"All right," Revathi said. "Do you think you can distract her, help her keep her human form while we tend to her wound?"

Mara moaned, and the pain in her face made Emil's heart twist.

"Tell me what to do," he said.

43

Mara

EMIL WAS BACK. Mara didn't care how or why, but he was back and he was sliding onto the bed, easing her into his arms, supporting her. She felt the light weight of a blanket on her hips. Her mind began to clear.

But the pain was still there, along with the magic, both of them snarling and growling just under her skin. And she was tired, so tired.

"You shouldn't be here," she murmured. "I could kill you."

Emil's voice was low and soft in her ear. "I don't care."

"You don't understand," Mara said, burying her face in his shirt. The words came out muffled and thick. "I'm a monster."

"No." Emil said. He slid a hand along her jaw, cupping her chin with his palm. "Even if you changed, you wouldn't be a monster." The faith in his voice was like a physical force, shattering and holding her together at the same time. "You can do this, Mara."

He held her close, keeping her from turning her head as someone started to cut away the shirt from her bloody back.

There was a sudden flare of pain, and Mara hissed through her teeth. "Emil," she said. "Talk to me. Please."

"What do you want to know?" Emil asked.

"Tell me about your people," Mara asked. "The Kildi. Are all of you herders?"

"Not all of us," Emil said. "Kildi clans can do a lot of things. There's a clan in the East that specializes in gathering rare mushrooms and tubers, and one based near Deshe that trains songbirds for pets. But we can only sell what we raise or make with our own hands. We don't grow anything because we're forbidden to own land. We live on what we hunt and on what we buy with the money we make from trading our wares. . . ."

Mara relaxed, feeling his words wrap around her like sturdy cords. Emil's shirt smelled like spices and his own special earthy scent, and his chest was warm and solid under her cheek. The smell and the touch were a rope of their own, leading her back to herself, keeping her human.

I can do this, Mara thought. *I can do this.*

44

Emil

EMIL LOOKED DOWN at the girl in his arms. He'd settled with his back against the wall and Mara half in his lap. She felt warm and solid in his arms, but her skin had a grayish cast, and she trembled as Revathi and Garen took turns working on her shoulder. The stab wound looked deep and angry to Emil, but Garen assured him that Sune healed quickly.

"You just keep talking to her," he said. "Let us worry about the wound."

It should have felt strange, holding Mara like this. He barely knew her after all. But it didn't feel odd. It felt . . . right. It felt like a good session of bargaining. Like lying by a stream on a hot, muggy day. Like home.

Mara curled into him, her face buried in his shirt, and Emil stroked her short, soft hair. And he talked. He told Mara about his camp and his family. He told her of the time that Stefan tried to catch the biggest male goat in camp, and how he was butted into the river while Emil laughed himself sick on the bank. The time the two of them had snuck out of camp and gotten lost trying to find just the right flowers for their mother's name day. How when they were small, they looked almost identical, and how they used that to play tricks on villagers and merchants.

And he told Mara the stories his mother had told him and Stefan when they were very little. He told her the legends of the Kildi and the Horned God, he told her the story of Pillaiyar, the Ancestor who watched over travelers and strangers. When she cried out in pain, he whispered soothing lullabies, singing them softly in her ear.

When the wound was washed with wine and herbs and the edges were stitched together, Garen bandaged Mara's shoulder, while Revathi made a strong-smelling tea. She handed it to Emil.

"This will keep you awake," she told him. "Garen says Mara needs to keep a clear head, which means no pain herbs for her, and more talking for you."

Emil glanced pointedly at the teacup. "That's not poisoned, is it?"

To his surprise, Revathi smiled. "Poison's not my style." She leaned down and put her mouth close to his ear. "I meant what I said before," she whispered. "About what happens if she dies."

Emil's arms tightened around Mara. "She's not going to die," he snapped. "Give me the damn tea."

Revathi handed him the cup. Still looking at her, Emil sipped the tea, tasting it. It was smooth and dark, with a faint sweet undertone, hot, but not scalding. He drank it down in one draught, then handed the cup back to Revathi.

"Not bad," he said. "Could have been a little stronger, though."

Revathi snorted, then went to help Garen, who was gathering up the medicines. She collected the bloody towels and started to pick up the scraps of bandage. Esmer was curled up near the door in cat form, her long spotted legs tucked underneath her. Her golden eyes seemed to take in the whole room, and her ears twitched with every sound.

"Standing guard?" Emil called to her softly.

The cat stood, stretched, and trotted over, the black tip of her tail twitching. When she shimmered back into human form, she was smiling.

"Someone had to do it," she said. "And I'm no good with sick people. How is she?"

Emil looked down at Mara, whose eyes were half-closed. "She's in control, and I can help her stay that way." He paused, glancing at Revathi and Garen. The two were talking in low voices and didn't seem to be listening to him and Esmer.

He lowered his voice to a whisper anyway. "Esmer, I found them."

Her eyes widened, understanding. "Where?"

Emil motioned for her to lean over. "Next to the house Mara was stabbed in," he breathed into her ear. "I almost got caught by someone there, and I know I heard Rajo's voice. Can you check?"

Esmer nodded. "I'll go now." And before anyone could stop

her, she flashed into cat form and leaped out the window.

"Where is she going?" Revathi asked.

Emil just shrugged. Revathi frowned.

"She'd better not tell anyone what's happened here," she said. "It could put Mara in danger."

"Esmer's not stupid," Emil said, sharper than he intended. "And she cares more about Mara than you do."

Revathi smiled again, but Emil thought her eyes were sad. "Emil, I've defied my fiancé, allowed an injured tiger-Sune into the palace, and lied to my grandmother. That's more than I've ever done for anyone before."

Garen straightened, his arms full of glass herb jars. "Revathi," he said. "Will you help me return these to the palace healers?"

"Of course, Garen," Revathi said. "I have to figure out a good lie to tell them anyway." She set a cup of water on the table by the bed. "Try to get her to drink this," she said to Emil. "I'll try to keep the servants and my grandmother away as long as I can."

Emil watched as they walked out.

Mara shifted a little in his lap, and Emil looked down to find her eyes were open and fixed on his face. There were subtle golden flecks in them that he hadn't seen before, the mark of a Sune. He was suddenly very aware of the weight of her body resting in his arms, of the heat of her cuddled against him.

"Hello, you," he said, covering his confusion. "How are you feeling?"

"Like I was stabbed," Mara said, her voice soft and hoarse. "But it could have been worse." Her eyes closed, tears slipping out from the corners. "It could have been so much worse."

"But it wasn't," Emil said. Without thinking, he wiped the damp trails from her cheek with his thumb. Her skin was soft under his hand, and she leaned into his touch in a way that made his mouth dry. "No one else was hurt, and you're still here."

"Thanks to you," Mara whispered. A spasm of pain twisted her face. "I'm still . . . could you talk to me some more?"

"I'm out of stories," Emil said.

"Not quite," Mara said. "You haven't told me why you're here."

"Well," Emil said, shifting so Mara could look up at him more easily. "I saw this girl I know attacked and . . ." He waved an arm. "Here I am."

Mara's mouth curved into a shaky smile, the first real one he'd seen on her since the Clothing Fair. "Not why you're in the palace," she said. "Why are you here in Kamal? It doesn't seem like the sort of place you'd be comfortable living."

"It's not," Emil said. "I mean, it's nice but . . ."

". . . there are too many people," Mara finished. "And not enough sky."

"Exactly," Emil said. "I can't wait to go home." A memory of his father's angry face rose up, and he swallowed.

"Must be nice," Mara said. "Having a home to go to."

Emil didn't answer for a moment. "I don't know if I do," he said at last. "Have a home, that is. I had a bad fight with my father right before I left."

"A fight about what?" Mara asked. And the words were like a key turning in a lock. Emil told her everything: Stefan, his father, the mercenaries, even his search across the roofs of the Flower Circle.

"So I don't know," Emil concluded. "Even if I find Stefan, and he's willing to come back with me, I don't know what our father will say. Stefan ran away, and I . . . I defied him. He might not welcome us."

He waited for Mara to reassure him, to tell him that of course his father would accept them again.

"Why *did* you defy him?" she asked instead. "It wasn't just because you were worried about Stefan, was it?"

"No," Emil said, caught off guard. The truth spilled off his tongue. "I couldn't stand the idea of losing Stefan like I lost my mother. Sacrificing him for the good of the camp."

Mara looked up, her eyes very wide and dark. "Tell me."

So Emil did. "It was the coldest Earthsleep anyone in camp could remember," he started. It was a relief to say the words out loud, words that had been swirling inside him for years, carving out hollow space. "The fog was so thick you could get lost, and it went straight through to your skin, no matter how many layers you were wearing. The wild animals either fled to the deep forest or died of cold and lack of food. I don't know what we would have done if Esmer's Tribe hadn't helped us. They hunted small game and birds for us in return for a share of our meals." He smiled at the memory. "Esmer said we were doing them a favor, that no one in her Tribe could cook properly."

"She must care about you a lot," Mara said. "To treat you like Tribe that way."

"We've been friends since we were kids," Emil said. "Esmer's the most loyal person I've ever known."

Mara coughed again, and Emil helped her take a drink of the water Revathi had left. "Sune don't give their loyalty lightly," she said. "You're lucky. What happened to your mother?"

"Right," Emil said. "The story." He settled Mara up on some pillows and stretched out next to her, propping himself up on one elbow so he could face her.

"We were doing all right until the sickness started. It started off as a cough that just never went away–people had trouble breathing. . . ." He swallowed. "Most of us got over it. Some, though, some just got sicker. My mother was one of them. Medicine is expensive, and we were spending too much money, money we needed to get us through the rest of Earthsleep. So my father decided to split the camp. He took half the family, including Stefan, and all the goats down to Deshe. He hoped to do more trading, maybe even sell some of the flock. I know he planned to return for the rest of us as soon as he could."

Emil took a deep, steadying breath. "I tried to take care of my mother, but without my father, she just . . . lost the will to fight. A few days after he left, she died."

He felt Mara move her hand, sliding it into his. He squeezed her fingers.

"I think that's when I realized what being a leader really meant," he said. "And I wanted no part of it." He looked away from her eyes, feeling oddly ashamed. "Stefan thinks I'm spoiled, that everything just falls into my lap. My father thinks–thought–I was a good, responsible son. I don't think they have any idea . . ."

"Of what?" Mara asked.

"Of how afraid I am," Emil said, his voice raw with the unaccustomed honesty. "Stefan is so much stronger than I am, even with all his flaws."

"I don't know about that," Mara said. Emil looked up, surprised, as she went on. "You're right, a leader should be able to think of the good of his Tribe first. But that's not the only kind of strength. Your father chose the family. You chose Stefan. What makes you a lesser leader has made you a better brother and friend."

Something rose in Emil's throat, something sweet and tight and suffocating. He tried to speak, but nothing came out.

Mara let his hand go and put her arm under her head, rolling to face him. "No one can save everyone, Emil. Some people choose to save as many as they can. Others choose to save the people most important to them. But we've all left someone behind."

Emil finally found his voice. "Who did you leave behind?"

The answer was as brief as it was sad. "Myself," Mara said. "I left myself behind."

Emil reached over, resting his hand lightly on the curve of Mara's hip. Her free hand reached up to linger on his shoulder. Emil leaned closer and Mara mirrored him, until their foreheads touched. Neither of them spoke. Emil could hear Mara breathing softly, feel the brush of her exhale on his lips. All he'd have to do was lean in a little. . . .

And kiss a girl who's injured and depending on you.

Emil opened his eyes and moved back a little. "Do you need anything?" he asked. "Another blanket? More water, maybe?"

"More water would be wonderful," Mara said, clearing her throat. "Thank you."

She doesn't belong to you, Emil reminded himself firmly, pushing down his disappointment. "Of course. I'll get you some."

He moved to get up . . .

. . . and Mara put out a hand to stop him. "Emil, wait."

Like a noose underfoot,

Or a poison that weakens the blood,

Love is dangerous to women.

Like a roaring lioness,

Or a flash flood in the high mountains,

Is the woman who still loves unafraid.

Flower caste poem

45

Mara

"EMIL, WAIT."

The words spilled from Mara's mouth. Emil gave her a concerned look.

"Are you all right?

"I just . . ." Mara trailed off. She suddenly felt cold without Emil's solid presence next to her. *Stay with me. Don't go.* The plea sat heavy on her tongue, but she swallowed it down. Emil would go eventually. He'd have to. Kildi weren't even supposed to be in the palace.

But Emil had saved her. He'd held her and talked to her and risked his life to be at her side. And she wanted . . . she needed to thank him. If nothing else, she wanted him to know how much he mattered to her.

Emil was studying her, that analyzing gaze that saw so much

more in people than Mara ever could. "What's wrong?" he said. His fingers brushed her cheek, and Mara had to fight not to press her face into his hand. "Is the pain bad again?"

"No," Mara said. She pushed herself up into an almost sitting position. "It's . . . it's bearable now. I won't be dancing anytime soon, but I'm in control."

"Good, that's good." Emil shifted around so he was facing her, his legs folded cross-legged on the bed. A smile tugged at his mouth. "Can you dance?"

"Nishvana, no," Mara said with a small laugh. "But it sounded good." She plunged forward before the moment of easy laughter was gone. "I wanted to say thank you. You have no idea how much you helped me tonight. I couldn't have . . . stayed without you."

Emil put his elbow on his knee and his chin in his hand. "I'm glad," he said, and it was all Mara could do not to reach out and touch him. "I think you're the bravest person I've ever known."

Mara felt her chest squeeze, choking off her air. "I'm not. Really, I'm not."

"I think you are," Emil said.

Mara shook her head so hard she was dizzy. "You don't know what I've done," she said. Her fingers moved to the leather cuff protecting her ear, and her voice was strained. "You don't know. . . ."

"Stop that." Emil reached up and pulled the cuff off. He ran a finger along her scarred ear, and Mara shivered.

"You're right. I don't know what you've done," he said. "But I just spent most of the night watching you fight every instinct you have so you wouldn't hurt us." His finger drifted down her jawline and tilted up her chin. "You are so much stronger than you think you are, Mara. Anyone can fight when they're unwounded. It takes a special sort of person to keep fighting when they're broken."

Mara felt like she was drowning. She couldn't take in his words, couldn't understand them. "You wouldn't think that," she managed. "Not if you knew."

Emil's voice was firm. "I know everything about you I need to know. Maybe someday you'll tell me what you've done, why you entered the Order. But Mara . . ." His voice was soft. "I can promise it won't change how I see you."

Mara dropped her eyes, unable to bear the tenderness in his gaze. "I wish I could believe that," she whispered.

"I wish you could too," Emil said. He leaned over and dropped a light kiss on her forehead. The touch of his lips seared Mara's skin, sending waves of warmth through her. She wanted to purr, to rub her face on his shirt, to curl up in his arms again and listen to his heart beating . . .

She jerked back to the present. Emil was looking at her expectantly.

"Did you say something?" she asked.

Emil flushed. "Yeah, I just wanted to know . . . why me?" He stroked her cheek, a curious wonder in his eyes. "You had friends here, you had help already, but you were calling for me. Why not

Revathi or Esmer or Garen? Why did you need *me?*"

Mara flushed. She thought of the wooden tiger, safe under her pillow in her room. The way she fell asleep every night with it in her hands, dreaming of a boy with deep-brown eyes, a boy who had been kind to her.

"My family," she said at last. "We were wild Sune. We stayed in animal form most of the time. I haven't changed since I left my Tribe, but sometimes . . . sometimes I still feel more cat than human." She forced herself to take a deep breath. "When I was hurt, it felt like being back there, the day I lost my family. I've never been less human than I was that day, and the memories—they were bad. I needed something to hang on to."

She looked down at her hands. "When we met, you touched me, took my hand. I hadn't felt a touch like that since . . ." She swallowed. "And you gave me the carved tiger and you smiled at me like we were friends. So when I was hurt, I hung on to that and tried to remember how it felt. Then you were there and I could hear your voice and it made me want to stay human and I know that makes no sense but–"

"Mara," Emil said, and the weight of her own name felt like more than she could bear. She looked up, ready to see him suppressing amusement, or even worse, prepared to be kind to her.

But he wasn't smiling. Instead he was looking at her with an expression that she couldn't read. Slowly, he leaned forward.

"Mara," he said, his voice rough. "You don't have to explain anymore." His fingers slid along her neck and into her hair. Heat spread through Mara's skin, and her breath caught in her throat.

"You make me feel more human too," he whispered.

He brushed his lips against hers, a light touch that made Mara's eyes close. His breath mingled with hers, his mouth was achingly gentle. She leaned into it–

Just as Emil started to pull away.

Mara growled in protest. Forgetting the Order, forgetting her promises, she grabbed the front of his shirt and pulled him back to her. For one horrible moment, she thought he was going to stop her, but then the hand on the back of her neck tightened, and he returned the kiss, matching her need with his own.

It was like staring into a fire pit at close range, all sparks and flame and flushing heat. Mara felt like her bones were melting. The magic curled in her stomach again, but this time it wasn't angry. It was . . . satisfied.

Mine.

Mine. Mine. Mine.

Her fingers traced the stubble on Emil's jaw, the long muscles of his back, his shock of thick, dark hair. She'd had a few kisses before as a human, but those had been shallow, experiments with no real feeling behind them. This, though, this was *want*. Want and need and a kind of connection with someone else she'd never imagined. She felt like all the debris and dust of her lonely heart were washing away, leaving only happiness and belonging.

Emil twined his hand deeper into her hair. Without breaking the kiss, he brought his other arm around her waist, wrapping her in warmth. It was the safest place Mara had ever known.

Their bodies fit together like puzzle pieces until Mara couldn't tell where one of them ended and the other began. She clung to him, never wanting it to end. And all that time the steady, satisfied growl inside her.

Mine. Mine. Mine.

46

Emil

IT WAS EMIL who pulled away first. His breath was ragged in his ears, and his head felt light. "Uh . . . ," he said, his tongue fumbling for words. "That was . . ."

"Yeah," Mara said. Emil saw her swallow. Her lips were flushed and her eyes were very dark. "It was."

"I really . . ."

"Me too."

The first chuckle caught Emil off guard, bursting out of his throat and filling the room like a stream of light. Under his supporting hand, he could feel Mara start to giggle. And then he was laughing and he couldn't stop. The laughter bubbled up, easing the tension in his chest. Mara's laugh mixed with his, as warm and real as her skin under his fingers.

"Why are we laughing?" Emil said, leaning his forehead against hers.

Mara giggled. "I don't know." She took a deep breath, then winced. "But I shouldn't, it hurts." She curled into Emil's shoulder, making a contented noise, very like a purr. Emil stroked her arm, feeling awkward and bizarrely happy at the same time.

"So, was that all right?" He fumbled with the words. "The kiss? I didn't just make you break an oath, did I?"

"What?" Mara put a hand to her scarred ear as if just remembering it was there. "Oh, no. We're not supposed to let relationships interfere with our duty, but that's just after we pledge to a charge. I haven't pledged yet."

"But I thought you and Revathi . . ." Emil heard the hope in his own voice and hated himself for it.

"No. I'm just working for her as a guard for hire. Until I find someone to pledge to." A frown crossed Mara's face, but it was gone too fast for Emil to examine it. "I think I'm going to stay in the palace for a while, though. There are some things I need to figure out."

Emil pushed down the jagged shards of disappointment. "I hope one of those things is getting that woman who stabbed you arrested," he said.

"Aari." Mara tensed under his arm. "Emil, promise me you'll stay away from her. Please."

"Why?" Emil said, pulling back a little to look down at Mara's face. "Who is she to you? And why did she attack you?"

"It's hard to explain," Mara said. "She's Sune as well, and we had a . . . philosophical disagreement. She wasn't trying to kill me."

"Really?" Emil said. "It didn't look philosophical from where I was standing."

Mara reached up, curving her fingers around the back of his neck in a firm grip. "Just promise me you won't go after her. She likes to hurt people for fun, and I don't want her anywhere near you."

"All right," Emil said. He pressed his cheek to the top of her head. "Mara . . . even if you leave the palace, you'll still be bound to the Order, won't you?"

He felt Mara sigh against him. "Yes," she said. "That's the oath I took. I can't break it."

"I understand," Emil said, rubbing his thumb along the back of her neck. "I've got promises of my own to keep."

"Your brother."

"Yes."

"So what does that mean for us?" Mara asked, calmly straightforward.

A smile twisted Emil's mouth. "It means we're in one of those romantic story-songs. Lovers torn apart by cruel fate."

"I hate those songs," Mara grumbled. "Everyone dies at the end."

"I know," Emil said, pulling her close and brushing another kiss across her lips. If Mara was released from her oath, if Emil found his brother and got him out safely, if somehow they found each other again, then maybe . . . but there was no comfort in ifs and maybes. And they didn't change the good-bye that Emil could feel creeping up on them.

"You know we wouldn't have this problem if we weren't both so honorable," Emil said, trying to lighten the mood. He was rewarded by a soft laugh. Mara put her head back on his shoulder, and Emil rocked her, careful of her bandage.

"I don't like being honorable," Mara said after a long moment.

"I know," Emil said. "Me neither."

They sat like that until the cold gray light began to seep around the drawn curtains. Revathi finally came back in, looking surprisingly apologetic.

"I'm sorry, Mara," she said. "I can't keep my grandmother out much longer, and I don't want her to find Emil here." She looked at him. "It's time to go."

Emil nodded. He slid away from Mara and helped tuck her into a comfortable position on the pillows. "Are you sure you're going to be all right?" he asked her, his fingers curling over hers.

"I will now," Mara said. "Thanks to you."

Emil kissed her gently, lingering over her soft lips. "Be careful," he said, teasing. "I don't want to have to rescue you again."

"I'm the reason you're not in a cell right now," Mara said with a lopsided smile. "I think we rescued each other."

Emil laughed. "All right, we're even."

Revathi cleared her throat.

Emil swallowed. "Well . . ." The word *good-bye* caught in his throat, and he thought he would choke on it. "I'll come back to see you," he said instead, hoping it was a promise he could keep. Then he rose and almost ran out the door.

Once he got out into the hallway, Emil stopped and leaned

against the wall. His legs felt wobbly and he had to fight the urge to go back inside, to stay by Mara's side as long as she would have him.

Revathi came out. "Did you have fun?" she asked, with a lift of her eyebrows.

Emil flushed. "It's not polite to spy on people."

"I am not concerned with being polite at the moment," Revathi said. She folded her arms. "Do you love her?"

"I don't see how that's any of your business."

A small, tight smile crossed Revathi's face. "That's not an answer."

Emil pushed himself away from the wall, deliberately towering over Revathi so that she had to tilt her head back to look him in the face. "It's all the answer you're going to get," he said. "I don't like nobles and I don't trust you, and I would take Mara away right now if I thought she would go."

Revathi met his gaze without flinching. "Why don't you? You clearly don't like leaving her here."

"It's her choice," Emil said, flexing his fingers. "I have to respect that."

Revathi pursed her lips, then nodded. "I see," she said, and her voice was thoughtful. She pulled a rolled piece of paper with a noble seal on it out of her asar. "This is a pass. It'll show the guards you have permission to be in the public areas and on the grounds of the palace complex."

"Thank you," Emil said, accepting the paper. He didn't like being beholden to Revathi, but he didn't want to get arrested, either. He looked around the ornate hall. "Where am I, exactly?"

"Oh, this is the Palace of Rippling Leaves. It houses the throne room, council rooms, and my family's quarters." Revathi pointed down the hall with her thumb. "Go that way, then take the third left, the first right, and then left again and you'll see the front door. I'd show you myself, but I don't want to leave Mara."

"Third left, first right, and then left again," Emil repeated.

"If you get lost, just look for a servant to direct you," Revathi said. She paused. "And don't wander into the throne room or you'll be beheaded."

Emil narrowed his eyes, but Revathi's face was completely neutral.

"I won't," he said finally.

"Good," Revathi said. She hesitated. "Thank you for your help, Emil. I'm sorry I had you arrested."

Emil nodded. "Take care of Mara."

"I will," Revathi said. She put her hand on the curtained doorway and looked back. "You can count on it."

Then she was gone.

47

Mara

MARA BURIED HER face in the silk bedcover. It smelled of Emil's earth-and-wool scent, and she breathed deeply, trying to brand it into her memory. Her cuff still lay on the bed, and she picked it up and slipped it back onto her ear. Her chest felt hollow and achy, as if Emil had taken part of her with him.

But he'd left something behind, too. Words that settled deep inside her, warm and solid as a summer-warmed stone.

I think you're the bravest person I've ever known.

Those words curled together with the memory of the kiss, and Mara felt like there was firm ground under her feet for the first time in years. Even if she never saw Emil again, she had his belief in her.

She looked up when Revathi came back in. The girl had changed her clothes, choosing a knee-length tunic and trousers patterned in dark red and cream. She'd also washed her face and taken down her hair, putting it in a simple braid. Revathi's face was thoughtful, but she smiled when she saw Mara.

"How are you feeling?"

Mara sat up, moving slowly. "I was about to ask you the same thing," she said. "How's your head?"

Revathi reached up and scrubbed her fingers lightly through her scalp. Her fingers came away spotted with dried blood. "Haven't gotten around to taking a bath yet," she said, when Mara frowned. "It doesn't hurt that much."

Mara patted the bed beside her. "I want to see. Come here."

Revathi hesitated, then walked over and sat down next to Mara. "I'm glad you're all right," she said. "What happened?"

"I forgot to watch my back," Mara said, preoccupied with examining Revathi's head wound. The gash had stopped bleeding, but it was still raw and red, and the blood had dried into her hair. "Have you let anyone look at this?"

Revathi shook her head.

Mara huffed out a breath. "Don't move," she said. Carefully, she slid her feet onto the floor and stood up. Her shoulder complained at the movement, sending a jolt of pain through her. Mara ignored it. Pain no longer meant danger. She was safe, and she would heal. She found the room's washbasin and dipped a towel into the water.

"How long has this been going on?" she asked.

Revathi didn't ask what she meant. "A while." She looked down at her hands. "That was only the second time he actually hit me."

"So it's getting worse," Mara said, wringing out the towel. She came back to the bed. "Does your grandmother know?"

"Ancestors, no," Revathi said, and shuddered. "She'd probably geld Tamas if she ever found out. That or hire the Black Lotus to make him disappear."

"The assassins?" Mara said. "I thought they were just a story."

"Oh they're real, all right," Revathi said. "Mostly they work for the Emperor, but they can be . . . persuaded to take an outside job now and again. I don't know any of them personally, but I'm pretty sure Grandmother does." She winced as Mara dabbed the wet cloth on her scalp. "That stings."

"So why not tell her?" Mara asked. She began to clean the dirt and crusted blood from the gash. It started bleeding again, and Revathi grimaced.

"It's complicated."

Mara folded the cloth into a compress, placing it on Revathi's head. "Hold this."

Revathi obeyed. Mara sat back and put her hands in her lap, waiting.

"When I was younger," Revathi said at last, "I fell in love. With someone I shouldn't have. Someone I would never have been allowed to marry. We tried to run away, but . . ." She swallowed.

"One of my friends suspected I was seeing someone and spied on me. She told my parents, and they caught me sneaking out of the city. It was this huge scandal. Mother and Father tried to hush it up, but my friend, she told everyone. If my family wasn't related to the Emperor, we might have been completely ruined." Revathi took the cloth from her head.

"Since then no one has come forward with an offer of marriage for me. No one except Lord u'Gra."

Mara took the towel from Revathi and went to the basin to rinse it. She also picked up a comb that was lying nearby.

"Do you *have* to get married?"

"I'm afraid so," Revathi said as Mara came back. "My family is very high socially, but we don't have a lot of money. There was some flooding in our farmlands and a couple of bad cold seasons, and our revenue just sort of . . . dried up." She looked up. "That's actually what my father and brother are doing this summer. Visiting our holdings, trying to figure out what can be salvaged, or if we need to sell some property. Some of the land in question is my mother's; it was part of her dowry. That's why she went with them. We're all making sacrifices."

"And marrying Tamas is yours." Mara took the comb and started to clean the dried blood flakes from Revathi's hair.

"Yes," Revathi said. "My grandmother might talk about breaking the betrothal, but the truth is, we need this alliance. Lord u'Gra is one of the richest men in the city, and he wants to be related to Emperor Saro very badly, badly enough to overlook the scandal and the fact that my dowry is smaller than it should be. He's even promised to clear some of my family's debts."

"I wish you had told me," Mara said, keeping her fingers gentle.

"I know," Revathi said. "I'm sorry. But there wasn't anything you could have done."

She slid off the bed and onto the floor. "Sometimes I wonder if that's why Tamas is so angry," she said. "Because he knows I'm only marrying him for his money. I like him, but . . ."

"But your heart is somewhere else," Mara said.

Revathi smiled, sad and distant. "Always."

Mara carefully joined her on the floor, settling her back against the bed.

"You know he won't stop, right?"

"I know." Revathi leaned her head on Mara's good shoulder. "I'm sorry I got you stabbed."

"That wasn't your fault," Mara said. "That was all Aari."

"Garen went looking for her," Revathi said. "But no one can find her."

Mara inhaled, deep and slow, feeling her shoulder ache. "I'll find her," she said. "But not tonight."

There was a moment of silence; then Revathi spoke again, her voice hesitant.

"Mara? Why don't you want to change back into tiger form? You don't have to tell me," she added swiftly as Mara stiffened. "It's just . . ." Her fingers twisted in her lap. "I've always wanted to be dangerous, you know? At least a little. Like my grandmother, or one of the Jade warriors. If I could turn into something like you, something strong and wild and free . . . I don't think I'd ever change back."

Mara forced her muscles to relax. Revathi didn't know, couldn't know, what she was asking. She didn't understand.

But maybe she could. Maybe it was time to tell someone. And

if Mara could tell Revathi . . . maybe someday she could bring herself to tell Emil as well. If she ever saw him again.

"It's not a nice story," Mara warned.

"It's the Empire," Revathi said, shrugging. "I'm not sure there are any nice stories."

Mara had to smile. Then she closed her eyes, gathering her courage. If she was going to tell this story, she would tell all of it, every shameful bit.

"You were right about one thing," she began. "My Tribe doesn't care for human form. We only changed to speak to humans, and there weren't many people in the Whispering Forest, where we lived. We were used to being left alone, and we got careless. One day"–she swallowed–"one day a party of strangers came into our woods. Tiger hunters. They found my family sleeping, my father and mother and two brothers. I was off somewhere, stalking a bird."

Mara stared out the window at the garden. "The hunters were smart as well as lucky. They had brought poisoned arrows with them and shot my family while they lay sleeping. My family tried to fight back, but the poison was powerful, and they were too weak. The hunters cut their throats and skinned them. I heard their cries, but I couldn't run fast enough."

"So you killed the hunters?"

"I ran at them," Mara corrected. "I thought maybe I could scare them away. But one of them . . . he stabbed me with his sword." Her fingers crept to the thick scar in her side, the past carved into her skin.

"He stabbed me, and everything went red. I've never felt such rage in my life. I killed the first hunter, and it felt good. I was glad that he was dead and I was glad I had killed him, but I was still hurting. I had blood in my mouth and a wound in my side and the bodies of my family around me. And the rage, it didn't go away. It just got worse." Mara took a deep breath. "I tracked them, Revathi. The rest of the hunters. I tracked them down and I ripped them all apart."

"That's . . . understandable," Revathi said.

"Understandable doesn't make it right," Mara said. "And that wasn't the worst part." The words stuck in her throat like thorns. "One of the men I was tracking sought shelter with another party of hunters from another village, out hunting for deer and rabbits to feed their families. These hunters tried to protect him. But I . . . I killed all of them."

Tears burned in her eyes, and she blinked them away. "I killed them all," she repeated. "They didn't understand what was going on. I'm not even sure they knew I was Sune, and I was so full of rage and pain that I didn't care. So they fought, and instead of trying to change and explain, or telling my Tribe's Elders and try-ing to get justice that way, I just . . . killed them."

Mara was shaking. Something inside her was crumbling like the muddy bank of a river in flood, collapsing under the onslaught of memories. "I killed them," she repeated again. "I killed them." Her breath was coming in ragged gasps and she couldn't stop talking, couldn't stop saying the horrible, horrible words. "I killed them. I killed them. I killed them. . . ."

An arm went around her, pulled her in. "Shhhh," Revathi said. "I know. It's all right. I understand."

Mara buried her face in Revathi's shoulder, as if the tiny girl was a rock that could keep her from being swept away. Hot tears trickled from her closed eyes. Revathi stroked her hair and made hushing noises until Mara stopped shaking.

"I think I can guess what happened next," Revathi said. "Your Tribe couldn't leave you unpunished, not if they wanted peace with the humans. If you'd just killed the ones who killed your family, it might have been different. But as it was, they had to punish you, so you were sent away. And you wanted to make it right, you wanted to atone. That's why you joined the Order."

Mara nodded. "That's exactly it." Her throat was raw, and her eyes burned, but at least she was no longer trembling. "I didn't realize you knew so much about Sune justice."

"I don't," Revathi said. "But I know a lot about politics. And a little bit about consequences." She rested her cheek against Mara's hair and sighed.

"You know, ever since . . . ever since I tried to run away and got caught, I've been alone. I couldn't trust my friends, I couldn't trust anyone. Except maybe my grandmother. And now you."

She took a deep breath.

"Mara, you're dismissed from my service."

48

Emil

EMIL WAS LOST. There was nothing but richly decorated hallways around him, and not a servant in sight to ask for directions.

Maybe if I can get to an outside door, he thought, *I can find my way out of the palace from there. And then I'll go get Stefan and we can go home.*

But for the first time since Emil had left the Arvi camp, the words rang false. His arms felt cold and empty, and suddenly he wondered if he wasn't giving up just as much for his family as his father had.

No one can save everyone.

Emil shook the thought away and shoved open the nearest door, then stopped, looking around in confusion.

He was outside at least, but where outside? Emil clearly

remembered walking through a spacious garden before reaching the Palace of Rippling Leaves. But now he found himself surrounded by shrines. They were made of stone and shaped like miniature pavilions, and their domed roofs were as high as his head. Each shrine held a bronze statue of a different Ancestor. Many had offerings of fruit or flowers lying at their feet.

On an impulse, Emil went farther into the statue garden, looking for a particular face. He knew the Horned God wouldn't be among them. Only the Kildi still worshipped the gods from before the Barrier. But there were Ancestors that they respected, like Pillaiyar.

And there was his statue, with his round belly and his broad laughing face from the shadows. Emil made a gesture of respect.

Please watch over my brother and Mara, honored Ancestor. For they are strangers to this city, and I cannot protect them both. The statue's smile didn't change, but Emil felt a little comforted.

He turned to find his way out of the garden, and something bright caught his eye. At the base of one of the statues was a pile of bloodred hibiscus. Emil bent to touch them. They looked fresh picked, and the petals seemed to glow against the stone. Emil couldn't resist picking one up. He looked up to see which Ancestor had inspired this devotion.

The bronze statue was of a woman, her neck draped in demon heads and her mouth stretched in a terrible smile. Her left foot was extended as if she was going to step out of the shrine, and there was a sword in her left hand.

Kalika the destroyer.

Emil dropped the flower he was holding as if it were hot. It was bad luck to disturb anything that belonged to Kalika.

Emil wiped his hands on his tunic and headed back toward the Palace of Rippling Leaves. Maybe if he circled the building, he could find a guard or servant to direct him out. . . .

There was a flash of movement in the corner of his eye. Before Emil could react, something soft and smelly was clapped over his nose. He struggled, but hands held him down, held him still. The smell filled his nose and scraped down the back of his throat. The world tipped, turned dark.

And disappeared.

49
Mara

"DISMISSED?" MARA PULLED away and stared at Revathi. "What do you mean, dismissed?" Shame twisted inside her. "Is it because of what I told you?"

"Ancestors, no!" Revathi looked startled. "No, I just . . . I'm letting you go, Mara. I mean, look at you." She gestured to Mara's bandaged shoulder. "Look at what we've done to you. You should be defending someone noble and true, or finding that Kildi boy of yours and pledging to *him*." She put a hand on Mara's arm. "You tried to be my friend and for that I'll always be grateful, but your life isn't here, Mara. It's out there." Her voice softened. "Go. Go and be happy."

"But if I go," Mara said, "what happens to you?"

Revathi lifted her thin shoulders in a shrug. "I'll marry Tamas. I don't have a choice. But it will be all right."

"I could stay a little longer," Mara offered.

"It wouldn't do any good," Revathi said. "Once Tamas and I marry, he'll have the authority to dismiss any of my personal servants he chooses. You'll be gone before the ink on the marriage contract is dry."

Mara wanted to argue, but Revathi was right. Once they were married, Tamas would have the right to treat Revathi however he chose, and there was nothing Mara would be able to do about it.

Revathi took Mara's hand and gave it a hard squeeze. "Mara, you can't save me. But it means a lot to me that you wanted to. Thank you."

Mara looked down at Revathi's hand in hers. It looked so small. She thought about how Tamas had refused to call a healer when Revathi had gotten hurt. If he hurt her again . . .

An idea began to grow inside her, an idea as solid and rough and true as a teak tree.

"What if I pledged to you?"

"What?" Revathi jerked back. "That's a terrible idea, Mara. You'd be bound to me until I died."

"But it would work," Mara said, feeling the words out as she spoke them. "In fact, it's the only thing that would. If you were my charge, then no one, not even the Emperor, could send me from your side. I would be required by oath to defend you, even from your husband." She paused. "Unless you don't want me."

"No, it's not that." Revathi hunched her shoulders. "It's just . . . I can't do that to you. You shouldn't be stuck here playing court games. You should be guarding some great singer or healer. I'm not worthy."

"You don't have to be," Mara said, her certainty growing. "I didn't understand that before, but I do now. My oath isn't just about me and my honor, it's about defending someone who needs me. And I don't know anyone who needs me more than you."

She knelt before Revathi, took her dagger from her belt, and offered them up, her hands open.

"I would swear to you, Revathi sa'Hoi. I will guard you to the last of my strength, protect you to the last of my breath, and follow you even to the Mountains of the Dead."

Revathi closed her eyes, her face crumpling. "Mara, please," she said, the words a whimper. "Don't do this. I'm just selfish enough to accept, and I'm not worth throwing your life away."

"Yes, you are," Mara said. "Revathi, look at me." She reached out and wiped a tear from Revathi's cheek. "No one should have to face what you're facing. Not alone."

Revathi drew a shuddering breath. "What about Emil?"

"I don't know what my relationship with Emil is going to look like," Mara said. "I don't even know if he's coming back. But I think . . . no, I *know* if I told him why I was doing this, that he'd understand."

"You trust him," Revathi said softly.

Mara nodded. "I do," she said. "He didn't ask me to walk away from my oaths when I was free. He won't ask me to leave you if we're bound."

"I envy you," Revathi said. She leaned her head back against the bed. "It's been a long time since I felt that way about anyone."

"You don't have to be alone anymore," Mara said. Revathi jerked at the words. "Please, let me protect you."

Revathi blinked rapidly. "You're crazy."

"Probably," Mara said. "I'm also stubborn. It's a bad mix."

Revathi started laughing, tears still streaking her face. Mara felt a smile bloom on her own face. It wasn't what she had planned or wished for, but it felt right. This was where she needed to be.

Revathi rubbed her eyes on her sleeve. "Fine, have it your way, you insane creature. What do I need to do?"

"Take the dagger," Mara said. "And this . . ." She reached into the small pouch on her dagger belt and pulled out the bronze ear hoop. "Pierce my ear with the dagger point, put the earring in it, and say this. . . ." She rattled off the words.

Revathi took the dagger from Mara's hand. Mara turned her head, feeling Revathi's light touch on her ear, then a swift dart of pain.

"I accept your oath," Revathi recited as she fastened the earring into Mara's ear. "Be the hand that guards me in the night and the blade that shines during the day. I give you back your honor. Wear this so all will know that you have atoned for your wrongs. I welcome you to my family. Rise, Mara t'Riala, and be no longer t'Riala, but sa'Hoi, member of my family and blood of my blood."

Revathi reached forward with the cloth she'd been holding earlier, dabbing away the blood from Mara's ear. A tiny smile twisted her mouth. "And the Ancestors help us both."

50

Emil

THE SOUND OF hinges creaking made Emil bolt to his feet. He didn't know how long he'd been in the darkness, or even how he'd gotten there. All he remembered was standing in the middle of the statue garden and then waking up in a heap on a cold floor, in a place that smelled like a wet tunic left in a chest for too long. He'd hurt himself on several stone . . . things before finding his way to a thick wooden door, a door that would not open no matter how much he banged on it, no matter how much he shouted.

Now the door was opening.

A beam of light shot in from the hallway, blinding him. Then there were rough hands on him, holding him tightly, shoving him into a chair. Before he realized what was happening, a rope was dropped over his chest and his hands were tied.

Emil struggled until someone cuffed him in the head, sending sparks through his vision. As his eyes adapted, the torchlight grew less painful and the room around him became sharper. In the middle of the room, three stone boxes were laid out in a row. Each rested on a stone base and was about the length of a human being. Low benches lined the walls.

There was a man sitting on the nearest bench, a small man with narrow shoulders and a neat beard.

"I'd say welcome," the man said. "But you really aren't."

Emil blinked the remainder of the sparks from his eyes. "Karoti."

"Don't sound so surprised, Emil. You were looking for us, and you found us. Or rather we found you." He nodded to the men guarding the door.

"Untie him," he instructed. "And give him something to drink."

Emil sat still while they took the ropes off him and handed him a clay cup of tepid water. "So what happens now?" he asked, trying to look as calm as the mercenary. "You torture me to find out what I know?"

"Heavens, no," Karoti said. "Too messy, and the screams are bad for morale. No, I thought I'd try something else." He smiled, pale in the darkness. "Would you like a job?"

There was a moment of silence.

Emil set down his cup. "You kidnapped me out of the palace because you want me to join you?"

"Well, we'd rather have you here than crawling all over the

Flower Circle drawing attention to us," Karoti said. "So yes."

"What are you even doing in the Flower Circle?" Emil asked.

Karoti tsked at him. "As if I'd tell you before you agreed. Come now, Emil, I thought you were brighter than that."

"Where's Stefan?"

Karoti stretched out his feet with a lazy smile. "Safe. But he thinks you're off with the rest of his family, herding goats and enjoying yourself without him."

Emil felt his mouth tighten. "So I could just . . . vanish. And he would never know I was even here."

"See, I knew you were smart." Karoti sat up. The torchlight made shadows shift and twist over his face.

A cold fury overtook Emil. "I'm not agreeing to anything until I see Stefan." He leaned forward, put his face closer to Karoti's, and spoke, every word slow and savage. "Where is my brother?"

Karoti smiled.

Karoti led Emil down a long, decorated stone passageway until they stopped at a dead end. Torchlight played on a carved relief of spirals and whirls.

"Where are we?" Emil asked.

"The noble crypts," Karoti answered. "Nobles are allowed to keep their dead; they don't have to cremate them like the rest of us. Every noble house has a tomb below it."

"I didn't know that," Emil said. He'd found a few locked doors in the noble houses, but he'd assumed they were treasure rooms or cupboards or something.

One of the guards put his hand on a stone decoration and pressed. With a rumble, a section of stone swung inward, making a doorway.

"This is the best part," Karoti said. "All theses noble crypts are connected. We think it's a holdover from the old Empire, before the Barrier rose. Back when the people actually had to worry about armies from other lands. You'd be surprised at how many people we can fit down here."

Emil's skin went cold at the thought of a force of armed mercenaries hiding in the crypts and tombs of the Flower caste. So close to the Imperial palace.

So close to Mara.

Karoti didn't seem to notice his reaction. He led Emil down yet another hall to a brightly lit crypt.

Stefan was there, standing with some other men around one of the stone caskets, a map spread out before them. He was dressed in a nondescript brown tunic and trousers, a dagger at his hip. His arm was still in a sling, but the bandage looked clean. And he seemed . . . relaxed. His mouth curved up, and his eyes were bright as he pointed out various parts of the map with his free hand.

"Here are the lines of retreat I've worked out. The primary one leads over the Flower Bridge. It's more easily defensible, and there are all those little side streets in the Jade Circle to scatter into if worst comes to worst."

"Plus healers for our wounded," one of the men said. "If you can get behind their walls and get them to help you."

"If you do manage to get inside, tread carefully," Stefan cautioned. "No pillaging, minimal force. They may heal you just because it's what they do. But we're also criminals and traitors. And healers have a lot of ways to kill people." He lifted his injured arm a little. "I was threatened with several of them when I wouldn't stop squirming."

The men around him laughed. Stefan looked up, still smiling, and saw Emil. His face went blank in an instant.

"Emil," he said, and the room fell silent.

"Hi, Stefan," Emil said, conscious of all the eyes on him. "How have you been?"

"What are you doing here, Emil?" The familiar sight of his brother's scowl made some of the long-held tension in Emil's chest leak away. His twin was healthy and safe and as grumpy as ever.

"Looking for you."

Stefan came around the corner of the casket and grabbed Emil's arm. His fingers dug in, and Emil winced. "Will you excuse me?" he said to Karoti. "I think my brother and I need to talk."

"Of course," Karoti said, his eyes crinkling with amusement.

Stefan pulled Emil down the corridor, shoving him into a small side room.

"It's good to see you, too," Emil said, stumbling over the rough floor. Stefan stood between him and the doorway, his solid arms folded.

"You shouldn't be here."

"I was worried about you." The words seemed as thin as weak

broth, and Emil suddenly felt very stupid. Stefan was clearly doing well on his own.

"Worried about me," Stefan repeated with a snort. "Right. Does Father know you're here?"

"Yes."

"And he let you come? I find that hard to believe." A bit of the old bitterness crept into Stefan's voice.

Emil sagged against the wall. "He didn't let me," he said. "I tried to get permission to come after you, but he ordered me to stay with the camp. I left anyway."

Stefan's head snapped up. "You defied Father. You."

"It was mostly just walking away, but yes."

"Why?"

Emil leaned his head back, feeling the stone scrape against his scalp.

"Because you're my brother," he said. "I didn't know who these men were, what they had planned, how dangerous it would be. I just . . . I knew I couldn't let you go alone."

Stefan started pacing, his steps restless and angry. "I don't need you to save me, Emil."

"I'm starting to understand that," Emil said. And he was. He had been so used to thinking of Stefan as rash and foolish that it had never occurred to him that his brother could actually find a place here. *I'm as bad as Father,* he thought. *We never gave him enough credit.*

"I needed to come after you," Emil finally said. "Not for you, but for me. With everything that happened, everything I said . . ." He spread his hands. "If I hadn't come after you, I don't think I'd have ever slept well again. I'd have just stayed up every night, replaying our last conversation over and over." He forced himself to smile. "You're enough of a pain in person, I don't need you haunting me for the rest of my life."

"It would serve you right," Stefan muttered, but his voice lacked its usual edge. "Well you're here now. Just . . . please don't make trouble. These men would kill you as soon as look at you, and I don't want to see you die. Please."

Emil stopped, mid-answer. Stefan never said please.

"All right," he said after a moment. "I'll cooperate." He clapped his hands together and pasted an eager look on his face. "What are we doing, anyway?"

"Should we tell him?" Karoti said from the doorway. He was looking at Stefan.

"Might as well," Stefan answered. "Since he's involved now." He gestured at the door, and Emil saw one of the men who had been guarding him leaning against the hallway wall outside it. "Besides, who is he going to tell?"

"There is that," Karoti said. He turned to Emil.

"We've been hired by an interested party to . . . assist in a regime change. He wishes to sit on the throne, and we've agreed to help him do it."

Emil stared at him. "A coup. You're going to try and overthrow the Emperor. Are you mad?"

"Probably," Karoti said. "But we're well-organized madmen and our plan is sound. We're going to start a riot in the Outer

City, provide a distraction. Once the city guards are occupied, we'll attack the palace."

"A riot?" Emil thought of Heema, of the children under her care, of the unrest already growing in the Wind Circle. "Do you have any idea what that could do?" he said. "How many people it could hurt?"

Stefan shifted uncomfortably, but Karoti only nodded.

"There are plans in place," he said. "We're going to try to do this as quickly as possible."

"Plans?" Emil said. "What plans?"

"You don't need to know that," Karoti said firmly. "Now, is anyone going to be looking for you? Anyone we should be watching out for?"

"No," Emil said. They could threaten him all they wanted, but he wasn't giving them any information about Esmer. An idea came to him. A brilliant, stupid, horribly risky idea.

"Actually, there is someone," he said, keeping his face relaxed. If there was ever a time to lie, and lie well, it was now. "Someone who might be looking for me, I mean. I hired a tea seller to smuggle me into the Flower Circle. I promised him more money after I got out. If he thinks I left the city without paying him, I don't know what he'll do."

"That could be a problem," Karoti said. "If he feels cheated, he'll start talking. Those tea sellers gossip like a flock of marsh geese, and I wouldn't be surprised if they sell information to the highest bidder." He thought for a moment. "Tell me his name. I'll send him the money."

"I don't know his name," Emil said. "He wouldn't tell it to me. He was afraid I'd tell the guards if I got caught. But I know his face."

"Nice try," Karoti said with a smirk. "But I can't let you go wandering around looking for some tea seller who may or may not exist."

"I don't have to go far," Emil said quickly. "He said I could leave the money with an associate of his in the Jade Circle. A cook he knows."

Karoti studied him for a long moment. Emil kept his expression bland.

"All right," Karoti said. "We'll go today. Stefan, as long as Emil is in the crypts, you're responsible for him. Understood?"

"Yes, sir," Stefan said.

"If you try to escape," Karoti said to Emil, "or do anything to threaten our plans, the blame will fall on Stefan. Do you understand me?"

"Yes." Emil's face felt stiff and stretched from trying to look harmless. "I understand."

"Good," Karoti said. He looked like he was about to say more, but Emil's stomach chose that moment to make a loud, angry growl. Stefan grinned.

"No breakfast, brother?"

"I've been a little busy," Emil said. "Being kidnapped and threatened and all."

A smile twisted Stefan's mouth. "Come on then," he said. "Let's get you some food."

51
Mara

"OUCH!" REVATHI BARELY ducked the bamboo staff that grazed her shoulder. Across from her, Prince Paithal grinned and twirled his weapon. "Come on, Revathi," he said. "You're not supposed to go easy on me."

Revathi rubbed her shoulder and looked over at Mara, who grinned. "He has a point," she said. "You do look like you're holding back."

"He has a staff," Revathi pointed out. "I've only got a knife."

"So?" Mara said, folding her arms.

Revathi scowled at her. Her face was flushed and her eyes were bright. "Aren't you supposed to be guarding me?" she complained.

"I'm making sure you can defend yourself," Mara said. "It's part of the job."

"A job you've only had since yesterday."

Mara's grin widened. Revathi sighed and turned back to the prince.

Paithal swung at her again, and this time Revathi blocked him. She brought her knife down and whirled out of the way of the staff, her movements as smooth as a shadow across the wall. Mara resisted the urge to cheer. Revathi had a natural talent for blade fighting. She could be a master if she kept practicing.

Revathi prowled around the prince, looking for an opening. The door creaked open, and Suni came in, Sudev following behind him.

Paithal looked over at them, and Revathi pounced, grabbing his staff and twisting it out of his hand. The padded edge of the knife tapped him sharply on the chest.

"You're dead," she said. "I got you."

"Not fair!" Paithal protested, rubbing his chest. "Suni distracted me."

"People who are trying to kill you don't play fair," Mara pointed out, smiling proudly at Revathi.

Suni nodded. "She is right, Paithal," he said. "You should never take your attention off your opponent. Still, you have done well today. After your balance exercises, you may go play."

Paithal put one hand on his chest and bowed to Revathi. "Thank you for the match," he said. Revathi bowed back.

"The pleasure was mine," she said. "Shall we go cool down?"

Paithal nodded and took Sudev's hand. "Come on, Sudev," he

said. "You can show me your new tumbling trick, too."

They headed for an outside door. Mara watched through the window as they found an empty spot in the yard and started the meditation and balance exercises. Sudev's round face was furrowed in concentration as he followed his brother and Revathi through the forms.

Suni came to stand beside Mara at the window. "They are strong children. Paithal will make a good Emperor someday."

"They're good boys," Mara agreed. "Sudev takes himself a little too seriously, but I think he'll grow out of it." She turned to look at Suni. "You know, when Garen told me the boys took lessons here, I was surprised. Samara always talked about how secretive Jade warriors were. Said they were like little marsh birds, always just out of sight and never where you thought they should be."

"That sounds like Samara," Suni said, chuckling. "She and I had many differences of philosophy when we knew each other. Once those differences ended in a bout that left both of us bruised and exhausted. We never did figure out who won."

He smiled at Mara's look of disbelief.

"But what Samara considers secrecy, we consider merely . . . discretion. Especially when it comes to our fighting skills. Few people believe we are as good as we are." His smile widened. "After all, we haven't left our walls in over a hundred years."

"That does confuse me," Mara confessed. "Why would you learn fighting skills and never use them?"

"Partly to be ready should the Empire need us," Suni said.

"Only the Empower can call us out, and then only in times of dire need. But also because these fighting forms require absolute control over both emotions and body. Battle is the ultimate moving meditation."

Mara nodded. She'd hated sitting still for meditation in the Order. Moving meditation did sound more appealing.

"There are many different aspects to the Jade caste," Suni continued, his voice taking on a lecturing tone that reminded Mara of her teachers. "But all of them have the idea of meditation and self-control at their heart. Scholars use their mental discipline to preserve the past. Healers use it to help people in the present, and the warriors . . ." He frowned. "We use our discipline to safeguard the future. Someday the Barrier may come down, and who knows what will be on the other side?"

Mara shivered at the thought. "My Tribe used to say that there were monsters in the mountains. My father even had a scar he said he got from a giant serpent. Do you think it's true?"

Suni considered this. "As long as they stay in the mountains, it doesn't matter, does it?" he said. "And if they don't . . . well, that's what we're here for." He bowed to Mara. "You and your friend are welcome to visit anytime."

"Thank you," Mara said, reaching up to touch her earring, still heavy and unfamiliar. "I think we will."

In the courtyard, Revathi was doing a ridiculous balancing act, standing on one foot while making faces and jumping up and down, while the two boys were laughing. Mara and

Revathi hadn't seen Tamas since the incident at his house, but he'd been sending flowers and notes of apology. Mara hoped he was doing some serious thinking.

Either way, Revathi was safe now, and she seemed . . . happier. Freer.

The door to the practice area creaked open. Mara tensed, then relaxed as Garen's voice touched her mind.

All safe, cousin?

All safe, she sent back.

"Suni!" Garen said, stepping inside. "How are you?"

"Ah, my old bones are not what they used to be," the man said, with a mournful look. "But still I hobble about. Such is the price of living to a great age."

Garen laughed. "Well, straighten your step, teacher. Saro is here to visit with the boys. Are they done with lessons?"

"Just finished," Suni said. "They'll be happy to see him. It was good of you to suggest that he come and spend time with them here."

Garen smiled at Mara. "Someone told me the boys missed him," he said. "I thought behind the walls of Jade caste, there would be fewer painful memories of the Empress."

"Well thought," Suni said. "I will go and show him the way to the courtyard." He bowed and walked out.

Mara turned back to the window, and Garen came to stand with her, warm and solid at her back.

The door on the far side of the courtyard opened and the Emperor came in, wearing a simple dark-blue tunic. Revathi knelt, and the boys shrieked with joy, throwing themselves into their father's arms.

Emperor Saro smiled and held them close. Mara thought she saw the glimmer of tears in his eyes, but then Sudev said something and the Emperor laughed. Paithal started showing him some of his new fighting moves, and soon all three were wrestling like tiger cubs.

Mara's smile slipped at the thought. Behind her, Garen put one heavy hand on her shoulder.

"I miss my family too," he said.

Mara turned her face up to his. "Where are they?"

"Far away. In the Eastern Forests, somewhere."

"Are you ever going to see them again?"

"Probably not," Garen said. "I am bound to Saro and his family by vows no less strong than the ones that bind you to Revathi." His mind touched hers again, his voice soft inside her head. *Choosing one life doesn't mean you don't regret the one you had to leave behind.*

Then he sent her a memory: a thick stand of trees, heavy with afternoon heat, the chirp of birds, the chatter of monkeys. Everything soothing and familiar.

Mara closed her eyes and leaned her head against Garen's upper arm, sinking deeper into the memory. She added her own details to his until they stood in a wild forest instead of a building. A warm, safe place with the gray sky of the Barrier above them and the forms of sleeping tigers and bears around them.

Home.

And for the first time, Mara's sorrow was mixed with joy, and the ache of losing her family eased. Not entirely, but a little. It was enough.

Mara!

The voice jerked Mara out of her memory-trance. Garen stiffened. "Someone's here," he said. "Someone who shouldn't be."

Mara, help me!

Three Jade novices burst through the door, chasing something slim and gray that darted here and there. Mara caught a glimpse of a black-tipped tail.

"Esmer?"

"CEASE!" Garen roared. The novices skidded to a stop, their faces identical masks of surprise and nervousness. Esmer dashed between Mara and Garen, hiding herself behind their feet.

Those Jade fellows are fast, she sent, panting. *They almost caught me a couple of times, and no one catches me.*

Garen spoke with gravity, though Mara saw a twitch at the corner of his mouth.

"The situation is under control," he said to the novices, drawing himself up to his full, intimidating size. "You may go."

The novices practically fell over one another trying to get out of the room. Garen and Mara turned to Esmer, who was licking her fur back into place.

"It would make me happy, small one, if you would change to human form," Garen said.

There was a shiver of magic over Mara's skin, and then the spotted cat flickered out of existence. Esmer ran her hand through her dark hair, patting it back into place.

"I'm sorry," she said, addressing Garen. "If I had realized the Emperor was going to be here, I would have waited. But I need to talk to Mara."

"What is it?" Mara asked.

Worry creased Esmer's face. "Mara, Emil's missing."

52
Emil

THE FOOD WAS a lukewarm bowl of stringy meat, lentils, and rice. Stefan didn't explain how they were able to cook in the crypts, and Emil didn't ask. He was too busy eating. Stefan sat on top of a stone coffin, making notes on a small parchment map with a charcoal writing stick.

"Not that way," he muttered to himself. "There's a dead end there. Maybe if the archers can cover a retreat here . . ."

One of the mercenaries, a solid-looking man carrying a mace, stuck his head in. "Stefan, when you're finished babysitting your little brother here, we need you in the planning room."

"Of course, Biren," Stefan said. "I'll be there in a moment." He was grinning, whether because of the "little brother" comment or some other reason, Emil couldn't tell. He set down the writing stick and rolled up the parchment, stuffing it into his shirt.

Then he looked at Emil, who was scooping the last of the rice out of his bowl with his fingers. "You should wash up," he said. "I can't offer you a bath, but there should be a washing basin and towel around here somewhere."

Emil set the bowl down, right in front of the writing stick. "Who's that?" he said, nodding toward the mercenary in the doorway.

Stefan looked at the man, and Emil put his hand down on the charcoal, sliding it up his sleeve.

"Someone who doesn't like you," the man said, frowning at Emil. "That's all you need to know."

Emil folded his arms, feeling the writing stick press against his wrist. "Fine, no one trusts me. I get that. Can I at least get cleaned up now?"

Stefan opened his mouth, then shut it again. "Let me show you where the washing area is," he said. "And . . . it might be better if you don't talk to anyone unless you have to."

"Trust me," Emil said, picking up his bowl. "The last thing I want is conversation."

The washing area turned out to be a tiny room lined with urns.

"Remnants of valued servants," Stefan said. He indicated a clay pot half full of water. "There you go. It's not the palace, but at least you'll be cleaner." Emil ignored the curiosity in Stefan's voice when he mentioned the palace. He wasn't ready to talk about Mara.

After a moment of silence, Stefan cleared his throat. "I have to go. Someone will come and bring you a set of clothes." Then he left.

As soon as Stefan was gone, Emil pulled the work permit Abhra had given him out of his tunic, along with the charcoal stick he'd picked up. Unfolding the creased, soft paper, he scribbled a hasty note on the back.

Riots coming, be warned . . .

He was going to write more, but footsteps echoing outside the room stopped him. Hastily Emil shoved the writing stick behind an urn and tucked the paper back into his tunic.

A woman with bored eyes and an unstrung bow in her hand entered the washroom. She tossed Emil a bundle of fabric, then turned and walked out without a word.

Emil didn't move for a moment. The paper felt hot against his chest, and his skin was tight with tension.

When no one came back, Emil pulled the paper out again. He folded it over and over again until it was a hard, circular disk the size of a copper coin. Then he slipped out of his bloody clothes and washed the worst of the dirt off with the tattered towel. He rubbed and rubbed until the water in the pot turned black. The scrape on his leg was less inflamed, but it still hurt. Emil ignored the pain and unwrapped the new clothes. It looked like they'd given him some of Stefan's things. They were too short, leaving his ankles and wrists exposed, but at least the cashmere felt familiar against his skin.

Emil had just slipped the paper coin into his pocket when he heard another set of footsteps. Grabbing his red scarf off the floor where he'd discarded it, Emil tied it around his neck.

This time his visitor was Karoti, holding a small bagful of coins.

"Here's the price you named," he said. "I'll come with you to make sure you don't get . . . distracted."

"Suit yourself," Emil said, with his best careless shrug. "I just want to get this over with."

"We all do," Karoti said, and Emil thought he sounded tired. "We all do."

Emil was expecting to come out in the house he'd seen the mercenaries in before, but instead he followed Karoti through a twisted maze of crypt passages that came out in another abandoned home, this one close to the Flower Bridge. Karoti peered through the door, then slipped out into the street. Emil kept his head down as they walked to the bridge.

"Just an errand," Karoti called, flashing a permit at the guards. "Need to pick up supplies." The soldier grunted at them, but let them through.

Emil followed Karoti in silence through the wide, spotless streets. They passed a gate, made of decorative metal, bent and twisted into the shape of a creature with eight legs, a lion's mane, and wings. Through the gate, Emil caught a glimpse of a young woman bearing two short swords.

"I thought healers didn't bear weapons," he said to Karoti.

Karoti gave a quick glance through the gate and quickened his step. "Not healers. That's one of the Jade warrior enclaves. Don't stare. They can't leave their walls, but I don't want any unnecessary attention."

"What do you mean, can't leave their walls?" Emil said. He'd heard stories of Jade fighters, but they always sounded like legends, tales made up to while away a frost-covered night. He'd never met anyone who even knew a Jade warrior, much less seen one himself.

"Just what I said," Karoti answered. "Once they pledge to their order, they cannot leave. Ever. I think even their ashes are buried somewhere inside those walls." His lips tightened. "And if you ask me, it's for the best. Rajo doesn't think they're much of a threat, but they make my skin twitch."

Emil decided to change the subject. "So I've been wondering about something," he said. "I get Rajo: he's a mercenary and he fights for money. And I know what Stefan's doing here. But you . . . you don't seem like the mercenary or revolutionary type. How did you get involved with Rajo?"

A smile twisted Karoti's face. "Rajo is my older brother," he said. "Someone had to keep him out of trouble." The smile softened, turned into something protective and fond. "You have to understand, Emil. Rajo is a remarkable person. He's impulsive and quick to lose his temper, and he's not always the most practical person. But he cares about his people. These men and women are his first priority, and they know it. Our employer has offered us land and money, and Rajo believes this will make a better life for us."

"What do you believe?" Emil asked.

"I believe he's my brother," Karoti said. Again, the dangerous look flashed across his face, like the flicker of a knife in the dark. "And I'll follow him to the Mountains of the Dead before I leave him to fight alone."

Emil swallowed. "I understand that."

"I know you do," Karoti said. "Now come on. I don't want you out here longer than necessary."

With a little searching, they found the side door Emil remembered. Emil rapped his knuckles on it, then shoved his hands into his pockets.

Manik opened the door. Spots of oil stained his tunic and apron. "What is it? I've got a very tricky almond cake in the oven. . . ." His eyes widened when he saw Emil. "Oh, it's you."

"Yes," Emil said, with just the right amount of anxiety. "I need you to do me a favor. You know our mutual friend, the tea seller?"

"I do." Manik folded his arms. "What of it?"

Emil looked directly into the cook's eyes. "I owe him money. And I *know* it would be stupid not to pay him back." He took his hands out of his pockets, palming the paper coin in one and taking the bag of copper from Karoti with the other.

Holding the bag in both hands to shield the paper coin from Karoti's view, he pressed the whole thing into the servant's palm. "Make sure he gets these coins," Emil said. "All of them."

Manik's gaze sharpened. Then he nodded. "I will. He comes by later today."

"Tell him I remembered our deal," Emil said, trying to keep his voice from sounding too urgent. "Tell him our bargain is fulfilled."

"Of course." Manik's eyes flicked to Karoti and back to Emil. "I will make sure he knows."

"Come along, Emil," Karoti said. "We have work to do."

Emil bowed to Manik. "Thank you," he said. As he turned away, he saw the cook slip the paper coin up his own sleeve. He hoped Abhra would get his message.

He hoped it would be enough.

53
Mara

MARA WAS PACING. Back and forth in the small meditation room that Suni had shown them, her feet following the same track over and over. Revathi and Garen and Esmer were speaking together and their voices washed over her, void of meaning. There was only the carpet and the walls and the restless need to keep moving.

Because if she stopped . . . if she let herself think about what Emil's being missing might mean . . .

She tried to focus on what the others were saying.

"I didn't hear from him after I left the palace," Esmer was explaining. "But I thought maybe he was still there." She glanced at Mara. "Anyway, I was tracking down something for him, and when I tried to find him to tell him what I'd discovered, he'd vanished. He hasn't been back to our room in the

Wind Circle, and no one's seen him."

Garen frowned. "I have to get Saro and the princes back to the palace," he said. "I'll check with the guards and the servants, see if anyone saw Emil leave." He patted Mara's uninjured shoulder, and she squeezed his hand, taking comfort in the solid *thereness* of him.

"Thanks, Garen," she said.

"I like Emil," Garen said. "He has a good heart. I would hate to see any evil befall him."

After Garen left, Revathi looked at Esmer. "What exactly were you helping Emil with?"

Esmer pressed her lips together. "I can't tell you that."

"Esmer, please," Mara said. Her voice didn't sound like hers; it sounded hoarse and a little wild. "You have to tell us something. I know a little, but not enough. And if those men have him . . ."

Esmer shook her head. "You can't ask me to do that, Mara," she said. And her voice was soft and so understanding that Mara wanted to scream. "Emil is family. I won't offer him up on a plate for the Emperor's men."

Mara started pacing again. She had the horrid feeling that she was free-falling, and only the thud of her feet on the carpet kept her in control. The magic was coiled tight and painful in her belly, a knot of worry and fear and tension that made her want to spill everything.

But Esmer was right. Mara didn't know what the mercenaries were up to. And if it was something illegal and she told Revathi, Revathi might feel like she had to report it. And even if Emil didn't go to prison again, Stefan certainly would. Emil might forgive her for turning him in, but he'd never forgive her if she betrayed his brother.

"Why would Emil be in trouble with the Emperor's men?" Revathi looked from one to the other. "Does this have anything to do with why he was in the Flower Circle in the first place?"

Esmer folded her arms and didn't answer.

Revathi ran her fingers through her hair, tangling them in her loose braid. "Emil's clearly not a thief, and he must have known what would happen if he got caught," she muttered to herself. "So whatever he was looking for, it was something that mattered more to him than his own safety."

Her eyes flicked over Mara. "He could have been looking for you, I suppose." She turned to Esmer. "But that doesn't explain why he sent you away. It couldn't have been to find Mara; she was right there. Someone else, perhaps?"

Esmer looked down at her hands.

"I'll take that as a yes," Revathi said. She bit her lip. "Look, I know you don't trust me. But I promise, I'll try to keep whatever you tell me a secret as long as I can. Please," she urged looking at Mara. "Let me help."

Mara looked at Esmer, imploring her with her eyes.

The cat girl threw her hands up. "All right, fine," she snapped. "I cannot believe the position these thrice-cursed boys put me in. Inconsiderate, hairless . . ." She trailed off in a stream of impressive swearing that made Mara's eyebrows rise. Finally Esmer ran out of steam.

"Emil's brother joined a mercenary band a few days ago," she said. "That's what Emil was looking for in the Flower Circle."

"Mercenaries?" Revathi said, in a disbelieving tone. "Mercenaries in the Flower Circle?"

"Yes," Esmer snapped. "And don't look at me like that. I know he found them, and I know where."

Mara's head jerked up. "You do?"

Esmer nodded. "In an abandoned house next to where Mara was stabbed."

Revathi made a small noise of surprise. "That's the tar'Vey house. They're in Deshe for the summer, like my parents. No one is supposed to be in there."

"Well, there isn't anyone there now," Esmer admitted. "But they *were* there. When I left you the first time, I found it and got inside. The house was closed and locked, and it stank of men and steel. I don't know where they went. So I came back to tell Emil, and that's when I realized he was missing."

Revathi tapped a finger on her chin. "There are connected catacombs and crypts all over the Flower Circle," she said thoughtfully. "If those men were there—"

"They were," Esmer said.

"Then they probably went underground," Revathi said. "Or moved to a different empty house."

"So we know where they were," Mara broke in. "But we still don't know what happened to Emil. Could he have gone back there?"

Esmer frowned. "No, there was some scent of him, but it was

fading, and only on the roof. Honestly, I'm not even sure he got out of the palace. I tried to pick up his trail on the Imperial Bridge, but it's had a coat of new pitch lately. Everything around it just smells like oil."

Revathi rubbed the back of her neck. "I should have called a servant to show him out," she said. "I just didn't want to call too much attention to him." She thought for a moment, then clapped her hands. "All right, this is what we're going to do. Mara and I will go back to the Palace of Rippling Leaves and see if we can trace Emil's footsteps from there. Esmer, can you go back to the tar'Vey house and wait for us? We'll find out what we can and meet you there."

"I can do that," Esmer said. "Emil might find his way there anyway." She flickered back into cat form.

I hope you know what you're doing, she sent to Mara. *I don't want to see Emil hurt.*

Me neither, Mara sent as Esmer padded out.

Revathi reached out and touched Mara's hand. "I'll help you find him, Mara," she said. "I promise."

It was easy to track Emil out of Lady Ekisa's room. No one had cleaned the carpet in that part of the palace yet. Emil's boots were heavier and rougher than the slippers and sandals the servants and nobles wore, and they still had more than a trace of grime and dirt from the prison he'd been in. Revathi and Mara tracked the distinctive smudges down the hall, then turned right when the passage to the main entrance went left.

"He went the wrong way," Revathi muttered. They followed the fading trace to a small outside door. Mara pushed it open and found herself surrounded by shrines and statues.

"What is this place?" she asked

"This is the outer Garden of the Ancestors," Revathi said. "It's here for the nobles and palace staff to leave offerings. There's another, more private one behind the Lotus Wall for the Imperial family, complete with peacocks to run off intruders." She looked at Mara. "I've heard Sune don't worship the Ancestors. Is that true?"

"Not your ancestors," Mara said. "Every group of Sune is different. Tigers follow Nishvana the Silent-Pawed. It is said she prowls the world, invisible and unseen, rewarding those who use power for good and punishing those who use it for evil. I believe Esmer's people follow someone they call the Long-Tailed Cat. The bears have Yaggesil the Strong, and so forth."

"The Ancestors watch over us," Revathi said. She knelt and touched the feet of one statue, a plump man with a gentle smile. "This is my favorite, Pillaiyar. He's the lord of new beginnings and the caretaker of travelers."

Something seemed to catch Revathi's eye, and she scrambled over to a pile of hibiscus flowers at the base of another statue, a ferocious-looking woman.

"That's odd," she said, bending over to examine them. "These are fresh. Someone left them recently."

"Why is that odd?" Mara asked, searching the ground for any sign of Emil.

"Kalika is the bringer of war," Revathi said. "She creates through destruction." She touched the bloodred flowers piled around the woman's feet. "There hasn't been a war in the Empire in hundreds of years."

Mara found what she was looking for. "Revathi. It looks like there was a struggle here."

Revathi came over and knelt down, running her hands lightly over the ground. "You're right. There was definitely a struggle here. And someone fell. You can see the marks where he was dragged for a few feet."

Mara knelt next to her and sniffed the ground. Her human nose wasn't as good as her tiger one had been, but she could just make out a harsh, bitter scent. "Where did you learn to track?"

Revathi didn't look at her. "My father taught me," she said. "He used to say, 'If you can read the forest, you can read the court. They're both dangerous and full of animals.'" She touched one of the scuff marks in the dirt. "Anyway, it looks like someone ambushed Emil here, probably by hitting him over the head or using a drugged rag."

"Definitely a drug," Mara said. "I can smell it."

"Good," Revathi said. "Hitting someone on the head is a risky move. Too light, they won't black out. Too hard and you can kill them. If someone drugged Emil, it means they want him undamaged." Mara raised her eyebrows, and Revathi blushed.

"My grandmother and her friends have some odd conversations. Anyway if they want him unharmed, it probably is the mercenaries."

Mara pushed a toe into the ground. "But how did they get into the palace?"

"That's what I want to know," Revathi said. "Unless . . ." She shook her head. "We need more information. We need to get into that house Esmer told us about and search it."

"How?" Mara said. "Esmer said it was locked."

Revathi cocked her head and gave Mara a lopsided smile. "Don't worry, Mara," she said. "I have a plan."

54

Emil

AFTER DINNER, EMIL went looking for his brother. He hadn't seen Stefan since he and Karoti got back from the Jade Circle, and he still had questions.

He wandered the stone corridors, ignoring the glares of the mercenaries. There were more of them than he had thought. In one room, several men were sharpening swords and mending armor. In another, a larger group was playing a game of dice on a coffin. The carved wooden dice rattled against the stone, and the mercenaries cheered. Occasionally, he'd pass an open arch with stairs going up, but those were always guarded. The guards did not smile as he hurried by.

At least the doors between the tombs were propped open. After walking through several dwellings' worth of crypts, Emil heard his brother's voice coming from a side room. He crept closer and peered inside.

Stefan and Rajo were sitting on a low bench carved into the wall. Rajo had his knife out and was carving designs in a dense ebony fighting stick. Stefan was studying a scroll, his forehead wrinkling with concentration.

"Stefan, you haven't put those plans down all evening," Rajo said. He lifted the fighting stick to his eye and looked down its length. "Don't you want to sleep? Or eat dinner? Or talk to that nosy brother of yours?"

"No," Stefan said. His head was down and his voice was muffled. "You put me in charge of this. Of what happens if everything goes wrong." His fingers moved over the parchment. "I just want to do it right."

Rajo reached over and plucked the scroll out of Stefan's hand. "I didn't give you this responsibility out of pity, Stefan. Or to test you. I did it because the newest member of my crew came storming up to me three days ago and demanded to know why we didn't have a solid retreat plan and a way to get the wounded to safety. And then he argued me into letting him form one. You earned this, and you've done a great job with it."

Stefan flushed with pleasure. He opened his mouth to answer, but then spotted Emil in the doorway. His face closed, his mouth tightening.

"Emil."

Rajo looked up too. "Ah, our reluctant addition. How do you find our little band, Emil?"

"They don't seem to like me much."

"Do you blame them?" Rajo stood and clapped Stefan on the shoulder. "I wouldn't worry about it. You're safe enough."

For now. The unspoken words hung in the air as Rajo left the room. Emil and Stefan stared at each other, the silence thin and brittle between them.

"You seem happy here," Emil finally said.

Stefan looked down at the scroll in his hand. "I feel like I'm doing some good. Like I matter."

You've always mattered. Emil opened his mouth to say the words, but his tongue betrayed him.

"By helping overthrow the Emperor?"

"Why not?" Stefan asked, his voice rising. "You can't tell me you like the way things are, Emil."

Emil thought of Heema's veiled face, the hungry, wary eyes of her children. He thought of Esmer, rubbing the black mark on her hand. Rebellion might not be the answer, but he didn't have another one to give.

"Are you going to stay?" he asked instead. "After? Or will you come home?"

Stefan stood, setting down the scroll. "I don't know," he said. "I haven't decided yet. You?"

"I'll go if they let me," Emil said. Stefan frowned at him, and Emil spread his hands. "I miss home," he said. "I won't apologize for it. I miss the trees and the tent and the sky. I miss being irritated by my family and cursing the donkeys and sorting out the rocks under my bedroll." Laughter clawed out of his chest, jagged and sad. "Horned God help me, I even miss the goat smell."

"Oh yeah, the goats." Stefan's mouth curled up, but there was a sheen to his eyes. "Makes unwashed mercenaries smell like wild-flowers. You ever wonder why it's only the male goats that smell horrid?"

"Meri says it's to attract the females, but I don't know. I wouldn't want to smell like that for *any* female."

The smile left Stefan's face. "Yeah, well. Not all of us have our mates handed to us," he said, turning to pick up the scroll.

"What?" Emil put a hand on his arm. "Hold on, Stefan."

Stefan tried to jerk away, but this time Emil wasn't letting go. "Why are you so angry with me? It's not just the leader thing, is it?"

"Nothing," Stefan said. His eyebrows were drawn down, and he wouldn't meet Emil's eyes. "I hope you and Kizzy will be very happy together."

Emil dropped Stefan's sleeve and stepped back. "Kizzy? What are you– Ohhhhh." He resisted the urge to rub his forehead, as a lot of things snapped into place. "You heard us talking. In Father's caravan."

"Maybe," Stefan said. "Maybe I did." His voice grew hot. "You don't deserve her."

"And you do," Emil said, finally understanding.

A dark flush spread over Stefan's face. Emil couldn't repress a grin. "Oh, Steffy."

"Don't call me that."

"Stefan," Emil said, and his brother turned to look at him. "I'm interested in someone else. And even if I wasn't, I've already told Father that I wouldn't marry Kizzy Yanora."

Stefan stared at him. "Really," he said, his eyes narrow. "You told him that."

"I think you missed that part of the conversation," Emil said gently. "And you also missed that part where I told him I didn't want to be leader. That I don't have the heart for it."

Stefan was looking at Emil as if he'd suddenly declared his intention to walk on the ceiling. "But . . . you've always wanted to be leader."

"No, *Father* wanted me to be leader. I want to apprentice to Uncle Pali and trade."

Stefan swallowed. "Why didn't you tell me?"

"I didn't think you'd believe me," Emil asked. "I had a hard time believing it myself. But it's true." He stepped closer, willing his brother to hear what he was saying. "Stefan, I don't want to be leader. I don't want to marry Kizzy Yanora. And I don't want to lose you."

His twin just stared at him.

"Stefan, I need your brother to come with me for a while." Emil's head snapped around at the sound of Rajo's voice.

"Why?" Stefan gave Rajo a suspicious look. "You're not going to—"

"Calm down, youngster," Rajo said, the corners of his eyes crinkling. The smile transformed his face. It radiated warmth, and suddenly Emil understood why these men might follow Rajo the Black into battle. Because when he smiled at you, you felt like you were important.

"I'm not going to hurt your brother," he continued. "In fact, I need his help."

"Oh." Stefan's shoulders relaxed. "Well, good." He picked up the scroll and shuffled his feet. "I guess I should go get some dinner then."

Emil put out a hand. "Will I see you later?"

Stefan looked at him, and for the first time in a long time, there was no bitterness in his smile. "Yeah," he said. "You will."

Rajo patted Stefan on the shoulder as he walked past, then turned to Emil.

"I've got a job for you."

55
Emil

EMIL FOLLOWED RAJO down a stone corridor to a small room full of supplies. Lifting up a chest, Rajo pulled out two coils of flax rope. The rope was stiff and dark, as if it had been soaked in something.

"This is fire rope," Rajo said. He wrapped the rope in some waterproofed skins and handed it to Emil. "Grab one of those packs, too."

Emil complied, slipping the rope inside, along with several pieces of iron and flint rocks that Rajo handed him.

"Keep those with you at all times," Rajo said. "You're in charge of them now."

"But what are they for?" Emil asked.

Rajo smiled. "You'll see."

"Rajo." One of the mercenaries poked his head into the supply room. "Have you seen the Imperial Guard parchment? Yatra wants to use it to run a couple of drills for her squad."

"I haven't seen it," Rajo said. "Not since we were meeting in the tar'Vey house." He paused, glancing at Emil. "We did leave in a hurry that night, thanks to all the disturbance. If you left it behind . . ."

"We'll find it," the man said hurriedly. "We'll go look for it now."

"See that you do," Rajo said, and smiled. This smile wasn't the warm, charismatic smile of earlier; it was full of teeth and threat. "If it falls into the wrong hands . . ."

"Going now," the man said. "I'm going right now." He ran off.

Emil raised his eyebrows. "You have an . . . interesting leadership style," he said.

Rajo grinned. "People don't become mercenaries because they like following rules, Emil. A little fear keeps things running smoothly." He took a work permit out of his pocket. "Now come with me. We've got a job to do."

Emil followed Rajo out of the crypt. The big man walked with purpose, his work permit in one hand and a sack slung over his back. The sack smelled strongly of wood and lamp oil and sloshed when he walked. Just as with Karoti, the guard merely glanced at his work permit, then waved him into the Jade Circle.

"What does that thing say?" Emil said, unable to hold his curiosity in anymore. He carried the pack Rajo had given him, along with a small bag full of stiff brushes and some dirty cloths.

"Says we've been hired to repair and repitch some of the bridges of the Inner City," Rajo said. "The permit covers our work on both the bridge to the Imperial Palace and the Jade Bridge, the one that links the Bamboo and Jade Circles. A small group of my men has been working on the Imperial Bridge for the last couple of days. It gives us a good excuse to watch the guards."

"That's it?" Emil said. "We're just going to the Jade Bridge?"

"First I need to show you something," Rajo said. He led Emil away from the main streets and to where the edge of the Jade Circle dipped into the canal that separated it from the Bamboo Circle. There was a low wall here, just the right height for a man to rest his arms on. Rajo followed the wall until he came to a small gate.

"The healing novices use this door to get down to the canal," he whispered when Emil caught up to him. He indicated a narrow set of stone steps below them. "There's a small landing at the bottom where they can dump some of their more pungent potions and rinse out the bottles."

"All right," Emil said, waiting for Rajo to explain the importance of the gate. But he didn't.

"Come on," he said instead. "Look busy, but stick to side streets. The less attention we draw, the better."

Emil followed Rajo to the wooden Jade Bridge, where Rajo showed the permit to the soldiers.

"Are you going to be done with this job anytime soon?" one of the soldiers asked. "The smell of that thrice-cursed pitch is giving me a headache."

"Very soon," Rajo said, ducking his head. "We have to let each coat dry before the next can be applied."

The soldier grumbled, but waved them along. Emil followed Rajo down another set of cut stone stairs and under the bridge. In the shadows, the stone was cold under his sandals. The edge of the canal was soft clay, and the water gurgled as it flowed past.

Rajo set down the pack and opened it. The smell came out in waves, and Emil felt a flash of sympathy for the soldiers. It did smell awful.

"What is this?"

"Dammar pitch mixed with lamp oil," Rajo said. "We've been painting the bridge with it."

"Why?" Emil asked.

Rajo pointed up. "See those iron hooks set in the bottom of the bridge? We put those there. That fire rope in your pack is soaked in a special mix of ashes and niter rock." He looked at Emil. "When I give you the signal, I want you to grab your brother and take some swords from the weapons room. Then leave by that gate I just showed you and swim to this bridge. Tie the ropes to the hooks, wrap them around the near legs of the bridge, and light them." He grinned. "The wood is so caked in pitch that it'll go up like a torch."

"You're going to burn the Jade Bridge?" Emil said. "Why?"

Rajo took the package of brushes from Emil and unwrapped it. "Karoti told you about the riot, right?" Emil nodded, and Rajo continued.

"Once the riot starts, the guards from the Flower Circle will be summoned to help control the crowd. As soon as they cross the Jade Bridge, you and Stefan light the fuse. That way we only have to worry about the Imperial Guard when we attack the palace."

"But I'm not an expert in arson," Emil said. "I wouldn't know what to do if something went wrong."

"Nothing's going to go wrong," Rajo said. He folded his arms. "You and I both know if your brother goes into this fight with an injured wrist, he's going to get killed. If he's here with you, he's not fighting. This is your chance to keep him out of it."

"He won't go," Emil said. "He's in charge of the retreat and the wounded, isn't he?"

"You leave Stefan to me," Rajo said. "He's been drilling the section leaders on this. Everyone knows what to do. And he'll follow orders."

"All right," Emil said. "Then I'll do it." He'd do worse to keep Stefan away from the fighting.

"Good," Rajo said. "Start painting."

Emil dipped his brush into the pitch mixture. The thick smell choked him, but he carefully applied the pitch to the nearest bridge leg.

Maybe he could convince Stefan to escape the city in all the commotion. If they swam the canal and found a way up into the far side of the Bamboo Circle, they might make it out alive.

If only there was a way Mara could come with them.

The thought made Emil's stomach tighten. Even if he and Stefan got out, Mara would still be in the palace, right in the way of the fighting. And she wouldn't leave Revathi if there was danger. Even unpledged, Mara took her duties seriously. It was one of the things he loved about her.

Emil's hand stilled.

Revathi was right.

In the middle of everything, with the most horrible timing in the world, apparently he'd fallen in love.

Ob for . . . Emil resisted the urge to bang his head against the wood. *You really are in a bad story-song.*

"Hey, keep working!" Rajo called. He'd climbed up one of the legs using a series of metal spikes set deep in the wood. He was painting the bottom of the bridge with pitch. "No time to day-dream."

Emil resumed painting. His hands and arms were getting sticky, and the fabric of his shirt was stiff with pitch. But he worked until Rajo climbed down from the leg and told him to stop.

Then he walked back to the crypt, his nose full of the smell of pitch and his thoughts spinning.

There was a message waiting for Rajo when they returned, a slip of parchment with a wax seal. A loose collection of mercenaries gathered around as Rajo broke the seal. He read the message, cursing under his breath.

Stefan came up behind Emil. "What's going on?" he asked. His nose wrinkled. "And what on earth have you been rolling in?"

Emil punched him lightly on his good shoulder. "I still smell better than you do," he teased.

Stefan smiled.

Rajo looked up, his eyes finding the man he'd spoken to earlier.

"Did you find the Imperial Guard list?" he said.

The man paled. "We went back and checked," he said. "Searched all around the room. Still not there."

Rajo looked at the parchment in his hand. "It doesn't matter," he said. "We're going back tonight anyway. Gather the men."

The men dispersed, and Rajo glanced over at Emil.

"Go wash that muck off and get a new tunic," he said. "It looks like you boys are going to meet our employers."

56
Mara

JUST AFTER DARKFALL, Mara found out what Revathi's plan was.

"What are we doing again?" Mara whispered, as she and Revathi crouched in a small alley on the inside edge of the Flower Circle.

"Waiting for the guard to pass," Revathi said, as if it were the most natural thing in the world. She was wearing a dark-colored asar, wrapped so that her legs were free, and her hair was braided and wound in a crown around her head. She'd given Mara a dark cotton tunic and trousers to wear as well.

Revathi peered around the corner, then ducked back.

"Here he comes."

Sure enough, a patrolling soldier passed, the wooden haft of his spear tapping at his side. Mara could barely hear Revathi's soft, shallow breaths beside her.

"Come on," Revathi whispered after the guard was gone. "This way."

She slipped out of the alley, staying away from the light cast by a nearby hanging lamp. Mara followed.

Everything smelled green and sweet as they moved through the Flower Circle. Voices drifted on the fragrant air, along with the flap and flutter of swooping bats. Mara kept one hand on her dagger hilt, trying to stay alert.

When Revathi had proposed sneaking into the Flower Circle after dark to meet Esmer, Mara had agreed, but privately she was worried. Noble girls weren't supposed to be out after dark by themselves, and even with Mara with her, Revathi would have a lot to explain if they got caught. And it was going to be hard not to get caught.

But now, following Revathi, Mara realized she's been concerned for nothing. Revathi moved as if she were made of smoke, her feet as silent as Mara's on the flat paving stones. She slipped through the darkness as if she'd grown up in its embrace. As if it was home.

Mara and Revathi crept between houses, keeping to the shelter of the high walls. Whenever they heard footsteps, they had to press up against the nearest wall, hoping the shadows would hide them.

Sometimes the footsteps belonged to a soldier, doing his rounds. Sometimes it was a group of nobles on their way to one party or another. Mara preferred the nobles; they held lanterns that swung wildly, and they chattered among themselves. None of them even looked in Revathi and Mara's direction.

Revathi finally stopped. "I think this is the house," she whispered. "Can you call Esmer to make sure?"

Mara reached out with her mind, finding the familiar bright presence on the other side of the wall.

Esmer, we're here.

Oh, thank the Long-Tailed Cat, Esmer sent. *I've found something. And I think the mercenaries might be back soon.*

Mara opened her eyes. "We need to hurry," she said. She started scanning the wall, looking for footholds. "Can you climb?"

"Probably," Revathi said. "But I don't have to." She reached into her asar and pulled out a large iron key.

"Where did you get that?"

Even in the shadows, Mara could tell Revathi was smiling. "Remember the keys Grandmother took off that guard? Well, the Imperial Guard keeps a copy of the key to every noble house. The keys are kept in a lockbox in the armory."

"And one of the keys your grandmother stole unlocked that box," Mara said. "She just gave it to you?"

Revathi coughed. "I might have picked it up when we were in her room earlier. I did have a backup plan, but keys are easier." She felt her way to the kitchen door and slipped the iron key in. It jammed, and Revathi cursed under her breath.

"Lock is stuck." She handed the key to Mara and reached into her asar again. "Looks like we need the backup plan after all." This time she pulled out a small pouch and several narrow pieces of metal. The smell of lamp oil filled the air.

Revathi oiled the lock and started probing it with the metal picks. After a few moments of jiggling, she pulled them out again and took the key back. This time it turned smoothly and noise-lessly. Revathi applied some oil to the hinges and pushed the now-silent door open.

"What was that?" Mara asked as they slipped inside the dark house.

"Something my brother taught me," Revathi said. "Lamp oil and lock picks. I've got a whole set of my own. He used them to break into his tutor's office and make sure he was getting high marks. I used them back when I was sneaking out all the time."

Mara shook her head. "Don't take this the wrong way, Revathi, but your family is terrifying."

"I told you," Revathi said.

There was a rustling noise. A small flame appeared, lighting up a doorway and Esmer's worried face.

"I'm so glad you're here," she said. "Come into the courtyard. You've got to see this."

This was a roll of parchment covered with narrow columns of cramped writing. Esmer had it spread out on a table. Revathi peered at it while Esmer held up the small clay oil lamp she was using for light.

"I found it on the floor while I was sniffing around," Esmer said. "It had fallen behind a large chest in the inside dining room."

Revathi ran her fingers over the parchment. "You think the mercenaries left this?"

"I know they did," Esmer replied. "Because they came back for it."

Mara's head jerked up. Esmer nodded. "I heard footsteps and so I ran into one of the bedrooms, jammed this under the mattress, and changed into cat form. I was out of sight when they came in, but I could hear them. They were grumbling about things getting left behind, and they searched right around the area where I'd found the parchment. Said Rajo would be angry if they didn't find it."

"I can understand why," Revathi said. Her voice was tight. "This is a summary of the Imperial Guard rotations. When the guards change, the patrol routes that they take through the palace, even the position of the night-lamps. Plus, there's a list of who serves on which shifts, along with notes on experience and fighting styles. All the information you would need if you wanted to attack the palace."

"The mercenaries are going to attack the palace?" Mara said. "Why?"

Revathi's lips thinned. "They're mercenaries. They've probably been hired to."

"They're definitely working for someone," Esmer agreed. "The mercenaries that came back for this said something about their employer. I thought about following them into the crypts, but they locked the door after them."

Revathi rolled up the parchment. "I'm glad you didn't follow them. There's not a lot of cover in those halls, and if they'd shut you in, you could have been trapped."

"Maybe." Esmer sounded unconvinced. "But I'm going to go

sniff around the crypt door anyway." She set the clay lamp on the table and vanished into the shadows.

"She's worried," Revathi said. "So am I. This could be very bad–" She stopped, her head snapping up. A metal clicking sound echoed through the house.

The sound of someone unlocking the front door.

57
Mara

MARA STEPPED IN front of Revathi as the front door creaked open. A dark figure stood in the opening for a moment; then a hand came up, holding a lamp. Weak, inconsistent light flickered over a familiar face.

"Tamas?" Revathi's voice behind Mara was incredulous, but there was a note there that Mara couldn't place, something sad and sharp. "What are you doing here?"

"What am I doing here?" Tamas said. "The tar'Vey family left the keys with me when they went to Deshe for the summer. What are *you* doing here?"

Revathi picked up the lamp. It cast light over her hands and lit up her dark, dark eyes.

"You lie," she said softly. "No one would leave a key with you, Tamas. They would have left it with your father. And your father would have sent servants to check on anything suspicious. What are you doing here?"

"I . . ." Tamas took a step back. "I don't have to justify myself to you."

"Can you justify this?" Revathi held up the parchment. The lines of writing seemed to twist and move in the flickering lamplight.

"Where did you get that?" Tamas blurted. The changing light distorted his features, his face a mask of anger and panic. A sick feeling twisted in Mara's chest. She pulled the dagger from her belt.

"I wondered," Revathi said. "After Emil vanished. No one in the palace would have a reason to grab him, and the mercenaries had no way of knowing he was there. Someone told them."

She waved the parchment, making it rattle. "And this? Only someone in the guard would know these things. Only someone who sparred with them, served with them, *lived* with them would know these personal details." She dropped the paper, letting it float to the ground between her and Tamas.

"Only someone like you."

Tamas snarled and lunged forward. But Mara was ready. She pulled Revathi behind her with one hand and stepped into his path, bringing her dagger up.

"Back off," she said. "Or I will gut you."

Anger, dark and ugly, twisted Tamas's features. "You don't know what you're dealing with, Mara," he said.

"I was about to say the same of you," Mara said, glancing at

Revathi. "But it doesn't matter. I've pledged to Revathi, Tamas. She's my charge, and I won't let you hurt her ever again."

"What?" Tamas's eyes flicked to the earring in Mara's ear. "You can't do that!"

"I think you'll find that I can," Mara said. She jerked her head toward the door. "Come on, Revathi. We're leaving."

Tamas put his hand on his sword hilt. "I'm afraid not," he said, and he suddenly seemed larger, more dangerous. "You're going to have to stay right here."

"What's going on, Tamas?" Revathi said. "What are you doing?"

"Proving myself," Tamas replied. "To you, to my father, to everyone." He pulled his sword. "Now sit down and be quiet."

Mara didn't move.

Tamas's face stretched in a wide, humorless smile. "Are you really going to die for her?" he said.

Mara tightened her grip on her dagger and dropped into a fighting stance. "If I have to."

Tamas lunged at her. His sword moved like quicksilver in the lamplight. Mara's blade met his, the ringing harsh and loud in the dark house.

"Just let us go," she said. "I don't want to hurt you."

"You won't," Tamas said. He fell back, twirling his sword. Mara circled with him, careful to keep herself between him and Revathi.

This time Tamas tried an overpowering rush, striking her dagger so hard that Mara almost dropped it. He was good.

But Mara was better.

Instead of stumbling back, like he was probably expecting, Mara turned her momentum into a pivot, ducking under his attack and jamming her elbow into his gut. Then she snapped her head back, striking him in the face.

Tamas staggered back, his hand to his face. He blocked her next two attacks, then rushed her again, swinging his sword in an overhead arc.

Mara blocked it, catching the edge of the blade inches from her nose.

Tamas pressed down. He was very close now; she could see the sweat-damp strands of hair clinging to his forehead.

"You shouldn't have pledged to her," he said, low and savage. "Now I have no choice but to kill you."

Mara's skin was cold. The darkness of the house seemed to press closer, the light narrowing to the shine of Tamas's sword and the glimmer of her dagger. Her muscles strained and the wound in her shoulder burned.

Suddenly Mara heard a sound that made her stomach clench, the sound of feet and clanking swords and chatter. And it was coming from inside the house, from the direction Esmer had disappeared to.

The mercenaries were coming back.

The knowledge gave Mara new strength. With a snarl, she shoved Tamas away. He grabbed the neck of her tunic as he stumbled back, and Mara felt the fabric tear. She ignored it and followed up with a whirling attack, keeping Tamas off balance.

Her breathing was loud in her ears. Tamas swung at her and she blocked his sword, aiming a kick at his knee. It connected with a solid crack. Tamas fell with a howl of pain, and Mara leaped on top of him. She dug her knee into his chest and put her dagger to his throat.

"Revathi, run!" she gasped. "Get out of here!"

"Mara." The sound of Revathi's voice, choked and afraid, made Mara look up.

The room was filling up with people, silent shadows lining the walls. Revathi was staring at Mara, her eyes wide and dark. She had the clay oil lamp in her hand . . .

And Aari's hand on her throat.

"Let him go, Mara," Aari commanded. Her hand tightened, and Revathi gave a pained whimper.

Mara stepped back, letting Tamas get to his feet. The room was full of mercenaries now; their torches filled the house with strong, warm light. Mara caught a glimpse of a familiar tall figure in the crowd.

It was Emil. He looked as stricken as she felt.

"Put down the dagger, Mara," Aari said. Her eyes flicked to the earring in Mara's ear. "Don't make me hurt your charge."

Revathi made a strangled noise that pierced Mara's chest like an ice shard.

Mara let the dagger drop.

Tamas was breathing heavily. He sheathed his sword. "You're better than I thought." He made a gesture to his men. "Take her."

Mara struggled, but two of the mercenaries grabbed her and

held her fast. Her eyes flicked up, meeting Emil's for a moment, and she shook her head slightly. It wouldn't do for Emil to get caught as well.

Aari released Revathi, who fell to her knees. She barely managed to set her lamp down on the floor before a wave of coughing overtook her. Mara pulled against the men holding her, trying to get to Revathi, to help. One of them grabbed her injured shoulder and squeezed, the pain turning her knees to water. She stopped struggling but didn't take her eyes off Revathi.

Revathi finished her coughing fit and glared at Aari. "Since you're here, I assume Lord u'Gra is involved in this too," she said, her voice hoarse. "Of course he is. Tamas couldn't be paying these men otherwise."

"My father has nothing to do with this," Tamas said.

That's what he's supposed to say, Aari drawled inside Mara's head. *I have to hand it to Sathvik. He knows exactly what carrots to dangle to get his son to do what he wants him to do.*

Why are you telling me this? Mara sent.

Consider it an open invitation. I want you on my side, Mara. We should be allies, not enemies. Something changed in Aari's voice, and for a moment she almost sounded wistful. *I miss the company of other tiger-Sune. Don't you?*

Mara didn't answer.

"This wasn't how this was supposed to happen," Tamas was saying to Revathi, as he limped over to her and lifted her to her feet. "I was going to tell you after it was all over, after I'd taken the throne. When you could take your place beside me as my Empress."

"No," Revathi said. The marks of Aari's hands were still visible on her neck. "Tamas, this is wrong, this is treason. Don't do this."

"Treason?" Tamas said. "I'm trying to protect the Empire! We'll be good rulers, Revathi, better than the Emperor is now." He ran a hand over her cheek. "Don't you want to be Empress?"

"Not this way," Revathi said, shaking her head. "Tamas, please . . ."

"It'll be over quickly," Tamas promised. "I have a plan to keep the bloodshed to a minimum. All I need to do is get into the Palace of Flowing Water while the Imperial Guard is busy with the battle, and the Emperor will give me the throne."

"You're crazy," Revathi said, her voice strengthening. "Emperor Saro isn't going to hand over the Empire just because you threaten him."

"We're not going to threaten the Emperor," Tamas said. "We're going to offer him a trade. The throne for his most precious possessions."

Mara saw Revathi stiffen, saw the panic that crossed her face. "The princes," she whispered in horror, pulling away from Tamas. "You're going after the princes."

58

Emil

EMIL WAS FURIOUS. It had been hard enough coming up into the house and seeing Mara taken captive. Only Stefan's hard grip on his arm had stopped him from throwing himself forward. Now he stood, feeling sick and angry as Tamas explained his plan.

"That's right," the nobleman said, and he actually sounded proud of himself. "This attack is only a distraction, a way to keep the palace soldiers away from the real coup. Once I take the princes hostage, the Emperor will give me anything I want. He's tired, he has no heart for ruling, and he won't want to lose the rest of his family."

"*That's* how you plan to take over the Empire?" Emil whispered to Karoti, who was standing next to him and Stefan. "By threatening children?"

"Not us," Karoti said, but Emil thought he looked uncomfortable. "We've just been hired to fight. Tamas has assured us the princes won't be harmed."

Emil turned to Stefan. "Did *you* know you were working for him?"

Stefan shifted from foot to foot. "No, I didn't." He glanced at Karoti. "I wouldn't have joined if I'd known."

"Is this going to be a problem for you two?" Karoti said, putting a hand on the hilt of his knife.

Stefan's face was strained and miserable, and Emil felt a stab of pity for his brother. Stefan had wanted to change the Empire. He'd wanted justice. And now he was being forced to fight for the very person who'd humiliated him.

"You." Tamas's voice cut through the crowd and Emil turned to see that the man was looking at him. "The tall one with the red scarf. Come here."

Stefan cursed under his breath. Emil felt like swearing too. He'd forgotten he was even wearing the scarf.

"Well?" Tamas said. "I said, come here."

Emil moved forward. He kept his eyes down and tried to put a vacuous look on his face, the way Abhra had taught him. But his shoulders were tight. He was wearing different clothes and he was cleaner than before, but surely that wouldn't matter. Tamas was surely going to recognize him.

But he didn't. In fact, the noble didn't even look at his face. He simply waved a hand in Revathi's direction.

"Give the lady the scarf around your neck. And give the other one your shirt before you tie her hands. I have plans for them, and I want them to look presentable."

Emil let out the breath he'd been holding and untied the red silk scarf. The gold-embroidered tigers glistened in the light as he tied it loosely around Revathi's bruised neck. The girl's ink-dark eyes watched him without expression.

"I'm sorry," Emil whispered to her. "They have my brother."

"They seem to have us all," Revathi replied, her mouth barely moving.

Emil turned his attention to Mara. Her tunic had been ripped down the shoulder, and it hung loose and ragged on her. She hadn't been tied yet, but two mercenaries held her tightly, one on each side. One of them handed Emil Mara's dagger and a length of rough rope.

"Just cut the rest of the shirt off," Tamas ordered. "We don't have time to waste."

Nausea rose in Emil's throat. He pulled his loose shirt over his head and placed it over his shoulder, feeling the cool night air on his bare chest. The weight of all the eyes on him felt like it was crushing the breath from his lungs. He reached for Mara's tunic.

"Does this have to be done in front of everyone?" he blurted before he could stop himself.

"I'm sure I can find another volunteer to undress her," Tamas said. He looked at the crowd of mercenaries around him. "Any takers?"

Someone hooted, and Emil saw Mara flinch.

"I'll do it!" Stefan pushed himself forward. His head was up, and his pale-brown eyes shone in the torchlight. "I'll do it."

Tamas's head swiveled around. "You," he said, and anger twisted his face. The watching mercenaries fell silent. "I *know* you. You struck me."

"Yes," Stefan said, lifting his chin. "That was me."

Tamas stepped up to him and dealt Stefan a blow to the face that made Emil wince. Stefan rocked back on his heels, then wiped the blood from his lip.

Tamas moved to hit him again, but Rajo stepped in.

"This boy is a member of my crew, Lord Tamas," he said, and his voice was a sword's edge. "I will not stand by and see him beaten."

Tamas collected himself with an obvious effort. "Of course not. But he does owe me something." He held out a booted foot. "Like a clean set of boots. I'll even let him spit on them instead of licking them clean." He gave Stefan a victorious smirk. "Isn't that generous of me?"

Stefan took a deep breath and looked over at Emil. Their eyes met, and a corner of Stefan's mouth turned up.

"Yes, sir," Stefan said, and wonder of wonders, he actually managed to sound *humble.* "Thank you, sir."

Then, with every eye in the room on him, Stefan knelt before Tamas. He spit onto the leather of the nobleman's boot and started to clean it with his sleeve.

Thank you, Steffy, Emil thought. His brother had given him the distraction he needed. Carefully, he slit open Mara's tunic, the dagger cutting through the material as easily as if it had been made of paper.

Mara didn't resist as he slid the ripped tunic off her shoulders. She looked so vulnerable standing there in just her breast band and trousers. Something tender and painful twisted in Emil's chest.

Shielding her from view as much as he could, Emil slipped his own shirt over Mara's body. His fingertips brushed the skin of her upper arms, her waist. She was warm and smooth under his hands, but every touch felt like a violation. Like he was stealing something that should be given freely.

He reached behind her to adjust the shirt, keeping her in the protective space of his arms. "I'm sorry, Mara," he breathed in her ear. "I didn't want them to touch you."

Mara lifted her face. "I'd rather it were you," she whispered. Her eyes were huge and dark. "Oh, Emil, what are we going to do?"

"I don't know," Emil said. He took the rope and bound her hands in front of her, careful to make knots that looked tight but could be easily undone. He kept his voice soft. "But we can't give up."

Everyone was still watching Stefan spit-clean the noble's boots. Emil moved behind Mara and slipped the dagger into the back of her trousers. His shirt was long and loose on her and covered the hilt completely. She stiffened at the feel of the metal.

"May the Horned God protect you," Emil murmured in her ear. Then, without looking at Mara again, he went to stand next to Karoti.

Stefan finished polishing Tamas's boots with his sleeve and stood up. His face was flushed and defiant.

Tamas looked pleased. "Glad to see your time with the mercenaries has taught you some respect," he said. "You may go."

Stefan came back to where Emil was standing. Emil put a hand on his arm.

"Thank you," he breathed.

Stefan shrugged. "I owed her," he said, low and soft. "And you're my brother."

Emil squeezed Stefan's arm, and shoulder to shoulder, they turned back to listen to Tamas.

"We have to move up the schedule," Tamas said. "People are going to come looking for Revathi as soon as they realize she's missing. Send messengers to your men in the city, Rajo. We attack at Firstlight."

A rumble swept over the crowd of mercenaries.

"That wasn't in the plan," Rajo said, folding his muscular arms. Tamas stepped up to him, matching the big mercenary glare for glare.

"I'm changing the plan," he said. "And I'm the one who pays you. If I say you fight now, then you fight now. Now give the girls to me and get out of here. Leave a few of your men, too. I'll need them when I get into the palace."

Rajo's mouth was a tight line. "Yes, sir," he spit out. "Come on men, we have work to do." He gestured to a small group of the men. "Except for you. Do what he says." The unspoken *within reason* hung in the air. Then, without a backward glance at Tamas,

Rajo stomped away toward the crypt entrance. The mercenaries trickled after him. With one last glance at Mara, Emil followed.

Be careful, he thought in her direction, wishing for a Sune's mind-speaking powers. *Stay safe.*

I love you.

Beware the man whose hands are full and whose heart is empty.

Hearth caste saying

59

Mara

MARA WATCHED EMIL go, her eyes following him until he was through the doorway and gone. She felt small and shattered and very, very alone.

But his scent still clung to the shirt she wore, the rope was loose and flexible around her wrists, and her dagger was a solid weight against the middle of her back. Emil was gone, but he hadn't left her defenseless. He couldn't save her, but he'd given her a way to save herself, and Revathi. He trusted her to do that.

If she could only figure out *how*.

Mara closed her eyes, flexing her wrists in their loosened bonds. If she could get free quickly enough, maybe she could grab Tamas, hold him at dagger point, and make them let Revathi go. . . .

Her tentative plan was shattered when Aari moved next to Revathi, her smile wide and gleaming in the lamplight. "I think we should hold these two separately," she said to Tamas. "Hold them as hostages for each other's good behavior."

Try to escape or change to tiger form, and she dies, she added to Mara. *I'll rip her open with my own claws and sink my teeth into her soft flesh.* Her tongue flicked out, licking her lips.

"I'm sure Revathi won't be any trouble," Tamas said. His voice was almost pleading as he reached out to touch her face. "I know this is hard to understand, love, but everything's going to be all right. And you and I? We're going to rule the Empire."

Revathi jerked her face away. "Tamas, I swear," she said, and her voice was velvet soft and cold, cold in a way Mara hadn't known Revathi's voice could be. Cold enough to burn. "If you harm those boys, there will be no place in the Empire that can hide you."

Tamas stepped back.

"You'll come around," he said. Something hard and ugly flashed across his face, and for a moment, he looked very like his father. "When you have to choose between being Empress and the dungeons, you'll change your mind."

One by one the few torches the mercenaries had left started to sputter out. Tamas spoke to the handful of armed men who remained. "I want a constant watch on that roof, rotated every hour. You and you, come with me. I'll show you where the uniforms are."

"Tamas, I do think we should separate the girls just to be safe." Aari kept her eyes on Mara as she spoke. "I'll watch out for Revathi here, and we can put Mara in a storage room. There should be one around that we can bar from the outside."

Tamas looked up from where he was speaking with one of the remaining mercenaries. "If you think that's best," he said. "Just keep them out of trouble and undamaged until it's time to move."

"With pleasure," Aari purred. She jerked her head at Mara. "Lock her up," she told the mercenaries. "Make sure the door is sturdy and there are no windows."

And don't you cause trouble, she warned Mara. *I've still got your little friend.*

Mara clenched her fists, helpless fury crawling under her skin as the guards hustled her into a small, unlighted storage room that smelled of mice and dust and a few spoiled vegetables. *You're insane, you know that, Aari? No wonder your Tribe didn't want you around.*

Aari put a hand on Revathi's shoulder and smiled down at her. The girl didn't smile back. *Nice try, Mara. But I prefer to think of myself as practical. Sathvik and I have worked very hard to make this rebellion happen. He provided the money for the mercenaries, and I made sure Tamas did his part. We've been planning this for a long, long time.* Her mind-voice was a low purr. *You'd be better off joining us, you know. These humans are never going to understand you the way I do. They have no idea what you're capable of.*

Do you? Mara snapped.

Aari just laughed. The door slammed shut between them. There was a thud as a bar went across it.

Mara stood for a moment, letting her eyes adjust to the darkness. The storage room was cold, and she huddled deeper into the sheltering cashmere of Emil's shirt.

I have to warn someone. It was risky, but if she was careful enough, maybe she could make it work.

Mara settled down onto the dusty floor. She curled her feet under her, relaxing her bound hands. A couple of deep, calming breaths, and she was feeling . . . well, not centered. But at least less shaky.

Carefully, slowly, Mara spread out her mental awareness. Not trying to connect, not yet, just searching. The house and the city outside it scrolled away from her, like a dark map. She felt the dim gray lights of humans' thoughts around her, and the sparkle of Aari's mind like a gleaming fleck of copper. Mara tread carefully around it, trying not to brush against Aari's awareness.

She didn't sense Esmer anywhere, which was worrisome. The cat might have gone with the mercenaries, or she might be on her way to warn someone herself.

Either way, Mara had to try and reach Garen. The chill of the floor reached through the seat of her cotton trousers, making her shiver. She forced herself to breathe, refocus, then directed her thoughts toward the palace, toward a light that burned there, just beyond the edge of her reach.

Garen?

She was still too far away. Mara forced her curled fists to relax. If she could just push a little harder . . .

Garen, can you hear me?

The bar scraped against the outside of the door, loud and harsh. Mara jerked her head up just as Aari yanked the door open.

The tiger-Sune was holding a lamp in one hand and Revathi in the other. The shadows made her face look sharp and hollow, and her eyes were utterly without pity.

"I heard that," she said. "Try to send for help again and I will kill her. I don't care what Tamas wants. And I won't warn you again."

"Don't listen to her, Mara," Revathi said. Her voice was shaking. "You have to warn Garen. You have to warn the palace. It doesn't matter what happens to me."

Aari twisted her arm, and Revathi cried out.

"I hate it when you vermin get all sacrificial," Aari said. She looked at Mara. "I'll kill her, you know I will. And I'll make it hurt. I'll make it last. And you'll hear every scream she makes."

Mara? Garen's uncertain voice was soft as a breath in her mind. She'd made it.

Too late.

Mara, is that you?

Aari tensed, her fingers digging into Revathi's shoulder.

Mara pulled back her mental reach. Garen's voice vanished from her mind, leaving only silence. Mara's eyes stung, tears trickling cold down her cheeks. She met Revathi's eyes.

"I'm sorry," she said. "I can't . . . I'm sorry."

Aari smiled. "That's better. Now just stay here, like a good little kitten, and I'll let you see how this ends." She pulled Revathi back and shut the door behind her.

Mara drew her legs up and buried her face in her knees.

60
Emil

AS SOON AS they were inside the crypt, Stefan turned to Karoti, his face a mask of betrayal.

"Why didn't you tell me?" he said. "Why didn't you tell me who we were working for?"

Karoti's voice was unusually gentle. "Rajo and I decided that it was better for everyone if we kept the identity of our employer a secret from the crew until it was time. This isn't the first time we've done that, and it won't be the last."

"But he–he–"

Emil watched as Karoti stepped forward, placed a hand on his brother's shoulder. "This is just a job, Stefan. Jobs come and go. What matters is our loyalty to each other. What matters is that we have each other's backs. This isn't just a mercenary band," he said, shaking Stefan lightly. "It's a family. We need you, Stefan. Are you with us?"

Stefan swallowed. Then, after a long moment, he nodded. "All right," he said. "I'm with you."

"Good." Karoti released his shoulder. "Now go get your orders."

With a glance at Emil, Stefan hurried off. Karoti turned to Emil.

"And you?" he said. "Are you with us?"

Emil pressed his lips together. "And if I'm not?"

"I tie you up and shut you in a crypt," Karoti said. "And you pray that someone remembers you're there and comes to let you out before you starve to death."

He couldn't keep anyone safe if he was locked up.

"I'm with Stefan," Emil said. "Not you."

Karoti nodded. "Go."

Emil went.

He'd just retrieved his pack and was jogging down the corridor, when he heard the meow. There was a flash of gray-and-black fur and Esmer leaped into his arms.

"Esmer!" Emil held her close. He could feel her heart pounding under her fur, the thin bones of her ribs.

"How did you . . . what are you doing here?" he asked. Esmer purred and rubbed her nose against his fingers.

"Emil!" Karoti called down the corridor. "Are you ready?"

Mercenaries ran past them with weapons, leaders barking orders. Emil stepped out of the way and opened his pack. Esmer jumped in without hesitation. It was a tight fit, but hopefully she'd be all right.

"I've got everything," Emil called back.

"Good." Karoti made his way over. His eyes were narrow and sharp. "If either you or Stefan do anything to screw this up, I will find you. Betray us, and I will take a pound of flesh for every man we lose. Understood?"

"Understood," Emil said. "Where is Stefan?"

The sounds of a sudden argument spilled down the crowded corridor, and Karoti gave a grim smile. "Getting his orders, it sounds like."

Stefan pushed his way through the flow of mercenaries. "Did you know about this?" he demanded, scowling at Emil. "Did you talk Rajo into keeping me out of the fight?"

"Stefan!" Karoti's voice cut across the crowded corridor, and Stefan fell silent.

"Emil had nothing to do with this." The small man's voice was flat. "You have your orders."

"But *why*?" Stefan said.

"We don't owe you an explanation," Karoti said. "We don't owe you anything. You either follow orders or you don't. But decide now and stop acting like a spoiled child."

Stefan flinched. Then he drew a deep breath and let it out.

"Understood," he said. "I'll do my part."

"Good boy," Karoti said. He reached into the sack he was holding and pulled out two gray servants' tunics and two pieces of parchment. "Pushing up the timetable creates . . . complications," he said. "The old cover of bridge repair isn't going to work at night. So we're improvising. Put these on. They won't match your trousers, but hopefully the soldiers won't notice in the dark."

Emil slid the tunic on. It barely fit his long torso, but if he kept his arms down, it looked all right. Karoti kept talking, his words coming fast. He gave Emil the parchments. "These are backup work permits identifying you as belonging to a noble house. If they ask, tell them you're picking up medicines for a sick noble."

He pushed a lantern into Stefan's hands. "Now go. The two of you need to be in position before Firstlight."

Much to Emil's surprise, the servant's tunics and work permit actually worked. The soldiers waved them into the Jade Circle without a problem. Emil darted down a side street, stopped, and opened his pack.

"What are you doing—is that Esmer?" Stefan held up his lantern as the cat leaped out. "What is she doing here?"

Esmer shook herself and flashed into human form. She looked tired, Emil thought, lines digging into her face like claw scratches. "Where else would I be?" she said, patting her hair back into place.

"In the palace, for one thing," Emil said, trying not to sound snappish. "You could warn Garen."

"Emil!" Stefan sounded horrified. Esmer ignored him.

"I *tried*," she said, throwing up her hands. "As soon as I was underground and out of Aari's reach, I tried to get through to him. But I couldn't reach all the way to the palace. And I'm not leaving you two," she said as Emil opened his mouth. Her voice was low and fierce, and she stepped forward, poking Emil in the chest with her finger. "Every time we get separated, you vanish or get arrested or something. I don't care if the Empire burns, *I am not leaving you again.*"

Stefan picked up the pack. "I don't care what either of you do," he said. "I have orders, and I'm going." He stalked off, the lantern swinging as he walked.

Emil stared down at Esmer. "Mara . . . ," he started.

"I know." The retreating light reflected off the gold flecks in Esmer's eyes. "I know. But she's in just as much danger either way. The minute she and Revathi stop being useful, Aari and Tamas will kill them. You did what you could, Emil. You have to let her do the rest."

Emil's breathing was loud and ragged in his own ears, but he made himself nod. Esmer was right. He hated it and he hated her and he hated this whole thrice-damned city, but she was right.

"Stefan," he called, stepping away from Esmer. "Stefan, wait for us."

61

Mara

MARA DIDN'T KNOW how long she was in the dark, sour-smelling storeroom before the door opened again. But when she was pulled out, hands rough on her arms, the sky above the courtyard was the color of ash.

In the weak morning light, the figures gathered around were pale versions of themselves. Revathi looked exhausted, her shoulders slumped and dark hair tangled around her face. Tamas had changed into a silver-and-cream tunic, his sword at his side. He was probably going for regal, but he just looked faded and unhappy.

Aari, though, Aari was practically glowing. Energy seemed to radiate off her, and she bounced softly on the balls of her feet. When she saw Mara, she gave her a wide grin.

Mara looked away.

The handful of mercenaries had changed and now wore the blue uniforms of Imperial Guards. One of them wrapped a dark cloak around Mara, hiding her bound hands. Aari still stood near Revathi, her presence a silent warning.

Tamas was pacing, his steps echoing off the courtyard walls. "Anything yet?" he called up. A soldier's head appeared over the edge of the opening in the roof.

"Nothing yet," he called back.

"How long does it take to start a riot?" Tamas said, still pacing.

"Patience," Aari said. "It's going to take a bit for the soldiers in the Outer City to realize they need help."

"The timing is so tricky," Tamas said, rubbing his arms. "If we don't get past the Lotus Wall before the bridge blows, they'll be on the alert. But if we go too soon, we'll be fighting the Imperial Guard ourselves. I don't like this."

"It'll work out," Aari said. "Thought I am worried about the Jade warriors. If they get to the palace before the Emperor steps down . . ."

"We'll just have to be fast," Tamas said. "Fast and persuasive."

Revathi's head came up. "What about the Jade warriors?"

"Nothing you need to concern yourself with," Tamas told her, a smile stretching across his face. "Just a little . . . modification I made."

Mara looked at Aari.

Oh, you'll love this, Aari sent, answering her unspoken question. *Tamas hasn't told the mercenaries that the Emperor can call out the Jade warriors. They have no idea they're walking into a trap.* Her laugh in Mara's head was rich and bitter, like blood. *It'll be a massacre.*

Mara felt stunned and sick. All those men . . . and Emil and Stefan were with them. *Why would he do that? They're on his side!*

Aari laughed in her head again. *Tamas isn't on any side but his own. He doesn't want to pay the mercenaries any more than he has already. When the Emperor steps down, Tamas will command the Jade warriors. They are sworn to the throne. He'll use them to wipe out the remaining mercenaries and bring the rest of the army into line.*

Bile stung the back of Mara's throat, and she swallowed it down. She didn't want to give Aari or Tamas any excuse to leave her behind. Or kill her.

"I see the signal!" The soldier came running down the roof stairs. He was carrying a long, thin metal tube. "The rioting has spilled into the Bamboo Circle."

"Excellent," Tamas said. "They'll have to call for help now. Time to go."

He turned to Revathi. "Make yourself presentable, love. Don't want the guards getting suspicious, now do we?"

Revathi's mouth tightened, but she replaited her hair into a loose braid and straightened her asar. Tamas put a cloak over her shoulders. The edge of his dagger rested across her neck, covered by her hair.

Mara felt a sharp blade press against her upper back. "Either of you make any trouble, and you both die," Aari said. She dug the dagger into Mara's still healing wound, and Mara gasped.

Revathi stepped out of Tamas's grip. "Don't do that again," she said, her voice taking on that new cold, tone. "If you want my help, leave my friend alone."

"Friend?" Aari said. "Don't you mean servant?"

"No," Revathi said, her chin up and her eyes steady. "I don't." She smiled briefly at Mara. Mara felt the corners of her mouth lift in response.

The sharp pressure on Mara's back lessened. *Not quite the meek little mouse she appears, is she?* Aari sent. *How delightfully interesting. Does she know you're Sune?*

Yes, Mara sent back. *Does Tamas?*

Oh, no. Aari laughed inside her head. *He'd kill you immediately if he knew who you are.* Her amused tone turned serious. *I'm not ready for you to die yet.*

Mara narrowed her eyes. Aari almost sounded . . . lonely. *I can't help you do this, Aari. And even if you do succeed, I won't join you.*

Aari looked away. *We'll see.*

Revathi yawned and rubbed her eyes. "I can't go into the palace like this," she complained, her voice suddenly sweet and overdramatic. "I'm sure I look a fright." Her eyes met Mara's briefly. Another tiny spark of hope bloomed in Mara's chest. Maybe, just maybe, they could fix this. Together.

"Tamas," Revathi said, "can someone find me a fan to hide behind?"

62

Emil

EMIL CLUNG TO the bridge support and slipped one end of the fire rope through the iron ring driven into the bottom. He tossed the end to Stefan, who started to wind it around the leg. Esmer, in her cat form, was crouched higher up the slope, just where the bridge met the earth. Her ears were up and her tail was still. She was listening.

Emil finished tying off his end and climbed down, leaping over the last few rungs. His still-damp clothes clung to his skin, making him shiver. He felt like he'd never be dry again. His arms and legs ached from climbing, his fingers were numb, and his shirt smelled like canal water and pitch.

Stefan was in no better shape. A permanent pain line had carved itself in his forehead, and he moved like an old man. They'd found the gate just fine, but the canal water was freezing, and unexpectedly fast. Stefan, never a very strong swimmer, had been hampered by his injured arm. Even with Emil helping him, it had taken a long time to reach the bridge. Then they'd huddled together, out of sight of the guards, waiting.

At least climbing up and down the bridge supports had warmed Emil a little. He stretched his stiff muscles and bounced in place. It wouldn't be long now. He could already hear shouts in the distance. He hoped Abhra had gotten his message and that Heema and her children were safe.

Stefan tied the ends of the flax ropes together and tied another rope to them to use as a fuse. Then he pulled two short swords out of his pack and handed one to Emil, who belted it on.

"Emil . . ." Stefan cleared his throat. "I'm sorry I got you into this."

"I'm not," Emil said, thinking of Mara. "Don't get me wrong, Stefan, I don't like the people you're working with and I don't like helping them. But I'm glad I came after you."

"Yeah," Stefan said. He nudged Emil with his elbow. "Me too."

There was a muffled pounding noise across the bridge, like someone running, and Esmer's tail flicked back and forth twice.

"Messenger's here," Emil said in a low voice. "Won't be long now." He prodded Stefan's shoulder. "Up you go."

He and Stefan crept up the bank to just under where Esmer was sitting. Emil held the fuse in his hand, as they waited, tense and silent.

Finally there were shouts and the rattle of rapid footsteps. A company of soldiers ran across the bridge, the sound loud and blunt over Emil's head.

Stefan started to move, but Emil put a hand on his arm.

"Esmer? Check the bridge."

The slender cat slipped out from under the bridge, as casually as if she were hunting mice. She crept up far enough to see it, then paused, the tip of her black tail quivering.

Emil waited.

The tail lashed three times. All the soldiers were off the bridge.

"Now?" Stefan asked.

"Now," Emil said. He took the flint and iron and chipped them together, making sparks against the fuse. The fuse lit and sputtered flame. Emil dropped the rocks and grabbed Stefan's hand.

"Esmer, go!" he shouted. He and Stefan skidded down the bank, rocks falling with them, and ran for the water. It was cold and fast, and Emil dove under, just as the fuse hit the pitch-soaked legs and the Jade Bridge went up in flames.

63
Mara

THEY HAD JUST passed the Lotus Wall when there was a
faint rumble far outside the palace and a column of black smoke
billowed into the sky.

"Stay calm, keep walking," Tamas told Revathi. He'd split the
mercenaries in their Imperial Guard uniforms into small groups
and sent them on ahead to avoid looking suspicious. "We need to
get to the princes' room."

"Promise me you won't kill them," Revathi said, stopping
so abruptly that Tamas almost slammed into her. "Right now,
promise me. Or I'll scream and you can kill us both."

"Of course I'm not going to kill the princes," Tamas said, his
voice a vicious hiss. "I don't want to start my rule as a child killer.
But I will kill Mara if you don't move *right now*."

Aari's arm went around Mara's neck, her blade pressing

uncomfortably into the fragile skin of her throat. "Do as he says," she ordered.

Then she let go, cursing as a familiar voice called across the garden.

"Revathi!"

Lady Ekisa came striding up. Tamas's hand slid behind Revathi, his dagger at her lower back. He whispered something in her ear.

Revathi swallowed.

"I've been looking for you all morning," Lady Ekisa said. "Where have you been?"

Revathi waved her fan gently. "I . . . went for an early-morning walk, but it was too dark and I fell." The fan fluttered. "I'm all right, but I was very shaken up. Tamas was caring for me until I felt strong enough to come back." Mara saw a flash as the fan made a complicated movement. "Everything is all right, though."

Lady Ekisa's expression did not flicker. "I'm glad to hear it. Are you tending to the princes today?"

Revathi nodded. "Yes." She lowered the fan, twisting it in her hands. Her fingernails scratched grooves into the wood. "Will I see you later?"

"Of course, Granddaughter." Lady Ekisa nodded. "I have my own duties to attend to right now, but I'll be around." The deep sound of an alarm bell sounded from the direction of the palace gates. Lady Ekisa looked up at the line of dark smoke still rising into the sky from the burning Jade Bridge. "What in the name of the Ancestors is going on?"

Everyone followed her line of sight. Out of the corner of her eye, Mara saw Revathi drop her fan.

"I don't know, but we should go," Tamas said. His hand tightened on Revathi's arm. "I need to get Revathi back to her room and rejoin the other guards."

"Of course," Lady Ekisa said, her face bland and pleasant. "Try to come to dinner, will you, Revathi? I'm cooking your favorite sweet rice."

"That sounds nice," Revathi said with a forced smile. "I'll try to make it."

"Crazy old woman," Tamas said as they walked away. "Talking about sweet rice at a time like this. She's more senile than I thought."

"In my Tribe, she'd have the decency to go off by herself and die quietly," Aari added. "She's just taking up resources now."

Revathi didn't answer. But as they moved off, Mara looked back to see Lady Ekisa pick up Revathi's fan.

64
Emil

EMIL PULLED STEFAN out of the canal, both of them gasping. From their landing point, they couldn't see the bridge burning, but thick, dark smoke drifted down the canal, filling the air with ash.

"Okay, I take it back," Emil said, rubbing the back of his neck, where a stray ember from the fire had seared him. The inside of his nose burned, and his mouth tasted like canal water. "I really wish I'd stayed home right now."

Stefan was bent over, his hands on his knees and his body shaking. "It's all right," he said, between coughs. "I kind of wish I had too." He managed several deep breaths and straightened up. "Now what?"

"We can't stay here," Emil pointed out. The soaked leather sword belt felt heavy on his hips. "They'll start looking for the people who set fire to the bridge. We have to get farther into Jade Circle. Besides, Esmer's waiting for us."

Stefan pulled his sword out of his damp scabbard and looked at it with disapproval. "Shouldn't we dry these off or something?"

"With what?" Emil asked. He squeezed the hem of his shirt, splashing cold drops of water on his feet. "We're both soaked."

"There is that," Stefan said. He started climbing the stairs to the gate. "I didn't realized the life of a mercenary would be so uncomfortable."

Emil following him up the steps, smiling despite himself. "Uncomfortable and surprisingly boring," he agreed. "Except for the explosion." A trickle of water dribbled over the burn on his neck and he winced. "That was exciting."

Stefan pushed open the gate, then let out a startled *oof,* as his arms were suddenly full of Esmer. The girl hugged him hard, then flung herself at Emil.

"I thought you'd drowned."

Emil hugged her back. "We're fine," he said. "Just a little wet."

Esmer drew back, wrinkling her nose. "You are wet." She brushed at a damp spot on her tunic. "The mercenaries are attacking the palace," she continued. "And every healer and scholar in this part of the city is looking out their front gate, wondering what is going on."

"So what are we going to do now?" Emil asked his brother. "Because I really don't want to fight anyone." Stefan bit his lip.

"The farther we are from the bridge, the better I'll feel," he said. "We can figure out the rest from there."

They hadn't gone too far, when Emil heard his name whispered from a doorway.

"Emil! Emil!"

Emil held up a hand. Esmer grabbed Stefan's sleeve, halting him. Emil peered into the doorway.

It was Manik. His hands twisted in the fabric of his apron, and his eyes darted from side to side. "I thought that was you," he said. "When the bridge caught fire, I said to myself, that boy Emil, he's got something to do with this." He reached out and caught Emil's arm in a strong grip. "I did you a favor, and now you owe me. What is going on?"

Emil hesitated, but only for a moment. Quickly, he gave the cook a sketch of what was happening, including the mercenaries' plan to put a new ruler on the throne. Manik's face grew more and more serious as Emil spoke.

"Oh my," he said, over and over. "Oh my." His fingers clamped down harder on Emil's arm. "You can't go back to the Flower Circle, any of you."

"Why not?" Stefan said. "We're already criminals, might as well see it through."

"Because, my dim-witted little grouse, you and your band of rebels forgot one very important thing. In matters of national importance, the Emperor can call for help."

"Who's he going to call?" Stefan said. "We've blocked the road out of here. The only armed men within reach are confined behind Jade caste walls."

"Unless the Emperor calls them out," Manik said. He gave

Emil's arm a shake. "You stupid children, the only way the Jade warriors can leave is *by Imperial decree.*"

Emil felt like someone had struck him on the side of the head with a board. If the Jade warriors joined the fight, they'd be coming at the mercenaries from the back, trapping them between enemies and driving them into the arms of the Imperial Guards. The Jade warriors might not be as good as legend painted them, but they wouldn't have to be. Not if they took the mercenaries by surprise.

Emil could tell by Stefan's look of horror that the same thoughts were running through his twin's mind. Manik looked at them and nodded.

"Exactly. And if an Imperial messenger isn't trying to reach the Jade Circle right now, I'll cook my sandal in butter and serve it to myself. If I were you," he said, glancing from Emil's face to Stefan's. "If I were you, I'd run."

Stefan was already moving, darting away. Emil gave Manik a nod of thanks and ran after him. Esmer was close on his heels.

"Stefan," he said when he caught up to his twin. "Where are you going?"

"I have to warn them," Stefan said. His eyes were wide and wild. "I have to find the section leaders and tell them not to use the retreat plan. We can't get over the Flower Bridge now, but there are other ways, routes back into the crypts where we can at least defend ourselves." He reached up, covering Emil's hand with his own.

"They'll all die, Emil. I know you don't agree, but I need to do this." His eyes were open and earnest. "Please."

Emil rubbed his forehead. Everything was moving too fast, spiraling out of control. "All right," he said, and it felt like ripping his own guts out, like cloth tearing through his fingers.

Like letting go.

Emil gripped his brother's hand. "All right, Stefan. Go. I'll find Rajo and warn him."

Some of the tension went out of Stefan's shoulders. "Thank you," he said, looking Emil in the eye. "I . . . thank you."

Emil forced himself to smile and ruffled his twin's hair. "Good luck, Steffy."

Stefan turned to Esmer. "I could use your help," he said. "You can move faster than I can through crowds."

Esmer bit her lip and glanced at Emil. He said nothing. It was her decision, and he'd already asked too much of her.

Esmer threw up her hands. "All right, fine. But so help me, Emil . . ." She yanked his head down with surprising strength and planted a brief, fierce kiss on his mouth. "If you get killed," she said, glaring at him, "I swear by the Long-Tailed Cat that I will *never* forgive you."

"Understood," Emil said. His eyes stung and he wasn't sure why. He shoved her in the direction of Stefan, who was grinning. "But we have to hurry."

65
Mara

THE PRINCES WERE still in bed. Sudev had crawled into
Paithal's bed, and even in sleep, Mara could see the difference
between them. Paithal slept on his back, face peaceful and mouth
slightly open, while Sudev was curled up tightly like a cat, his
dark hair messy against the silk pillows. Revathi went straight to
them, as Tamas ordered his men to secure the room.

Paithal woke first. "Revathi?"

"Shhh," Revathi said, sounding like she might cry. She ran a
hand through the prince's hair. "I need you to be very good, all
right? Very good and very quiet."

Sudev blinked at her sleepily. Paithal glanced around at Tamas's
men, at Aari, standing behind Mara. His eyes found Mara's
bound hands, and Mara saw him swallow hard.

"You're not here to play with us, are you?" he asked.

"I wish I was," Revathi said, falling to her knees. "I wish I was. Forgive me."

Paithal drew a deep breath, and his fingers gripped the bedspread. "Did they threaten you?"

"Both of us," Mara said. Aari poked her with the sharp tip of the knife.

Revathi buried her face in her hands. "I'm sorry. I'm so sorry."

Paithal slid off the bed, putting a hand on Revathi's head. "It's all right," he said. "Father and Garen will save us."

"No one is coming to save you," Tamas said. There was a wide grin on his face, and he couldn't seem to stand still. "I'm going to be Emperor and no one can stop me."

Sudev started to cry.

Paithal looked at Tamas. "I think you will make a very bad Emperor."

Tamas looked angry for a moment; then he laughed. "What do I care for the opinion of children? I'm about to have the Empire handed to me on a golden plate."

"Not if you don't stop talking," Aari interrupted. "As entertaining as this is, we have an Emperor to negotiate with." She gestured with her knife.

"You, prince. Get back on the bed. You and I are going to be very good friends."

"No!" Revathi shot to her feet, standing between them. "You promised," she said to Tamas. "You swore you wouldn't hurt them."

Aari rolled her eyes. "Grab her and tie her hands," she ordered the men.

Paithal climbed back up next to Sudev, who clung to him. "Why are they waving weapons?" the younger boy asked, his eyes wide. His voice shook. "They're scaring me, Paithal."

"Shhhh," Paithal said, rocking him. "Don't be afraid, Sudev. I won't let anything happen to you."

Sudev sniffled and buried his face in his older brother's tunic.

Aari pushed Mara into a far corner. "Now just sit there and be a good little Sune," she said. "And no sending."

Revathi made a pained noise as the men pushed her down next to Mara. Her hands had been tied tightly, and Mara could see the beginnings of rope burns on her wrists.

Tamas looked around the room and gave a satisfied nod. "You," he said, indicating one of the men at random. "Fetch the Emperor."

The man left the room. Aari sat on the edge of the princes' bed and started cleaning her fingernails with the tip of her knife.

Mara shifted, moving so that her head was almost on Revathi's shoulder.

"I think I can get my hands loose," Mara said in a whisper. "And I've got my dagger. I could cut you free and make a move for Aari. . . ."

Revathi shook her head. "Someone will grab the princes before we can get to them." She straightened her back, steadying herself with an obvious effort. "I hope Grandmother understood my message."

"I thought that's what you were doing," Mara said. "What did you tell her?"

"Well, there's no fan signal for treason." Revathi shifted so her mouth was right over Mara's ear. "But I was able to let her know that I was lying and warn her that Tamas was dangerous." Her breath tickled Mara's ear. "Grandmother is very resourceful. She'll find a way to help us if she can. . . ."

She trailed off, her eyes shifting to the large curtained window.

"Mara," she breathed. "Is it just me, or are those curtains moving?"

Mara followed Revathi's line of sight. The curtains *were* moving a little. It might have been a breeze from a nearby pond.

Or not.

There was another breeze-like movement, and a knife appeared on the edge of the windowsill, barely visible behind the curtain. It glinted a little in the light.

Mara moved her mouth back to Revathi's ear. "On the windowsill. Looks like a knife."

"Thank you, Grandmother," Revathi murmured. "Now if I could just get over there . . ."

Her whisper was interrupted by a bellow of pure rage from the hall.

"Tamas!" The building seemed to shake with the vibration of Garen's angry voice. "Tamas!"

Aari grabbed Paithal by the arm and yanked him off the bed. She put her knife to his throat and nodded to Tamas.

Tamas cleared his throat. "Garen, I have a blade to the heir's throat!" he shouted, just as something huge and heavy hit the door. "Break down that door and he dies!"

Sudev shrieked and reached for Paithal, but one of Tamas's

men grabbed him and held him fast.

"It's all right, Sudev," Paithal said. His lips trembled. "It's going to be all right."

Garen had stopped banging on the door. "What do you want, Tamas?"

"Is the Emperor with you?" Tamas called. "I don't deal with palace pets."

The growl that came from the other side of the door made the hair on Mara's arms stand up. "He is," Garen said.

"Prove it," Tamas said.

The Emperor's voice floated through the wood. "I am here."

Tamas looked at Aari.

"Open the door," she said. "Let them see."

"I'm opening the door," Tamas called. "Charge us and Paithal dies."

Tamas's men stepped forward and unlocked the door. It swung open, revealing Garen and Emperor Saro. Garen had his massive sword in his hand. His face was twisted into a snarl. The lines in the Emperor's face were deep, and his voice was quiet.

"What do you want, Tamas? You know you cannot hope to escape."

"I want your throne," Tamas said. "I want a royal decree, signed and sealed with your own seal, that declares me the new Emperor. Give me that and I will let you and your sons live."

"This is madness, Tamas," Garen said. "You can't hope to hold the throne like this. The army will tear you to pieces."

"I will have my own army," Tamas said. "One sworn to the

throne, no matter who holds it. Or have you not called out the Jade warriors yet?"

Garen sucked in a breath. Tamas laughed.

"You have a choice, Saro," he said. "You can try to stall me until the Jade warriors get here. My men and I will die, but we'll kill the princes first, leaving you without family and without heirs. Or you can quickly abdicate, hand over the official decree, and keep your sons."

"If I step down, what happens to me and my family then?"

"You'll be banished to the Eastern Forests," Tamas said. "After we ensure that you will never be fit for Flower caste again." He smiled. "Don't worry, I won't take anything you'll miss too much. Some fingers, perhaps, or an ear. The nobles will never suffer a deformed Emperor."

Emperor Saro pressed his lips together. "I need to think about this."

"Wrong answer," Aari said. And with a swift movement, she cut Paithal's throat.

The boy fell to his knees, choking, his eyes wide with shock.

Someone screamed, and Mara couldn't tell if it was her, Revathi, or Sudev. The scream mingled with Garen's roar, an unearthly sound of grief and pain and fury.

Emperor Saro reached out helplessly. . . .

Ignoring them all, Aari pushed the twitching Paithal out of the way with her foot and grabbed Sudev. She held him like a shield in front of her, her wet knife to his neck.

"Back off, Garen," she called, and there was no mercy in her voice. "And tell those soldiers with you to back off too. Unless you want the Emperor's last child to die like his brother."

Garen was shaking, his face twisted with rage. But he took a step back.

Tamas's men slammed the door shut.

66

Emil

EMIL'S FEET POUNDED on the smooth stone as he ran. He and Stefan and Esmer had split up once they crossed the Flower Bridge. Stefan and Esmer planned to circle behind the fighting, find a safe place for the wounded and retreating to go, and then spread the word among the others. Emil's job was to find Rajo.

Most of the fighting seemed to be centered around the palace, so he headed in that direction, following the sounds of battle.

The palace was well defended. Imperial archers stood on top of the smooth gray walls, their barbed arrows flying at anyone within range. The infantrymen were holding the Imperial Bridge against the mercenaries, their uniforms making a line of dark blue across the clear water. A few groups of Imperial Guards clustered together, back to back in the middle of the fight. Their short, leaf-shaped swords flickered as they battled through the mercenaries, cutting through the crowd like a throwing circle. The clash of blades rang out over the grunts and cries.

But the mercenaries weren't backing down either. There were mercenaries trying to swim the narrow canal, men trying to slide long planks across it, and a crowd fighting to get on the bridge. A group of mercenary archers, under the command of a brown-haired woman, were picking off the guardsmen. As Emil watched, an Imperial soldier went over the bridge railing, an arrow buried in his throat. Another group loaded flaming slings and threw them at the archers on the walls, trying to slow the rain of Imperial arrows.

"Soldiers on the left! Protect the archers!" It was Rajo's unmistakable bellow, and Emil ran toward it. Men with swords and staffs gathered in a loose, flower-shaped pattern around the archers, right as one of the circles of Imperial soldiers arrived. The two groups clashed in a mess of war cries, tearing flesh, and the smell of blood.

Bile rose in Emil's throat, but he forced himself to fight his way forward, using the pommel of his sword as much as he could instead of the blade.

"Rajo," he called. "Rajo!"

"Emil, down!" Rajo pulled out his throwing circle and threw it. Emil ducked and the metal circle whistled overhead, embedding itself in an Imperial soldier's throat behind him. Emil felt the spray of warm blood on his back. Somewhere inside him, panic gibbered.

He ignored it. "Rajo! The Jade warriors are coming!"

Rajo twirled his sword and blocked an Imperial blade. "What did you say?"

"The Jade warriors!" Emil was almost screaming, the words scraping his throat.

"What about them?"

"They're co–"

Suddenly from the Jade Circle came a sound like nothing Emil had ever heard. It was a horn, so deep and powerful that it stopped everyone on the battlefield for a moment.

"What in the name of the Seven Hells?" Rajo said into the sudden silence.

"That's what I was trying to tell you," Emil said. "The Jade warriors have been called out. They're coming!"

Rajo swore loudly. Then he punched his opponent in the face, laying the man out. Gesturing to a nearby group of mercenaries, he ran for the Jade Circle, Emil and the men right behind him.

But when Emil saw what was waiting for them, he realized that no amount of warning would have been enough.

Ranged on the other side of the broad stone Flower Bridge was an army. At least it looked that way to Emil. Rows of unsmiling men and women in green, each holding a spear or staff or sword. Muscled arms and straight backs and gleaming weapons. Eyes underlined with green dye. These were not people who fought for sport, Emil realized with a sick feeling. These were true warriors.

At their head was an old man with a cap of white hair and deep-set eyes. He leaned on his staff as if it were a walking stick, but his voice was clear and carrying.

"Lay down your weapons and surrender," he called over the bridge. "We do not wish for death to come to any of you."

"You seem very sure of yourself, old man," Rajo called back. "You might be surprised."

The man held up one hand. "Very few things surprise me," he said in a mild voice. "Now, surrender or die."

Karoti came running up. "Emil what is going . . . oh." He stared at the rows of warriors waiting on the other side of the bridge. "Shit."

"What happens to my men?" Rajo asked. "If we lay down our arms?"

"You'll be punished as befits traitors to the throne," the older man said. "Some of you will be sent to the copper mines; some will become bond servants. We will visit no retribution on your families, but you and your men must face justice."

"Justice," Rajo said, half to himself. His hand tightened on the hilt of his sword. "How can there be justice in an Empire that shelters the wealthy and abandons the ones who most need its help? Is it the justice of the Empire that makes us wander and beg and fight to survive?"

The man's voice was full of pity. "If you wish to die for your cause," he said, "I cannot stop you. But we serve the throne, for good or ill."

Rajo frowned.

"He's going to fight," Karoti said in a low voice. "That thrice-cursed idealistic bastard is actually going to fight." He whirled on Emil, shoving something into his hands. It was an oddly curved horn with a bamboo mouthpiece. "If those men get over the bridge, sound this."

"What is it?"

Karoti's mouth twisted. "Rajo calls it the Horn of No Hope," he said. "We have never used it, but every man and woman we take on has to learn the sound. It means everything is lost, and retreat impossible. They will know that, and surrender or fight as they wish."

Emil's throat was tight. He nodded.

"Sound the horn, then run," Karoti said. "That's an order."

Emil grabbed his sleeve. "You can't hope to survive this. This is madness."

Karoti shrugged. "He's my brother."

He pulled out of Emil's grip. Then he turned and made his way to the front of the group to stand beside Rajo. He looked up, and Emil saw him smile.

Rajo smiled back. Then he put a hand on Karoti's shoulder and held up his sword with the other. "Do what you must," he shouted. "I do not accept the Empire's justice."

The older man dropped his hand. A flood of green-robed Jade caste surged over the Flower bridge. Rajo yelled a battle cry and threw himself forward.

The two sides crashed together in a wavering line, the tattered mercenaries and the well-trained warriors. Swords and spears flashed, staffs and fighting sticks twirled in a deadly blur. Rajo was holding his own on one side of the bridge, holding off a group of Jade warriors by himself. Karoti moved through the crowd like a snake, taking down all in his path. The other mercenaries were doing well too, and for a moment, Emil thought they might be able to hold the bridge. . . .

Then Karoti took a spear to the gut.

"Karoti!" Rajo howled. Karoti sank to his knees, his fingers clasped over the spear still embedded in his belly. His mouth worked but no sound came out. He looked up, eyes searching the crowd, then—as if in slow motion—pitched forward.

"No!" Rajo swung his sword like a scythe, carving his way through the Jade warriors. His eyes were wild.

He never saw the blade that took him through the back.

Emil caught a brief glimpse of Rajo's blank, shocked face before the man stumbled forward and fell, lost in a sea of deadly green. Then they were both gone.

Emil felt like he couldn't move, as if he were stuck in some sort of nightmare. And the Jade warriors kept coming, kept fighting. There was no anger in their faces, only an implacable determination. Somehow that made them even more terrifying.

A woman standing next to Emil went down with a knife buried in her eye. The suddenness of it jerked Emil out of his horrified trance. He started backing away, hands trembling, his breath coming fast. Rajo's dying howl still echoed in his ears, but Emil had his orders, and one more thing to do.

As the first Jade warrior stepped off the bridge, Emil put the horn to his lips and blew.

67

Mara

"WHAT ARE YOU doing, Aari?" Tamas was pacing, hands fisted in his hair. "You weren't supposed to actually kill him!"

"They were stalling, and we're in a hurry." Aari shrugged her shoulders, ignoring the growing pool of blood that was darkening around her and Sudev's feet. "We still have the one."

Tamas glared at her. Then he went over and spoke through the door.

"Bring me the signed decree," he said. "Write it down, seal it, and slide it under the door. Now!"

"Someone has gone for parchment and the seal," Emperor Saro's voice answered. "Just don't hurt my son."

Revathi was trembling and silent. Her hands were clenched together as if she wanted to strangle Aari between them. Garen, on the other hand, was anything but quiet.

Aari! His voice cracked into Mara's mind like a whip, and she saw Aari's shoulders jerk. *Aari. Enough.*

I don't answer to you, Garen, Aari answered, and Mara didn't know how the tiger woman was still standing. Even from the next room, Garen radiated fury and challenge.

That child is mine, Aari. Release him. Mara felt Garen's push on Aari's mind, but Aari didn't move.

No. And if you try to take him, I'll kill him. You know I will.

Then you would have no hostage.

Test me. There was something dark and vicious in Aari's words, and Mara heard Sudev whimper as her fingers dug into his shoulder. *Please, Garen. Give me an excuse.*

Aari was going to kill Sudev, Mara had no doubt about that. And she was more than a match for Garen's mind-strength. Garen couldn't *force* Aari to change. After all, it wasn't like he was another tiger, challenging her for territory. . . .

The room and its inhabitants faded to gray around Mara.

Another tiger.

Challenging Aari for territory.

A spark of magic stirred inside her. But this wasn't the terrified, angry need that Mara had been fighting for three years. This was solid, comforting. Like a summer-warmed rock under her hand. She felt centered and present, and alive.

I can stop this. I can.

For the first time since she'd lost her family, Mara found herself reaching for her magic. It bloomed to life, a fire in her stomach and a tingle in her fingertips. She'd forgotten how it felt to have that strength humming through her, ready if she needed it. It wasn't everything she was—never that—but it was a part of her just the same.

Yes.

It was only a moment's work to free her hands, and as the ropes fell away, Mara felt something else fall away from her, too. Something that felt very much like fear.

"You want to get to that knife in the window?" she whispered in Revathi's ear. She pulled the dagger out and severed the girl's bonds. "Then be ready."

And she stood.

"Mara? Mara, what are you doing?" Revathi hissed, but Mara didn't look at her.

"Aari!" she said, sending every head in the room swiveling toward her. Aari jerked Sudev closer.

"Don't come any closer, Mara."

"I challenge you," Mara said. She shifted to face Aari full on and put her chin down, making sure not to break eye contact. She didn't have ears to flatten or a tail to thrash, but maybe this would do.

"I challenge you," she repeated, taking a step forward. She made her voice a low, soft growl. "I work in this room, I live in this palace. This is *not* your territory. It's mine. You are an intruder here."

Aari's fingers twitched on the handle of the knife. "You can't fight me," she said, her lips curling up to show her teeth. "You'd have to kill me, and your precious oath says you can only kill in defense of your charge."

"My oath does not define me," Mara said. She held up the dagger; then, with a deliberately dramatic gesture, she threw it in the opposite direction from the window. Every eye followed it as it clattered to the floor. Mara's back was to Revathi, but she had to hope the girl understood what she was doing.

"I'm not challenging you as a member of the Order of Khatar, Aari. I'm challenging you as myself. As Shar of the Kishna-Sune, tiger-blood and tiger-born."

Out of the corner of her eye, she saw Tamas jerk away, the blood draining from his face.

"You're not Kishna-Sune anymore," Aari said. She tried to smirk, but Mara could see she was trembling. Her instincts must be calling for blood right now. "You were exiled, remember?"

"Being outcast doesn't change what I am," Mara said. The anger was back now, mixing with her magic, a pure golden flame burning through her. Not the all-consuming rage of before, but a controlled anger. A useful one. "You told me that."

This is my home, she added mentally, stepping forward again. *I claim it by right of possession and by right of strength.* She sent the words with every ounce of will and dominance she possessed behind them and took one more deliberate step.

Either fight me or get the hell out of my territory.

With a snarl, Aari shoved Sudev at a nearby guard. "Watch him," she snapped. "I'm going to teach this arrogant kitten a lesson she won't forget."

Stupid move, she sent, her voice an angry growl inside Mara's head. *Very, very stupid, little girl.*

Mara smirked at her. *We'll see.*

And she let the magic burn.

It raged through her, stronger for all the years of being pent up, a welcome fire in her blood. One second Mara was in human form, the next her hands had become heavy, dark paws. Her back lengthened, her body falling forward. Her mouth was suddenly full of sharp teeth. And oh, Nishvana, her senses were back. It was like throwing a heavy wool blanket off her head. *Everything* was sharper, clearer.

It was glorious.

Mara saw Aari drop to four feet as well, and then there was no more time to think, as the other tiger attacked.

Mara rose up on her hind legs and met the charge, feeling Aari's ribs slam into hers. The impact shook them both, but Mara's broad rear claws dug into the carpet, holding her steady. She was bigger than Aari and blocked the other tiger's powerful swipes.

Aari fell back, her mouth open, the tips of her fangs showing. Her yellow eyes glowed with feral joy.

You're strong.

Biggest in my litter, Mara sent back. *You should have seen my father. He'd give you nightmares.*

You know what gives me nightmares? Scum-loving Sune like you, Aari sent, panting. Mara spared a thought for how they must look. Her dark fur and Aari's luminous bronze coat. So similar, but so different.

Well, come on then, she sent. *Teach me a lesson.*

They rose up and met again in a blur of snarls and roars and teeth. Mara was still stronger, but Aari was faster and more experienced. They fell apart and circled each other again.

This time when Mara charged, Aari was prepared. She ducked one paw under Mara's defenses. The blow rocked Mara's head back. Claws scored her cheek, scraping through her fur.

Aari took advantage of the momentary distraction to throw all her weight against Mara. Mara went down. Aari was on top of her before she could move, claws swinging. Pain tore through Mara's shoulder, and she roared.

With sheer effort, Mara managed to wriggle out of Aari's deadly embrace and to her feet again. But before she could retreat, Aari's mouth closed around the top of her head. Sharp teeth pressed painfully into Mara's scalp.

Give up, Aari sent, her growl rumbling through Mara's skull. *You're strong, but you've forgotten how to fight as a tiger. You can't win.*

Sparks of pain and pressure flickered across Mara's vision. She tensed her legs, resisting, keeping herself upright.

No, she sent, letting her lips lift up over her fangs. *Never.*

You can't win, Aari repeated.

There was a flash of metal and the guard holding Sudev dropped with a choked gurgle. Out of the corner of her eye, Mara saw Revathi grab the prince, pulling him behind her.

I don't have to win. Mara twisted her head, jerking out of Aari's grip. *I just have to keep you busy long enough for them to win.*

"Now, Garen!" called Revathi.

There was the sound of splintering wood. And the room was

suddenly full of swords and screaming and the roar of one very, very angry bear.

Mara kept her attention on Aari. The two tigers circled each other again, prowling, searching for weakness.

A distraction, Aari sent. *Very clever. But you're still going to lose this fight.*

She reared up, and Mara met her in another charge, almost losing her balance again. Aari's claws came perilously close to her neck.

Such a waste, Mara. You and I could have been so good together. But you chose the useless humans instead.

Not so useless. Mara lunged forward, but this time, instead of trying to strike at Aari, she dug her claws into the other tiger's shoulder. *They taught me this.*

And with that she flung herself backward. The move went against all her tiger instincts, but Mara's training from the Order held true. She rolled backward, taking Aari with her, and as soon as her back hit the floor, her hind legs were moving. She pushed up, deadly claws flailing . . .

Straight for Aari's exposed underbelly.

Aari shrieked in pain. Her momentum carried her over Mara, and she hit the flood with a hard thud.

Mara rose to her feet and stalked over to Aari, who was trying to rise. One of Mara's slashes had scored her hind leg deeply, and there were several deep gashes on her belly. Her cream-colored stomach fur was soaked in blood. She looked up at Mara with mad yellow eyes.

Do it. Go on. Do it.

Mara lowered her head, grabbing Aari's throat in her teeth. It would be so easy. Just a little pressure . . .

Do it, Aari snarled inside her head. *There's nothing for me here anyway.*

For a moment Mara stood there, feeling the other tiger's panting breaths, the warm pulse under the neck fur.

You know, she sent back at last, *you were right. We do have a lot in common. But you overlooked something.*

Really? Aari sent, with a weak effort at her old amused tone. *And what was that?*

I'm not you.

Mara released Aari's throat and stepped away, pulling the magic back inside her as she did so.

Coward, Aari spit, closing her eyes.

Once back in human form, Mara staggered and would have fallen if Garen hadn't caught her elbow.

"Well and bravely fought, Mara," he said softly.

"Revathi," Mara said, trying not to gasp. Her torn shoulder burned with pain, and her trembling legs didn't feel like they would hold her up much longer. She reached up to touch the shallow scratches on her cheek, feeling the blood trickle down her face. "Is Revathi all right?"

Garen nodded. "She fought well," he said. "Kept Sudev alive long enough for me and my soldiers to take care of the other men. She's making sure Sudev reaches the Emperor's quarters safely, and then she will return." He turned to look at Aari.

"What shall we do with this one?"

Mara looked down at the wounded tiger. Aari's gut wounds were bleeding freely, the ragged edges gaping. The tiger's sides heaved. Without medical attention, she probably wouldn't survive.

"Bandage her up and take her into custody. She should face justice for what she's done," Mara said.

Aari snarled at them, teeth bared. *I'd rather bleed out here on the floor than let traitors like you touch me,* she sent. Her head fell back onto the carpet. *Just leave me here to die.*

Very well, Garen sent, his mind-voice raw. Mara could sense the rage and grief thundering through him and marveled that he had been able to change back at all. *As you choose.*

Then he walked away. Mara turned her back on Aari and followed him.

Out in the hall, Garen pressed his palms against the wall and took a deep breath. Mara put a hand on his broad back, offering him her quiet sympathy.

"Will you be all right here?" Garen said after a moment. "I need to go help the Imperial Guard. There is still a battle going on outside."

"I'll be fine," Mara said. "I'm just going to wait here for Revathi. But . . . Garen?" She hesitated. "I know it's a lot to ask, but Emil's out there somewhere, he and his brother. They only joined the mercenaries recently and they didn't know anything about the plan to harm the princes. Could you . . . would you . . ."

"I see," Garen said. He stood up straight. "I'm not allowed to grant Imperial pardons, but I think I can arrange something."

Mara closed her eyes. "Thank you."

"You saved Sudev, Mara," Garen said. "It's the least I can do." He strode down the hall, then stopped and looked back. "How did you know that Aari would take your challenge?"

Mara leaned her head against the wall and felt herself smile. "I'm Sune," she said. "I knew."

68

Emil

EMIL WAS IN trouble.

He was still blowing the horn Karoti had given him. He didn't know why, except that some part of him thought if he kept blowing it, maybe more men would lay down their weapons, maybe people would stop dying, and maybe this whole bloody mess would just *stop*.

He was in an alley now, but he could still hear the screams and cries from the main battle. Some of the mercenaries had laid down arms, but not enough, not nearly enough. Emil had sounded the trumpet until his breath was gone, but people were still fighting, and the smell of blood and gore was getting thicker.

He put the horn to his lips and blew again, but the sound was ragged and weak. And the bamboo mouthpiece tasted like sweet copper and had dark, damp spots on it.

Emil threw the horn against a nearby wall. He was still staring at it when a commotion at the end of the alley caught his attention. One of the mercenaries was battling a small figure in Jade green. A young girl.

Emil's first thought was that the girl looked like his cousin Rona. She was about the same age, with the same sort of unruly dark hair confined in a braid down her back. But this girl had a cleft lip and fierce eyes, and she was wielding an iron-tipped *lati* staff. She was good, but the man she was fighting outweighed her, and his sword gave him just enough reach that he could avoid her twirling staff. As Emil watched, the man knocked the girl's weapon aside and swung under her guard. She cried out and staggered backward.

Emil was moving before he thought. He flung himself at the mercenary, tackling him to the ground. The two went down in a tangle of limbs and swords.

The man recovered quickly and tried to stand, but the girl wasn't out of the fight yet. She took advantage of her opponent's distraction and swung the staff. The heavy metal point struck the man in the stomach, and he fell to his hands and knees with the breath knocked out of him. She followed up with a kick to the face that laid him out entirely. Then she turned to Emil. He braced himself for her attack . . . but none came.

The girl's copper skin had taken on an unhealthy pallor, and she swayed on her feet. She pressed her hand to her side and Emil saw with horror that her tunic was dark with blood. She took a step toward him, then collapsed.

Emil was at her side in a second. Every nerve in his body screamed at him to keep running, to find Stefan and Esmer and get somewhere safe. But the girl was crumpled up in pain on the pavement, her face small and scared. Her resemblance to Rona was even stronger now.

He couldn't just leave her.

"Shhhh," Emil said, as the girl weakly tried to push him away. "I'm going to help you. It's all right." He found the wound easily, a long gash along her ribs. It was bleeding freely but wasn't deep.

Fortunately, the girl's oversize tunic was loose on her. Emil gathered the fabric into a careful handful and pressed it against the wound. The girl held her lips together but didn't cry out.

"I need you to hold this here," Emil said. "Can you do that?"

The girl nodded and put a hand over the wad of cloth. Emil put away his sword and helped her to her feet. She leaned on him, real and solid, with more trust than he probably deserved. The hard knot of panic in Emil's chest loosened. His breathing steadied and his thoughts cleared.

He couldn't stop this battle. He couldn't protect Stefan or the princes or the people who were dying all around him. But he could make sure this girl got to safety. He could do that.

"I'm going to find you a healer," he told her. "Come on."

The two started moving. It was slow and awkward, trying to support the girl without hurting her further. But Emil was determined. Carefully, they made their way down the alley and into a main street. The fighting here was dying down, but there were still pockets of combat, mercenaries battling against Jade warriors and Imperial Guards. Emil kept close to the wall, trying to stay invisible.

"You!" A mercenary with a mace and a scarred face pointed at them. His face twisted with rage and contempt as he saw the girl Emil was helping. "You did this, didn't you? You helped them!"

"No!" Emil said. "I can explain!"

The man advanced, the mace raised for a blow. "Liar," he snarled. "Traitor!"

The man swung his mace, and Emil turned, trying to shield the girl. . . .

Suddenly there was a roar, and a huge bear, bigger than Emil had ever seen in his life, crashed into the mercenary. The man's scream stained the air, then cut off abruptly.

The bear lifted his head and looked at Emil. His fur was a dark reddish-brown color, tipped with silver. His head was massive and shaggy, with two incongruously fluffy ears, and his paws were bigger than Emil's head. There was blood around his mouth.

Emil didn't move.

There was a flicker of magic, and then a man stood where the bear had been. It was Garen, the man Emil had met in the palace. But now he didn't look calm and solid, he looked . . . wounded. His dark eyes were mad and filled with grief.

"The heir is dead," he said.

The words hit Emil like a blow. One of the princes was dead, and he had helped make it happen. Nausea and guilt rose up in his throat.

"I'm sorry," he said. "I'm so sorry. If I could have stopped it, I would have." He nodded at the girl next to him, her face almost white with pain. "If you could just let me set her down . . . I don't want her hurt."

Garen stared at him. "I'm not going to attack you," he said, his words quiet, yet clear. "I'm letting you go."

"What?" Emil floundered, confused. "Why?"

"Because I made a promise to Mara," Garen said. "She seems to believe that you and your brother are worth saving."

Emil swallowed. "My brother," he said. "I think he's helping the wounded."

"We won't kill anyone we don't have to," Garen said. "All who ask for mercy will get it."

Emil thought of Rajo, choosing death over the justice of the Empire. He wondered if the mercy of the Empire would be any better.

He realized Garen was staring at him. "Thank you," Emil said, adjusting his grip on the wounded Jade warrior. "And . . . I am sorry."

Garen flicked into his bear form without answering. He took a few lumbering steps, then looked back.

Take her to the palace. The words rang inside Emil's head, and he jerked. *The Imperial Bridge is clear now, and there are healers already there, helping the soldiers. But you'll have to leave the sword.*

Then the bear gave a deafening roar and threw himself at a group of mercenaries.

Emil stood stunned for a moment, Garen's voice still ringing inside his head. Then with one hand, he pulled off his sword belt, leaving it on the ground. The girl moved her head slightly and murmured something Emil couldn't catch.

"It's all right," he told her, hoping it wasn't a lie. "We're all right now."

Turning his back on the carnage, Emil and the girl made their way toward the palace.

Regarding your question about our mutual friend: We all know what the Black Lotus family does, though propriety demands that we pretend that we do not. What you may not know is that though the members of the Black Lotus *are* assassins, they are not cold. They mourn at every death. When asked about this odd trait, our mutual friend merely said that a hard soul is a brittle soul and thus too easily broken. But I suspect it is more than that. Perhaps the sorrow itself is a kind of penance, a way to live with who they are and what they do. Or perhaps living so close to death has given them a vivid understanding of the value and wonder of life. I would inquire further, but I know I will get no answers. And it is rather rude to make your friends lie to you.

From a letter of Lady Ekisa to a friend

69

Mara

MARA WAITED IN the hallway for what felt like a long time until Revathi came back. The girl's asar was ripped and slashed in several places, and there was a smear of blood on her cheek.

"Are you all right?" Revathi asked. "Is Aari . . . ?"

"She's in there," Mara said, jerking her head toward the princes' room. "Wouldn't let anyone near her."

"Good." Revathi's voice was fierce, as she examined Mara's bloody shoulder.

"What about you?" Mara said, wincing as Revathi touched the slashes on her cheek. "Are you all right?"

"Just a few scratches," Revathi said. "Nothing serious, I promise. You're a good teacher." She held out her hand. "Of course this helped."

Mara looked at the knife. It was a wicked-looking thing, with a worn wooden handle and a serrated edge. The blade was dark, as if permanently stained, and it looked like it had been dipped in some kind of oil.

"Where did your grandmother get that?" she asked. "And what is that on the blade?"

"It's called nightshadow oil," Revathi said. "Don't touch it." She pulled a handkerchief out of her asar and wrapped the dagger in it. "Another present from one of my grandmother's friends. It's a nasty poison, paralyzes before it kills."

"Why on earth would your grandmother need something like that?" Mara asked.

Revathi shrugged. "She says she uses it to kill rats." She rubbed the back of her neck and winced. "Ancestors, I'm tired."

"Me too," Mara said. She peered into the princes' room. Aari lay motionless on the floor, and Mara could not tell if she was alive or dead. The bodies of the mercenaries lay scattered over the rich rug and the few survivors were being guarded by angry-looking Imperial Guards.

"Where's Tamas?" she asked.

"What?" Revathi's spine straightened, tight as a bowstring. She looked inside the room, her eyes darting from face to face. "He's not there. Why isn't he there?"

"He must have gone out the window during the fight," Mara said. "The other men stayed and died and he ran."

Revathi gave a hysterical half laugh. "Paithal was right," she said, choking on the words. "Tamas would have made a horrible emperor." She started coughing, leaning up against the wall, her breath coming in short gasps.

"Oh gods, Mara," she said, putting shaking hands over her face "What have I done? How did this happen?"

Mara took her by the shoulders. "Revathi, it's not your fault. We did everything we could. And it's over now. I took care of Aari, and the guards are hunting Tamas. Garen will tell them what he did. They'll catch him. And then they'll make sure he won't be able to hurt you or anyone else ever again."

Revathi took one deep shuddering breath, then another. "You're right," she said. "I know you're right. I should be grateful we managed to save one of them." She looked up. "You can let go now. I'm not going to collapse." Her voice was stronger, but her eyes were dark and unreadable, and Mara could not tell what she was feeling.

She let go of Revathi reluctantly. "Come on," Mara said, heading down the hall. "We'll take a bath, get our wounds looked at. You'll feel better when you're clean."

"I'm never going to be clean," Revathi said, so quietly that Mara barely heard her. Then she smiled, thin and cobweb fragile. "A bath does sound good, though." She put a hand on Mara's arm. "Thank you, Mara. For being my friend."

Mara put her hand over Revathi's and squeezed. "I'll always be your friend."

Revathi didn't answer, but Mara thought her smile grew a little more solid.

"Garen sent soldiers to Lord u'Gra's house," Mara told her,

pushing open the door to the bathing room. Steam rose from the warm bathing pools, but there were no servants in sight. "Aari said he was giving Tamas money to hire the mercenaries."

"Sending his son to do his dirty work?" Revathi said. "That's pretty cold. But it makes sense. This plan was way too detailed for Tamas to come up with on his own—"

There was a *crack* behind her, and Mara whirled around in time to see Revathi pitch forward. Tamas stood behind her, a bronze owl statue in his upraised hand.

Hiding behind the door. Stupid, stupid. Why didn't I check that?

Tamas was breathing heavily. "She never loved me," he said, looking down at Revathi's prone form. "It wasn't fair. We could have been so good together, but she never—"

Mara lunged for him, but Tamas swung the statue at her, making her step back.

"It's all your fault!" he shouted. "I could have made her love me if you hadn't interfered. We would have ruled the Empire together. It would have worked!"

Tamas threw the statue at her and ran. Mara ducked as the owl hit the floor behind her with a crash, skidding and rattling over the stone. Then she ran to Revathi.

The girl lay on the tile, her eyes closed. Blood pooled under her dark hair. Mara slipped her fingers under the scarf, feeling for the pulse in Revathi's throat. There was a flutter under her fingers. . . .

Then it stopped.

"Revathi!" Mara put her ear to the girl's mouth, trying to catch a whisper of life. But there was no brush of air against her skin. And no heartbeat under her frantic hands.

There was nothing.

"No." Mara shook Revathi, her voice rising. "No. No. Wake up. Wake up, Revathi." She was pushing at the still body, and there was water on her face and salt on her lips and she couldn't stop.

"Please. We won. It's over. Wake up."

But there was no response.

A broken wail filled the room, and Mara realized it was coming from her own throat. Cold grief filled her. Not the red fire of rage she'd felt when her family was killed, or the determined fury that had come at Paithal's death, no, this was something else. Something sharp and jagged and frozen. An icy pain that coated her insides and sharpened her mind.

When her voice ran out and her breath came back, Mara forced herself to her feet. Her eyes turned to the door where Tamas had vanished.

Tamas.

The magic was there almost before she reached for it, warm and sparkling, coming to her call. But not even magic could warm her now. She wrapped herself in it anyway, letting it change her, until her skin was covered with plush, protective fur, until she could feel the power in her coiled muscles and the tile under her huge brown paws.

She nuzzled Revathi's motionless form. The girl smelled of blood and poison, and Mara licked her forehead with a rough tongue. Then she raised her head, sniffing the air.

Tamas's scent was all sour sweat and fear. It left a clear trail, like a rope trailing after him. Marking him.

Mara growled, lifting her lips over her sharp canines.

It was time to hunt.

EMIL FOUND THE healers setting up a tent just inside
the palace gate. Servants ran back and forth, fetching bandages
and jars of salve. Imperial soldiers and unconscious mercenaries
were being laid out nearby.

"Help me," Emil called to a woman with tightly pulled-back
dark hair and a green asar. "Help me, please."

The woman paused, frowning at him. Her stern look dissolved
into concern when she saw the girl sagging against him.

"Wounded in the fight?" she asked. Her fingers probed the
girl's bloody side. The girl moaned.

"Caught the wrong end of a sword," Emil said. "It didn't look
too deep, but I didn't want to take any chances."

"I should say not," the woman said. Her hands and arms were
painted with green dye, like intricate vines over her skin. "She's too

young to be out there anyway. I don't know what Suni was think-ing." Her brow folded in concentration. "It's not life-threatening, but she will need stitching. Put her over there and I'll have one of the assistants see to her."

Emil followed her directions, setting the girl gently on the grass, next to an archer with a bandage around his head.

He turned to find the woman studying him. "Any of that blood yours?"

Emil touched his face. His fingers came away tacky and brown. His gray servant's tunic was streaked as well. "No," he said, swal-lowing.

"Then you don't belong here," the woman said, waving him away. "Uditi!" she shouted to a nearby assistant. "What are you doing? We don't need that bowl of cotton ash over here; it's for making burn salve. Take it to the other side of the tent. And fetch another jar of cold water while you're at it. We've got more coming in with hot oil burns." She shook her head. "As if people needed more ways to hurt each other."

"I've got a leg wound here and I can't stop the bleeding!" a voice called. Someone screamed in pain. The healer cursed and darted away.

Emil stood feeling lost and useless for a moment. Another passing healer shoved a basket into his arms.

"We need more bandages," he ordered. "They might have a stash in the Palace of Flowing Water. Ask there." He rolled his eyes at Emil's look of confusion. "Behind the Lotus Wall," he said, shoving him. "Go. Now."

Emil went, leaving the groans and cries behind him. He'd been mistaken for a servant, it seemed. But at least he was doing something to help now. Maybe he would find Mara in this vast palace complex.

The wall bisecting the palace grounds was high and unwelcoming. Emil was about to turn around when one of the guards spotted him.

"What do you want?" the guard said. He looked tired and angry. Emil wondered if he knew the heir to the throne was dead.

Emil held out his empty basket. "The healers want bandages," he said. The guard gave him a cursory up-and-down look and waved him through.

Once past the wall, Emil kept walking. He wasn't sure where he was going, but moving purposefully was better than looking lost.

He heard the sound of feet on grass and looked up to see a young boy–a bond servant–running toward him. "A tiger!" the boy cried, waving his hands. "There's a tiger in the palace."

Emil's stomach fell into his feet. He grabbed the boy, stopping his headlong rush.

"Are you sure?" he said, hearing the urgency in his own voice. If it was Mara and the soldiers found her first . . .

The boy's face had a sickly green cast. He looked about ready to faint from fright. "I–I saw it!"

"Show me," Emil said. "Show me now."

The boy shook his head. "I'm not going back there. It's huge."

Emil spoke as firmly as he could. "Listen to me," he said,

shaking the boy's shoulders. "You don't have to come with me. But you need to tell me where the tiger is. Now."

His tone of command must have penetrated the boy's panic, because he swallowed and pointed. "That way," he said. "It was headed for the Imperial Garden of the Ancestors. You can't miss it."

Emil dropped his basket and ran.

The Imperial Garden of the Ancestors was much like the one in the outer palace, a forest of shrines. Only instead of gray stone, these shrines were made of polished white marble, trimmed with silver overlay. The figures inside were painted ceramic, polished to a gleaming sheen. Fresh flowers had been heaped at every base.

Emil paused at the edge of the garden and listened. He heard nothing . . . but there was a waiting quality to the silence. He could see birdseed scattered at the feet of several Ancestors and a peacock feather in the grass, but the sacred birds were nowhere to be seen.

"Mara?" he called, moving cautiously between the shrines "Mara are you here? It's me, Emil."

There was a rustle and Emil caught a blow to the side of his head that made his ears ring. Someone kicked him in the back of the knee, and he fell.

When the sparks cleared from his vision, he found himself on the ground, looking up at Tamas. The noble's brows were high and drawn together, and his eyes looked like a terrified rabbit's. The tip of his curved sword rested on Emil's chest.

"Don't move," he snarled. Emil held his hands up and out, showing he had no weapons.

"I think you've mistaken me, honored lord . . . ," he started.

"Shut up," Tamas said. "Or I'll skewer you like the rat you are. Mara!" he yelled, moving slightly so his back was to a shrine. "Come out, or I'll kill this man." He prodded Emil with his foot. "See, I thought I recognized you earlier. You're the one who broke into my house. I should have killed you then, but since you're here, you can be useful." He raised his voice again. "I mean it, Mara! I know you're lurking somewhere. Come out in human form or he dies *right now.*"

"Give up, Tamas." Mara stepped around the corner of another statue. Her voice was flat, expressionless. She didn't look at Emil. "It's over. You lost."

"I was only trying to help the Empire," Tamas said, the panic pitching his voice higher. "We need strong leadership. And I could have done it. I could have made my father proud."

"I'm not here for the Empire," Mara said, in the same distant tone. "I'm here for Revathi."

"That was *your* fault!" Tamas shouted. "You turned her against me. Revathi belonged to me, she was mine."

"Revathi was never yours," Mara said. Her hands curled into fists. "If you had been married to her for a thousand years, she would never have been yours. And you knew it. That's why you tried so hard to break her. But Revathi was stronger than that. She was stronger than you."

Tamas pushed the point of his sword against Emil's chest, and pain radiated through his body. He groaned.

Mara took another step forward. "Revathi was my friend, Tamas. But more than that, she was my charge. Do you know what that means?" She smiled, but there was no humor in it. "It means by the laws of the Empire, your life is mine. When they catch you—and they will catch you—they'll give you to me."

Tamas was shaking, his eyes darting back and forth. He looked as if he was about to soil himself with fear.

"Revathi was an accident, I swear."

"It doesn't matter," Mara said. "You're not a hero, Tamas, you're just a man who wanted more than he was given and thought he deserved more than he had. And now it's over."

"Promise not to kill me," Tamas said. His sword trembled against Emil's chest. A small patch of blood stained Emil's tunic, where the tip had gouged him. "Promise not to kill me," Tamas repeated, "and I'll let him go."

Mara's eyes met Emil's, dark honey with golden flecks. And for the first time, Emil could read her expression clearly. He tensed.

"Tamas," Mara said. "Put down the sword."

"No!" Tamas shouted. "Get back!"

This is going to hurt, Emil thought. And then he moved. Grabbing the blade of the curved sword, he shoved up, taking Tamas by surprise. Emil rolled to one side, pain screaming through his hands. . . .

Just in time to see Mara leap at Tamas and change in midair. But this wasn't Esmer's light and graceful cat form. Mara *grew*, her massive bulk slamming into Tamas. They hit the shrine behind him with a deafening crash. Dust flew everywhere.

Then everything was quiet again.

Emil rolled to his knees, no easy task with his cut and bleeding hands. Deep slashes decorated his palm, and his chest throbbed. Dust stung his eyes.

"Mara?" he called, coughing. "Are you all right?"

A dark form limped toward him out of the clearing dust. Emil stared in awe.

The tiger's fur was a rich, velvety brown, contrasting with her creamy belly and black stripes. Her tail was as long as Emil's leg, her eyes were a dark, burning amber, and she moved with a grace and power that stole Emil's breath.

Emil held out one of his bleeding hands. The tiger came closer, swiping at his palm with just the tip of her broad, rough tongue. Emil reached up with his other hand and stroked the fur of her face. It felt like spun cashmere under his fingers. He opened his mouth to thank her for saving him, to ask if she was all right.

"You're so beautiful," he blurted instead.

There was a flicker and Mara stood there, her features streaked with dirt and tears. She looked behind her and Emil followed her line of sight. Tamas was lying in the wreckage of the marble shrine, his neck bent at an impossible angle.

"He killed Revathi." Mara's voice was soft and despairing, edged with raw grief. She dropped to her knees, her hands pressed into the dirt. "She's dead, Emil. I promised to protect her, and he killed her."

"I'm sorry, Mara," Emil said. "I'm so sorry."

"She trusted me." Mara raised a hand to her earring. She pulled it off and stared at the small bronze circle in her hand. "What am I, Emil? Am I a monster?"

"Of course not." Emil held out his hands to her again, crusted and dripping with blood. "You're someone who tries to protect the people she loves and doesn't always succeed. None of us are heroes, Mara. And none of us are monsters. We're just people who do the best we can."

Mara looked back at Tamas's glassy-eyed corpse. "I'm tired of killing."

"I know," Emil said.

"I don't want to be Mara anymore."

"All right."

There was another moment of silence; then, like a wall crumbling, Mara gave a deep, wounded sob and threw herself into Emil's arms.

71

Mara

THE AFTERMATH IS *always messier than the battle,* Mara thought as she took the jar of salve from the healer's apprentice. At least here, inside the palace walls, the mess was composed of living human beings. Groups of wounded were clustered on the grass, waiting for the green-clad healers to come and tend them. There was a faint reek to the air, a smell of medicine and blood and burned flesh. But these people were still alive. They would heal.

It was different near the front gate. That was where a line of bodies lay, most of them in Imperial Guard blue, and all of them with their faces covered. Mara didn't look at them as she passed, but her hand clamped a little tighter around the jar of salve.

Mara. Garen loped up, still in his bear form. *How are you doing?*

I don't know, Mara sent. *I keep looking for Revathi, and then* realizing she's not here. I can't believe . . . She trailed off, unable to finish even in her mind.

I should have done something, she finally sent, knowing she would choke on the words if she tried to say them out loud. *I should not have let it happen.*

I know, Garen sent. He leaned into her side, his mind-voice heavy and sad. *I'm pledged to protect Saro and his family, and I failed in that. I'll have Paithal's last moments in my head for the rest of my life.*

Mara stroked his shoulder, running her fingers through his thick reddish fur. *I'm so sorry, Garen. How is Sudev doing?*

He's in shock. Keeps asking why Paithal died, why his father couldn't stop it. I don't think he fully understands. And of course Saro is devastated. To lose his wife and son so close together . . . the echo of this is going to take a long time to die down.

For all of us, Mara sent. *Did you find Lord u'Gra?*

No, Garen sent. *He's vanished.*

Mara closed her eyes. *I didn't even get to say a proper good-bye to Revathi. Her body was gone by the time I returned to the bathing room.*

I heard, Garen said. *Saro is seeing to her burial personally. She'll be given the highest honors a citizen of the Empire can have. The two of you are heroes. In fact . . .* He hesitated. *I know this is a little soon, but I've been instructed to tell you that there is a job for you here if you so wish it. You could join the palace staff, or we could find you someone to pledge to, if you still wish to keep your Order vows.*

I'm done with vows. Mara took a deep breath and softened her snappish thoughts. *I'm not a hero, Garen. Please tell the Emperor I'm honored, but I am tired of blood.*

I understand. Garen nuzzled her shoulder.

Mara wrapped her arms around his neck and buried her face in his fur. And if a few hot tears leaked out, the bear didn't seem to care. Finally she pulled back and rubbed his fluffy ears.

Thank you. For everything.

Then Mara turned and walked out of the palace. Halfway over the Imperial Bridge, she stopped and looked back. Garen was still watching her. He lifted a paw in salute.

May Yaggesil guide your path, Mara. Safe travels.

You too, my friend, Mara sent back.

Out in the Flower Circle, everything smelled of iron and blood and death. Soldiers were everywhere, picking up the dead bodies for cremating and guarding a few small bands of captured rebels. Mara passed a crew loading bodies into a wagon and averted her eyes as she walked by.

Emil and Esmer and Stefan were sitting on the Jade side of the stone bridge, away from the stench of death. Mara walked to meet them. Her entire body ached, and she welcomed the pain. It was a distraction, keeping her thoughts from flying back to the Palace of Flowing Water and the crumpled body that she'd left there.

I'm sorry, Revathi.

"Mara!" Emil called. His face lit up when he saw her, and Mara felt some of the ache inside ease. "I was about to come and look for you."

"I was saying good-bye to Garen," Mara said, sitting down next to Emil. The stone was warm under her legs. "And getting this." She waved the salve jar. "It will help keep your hands from getting infected."

"Do you have enough for Stefan, too?" Esmer asked. She had a knife out and was carefully cutting off Stefan's blood-soaked sleeve. There was a shallow sword cut just above Stefan's wrist cast.

"It's a good thing these splints are so sturdy," Esmer said. "You're lucky the cast deflected the blade. Next time block with your sword, not your arm."

Stefan didn't respond to her teasing tone. There were deep lines around his mouth, and his eyes were haunted. "Better an arm than something else," he said. He rubbed his forehead. "I've never seen so many dead bodies before."

Esmer put a hand on his shoulder. "I know."

"I really thought . . ." Stefan took a deep breath. "I really thought we were going to change things."

"We will," Emil said, as Mara bent over his hands. "Someday. Someday there will be another chance."

Stefan shook his head. "Maybe," he said. "But all I want to do now is go home."

Esmer was examining his cast with disapproval. "This is filthy," she said. "When you go home, you should see a healer and get it changed."

"I hate healers," Stefan groaned.

Mara bent over Emil's hands. The hasty strips that she'd torn from the bottom of her shirt and tied around Emil's cut palms were stiff with blood. She peeled them away and rubbed the salve gently into the cuts. They were deep, but not dangerously so.

Mara ripped another few strips from her shirt, letting the warm air caress her waist and stomach.

"You don't have to do that," Emil said. "I'm sure someone around here has bandages."

Mara shrugged. "Bandages are always the first thing to run short in a battle," she said. "Besides, it's your shirt." She felt Emil's eyes on her as she worked. Mara rebandaged his hands carefully, then tossed the salve to Esmer.

"Where will you go now?" Emil asked softly.

Mara shook her head. She felt empty and oddly light, as if a feather could blow her away. "I don't know. I just know I don't want to go back to the Order. Or the palace." She thought with a pang of the wooden tiger, hidden under her pillow in Revathi's room.

"I'll make you a new one," Emil said, and Mara realized she had spoken her last thought aloud. "Wood can be replaced," he continued, brushing his thumb along her cheek. Mara leaned into the touch, careful not to hurt his bandaged palms. His touch was solid and real and made it easier to breathe.

"Come with me," Emil said. "Come back to the Arvi."

Mara jerked back, panic spilling through her. "Emil, I can't . . ." *I can't tie myself to someone else. Not now. Not while this still hurts so much.*

"Come as our guest," Emil said, as if reading her thoughts. "Stefan's and mine. At least stay until my hands heal and I can carve you a new tiger. I . . . we owe you that much." He reached over and put his hand on hers—not gripping it, just letting it rest there. "Mara," he said, and his voice was so tender that Mara could hardly bear it. "I'm not going to pretend that I'm being unselfish here. I don't want to lose you. But more than that, I don't want you to be alone. And I'll be your friend, no matter what you decide."

"Me too," Stefan said. There was the sound of a smack, and Mara opened her eyes to see Stefan rubbing his head and glaring at Esmer. The cat girl looked back serenely.

"That's what you get for interrupting," she said. Then her gold-flecked eyes shifted to Mara. "But he's right. We're all your friends. You don't have to be alone unless you want to be."

Mara took a deep breath, letting the word settle inside her. *Friends.*

"All right," she said, turning her hand palm up, so that Emil's bandaged palm rested against hers. "I'll come. On one condition."

Emil's smile was as warm as a summer afternoon. "What condition?" he asked.

"I want you to call me by my real name," Mara said. She curled her fingers into Emil's and smiled back at him. "I want you to call me Shar."

There are no beginnings, because everything is connected.

There are no endings, because nothing ever truly ends.

There is only where you choose to start the song,

And where you choose to stop.

The words of Elina the Bow-Singer, as told to her students

THE WOMAN CALLED Shar Arvi reached the shadowed brick building just before Firstlight. The small, flat-roofed structure was hidden in the middle of a tiny, tangled forest and difficult to find unless you knew where to look. Tree shadows played over every surface, clustering close as if to protect the secrets inside. She heard a rustle in the trees, a whisper of footsteps on the roof. The back of her neck crawled with the touch of unseen eyes.

Shar put her hand against the heavy wood of the door, gathering her courage. Then she knocked sharply.

The door opened, revealing a thin woman in a brown-and-gray tunic, with close-cropped black hair. Her eyes widened when she saw the visitor.

The two stared at each other, silence stretching between them like a binding thread.

"You still smell like jasmine and sandalwood," Shar said. Against her will, the corners of her lips curled up. "I would have known you anywhere."

The ghost of a smile passed over the other woman's face, then she snapped her fingers twice. The footsteps on the roof stopped. The rustle of movement in the trees died down. The feeling of unseen eyes vanished.

"They are very good," Shar commented.

"They are," the woman agreed. She opened the door wider. "You might as well come in."

Shar followed her inside, to a small room paneled in dark wood. She sat down in a narrow chair and folded her arms.

"You haven't changed as much as I imagined, Revathi. Even after ten years."

The woman turned away, staring at the thick mat of vines that clustered over the window. "I've changed more than you know," she said softly. "When did you figure it out?"

"Not for a long time." Shar swung her braid of black hair over her shoulder. "Not until Emil took over as Master of Trade a few years ago. He was here in the City of a Thousand Dolls on business and he saw you, going around the corner of a building. He couldn't believe it and neither could I. Then he started asking questions. He has a lot of . . . interesting contacts in Kamal. When he discovered that no one but me ever saw your body, that's when I knew."

"Revathi sa'Hoi had to die," the woman said very softly. "It was the only way, Mara."

"It's Shar now," Shar said, and then her voice broke. "Why did you do it, Revathi? *How* did you do it?"

"Grandmother helped me," the woman said. "She was waiting for me when I took Sudev to safety. It turns out one of her friends was a member of the Black Lotus family and a trainer on this estate. She was willing to take me in, if I joined them." The woman turned from the window and took the chair across from Shar.

"You have to understand, I might have helped save the princes, but I also helped Tamas get into the palace. Even with the Emperor's pardon, there would have been talk, people wondering, whispering. My family would have been shunned. No one would have been willing to marry my brother. It would have destroyed us."

"Unless you died," Shar said, starting to understand. "You could live under suspicion, or you could die a hero."

The woman nodded. "When Tamas struck me, I was still conscious. I saw my chance and pricked myself with the poison dagger. In tiny doses, the poison causes a brief deathlike state. It only lasts a minute or two, but that was all I needed."

"Why didn't you tell me?" Shar asked. "I would have come with you."

"I know." The woman's fingers tugged at the sleeves of her tunic. "This is a small, safe life, Shar. I answer only to Emperor Saro and I rarely leave the estate. It's freedom for me, but for you?" Her voice softened. "You did more for me than you can ever know, and I owe you more than I can ever repay. I couldn't see you miserable."

Some of the tension in Shar's chest eased. "I'm glad you said that. Because I need your help." She took a deep breath. "I need you to protect my daughter."

"You have a daughter?" Revathi's head snapped up. "How old is she?"

"Six," Shar said, and a smile crept over her lips. "She looks just like Emil. He dotes on her."

"And you're leaving her *here*? Are you mad?"

"No," Shar said. "Just desperate."

Revathi's eyes narrowed, grew hard. "Are you in danger? Who is threatening you?"

Shar put out a hand. "Revathi," she said. "Listen to me. I don't have a lot of time. Something is happening, something that could shift everything we know about the Empire. Emil and I have seen things. . . ." She trailed off, letting the wonder come through her voice. "Things you would not believe. Things out of the old tales. But we saw too much, and now someone wants us gone. I wish I knew who it is, but I don't."

Her hand tightened on Revathi's sleeve.

"We can't take our daughter with us, and it's too dangerous to leave her with Emil's family. The Matron in charge of the girls has promised to look after her, and Esmer is coming with her Tribe as well, to help. But that's not enough for me. I want someone on my daughter's side who will do anything to protect her. And I want that person to be you."

There was a moment of silence; then Revathi put her hand over Shar's and squeezed it. "I swear by the Ancestors and by the debt I owe, I will watch over your daughter."

Shar let out the breath she was holding.

"Thank you," she said, rising from her chair. "Emil left her by the front gate. She doesn't know I'm here. And you can't tell her that you know us, not unless . . ." Shar paused. "Unless you have to. If for some reason we can't come back, if she needs you . . ."

"I'll be there."

"Thank you." She turned to leave, pausing at the door. "You could have come with us," she said without looking at Revathi. "Emil and I would have welcomed you."

"I lost Paithal," Revathi said, her voice shadowed with old grief. "I failed my Emperor and my country. The least I could do was offer my own life in return."

"Penance," Shar said. She looked down at her hand, resting on the latch. "I understand that."

"I know you do," Revathi said. Her tone softened, until she almost sounded like the Revathi that Shar remembered. "This is who I am now. I've accepted that. But don't think I don't regret it."

Shar nodded. "I miss you too," she said, then pushed the door open.

"Wait," Revathi said. "What is your daughter's name?"

Shar told her.

The woman who had once been Revathi sa'Hoi watched from the door of the House of Shadows as Shar vanished into the woods.

Tilting her head up, she chirped, the fluted two-note trill of a songbird. There was an answering call, and a figure dropped from one of the trees that surrounded the tiny clearing. It was a girl of about fourteen, dressed in mottled gray-and-brown clothing. There was a bow and a quiver of arrows slung across her back.

"Zophia, spread the word to the others. The woman who just left is not to be bothered. Go quickly."

The girl put her hand to her chest and bowed, giving the warrior's sign of respect. "Yes, Shadow Mistress." Then she darted away, as silently as she had come.

The woman went back inside and upstairs to the tiny, private space that served as her bedroom. Kneeling swiftly, she reached into a chest at the foot of the bed and pulled out a bundle of red silk, a delicate scarf embroidered with gold. She unwrapped it, her shaking fingers finding the carved rosewood tiger inside. It was smooth and cool against her palm, the features worn from years of handling.

She cradled the tiger in her hands, breathing deeply for a moment, until she felt centered again. Then she quickly rewrapped the wooden figure in the scarf, shut the lid, and left the house.

Her teacher always said meditation worked better with a focus.

Revathi walked briskly out of the small stand of trees, past the shouts and drills of the House of Combat, past the hedge maze and the girls sitting in the gardens of the House of Beauty. Down the wide main road and out the gate.

There was a tiny girl sitting against the wall, dressed in a gray skirt and blouse and playing with a carved toy cat. She jumped up at the sound of footsteps, her eyes wide.

Revathi hid a smile. The child might have Emil's dark, unruly hair and rich brown eyes, but she moved with the same wary, unconscious grace that her mother did. And right now she was staring at Revathi as if she wasn't sure whether to run or fight.

Go swiftly and come back soon, my friends, Revathi thought. *And the Ancestors watch over you.*

Looking down at the little girl, she held out a hand. "Come inside, Nisha."

Acknowedgments

AGAIN, THE LIST of people to thank is too long for me to do justice to it.

Thank you to my husband, Dan, who was there for me through all the book two angst. You were my touchstone and my shelter, and this book would not exist without you.

Thanks to Fred and Cindy, for the gift of house and home, and for letting me scatter my work all over your living room. And thanks to my family for rooting for me this year. I love you all.

A giant thank-you to all the people who made this book better: my awesome and patient editor, Sarah Dotts Barley, Renée Cafiero and Valerie Shea, for putting up with my misuse of transitive verbs, and Erin Fitzsimmons and Colin Anderson, who made the book itself so beautiful. And thank you to my agent, Jennifer Laughran, for managing to be both hilariously honest and incredibly reassuring.

Thanks and hugs to the wonderful crew at Rediscovered Books in Boise for being the best thing about 2012. Thanks to the fabulous Jess K. for beta reading, and thanks to the Lucky13s for being amazing. And a final thank-you to all the people on Archive of our Own and elsewhere who write wonderful stories. Your words helped me rediscover my own love of reading and kept me sane during a very dry and difficult time. Thank you.